PORTSMOUTH
POLICE
0333

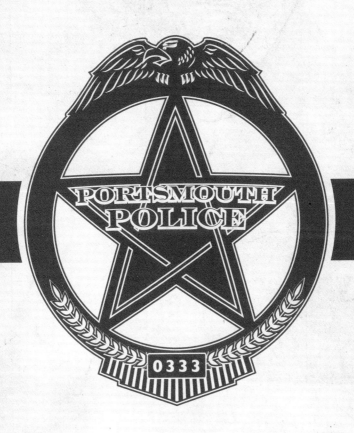

BLACK MAGICK ™

Created by Greg Rucka and Nicola Scott

VOLUME 2: "AWAKENING II"

Writer: GREG RUCKA

Artist: NICOLA SCOTT

Color Assists: CHIARA ARENA

Letterer: JODI WYNNE

Cover: NICOLA SCOTT
(with ERIC TRAUTMANN)

Follow Greg on Twitter: @ruckawriter • Follow Nicola on Twitter: @NicolaScottArt
Follow Alejandro on Twitter: @alejandrobot • Follow Eric on Twitter: @mercuryeric

IMAGE COMICS, INC.
Robert Kirkman—Chief Operating Officer
Erik Larsen—Chief Financial Officer
Todd McFarlane—President
Marc Silvestri—Chief Executive Officer
Jim Valentino—Vice President

Eric Stephenson—Publisher / Chief Creative Officer
Corey Hart—Director of Sales
Jeff Boison—Director of Publishing Planning
                      & Book Trade Sales
Chris Ross—Director of Digital Sales
Jeff Stang—Director of Specialty Sales
Kat Salazar—Director of PR & Marketing
Drew Gill—Art Director
Heather Doornink—Production Director
Nicole Lapalme—Controller
IMAGECOMICS.COM

Editor: ALEJANDRO ARBONA

Book and Logo Designer, "A" cover colors: ERIC TRAUTMANN

http://blackmagickcomic.tumblr.com

BLACK MAGICK VOLUME 2: AWAKENING II.

First printing, May 2018. Published by Image Comics, Inc. Office of publication: 2701 NW Vaughn St., Suite 780, Portland, OR 97210.

Copyright © 2018 Greg Rucka and Nicola Scott. All rights reserved.

Contains material originally published in single magazine form as **BLACK MAGICK** #6–11. "Black Magick," its logos, and the likenesses of all characters herein are trademarks of Greg Rucka and Nicola Scott, unless otherwise noted.

"Image" and the Image Comics logos are registered trademarks of Image Comics, Inc. No part of this publication may be reproduced or transmitted, in any form or by any means (except for short excerpts for journalistic or review purposes), without the express written permission of Greg Rucka, Nicola Scott, or Image Comics, Inc. All names, characters, events, and locales in this publication are entirely fictional. Any resemblance to actual persons (living or dead), events, or places, without satiric intent, is coincidental. Printed in the USA. For information regarding the CPSIA on this printed material call: 203-595-3636 and provide reference #RICH–787664.

For international rights, contact: foreignlicensing@imagecomics.com.

ISBN: 978-1-5343-0483-3

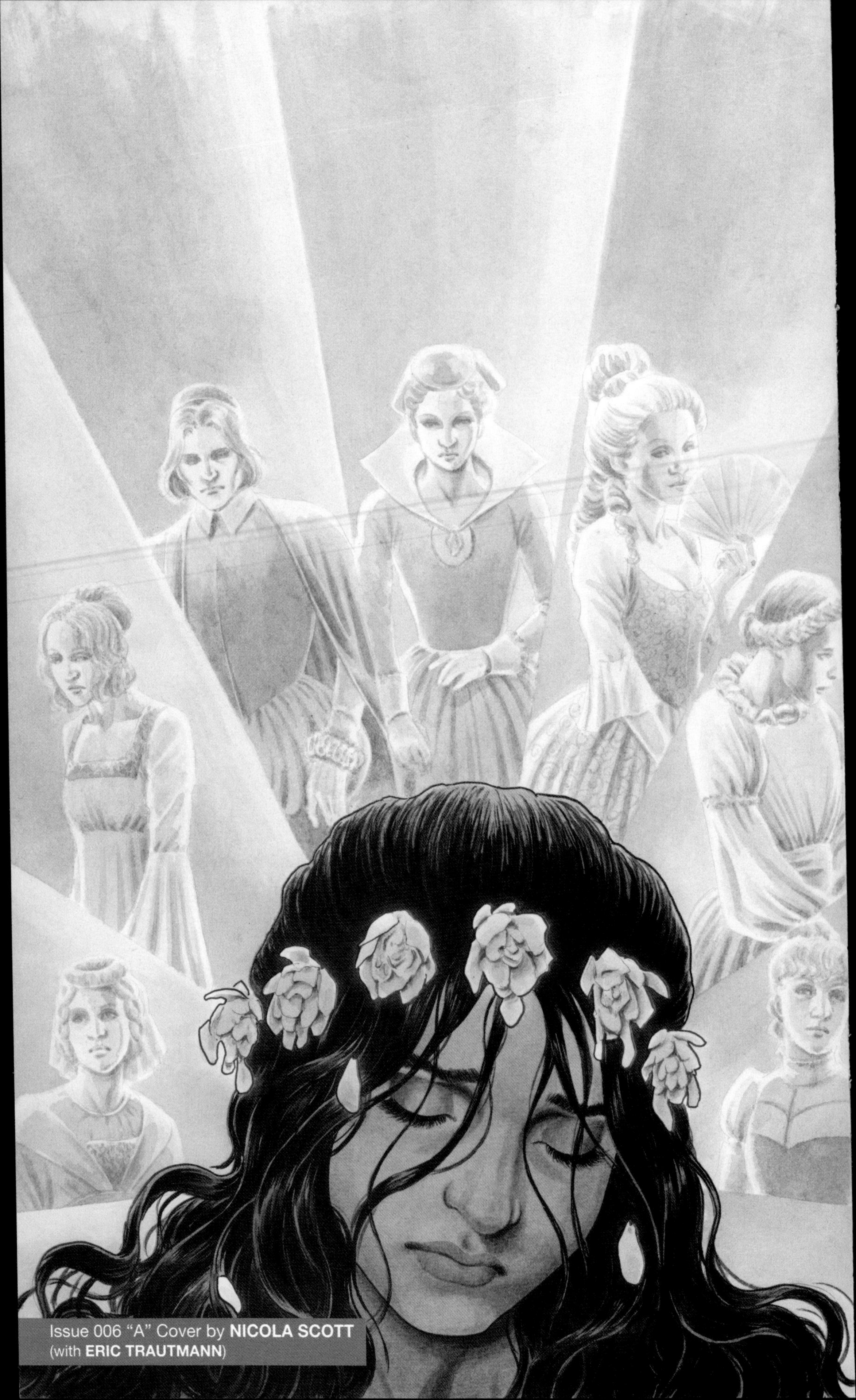
Issue 006 "A" Cover by **NICOLA SCOTT**
(with **ERIC TRAUTMANN**)

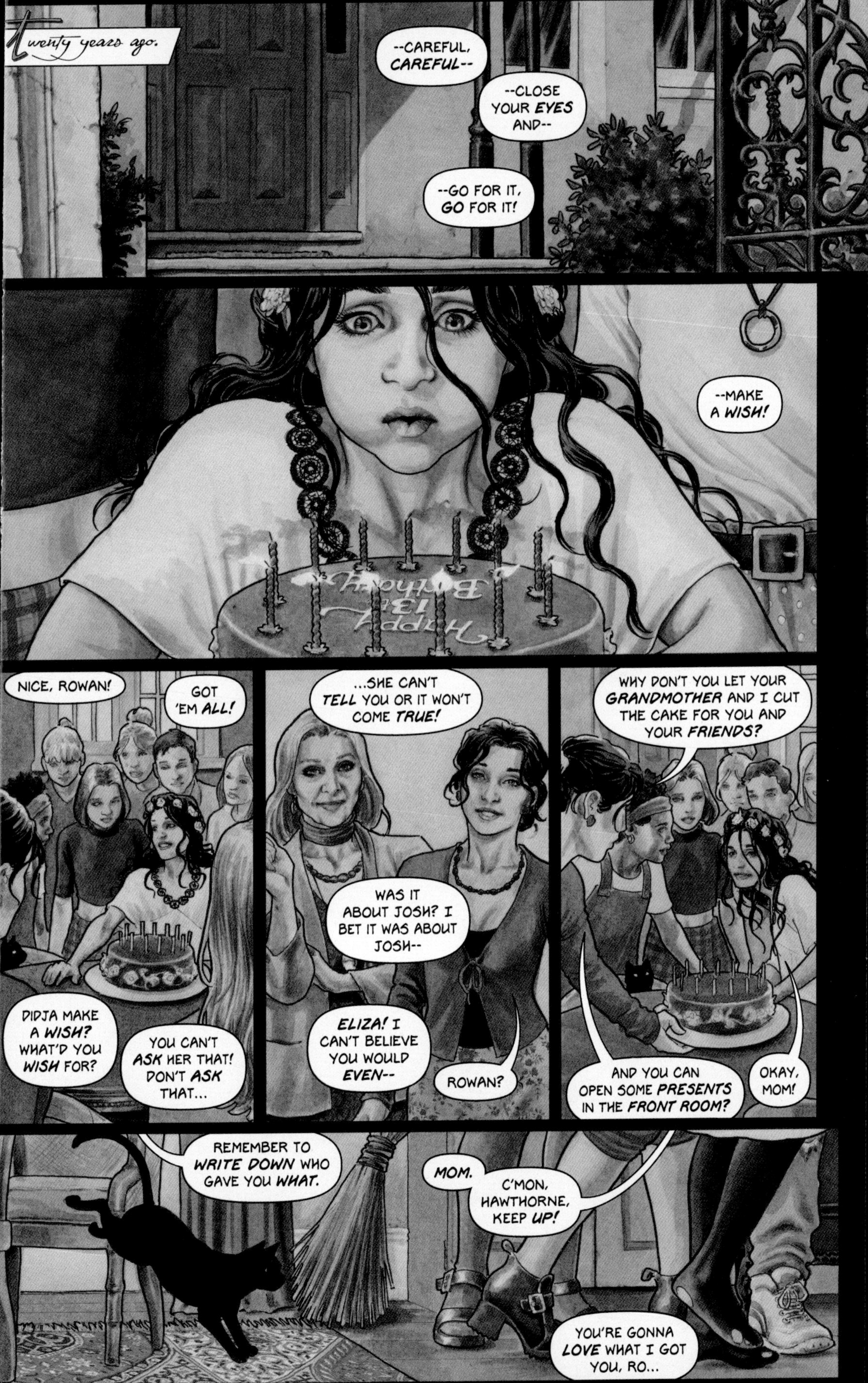
twenty years ago.
--CAREFUL, CAREFUL--
--CLOSE YOUR EYES AND--
--GO FOR IT, GO FOR IT!
--MAKE A WISH!
Happy 13th Birthday
NICE, ROWAN!
GOT 'EM ALL!
DIDJA MAKE A WISH? WHAT'D YOU WISH FOR?
YOU CAN'T ASK HER THAT! DON'T ASK THAT...
...SHE CAN'T TELL YOU OR IT WON'T COME TRUE!
WAS IT ABOUT JOSH? I BET IT WAS ABOUT JOSH--
ELIZA! I CAN'T BELIEVE YOU WOULD EVEN--
ROWAN?
WHY DON'T YOU LET YOUR GRANDMOTHER AND I CUT THE CAKE FOR YOU AND YOUR FRIENDS?
AND YOU CAN OPEN SOME PRESENTS IN THE FRONT ROOM?
OKAY, MOM!
REMEMBER TO WRITE DOWN WHO GAVE YOU WHAT.
MOM.
C'MON, HAWTHORNE, KEEP UP!
YOU'RE GONNA LOVE WHAT I GOT YOU, RO...

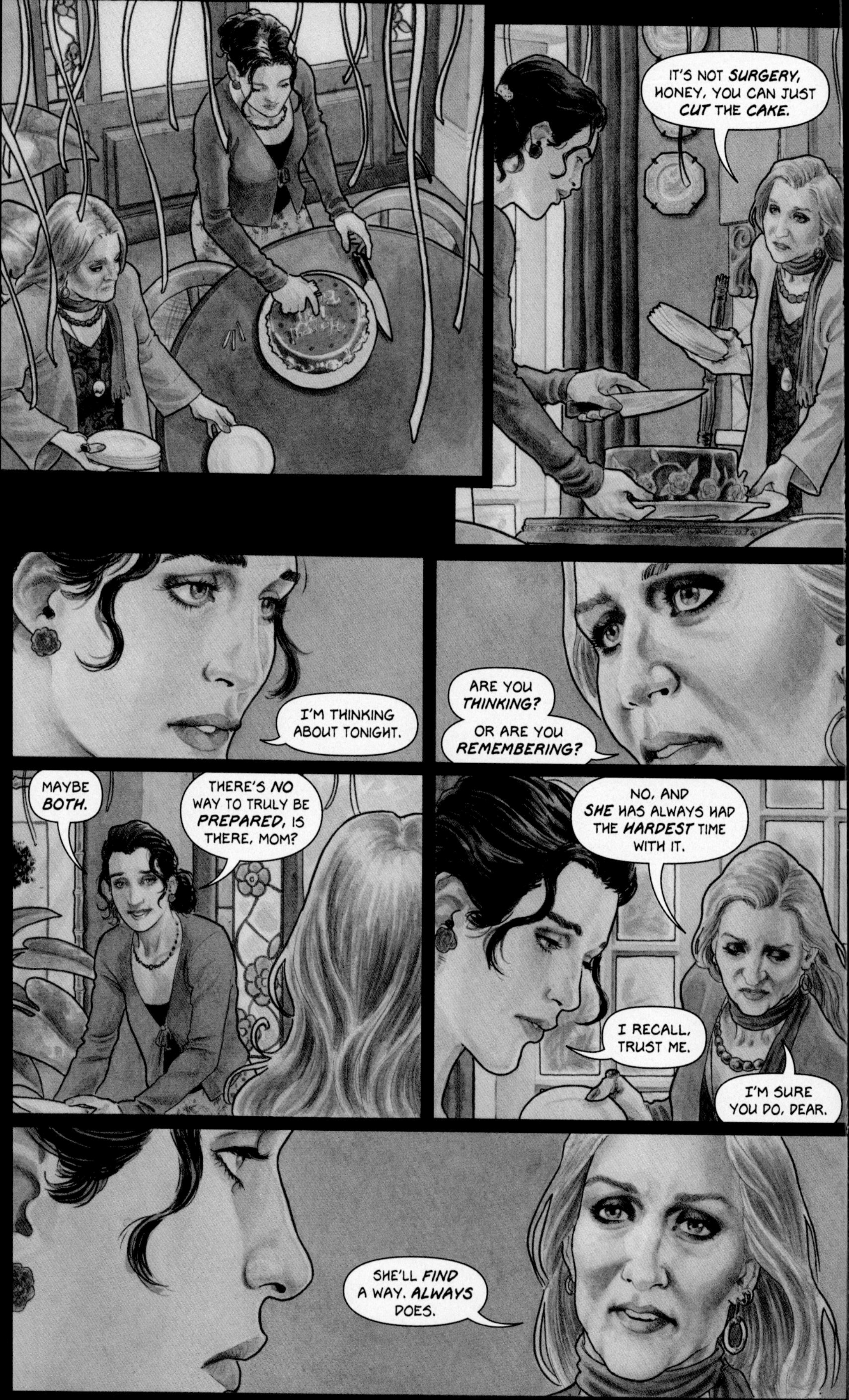
IT'S NOT SURGERY, HONEY, YOU CAN JUST CUT THE CAKE.
I'M THINKING ABOUT TONIGHT.
ARE YOU THINKING?
OR ARE YOU REMEMBERING?
MAYBE BOTH.
THERE'S NO WAY TO TRULY BE PREPARED, IS THERE, MOM?
NO, AND SHE HAS ALWAYS HAD THE HARDEST TIME WITH IT.
I RECALL, TRUST ME.
I'M SURE YOU DO, DEAR.
SHE'LL FIND A WAY. ALWAYS DOES.

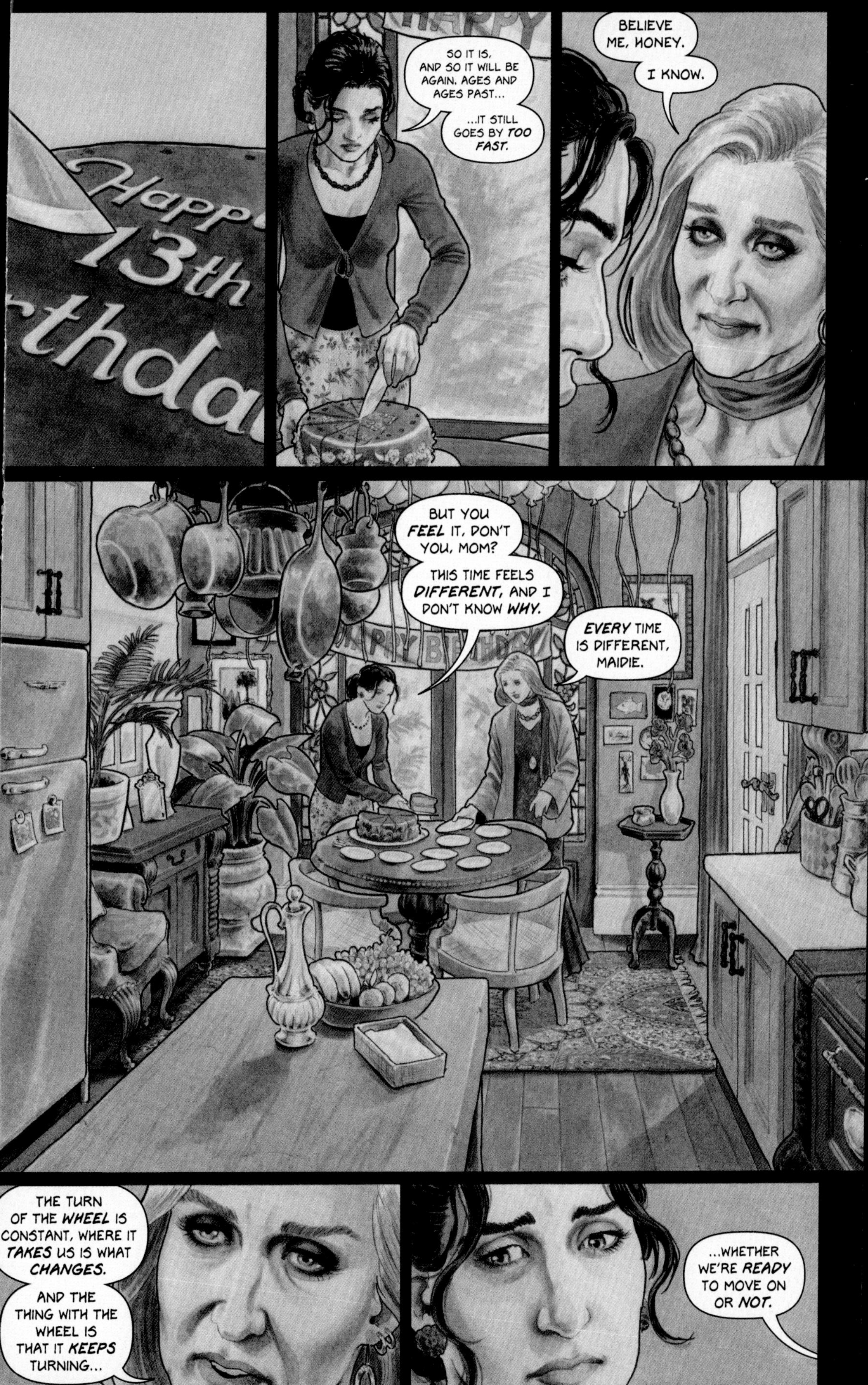
Happy 13th Birthday
SO IT IS, AND SO IT WILL BE AGAIN. AGES AND AGES PAST...
...IT STILL GOES BY TOO FAST.
BELIEVE ME, HONEY.
I KNOW.
BUT YOU FEEL IT, DON'T YOU, MOM?
THIS TIME FEELS DIFFERENT, AND I DON'T KNOW WHY.
EVERY TIME IS DIFFERENT, MAIDIE.
THE TURN OF THE WHEEL IS CONSTANT, WHERE IT TAKES US IS WHAT CHANGES.
AND THE THING WITH THE WHEEL IS THAT IT KEEPS TURNING...
...WHETHER WE'RE READY TO MOVE ON OR NOT.

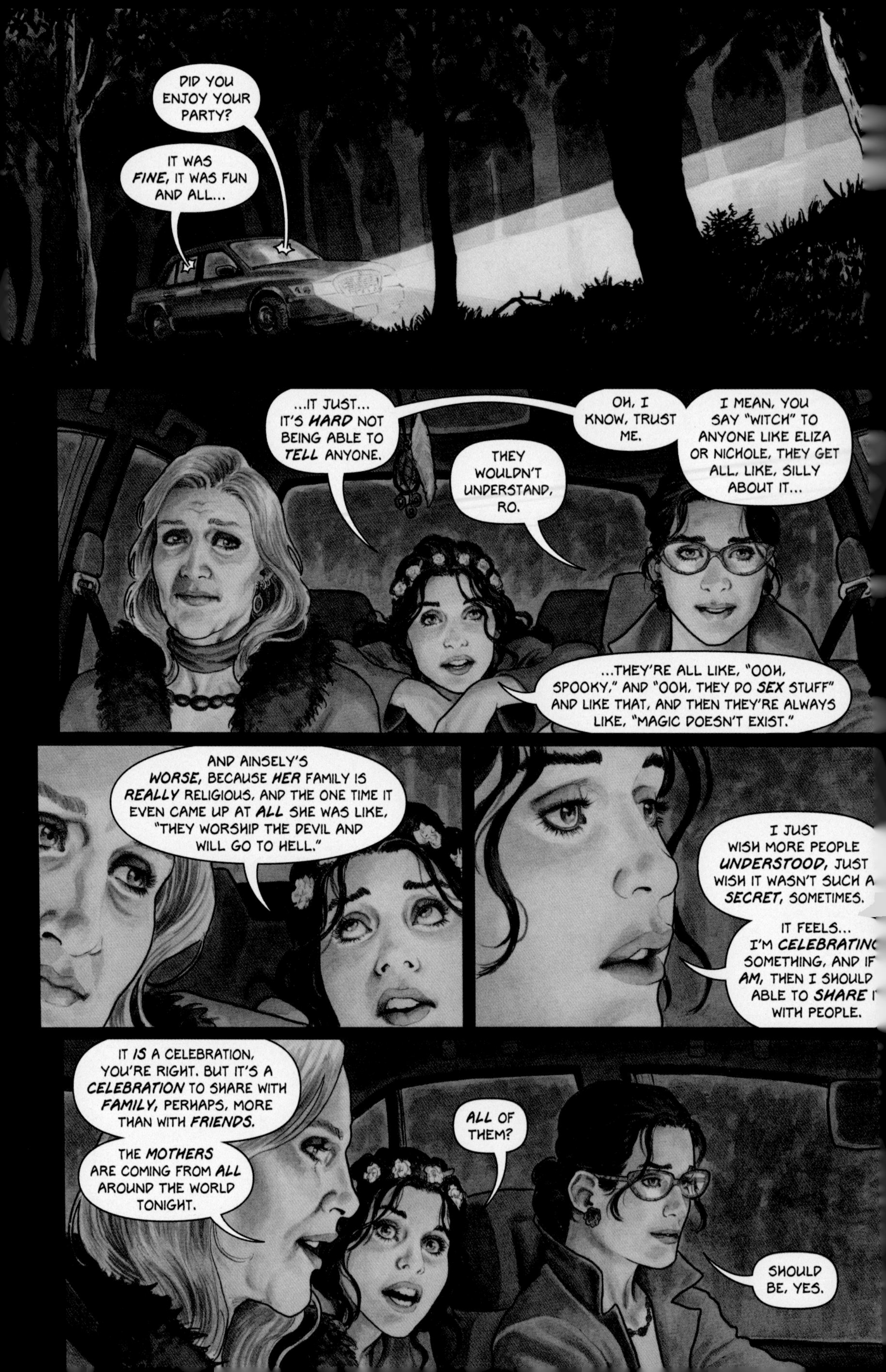
DID YOU ENJOY YOUR PARTY?
IT WAS FINE, IT WAS FUN AND ALL...
...IT JUST... IT'S HARD NOT BEING ABLE TO TELL ANYONE.
OH, I KNOW, TRUST ME.
THEY WOULDN'T UNDERSTAND, RO.
I MEAN, YOU SAY "WITCH" TO ANYONE LIKE ELIZA OR NICHOLE, THEY GET ALL, LIKE, SILLY ABOUT IT...
...THEY'RE ALL LIKE, "OOH, SPOOKY," AND "OOH, THEY DO SEX STUFF" AND LIKE THAT, AND THEN THEY'RE ALWAYS LIKE, "MAGIC DOESN'T EXIST."
AND AINSELY'S WORSE, BECAUSE HER FAMILY IS REALLY RELIGIOUS, AND THE ONE TIME IT EVEN CAME UP AT ALL SHE WAS LIKE, "THEY WORSHIP THE DEVIL AND WILL GO TO HELL."
I JUST WISH MORE PEOPLE UNDERSTOOD, JUST WISH IT WASN'T SUCH A SECRET, SOMETIMES.
IT FEELS... I'M CELEBRATIN SOMETHING, AND IF AM, THEN I SHOULD ABLE TO SHARE I WITH PEOPLE.
IT IS A CELEBRATION, YOU'RE RIGHT. BUT IT'S A CELEBRATION TO SHARE WITH FAMILY, PERHAPS, MORE THAN WITH FRIENDS.
THE MOTHERS ARE COMING FROM ALL AROUND THE WORLD TONIGHT.
ALL OF THEM?
SHOULD BE, YES.

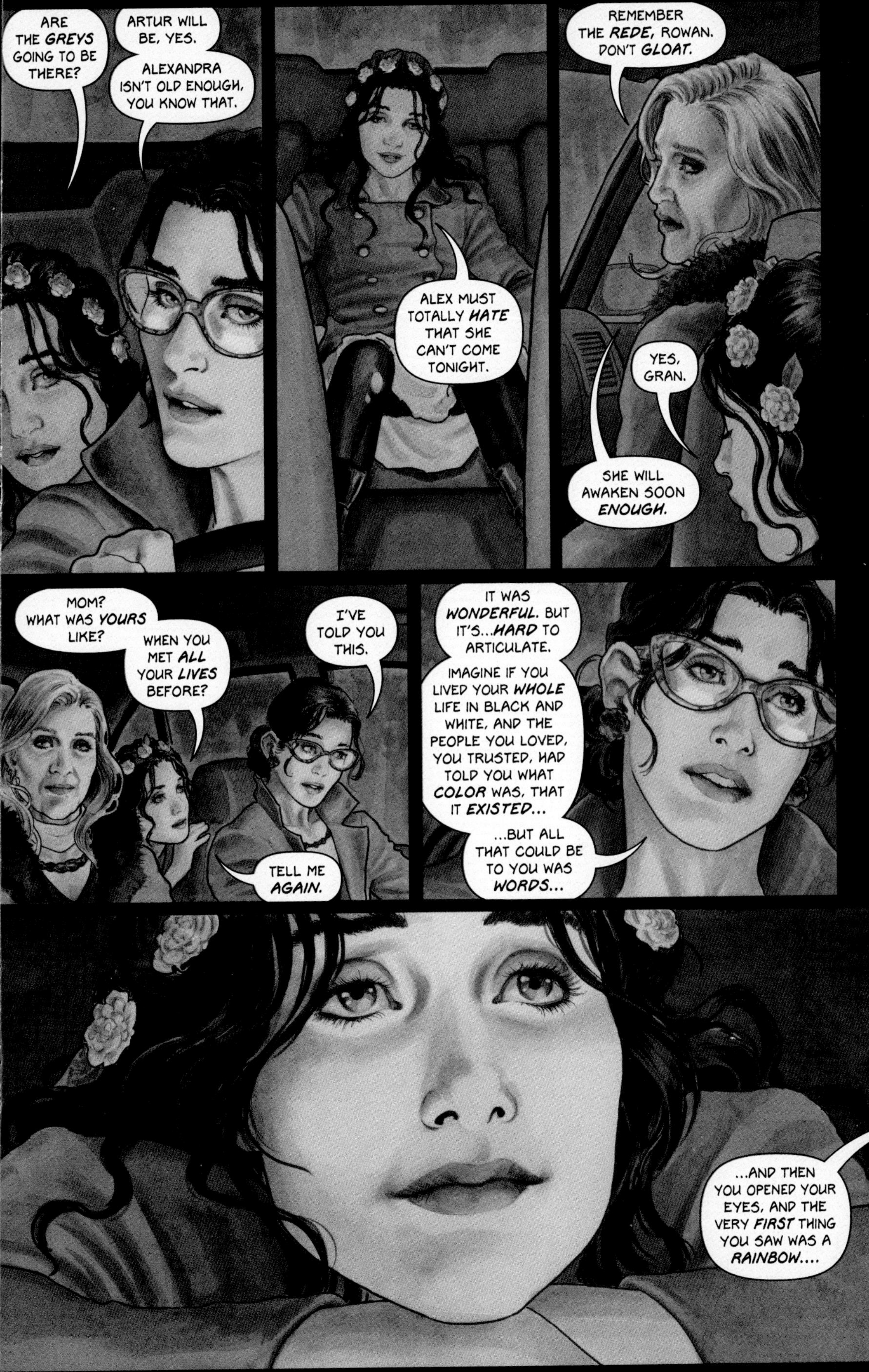
ARE THE GREYS GOING TO BE THERE?
ARTUR WILL BE, YES.
ALEXANDRA ISN'T OLD ENOUGH, YOU KNOW THAT.
ALEX MUST TOTALLY HATE THAT SHE CAN'T COME TONIGHT.
REMEMBER THE REDE, ROWAN. DON'T GLOAT.
YES, GRAN.
SHE WILL AWAKEN SOON ENOUGH.
MOM? WHAT WAS YOURS LIKE?
WHEN YOU MET ALL YOUR LIVES BEFORE?
I'VE TOLD YOU THIS.
TELL ME AGAIN.
IT WAS WONDERFUL. BUT IT'S...HARD TO ARTICULATE.
IMAGINE IF YOU LIVED YOUR WHOLE LIFE IN BLACK AND WHITE, AND THE PEOPLE YOU LOVED, YOU TRUSTED, HAD TOLD YOU WHAT COLOR WAS, THAT IT EXISTED...
...BUT ALL THAT COULD BE TO YOU WAS WORDS...
...AND THEN YOU OPENED YOUR EYES, AND THE VERY FIRST THING YOU SAW WAS A RAINBOW....

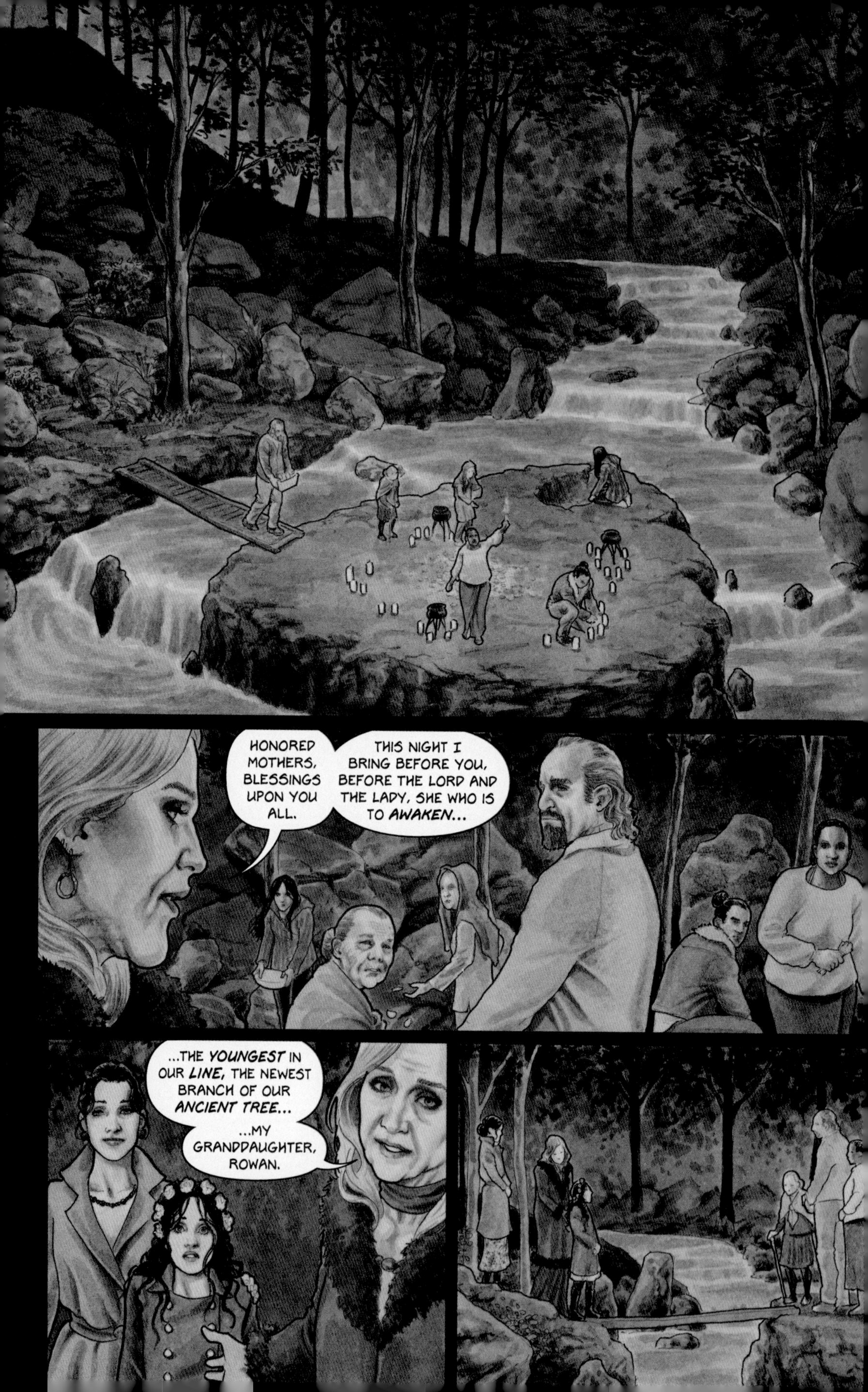
HONORED MOTHERS, BLESSINGS UPON YOU ALL.
THIS NIGHT I BRING BEFORE YOU, BEFORE THE LORD AND THE LADY, SHE WHO IS TO AWAKEN...
...THE YOUNGEST IN OUR LINE, THE NEWEST BRANCH OF OUR ANCIENT TREE...
...MY GRANDDAUGHTER, ROWAN.

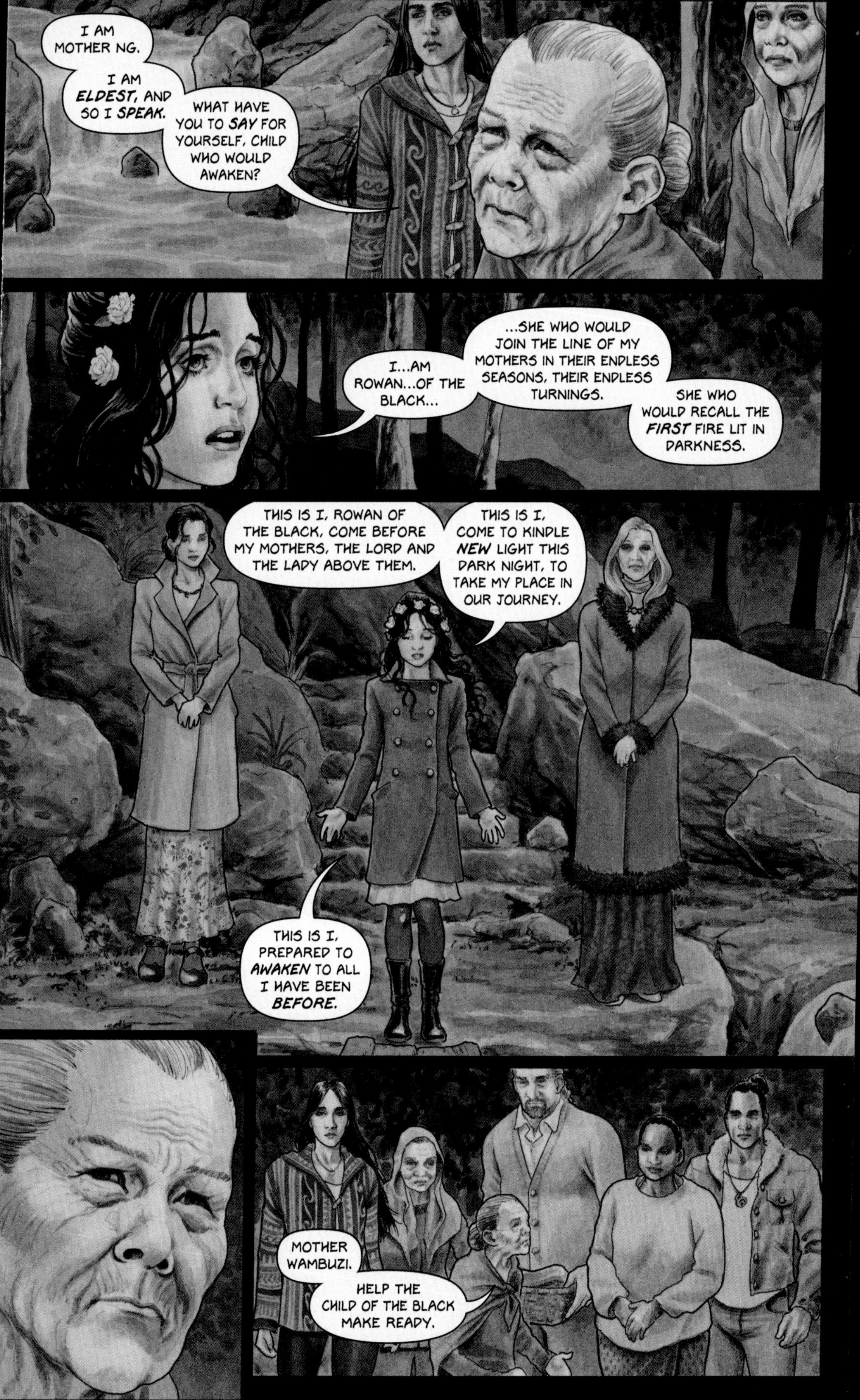
I AM MOTHER NG.
I AM ELDEST, AND SO I SPEAK.
WHAT HAVE YOU TO SAY FOR YOURSELF, CHILD WHO WOULD AWAKEN?
I...AM ROWAN...OF THE BLACK...
...SHE WHO WOULD JOIN THE LINE OF MY MOTHERS IN THEIR ENDLESS SEASONS, THEIR ENDLESS TURNINGS.
SHE WHO WOULD RECALL THE FIRST FIRE LIT IN DARKNESS.
THIS IS I, ROWAN OF THE BLACK, COME BEFORE MY MOTHERS, THE LORD AND THE LADY ABOVE THEM.
THIS IS I, COME TO KINDLE NEW LIGHT THIS DARK NIGHT, TO TAKE MY PLACE IN OUR JOURNEY.
THIS IS I, PREPARED TO AWAKEN TO ALL I HAVE BEEN BEFORE.
MOTHER WAMBUZI.
HELP THE CHILD OF THE BLACK MAKE READY.

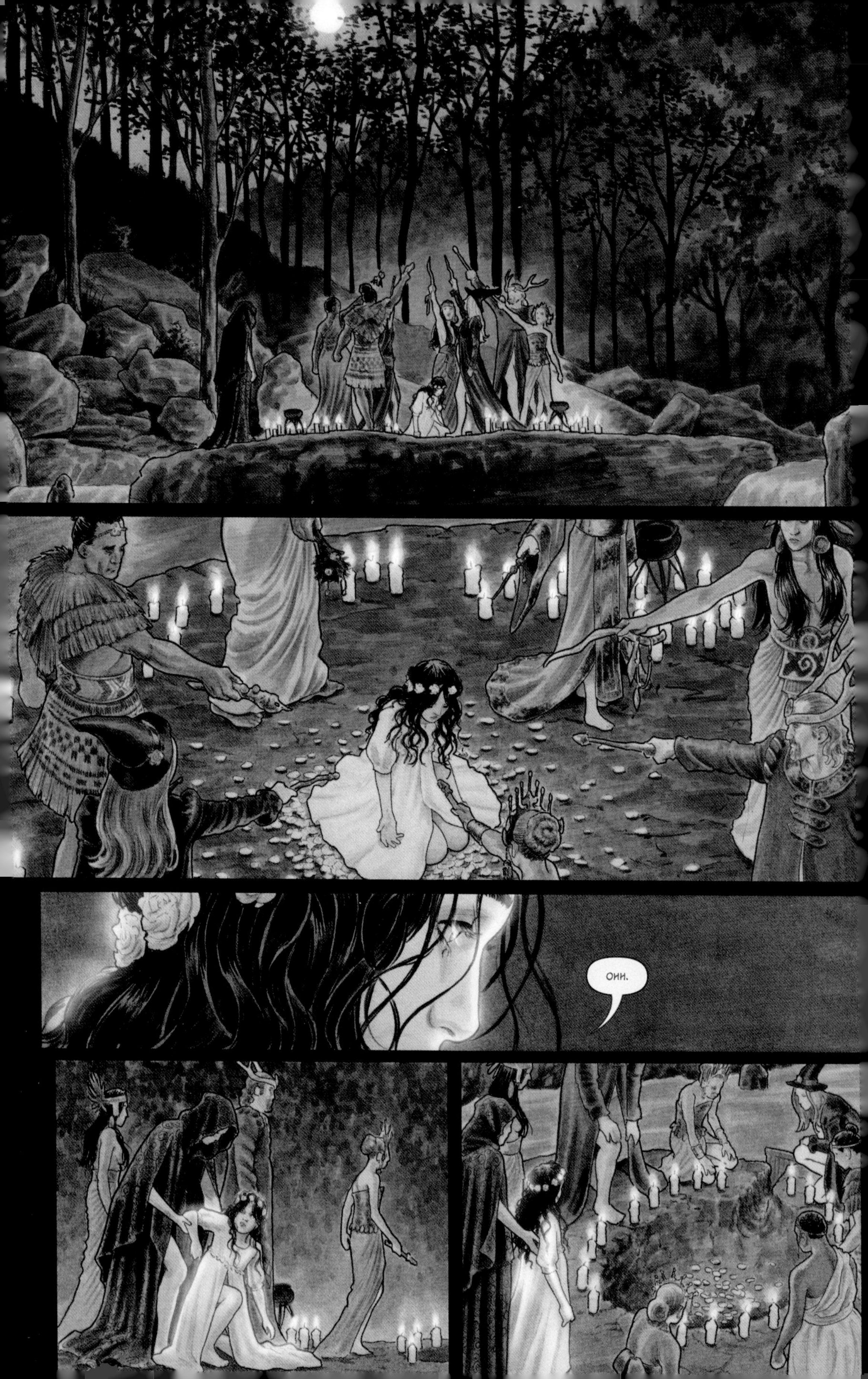
Они.

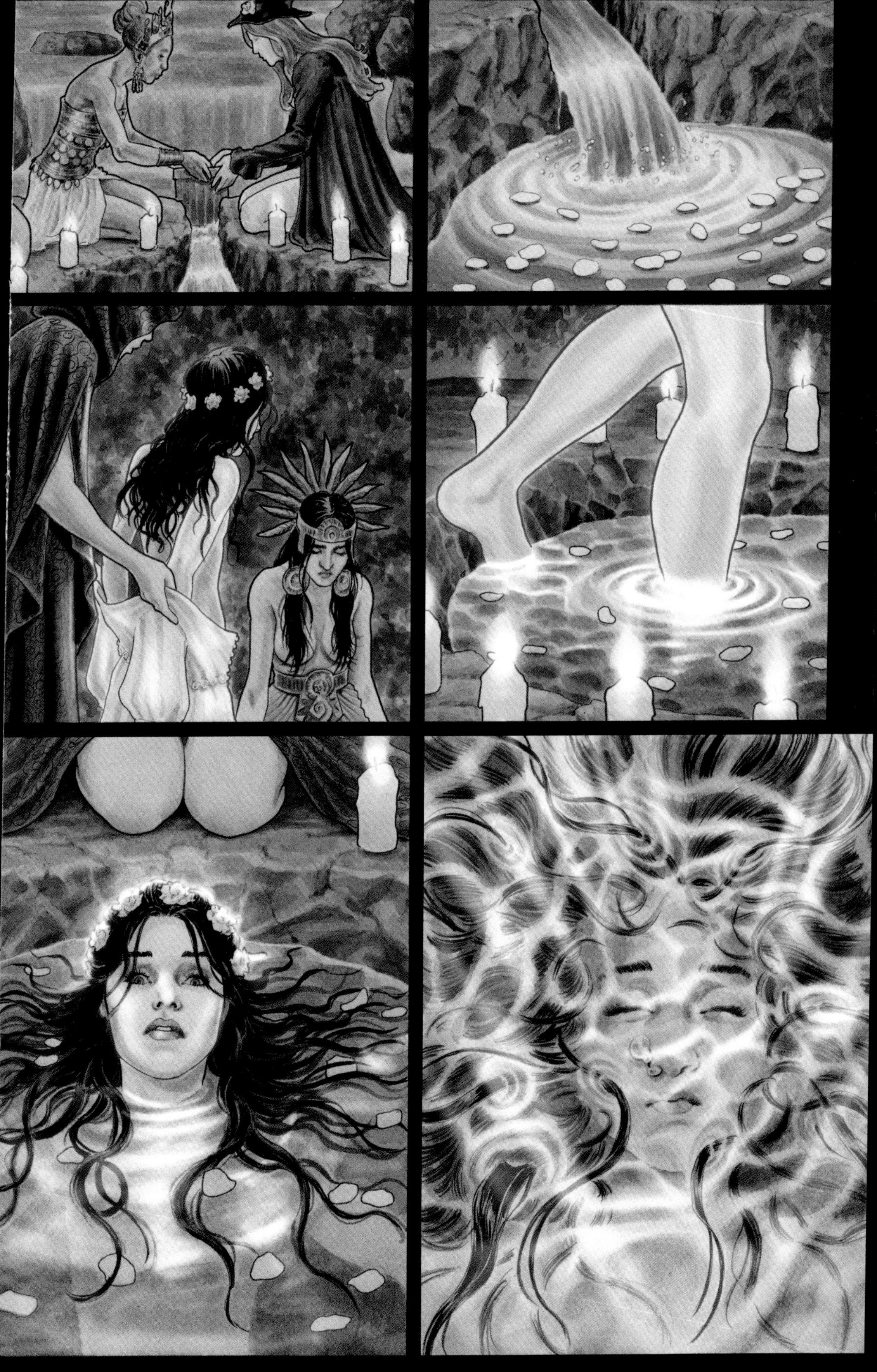

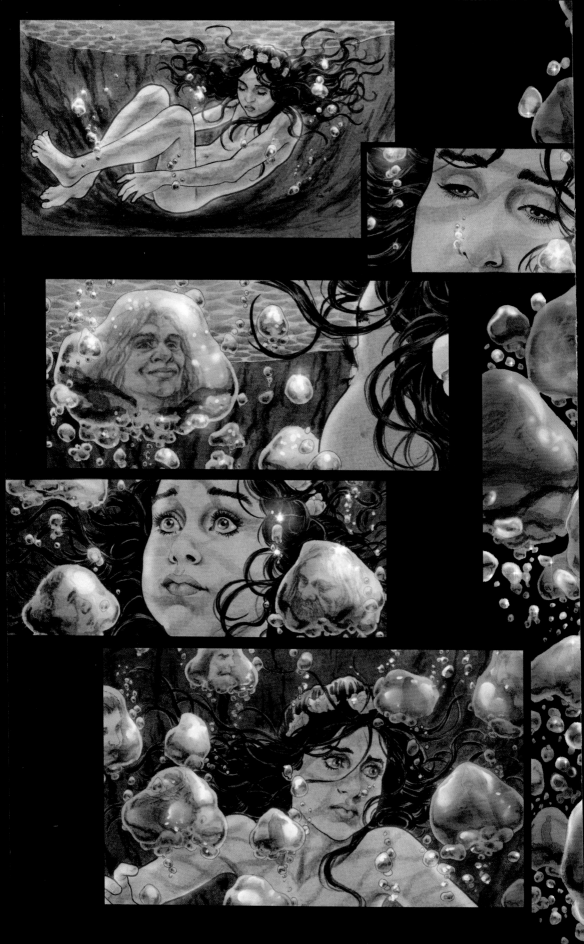

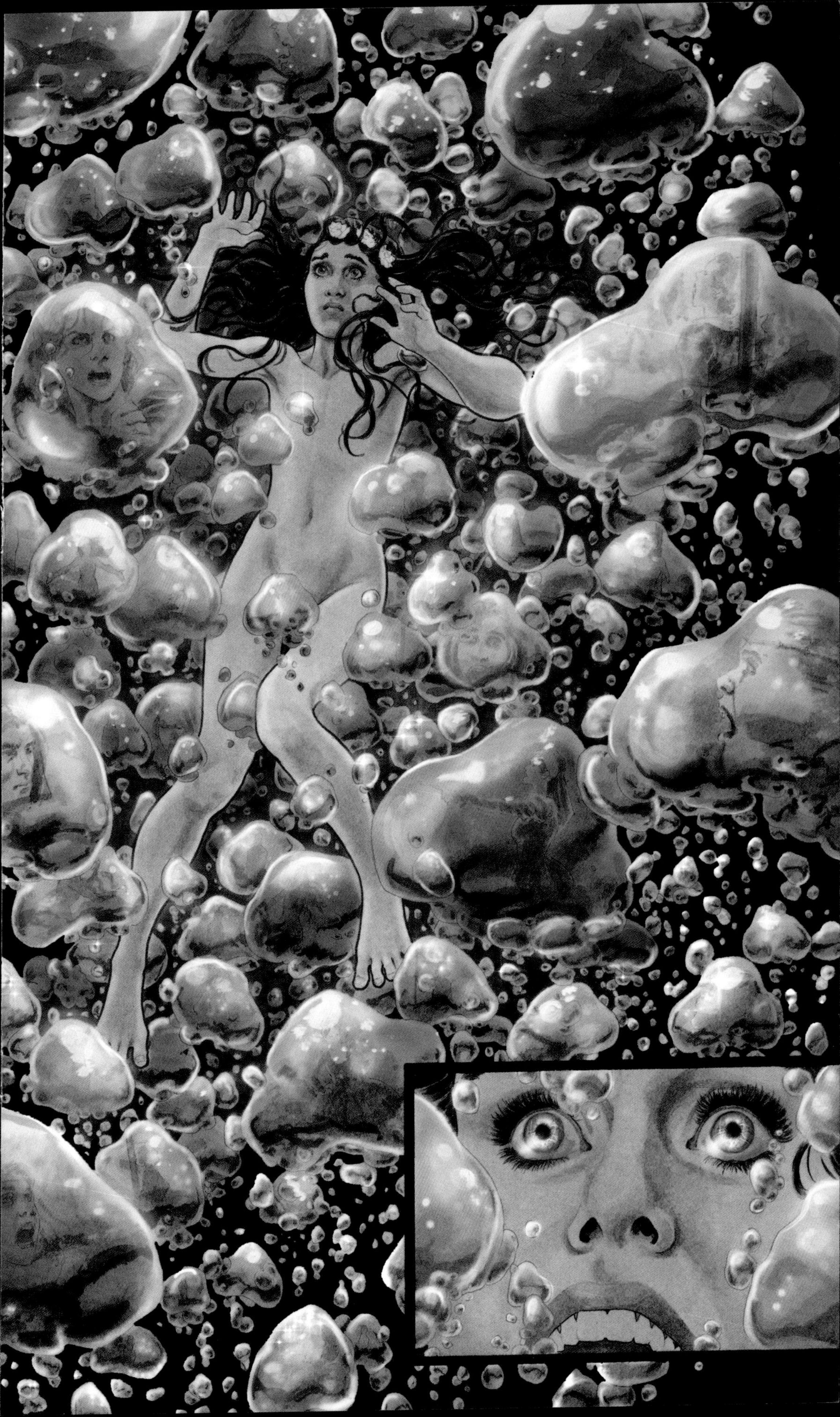

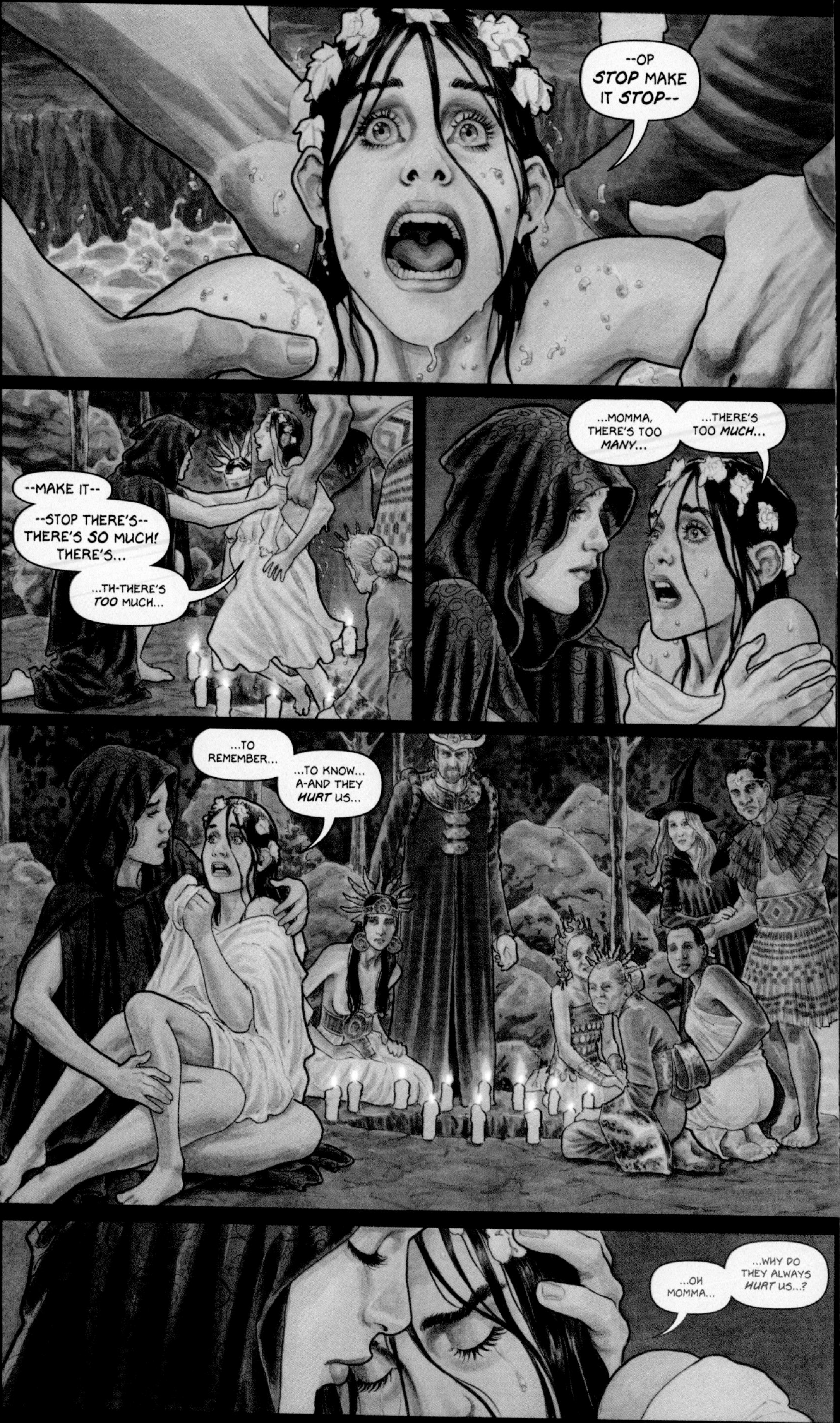
--OP STOP MAKE IT STOP--
--MAKE IT--
--STOP THERE'S-- THERE'S SO MUCH! THERE'S...
...TH-THERE'S TOO MUCH...
...MOMMA, THERE'S TOO MANY...
...THERE'S TOO MUCH...
...TO REMEMBER...
...TO KNOW... A-AND THEY HURT US...
...OH MOMMA...
...WHY DO THEY ALWAYS HURT US...?

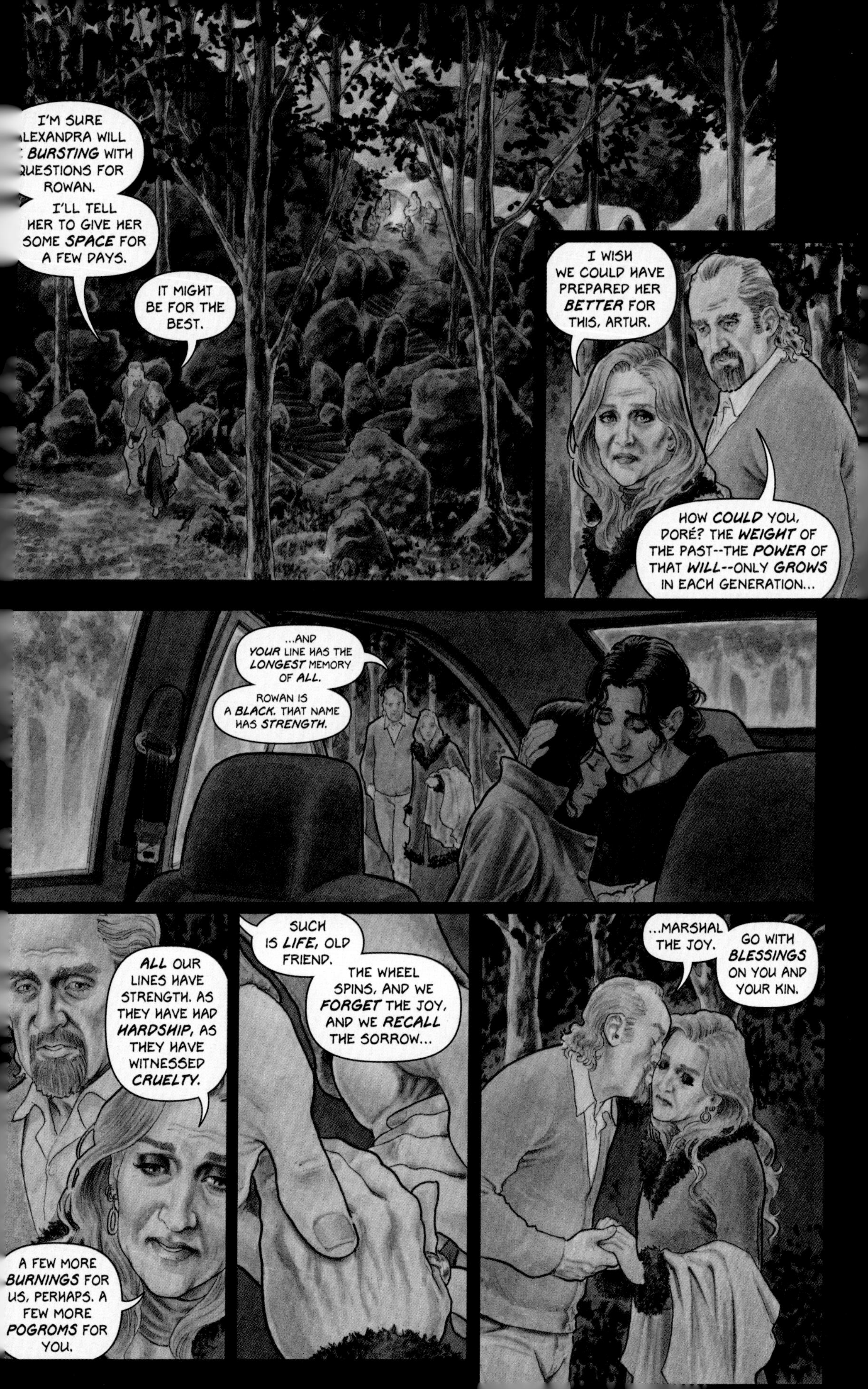
I'M SURE LEXANDRA WILL BURSTING WITH UESTIONS FOR ROWAN.
I'LL TELL HER TO GIVE HER SOME SPACE FOR A FEW DAYS.
IT MIGHT BE FOR THE BEST.
I WISH WE COULD HAVE PREPARED HER BETTER FOR THIS, ARTUR.
HOW COULD YOU, DORÉ? THE WEIGHT OF THE PAST--THE POWER OF THAT WILL--ONLY GROWS IN EACH GENERATION...
...AND YOUR LINE HAS THE LONGEST MEMORY OF ALL.
ROWAN IS A BLACK. THAT NAME HAS STRENGTH.
ALL OUR LINES HAVE STRENGTH. AS THEY HAVE HAD HARDSHIP, AS THEY HAVE WITNESSED CRUELTY.
A FEW MORE BURNINGS FOR US, PERHAPS. A FEW MORE POGROMS FOR YOU.
SUCH IS LIFE, OLD FRIEND.
THE WHEEL SPINS, AND WE FORGET THE JOY, AND WE RECALL THE SORROW...
...MARSHAL THE JOY.
GO WITH BLESSINGS ON YOU AND YOUR KIN.

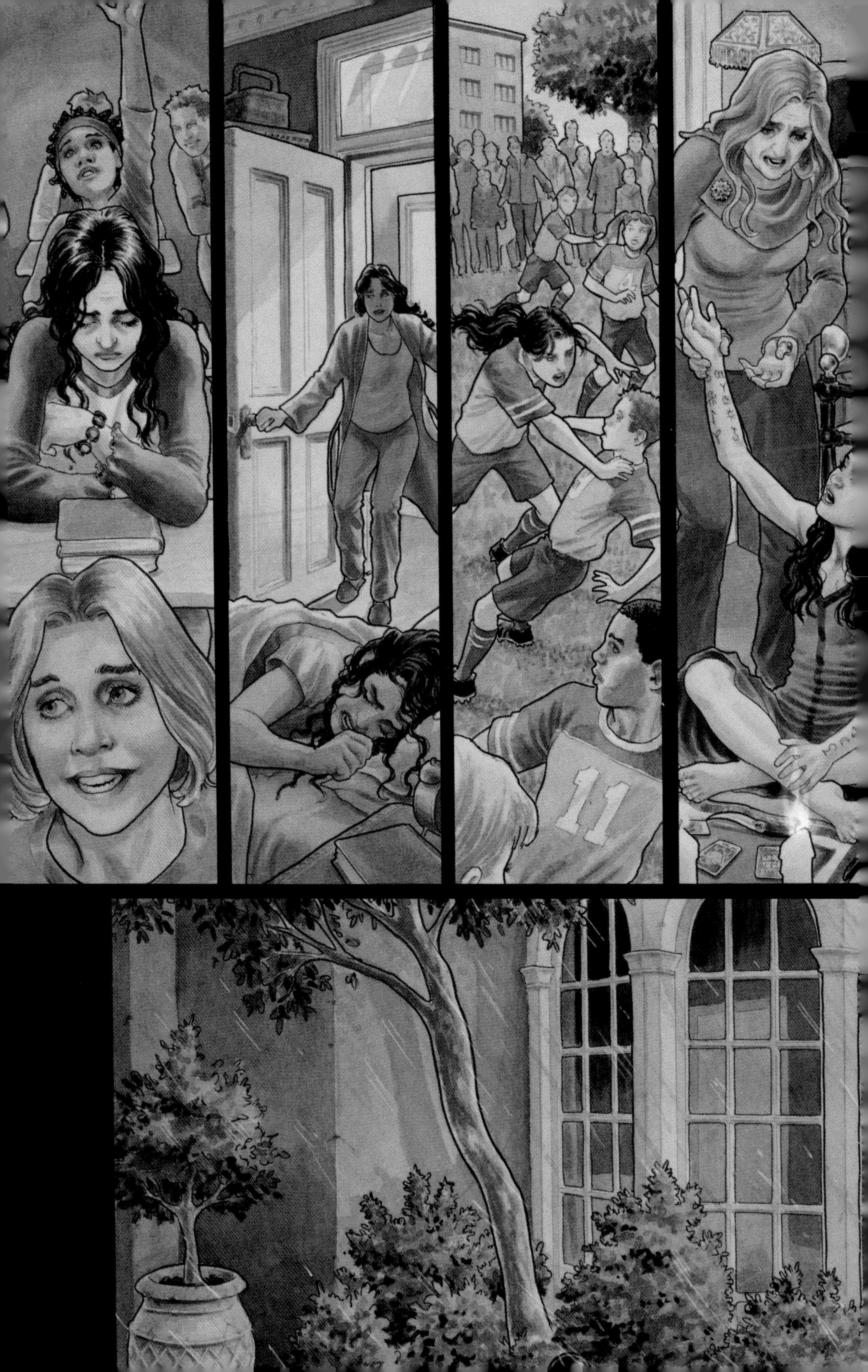

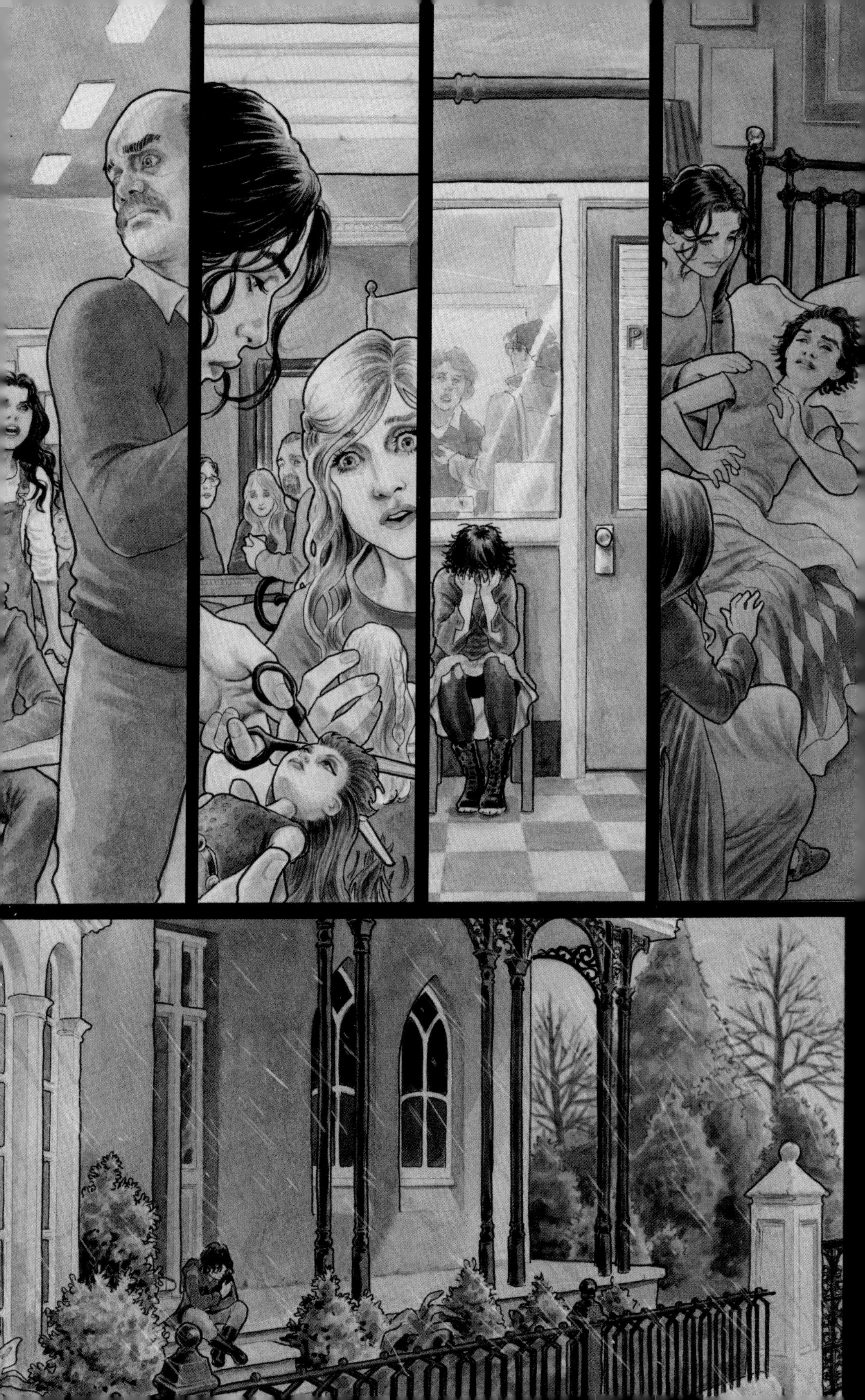

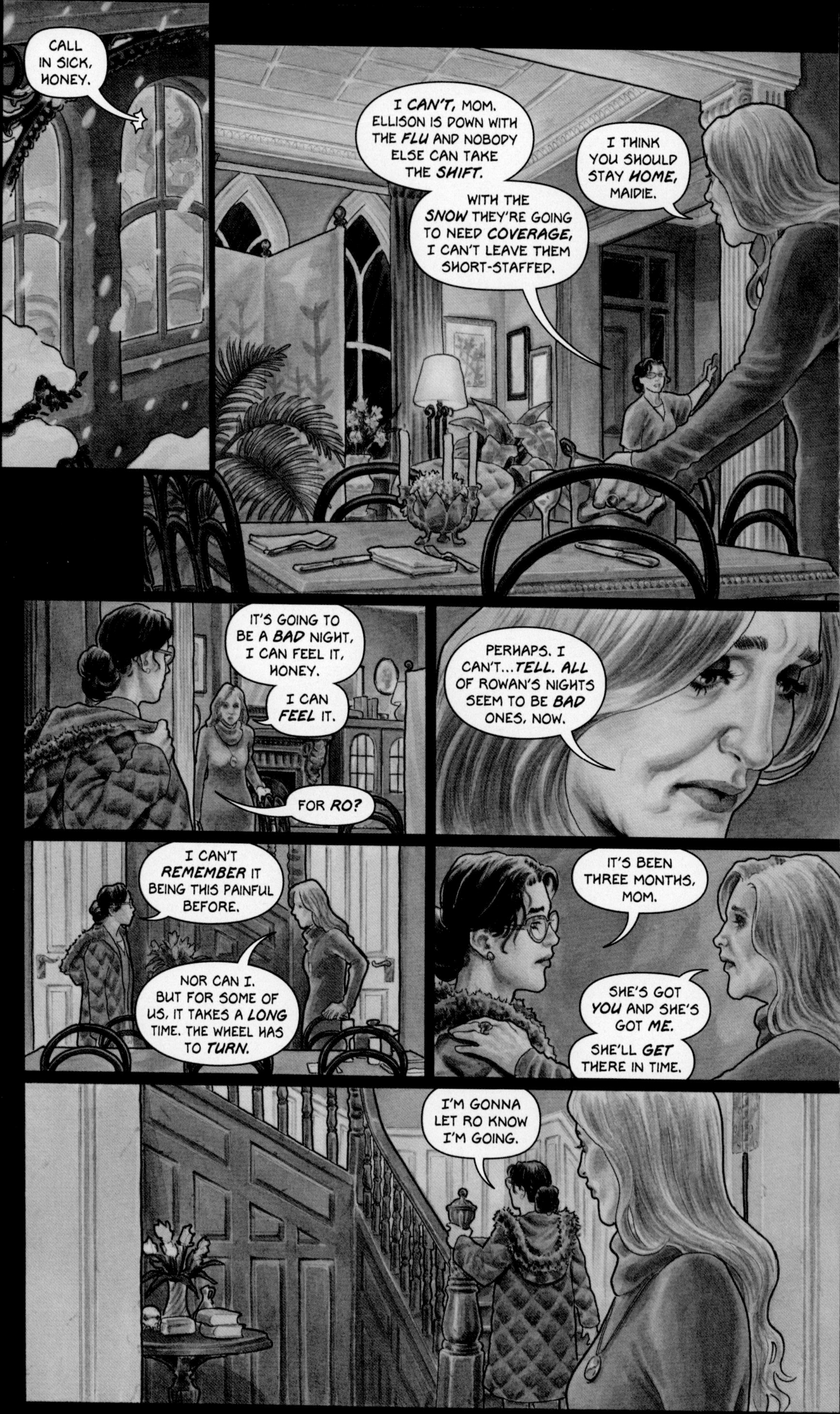
CALL IN SICK, HONEY.
I *CAN'T*, MOM. ELLISON IS DOWN WITH THE *FLU* AND NOBODY ELSE CAN TAKE THE *SHIFT*.
WITH THE *SNOW* THEY'RE GOING TO NEED *COVERAGE*, I CAN'T LEAVE THEM SHORT-STAFFED.
I THINK YOU SHOULD STAY *HOME*, MAIDIE.
IT'S GOING TO BE A *BAD* NIGHT, I CAN FEEL IT, HONEY.
I CAN *FEEL* IT.
FOR *RO?*
PERHAPS. I CAN'T...*TELL*. *ALL* OF ROWAN'S NIGHTS SEEM TO BE *BAD* ONES, NOW.
I CAN'T *REMEMBER* IT BEING THIS PAINFUL BEFORE.
NOR CAN I. BUT FOR SOME OF US, IT TAKES A *LONG* TIME. THE WHEEL HAS TO *TURN*.
IT'S BEEN THREE MONTHS, MOM.
SHE'S GOT *YOU* AND SHE'S GOT *ME*.
SHE'LL *GET* THERE IN TIME.
I'M GONNA LET RO KNOW I'M GOING.

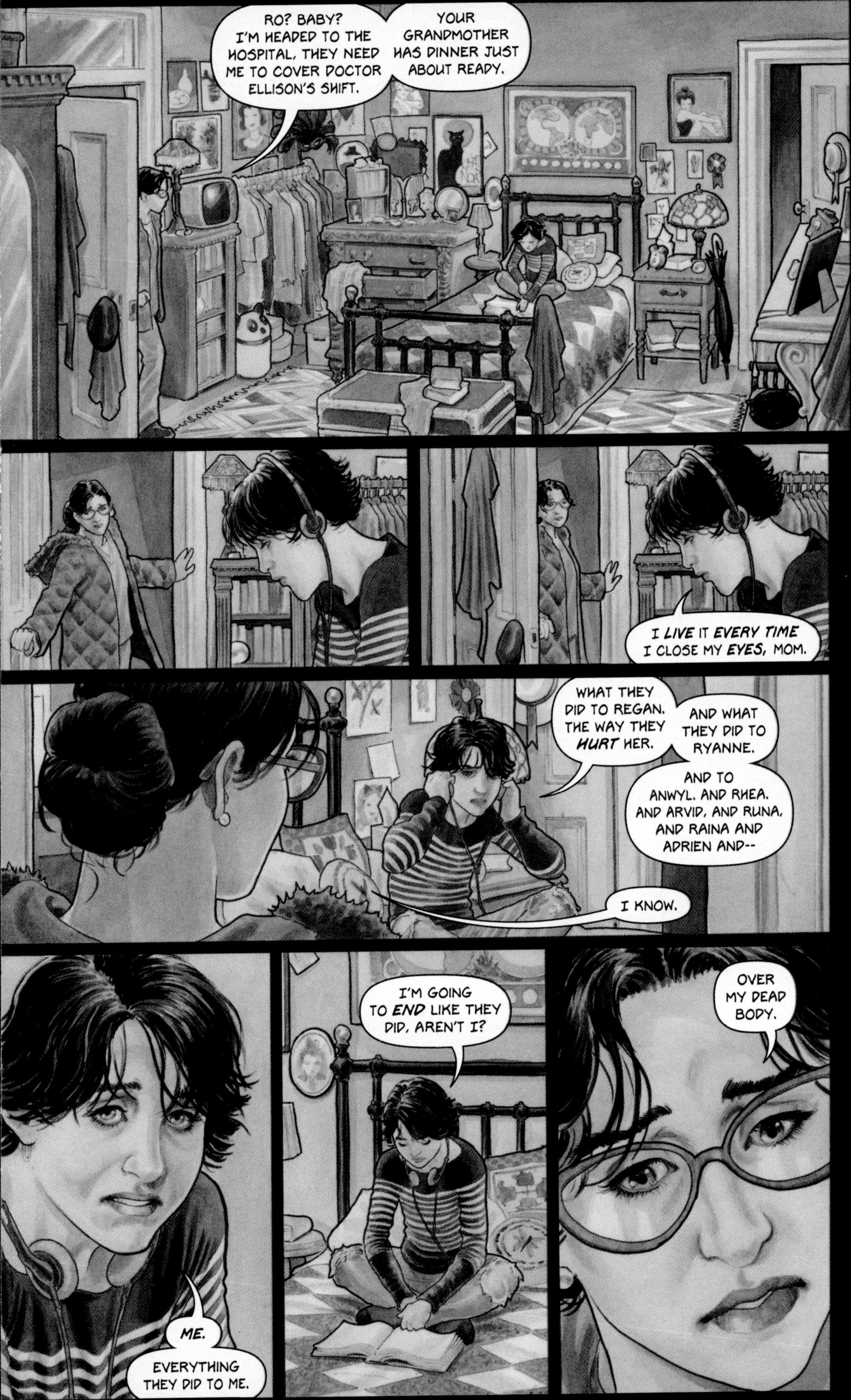
RO? BABY? I'M HEADED TO THE HOSPITAL. THEY NEED ME TO COVER DOCTOR ELLISON'S SHIFT.
YOUR GRANDMOTHER HAS DINNER JUST ABOUT READY.
I LIVE IT EVERY TIME I CLOSE MY EYES, MOM.
WHAT THEY DID TO REGAN. THE WAY THEY HURT HER.
AND WHAT THEY DID TO RYANNE.
AND TO ANWYL. AND RHEA. AND ARVID, AND RUNA, AND RAINA AND ADRIEN AND--
I KNOW.
ME.
EVERYTHING THEY DID TO ME.
I'M GOING TO END LIKE THEY DID, AREN'T I?
OVER MY DEAD BODY.

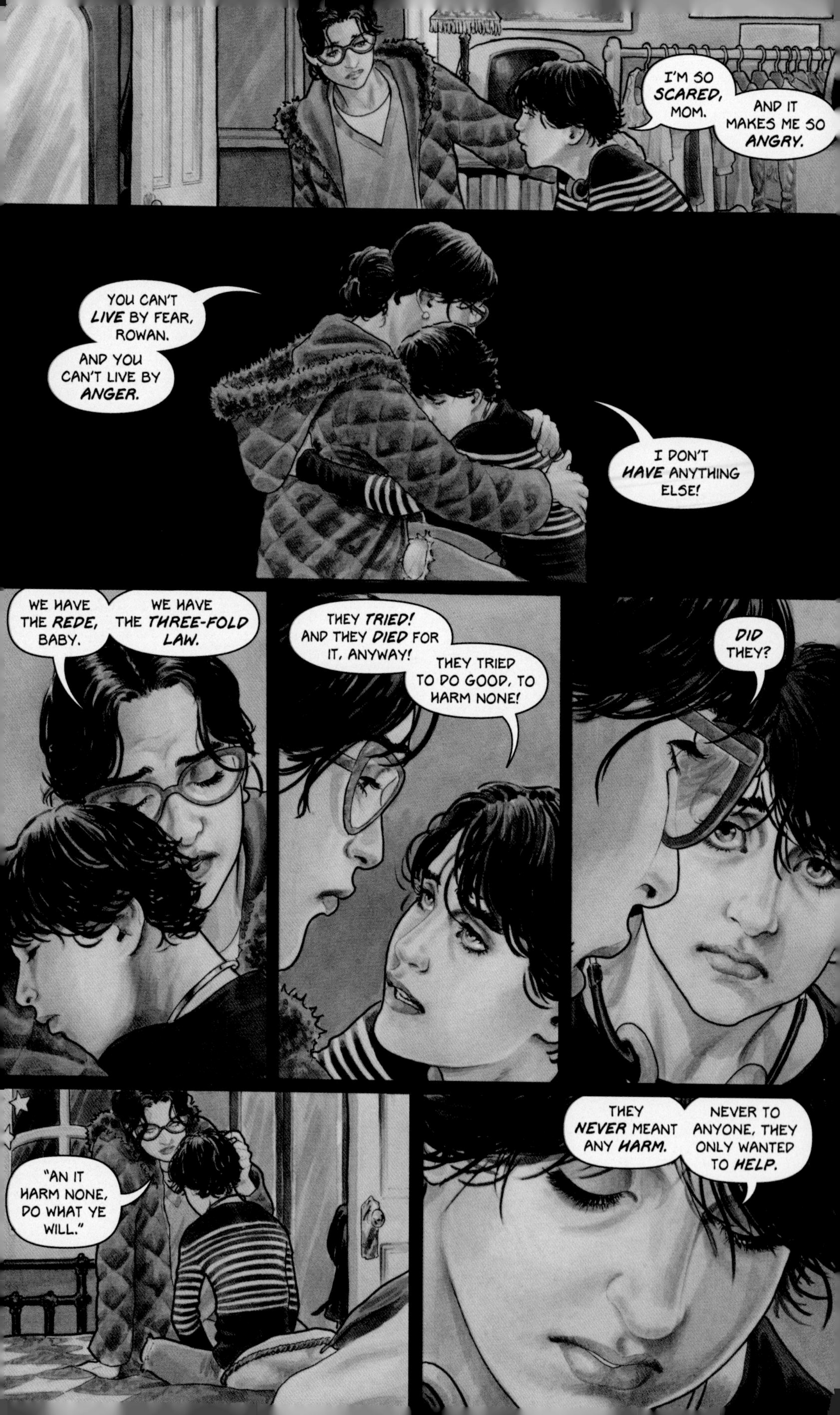
I'M SO SCARED, MOM.
AND IT MAKES ME SO ANGRY.
YOU CAN'T LIVE BY FEAR, ROWAN.
AND YOU CAN'T LIVE BY ANGER.
I DON'T HAVE ANYTHING ELSE!
WE HAVE THE REDE, BABY.
WE HAVE THE THREE-FOLD LAW.
THEY TRIED! AND THEY DIED FOR IT, ANYWAY!
THEY TRIED TO DO GOOD, TO HARM NONE!
DID THEY?
"AN IT HARM NONE, DO WHAT YE WILL."
THEY NEVER MEANT ANY HARM.
NEVER TO ANYONE, THEY ONLY WANTED TO HELP.

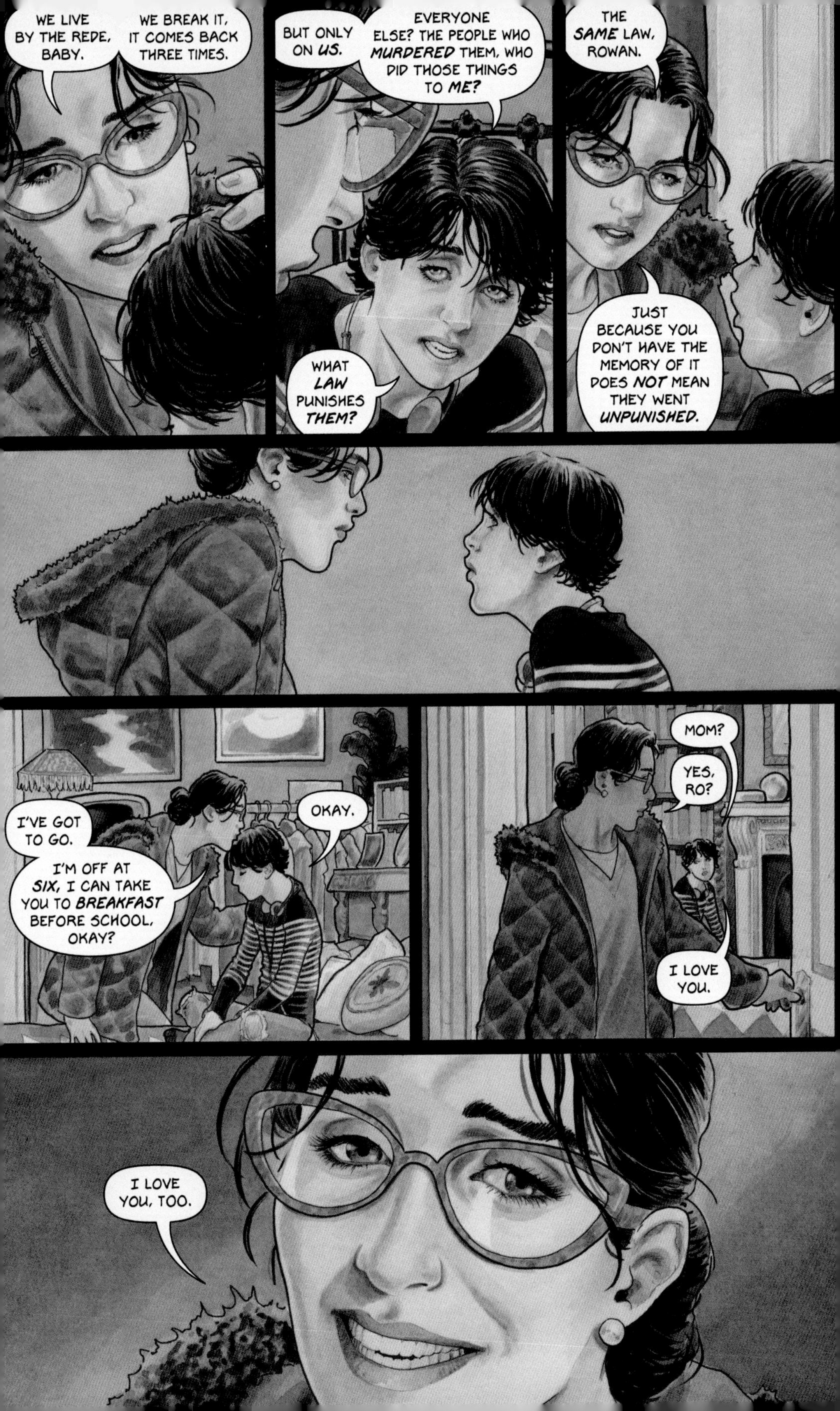
WE LIVE BY THE REDE, BABY.
WE BREAK IT, IT COMES BACK THREE TIMES.
BUT ONLY ON US.
EVERYONE ELSE? THE PEOPLE WHO MURDERED THEM, WHO DID THOSE THINGS TO ME?
WHAT LAW PUNISHES THEM?
THE SAME LAW, ROWAN.
JUST BECAUSE YOU DON'T HAVE THE MEMORY OF IT DOES NOT MEAN THEY WENT UNPUNISHED.
I'VE GOT TO GO.
I'M OFF AT SIX, I CAN TAKE YOU TO BREAKFAST BEFORE SCHOOL, OKAY?
OKAY.
MOM?
YES, RO?
I LOVE YOU.
I LOVE YOU, TOO.

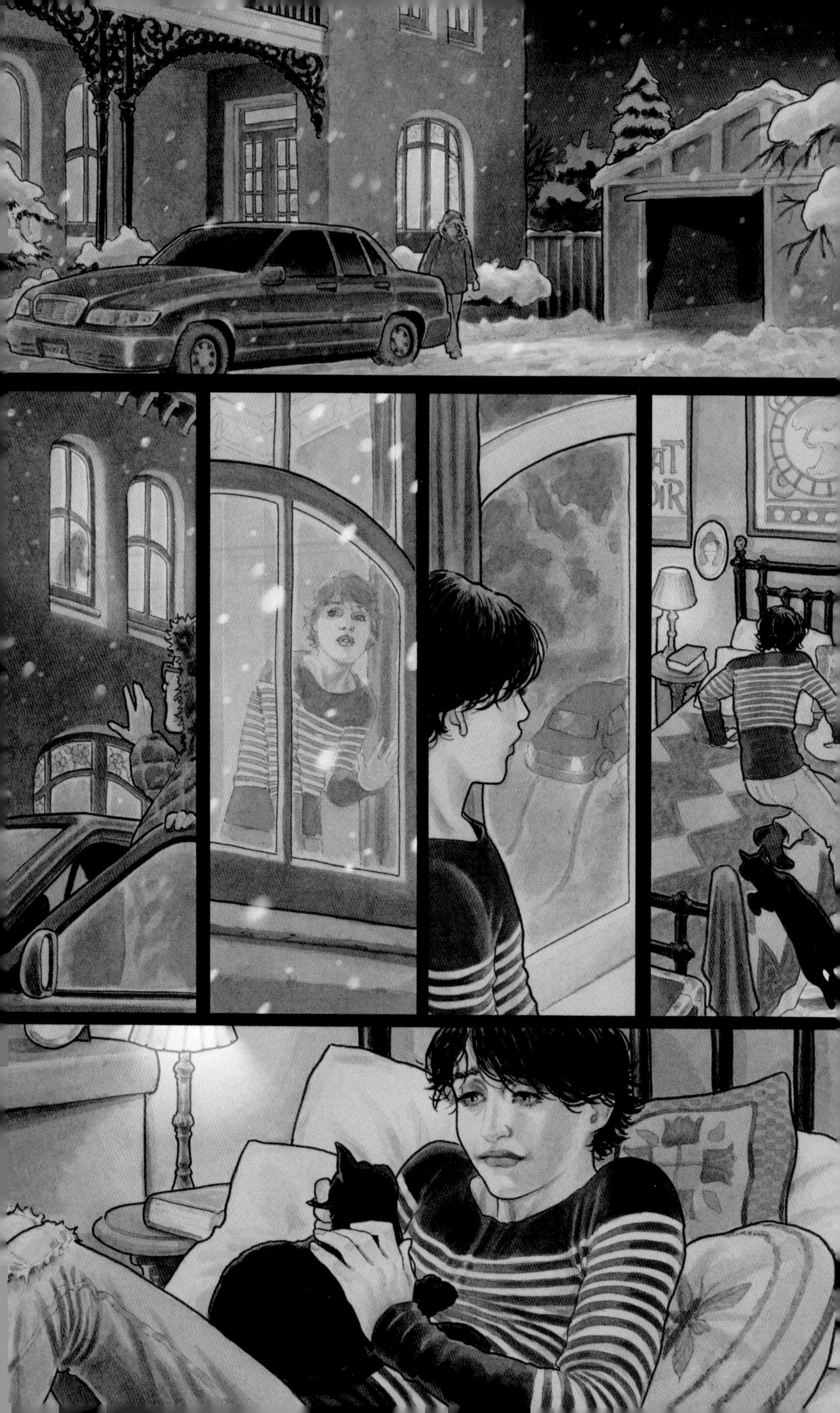

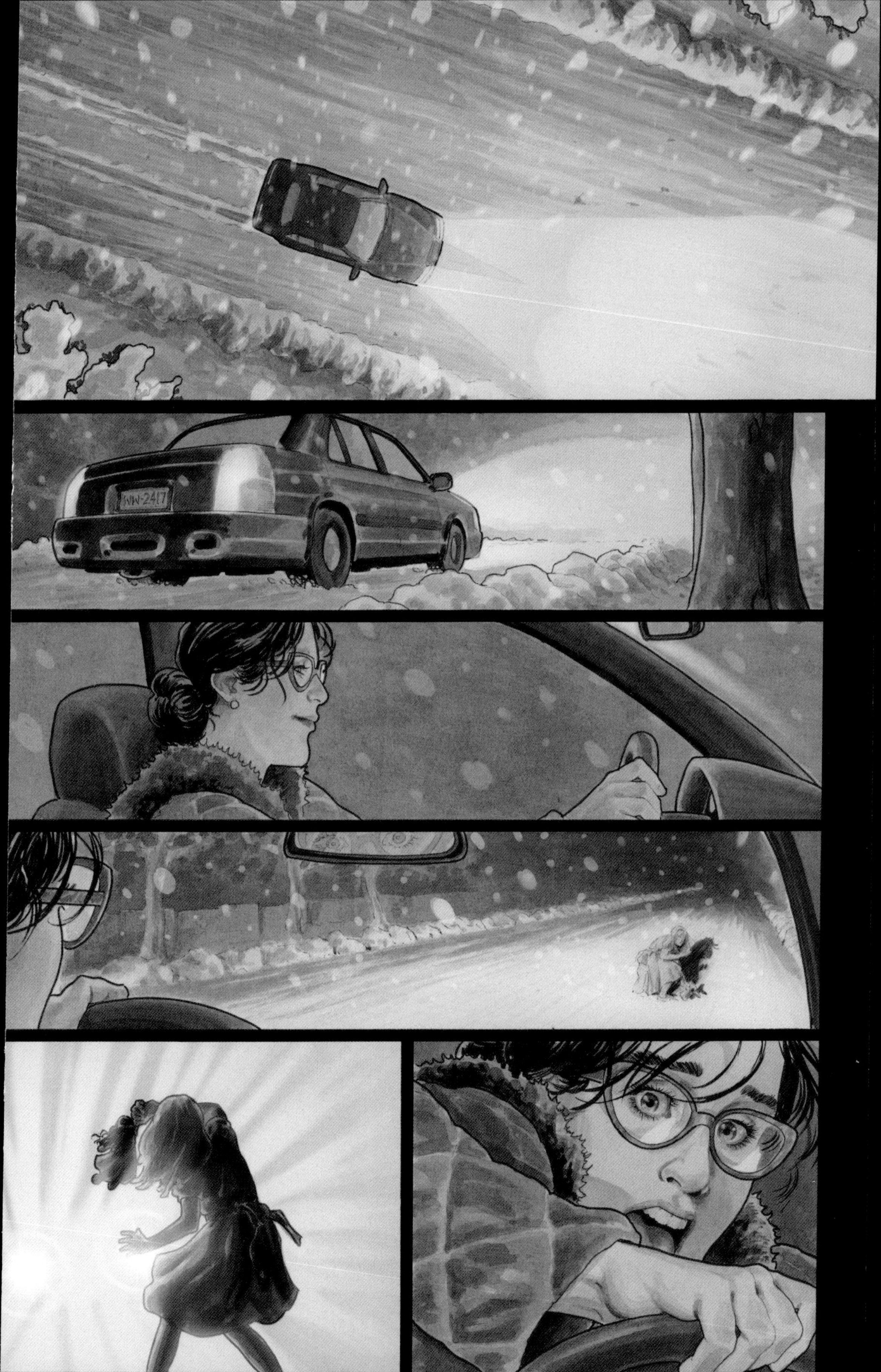
WW-2417

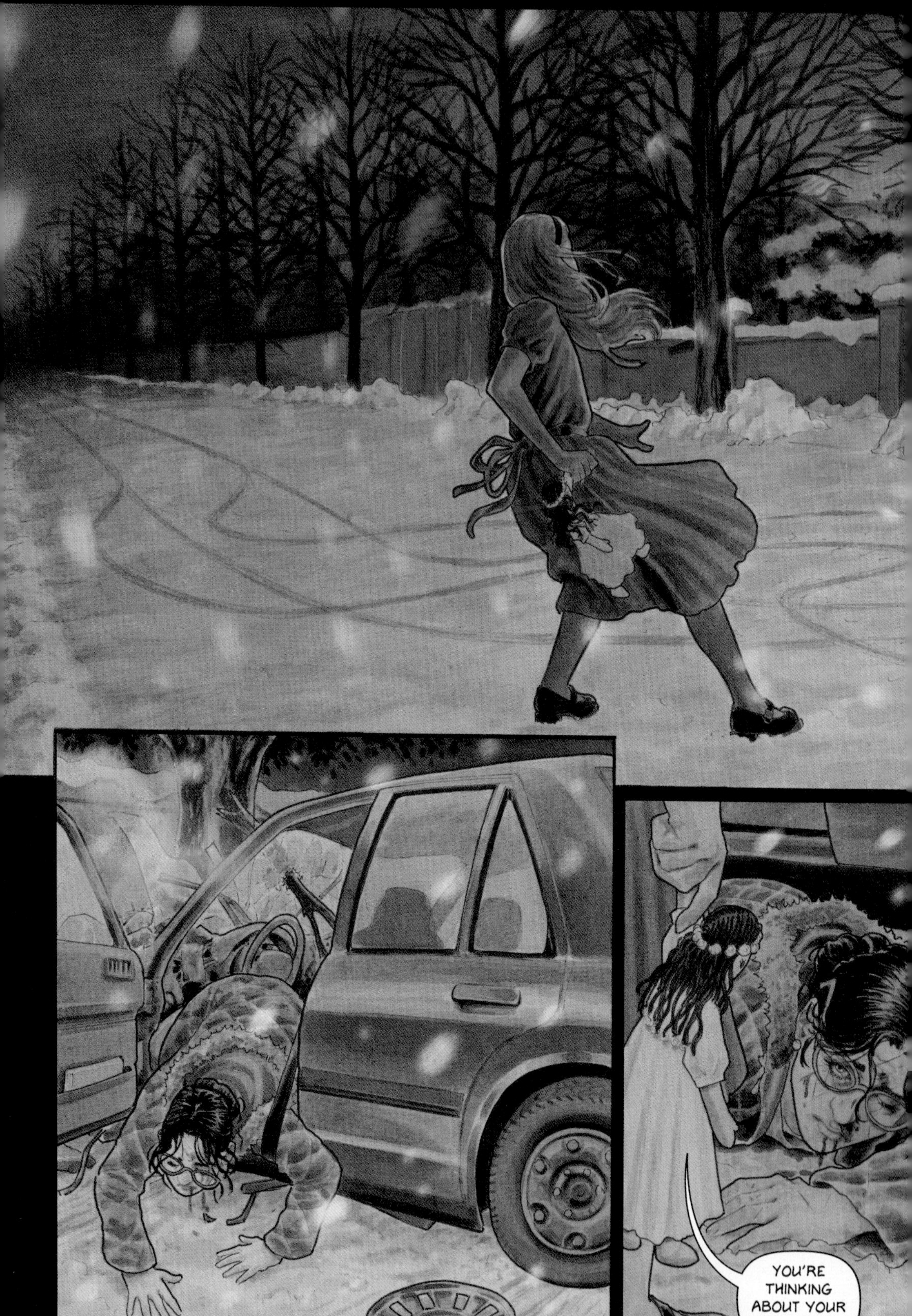
YOU'RE THINKING ABOUT YOUR DAUGHTER.
THAT'S SO SAD.

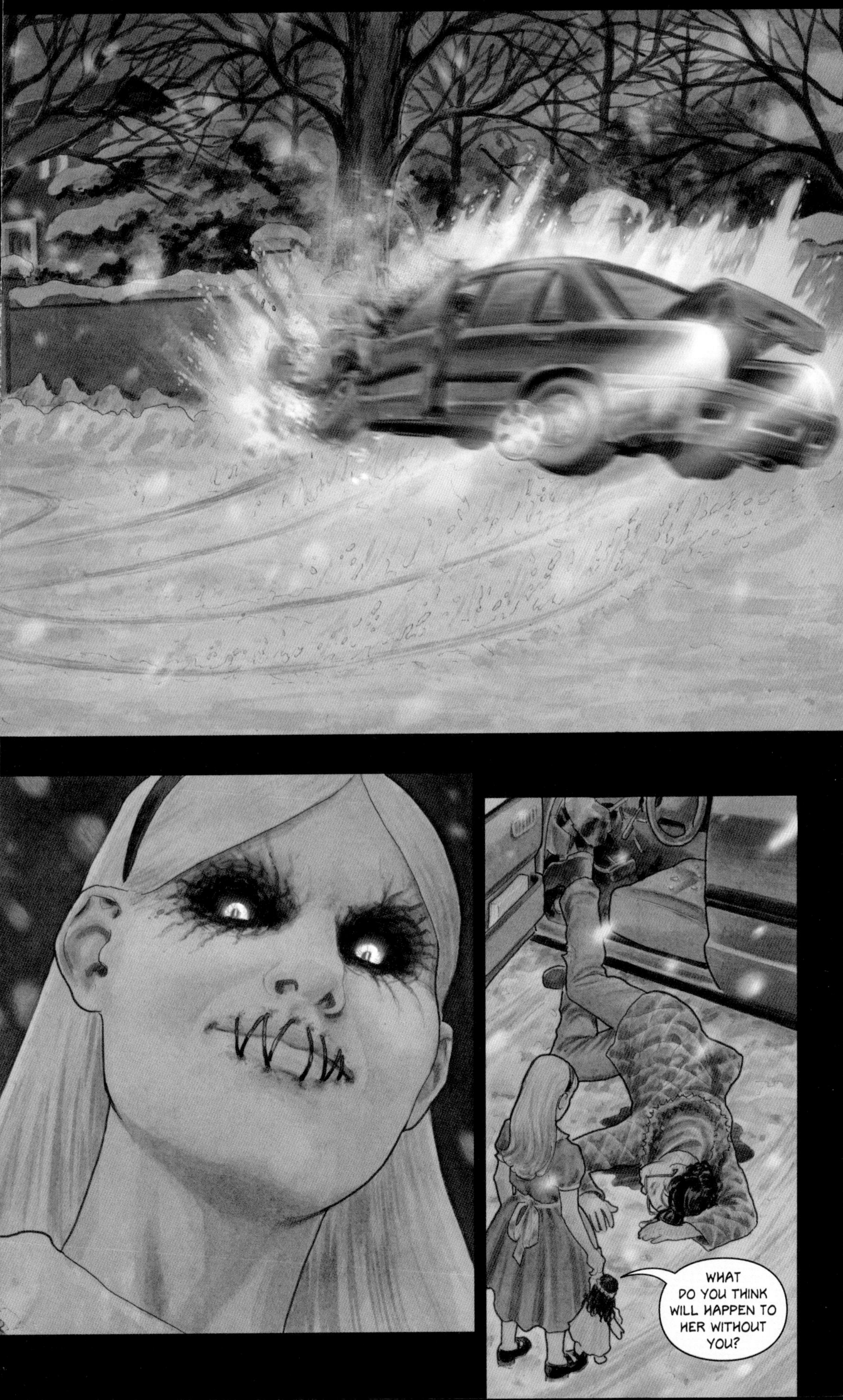
WHAT DO YOU THINK WILL HAPPEN TO HER WITHOUT YOU?

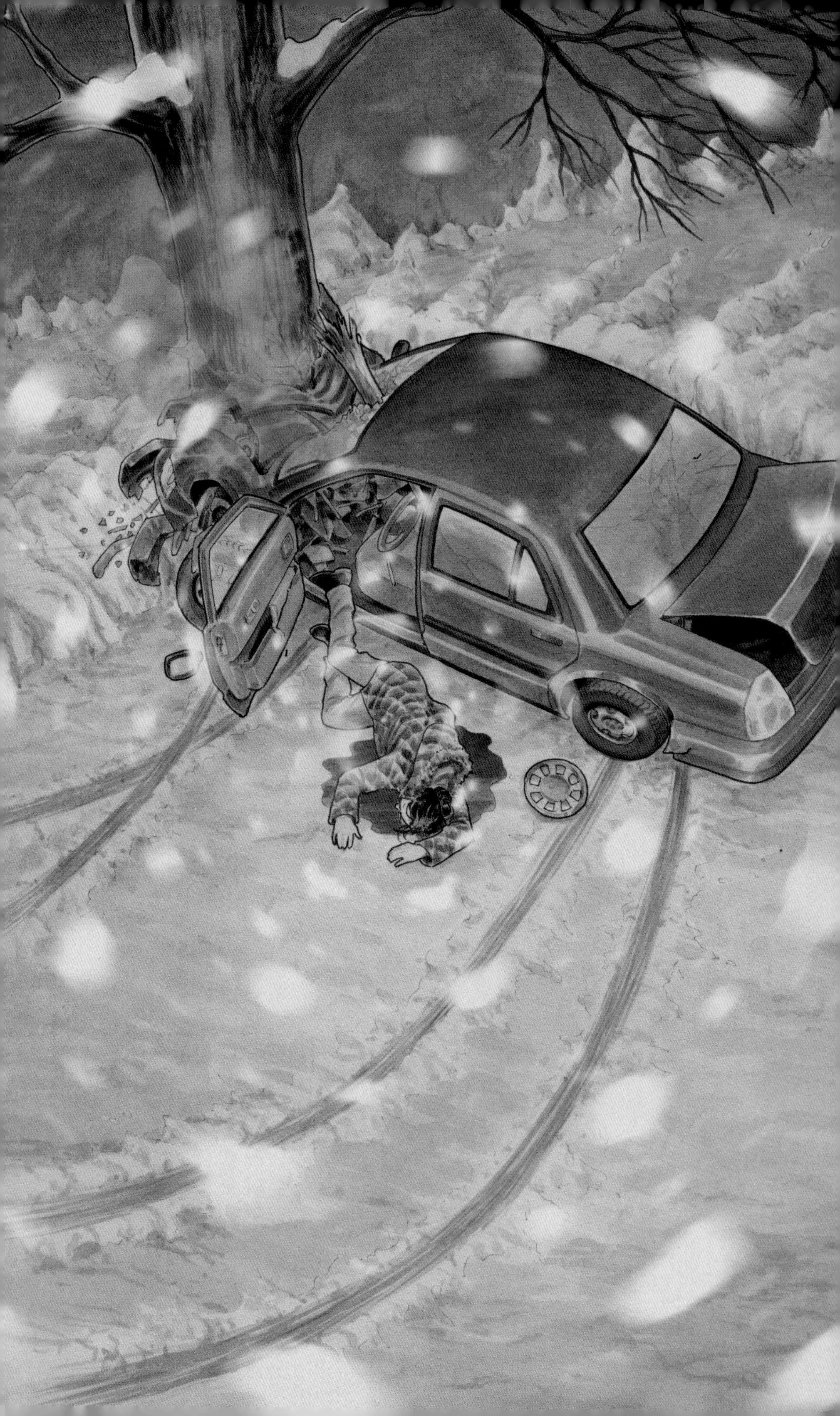

ARTMENT

CITY OF PORTSMO

ED   FIRST NAME   MIDDLE NAME   RACE   SEX   AGE   RESIDENCE OR PERSON KILLED   OFFENSE SERIAL N

                           TITLE OR RELATIONSHIP   RACE   SEX   AGE   ADDRESS OF PERSON KILLED   PHONE OF PERSON

ME)   AFTER INVESTIGATION CHANGED TO

STREET AND NUMBER OR INTERSECTION   DIVISION   PLATOON   BEAT   OFFICERS MAKING REPORT   I.D. NO.   NAME

OCCURENCE   TIME OF DAY   DATE REPORTED   REPORTED   REPORT RECEIVED BY   RECEIVED — TIME — TYPED

DESCRIPTION OF PERSON

T   EYES   HAIR   BEARD   LEXION   KS., ETC.   CLOTHING

          NAME OF CORONER   TIME OF ARRIVAL   AM   CUTOR ATTENDING — TIME OF ARRIVAL
                                                           PM

HYSICIAN   PERSON WITH WHOM ACCUSED   OR ASSOCIATED

CIRCUMSTANCES OF OCCURENCE OF OFFEN   IS INVESTIGATION)   USE   ES OF THIS SHEET

ODY   ADDRESS   ITNESS TAKEN INTO CUSTODY   ADDRESS

OSSIBLE MOTIVES

      ALIAS   ADDRESS   SEX   RACE   AGE   HEIGHT   WEIGHT   EYES   HAIR   COMPLEXION

OCCUPATION   DRESS AND OTHER MARKS   FOR SUSPICION

      ALIAS   ADDRESS   SEX   RACE   AGE   HEIGHT   WEIGHT   EYES   HAIR   COMPLEXION

OCCUPATION   DRESS AND OTHER MARKS   CAUSE FOR SUSPICION

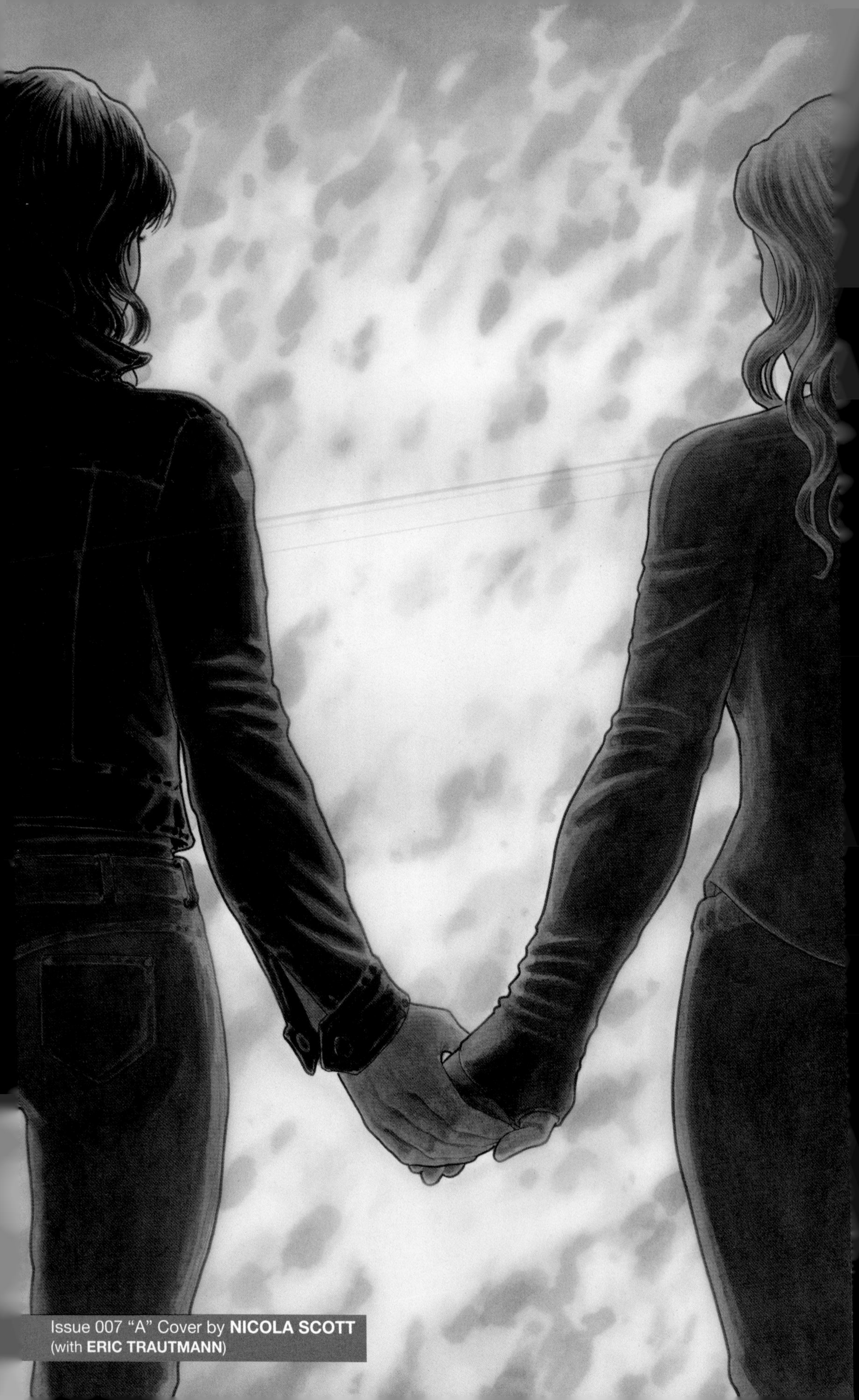

Issue 007 "A" Cover by **NICOLA SCOTT**
(with **ERIC TRAUTMANN**)

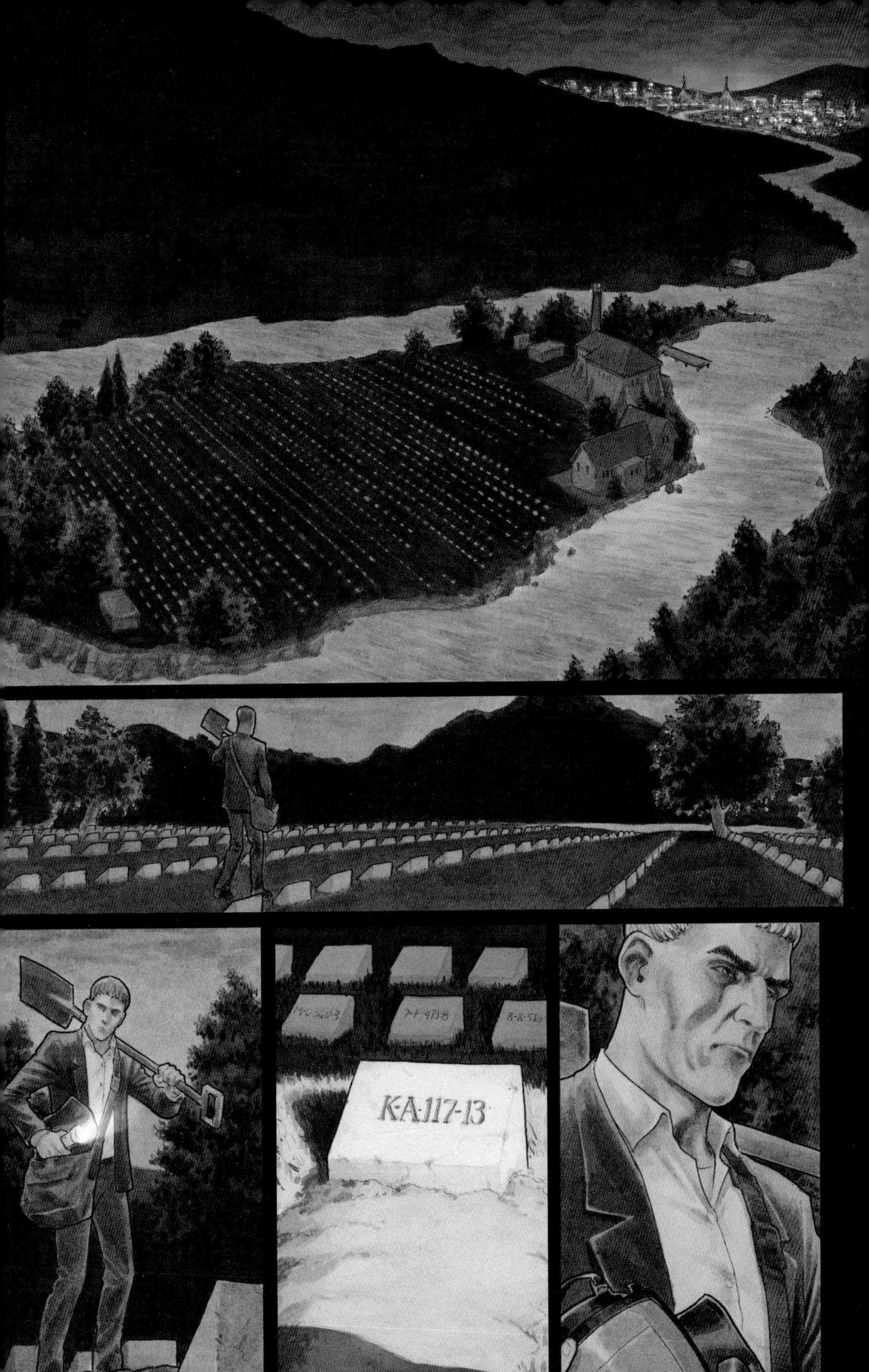
K-A117-13

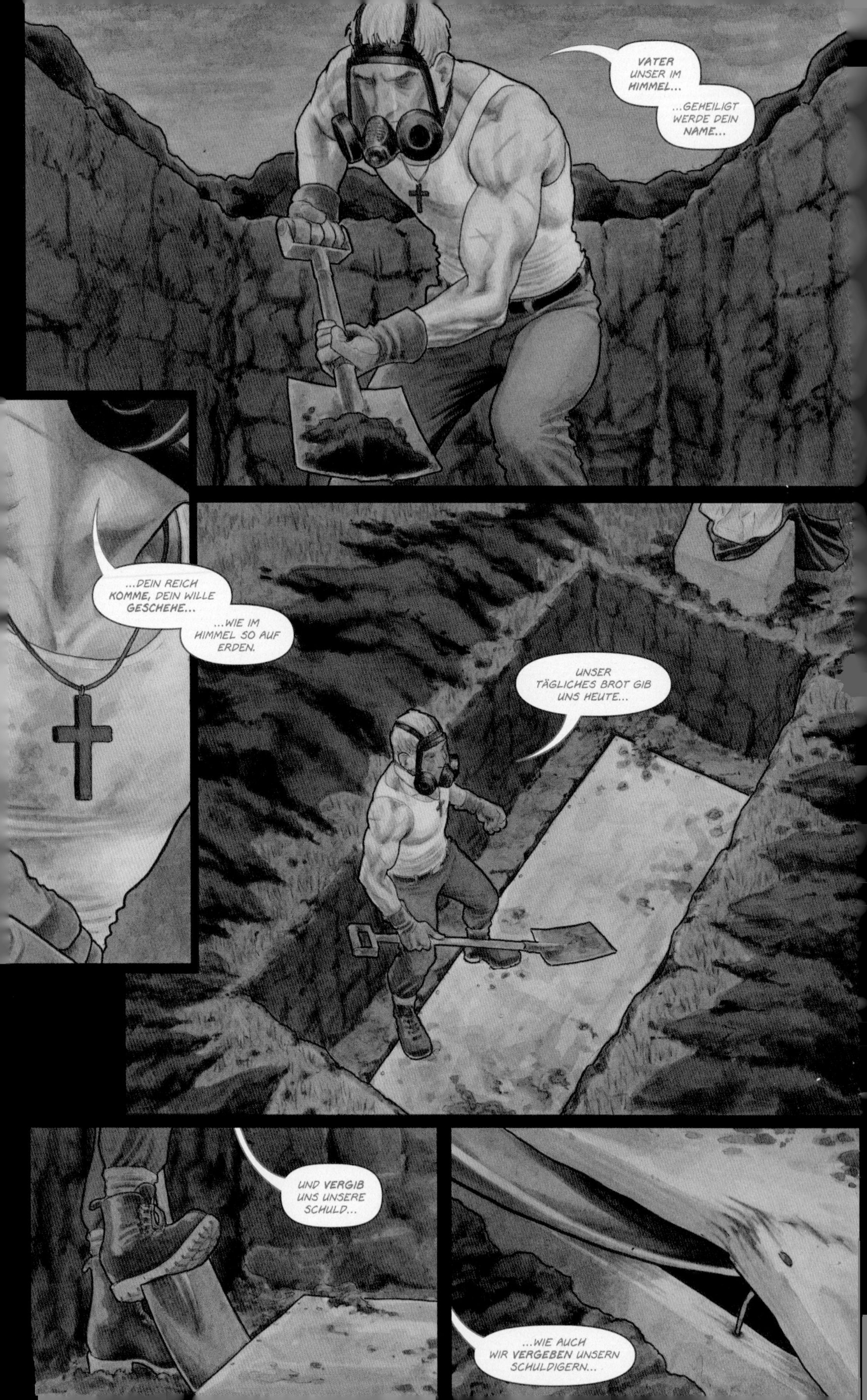
VATER UNSER IM HIMMEL...
...GEHEILIGT WERDE DEIN NAME...
...DEIN REICH KOMME, DEIN WILLE GESCHEHE...
...WIE IM HIMMEL SO AUF ERDEN.
UNSER TÄGLICHES BROT GIB UNS HEUTE...
UND VERGIB UNS UNSERE SCHULD...
...WIE AUCH WIR VERGEBEN UNSERN SCHULDIGERN...

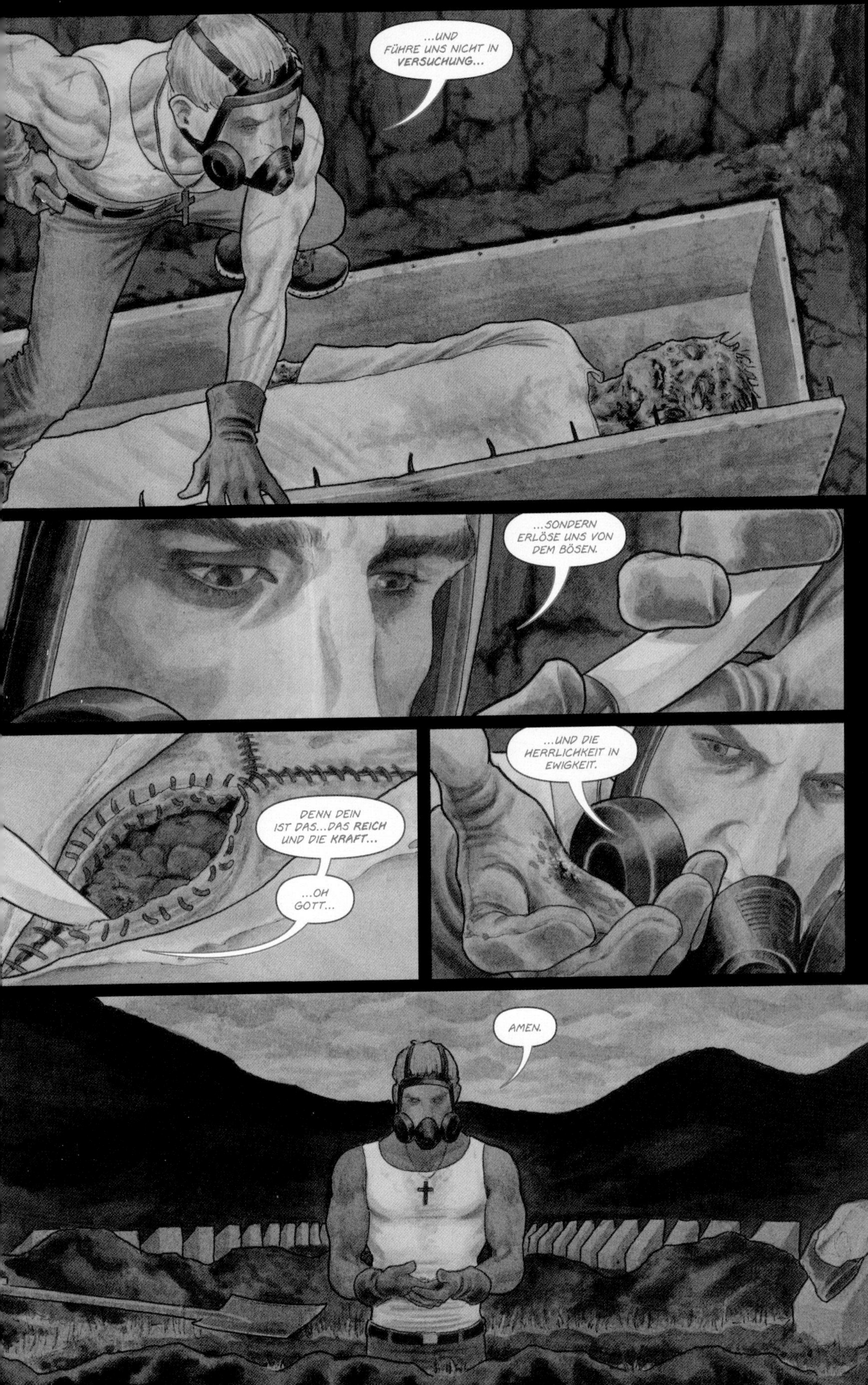
...UND FÜHRE UNS NICHT IN VERSUCHUNG...
...SONDERN ERLÖSE UNS VON DEM BÖSEN.
DENN DEIN IST DAS...DAS REICH UND DIE KRAFT...
...OH GOTT...
...UND DIE HERRLICHKEIT IN EWIGKEIT.
AMEN.

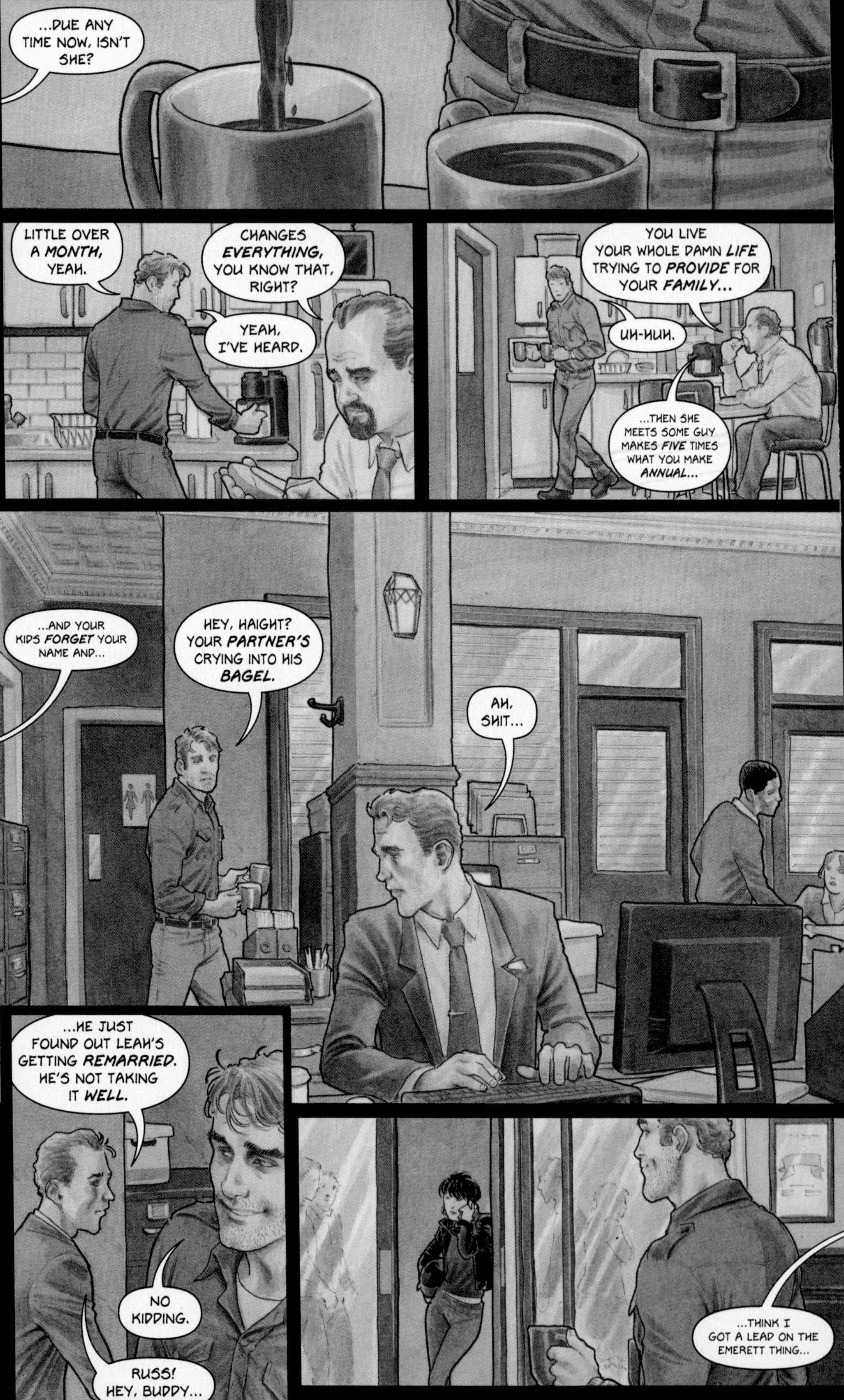
...DUE ANY TIME NOW, ISN'T SHE?
LITTLE OVER A *MONTH,* YEAH.
CHANGES *EVERYTHING,* YOU KNOW THAT, RIGHT?
YEAH, I'VE HEARD.
YOU LIVE YOUR WHOLE DAMN *LIFE* TRYING TO *PROVIDE* FOR YOUR *FAMILY...*
UH-HUH.
...THEN SHE MEETS SOME GUY MAKES *FIVE* TIMES WHAT YOU MAKE *ANNUAL...*
...AND YOUR KIDS *FORGET* YOUR NAME AND...
HEY, HAIGHT? YOUR *PARTNER'S* CRYING INTO HIS *BAGEL.*
AH, SHIT...
...HE JUST FOUND OUT LEAH'S GETTING *REMARRIED.* HE'S NOT TAKING IT *WELL.*
NO KIDDING.
RUSS! HEY, BUDDY...
...THINK I GOT A LEAD ON THE EMERETT THING...

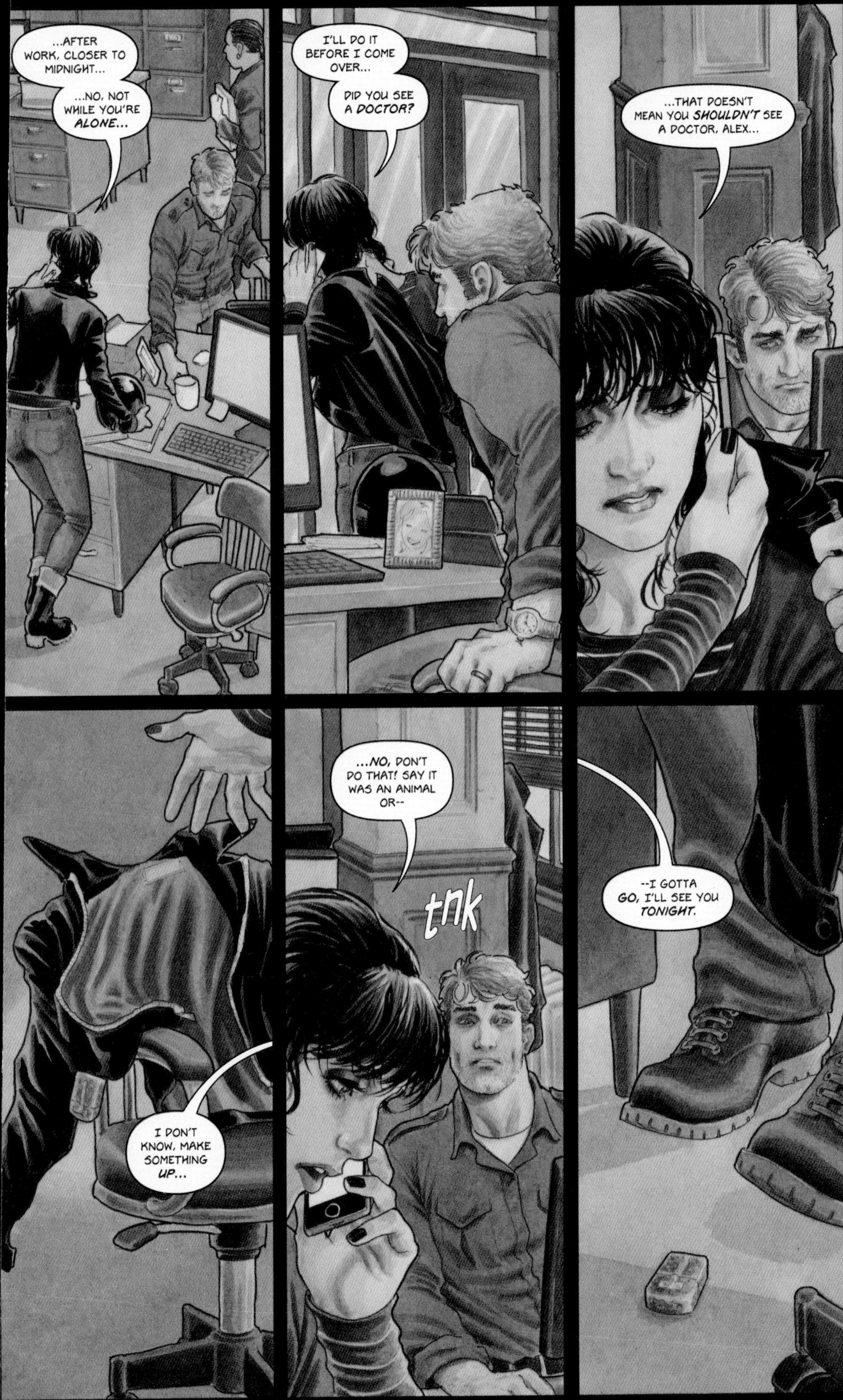
...AFTER WORK, CLOSER TO MIDNIGHT...
...NO, NOT WHILE YOU'RE ALONE...
I'LL DO IT BEFORE I COME OVER...
DID YOU SEE A DOCTOR?
...THAT DOESN'T MEAN YOU SHOULDN'T SEE A DOCTOR, ALEX...
I DON'T KNOW, MAKE SOMETHING UP...
...NO, DON'T DO THAT! SAY IT WAS AN ANIMAL OR--
tnk
--I GOTTA GO, I'LL SEE YOU TONIGHT.

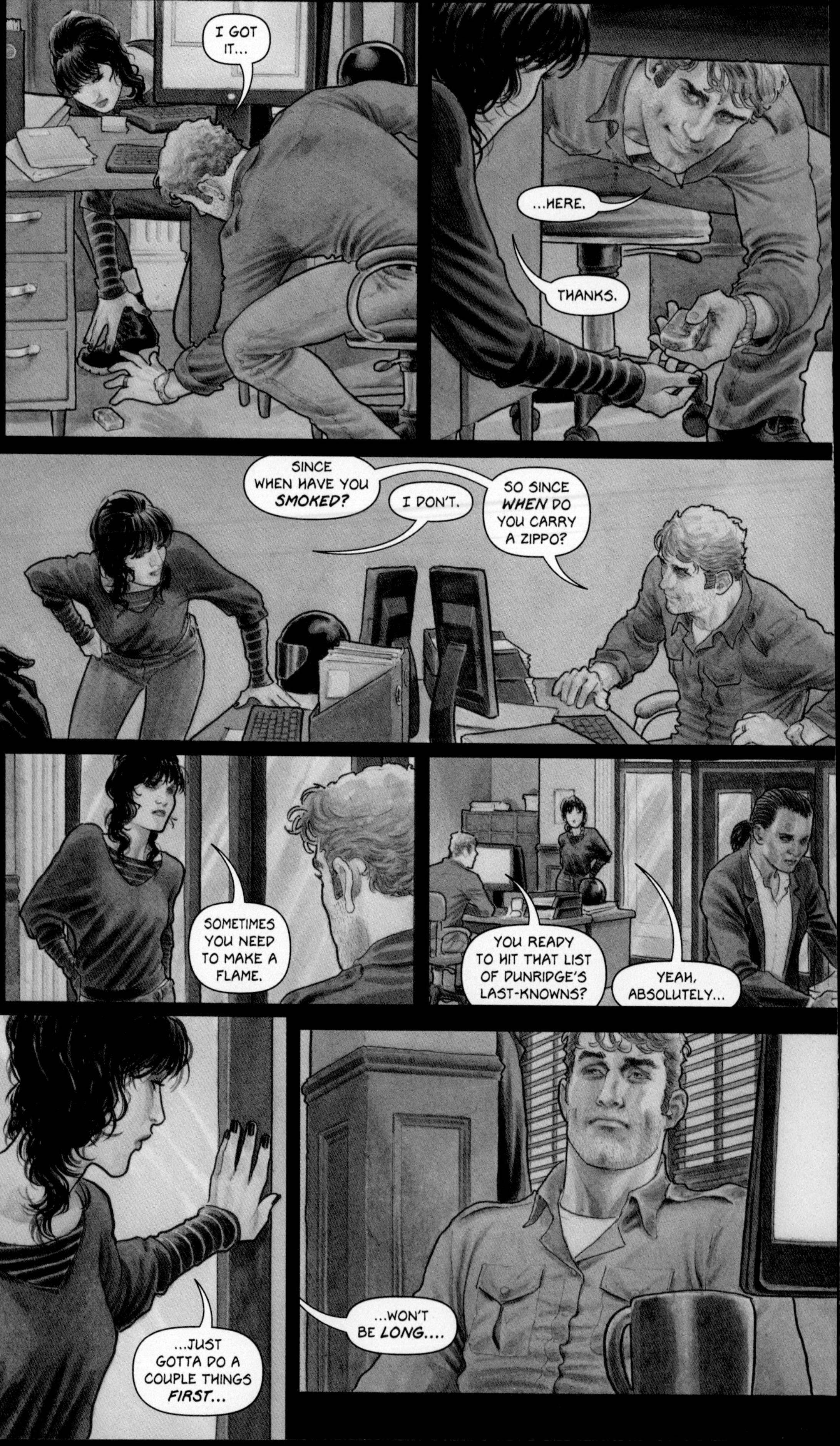
I GOT IT...
...HERE.
THANKS.
SINCE WHEN HAVE YOU *SMOKED?*
I DON'T.
SO SINCE *WHEN* DO YOU CARRY A ZIPPO?
SOMETIMES YOU NEED TO MAKE A FLAME.
YOU READY TO HIT THAT LIST OF DUNRIDGE'S LAST-KNOWNS?
YEAH, ABSOLUTELY...
...JUST GOTTA DO A COUPLE THINGS *FIRST*...
...WON'T BE *LONG*....

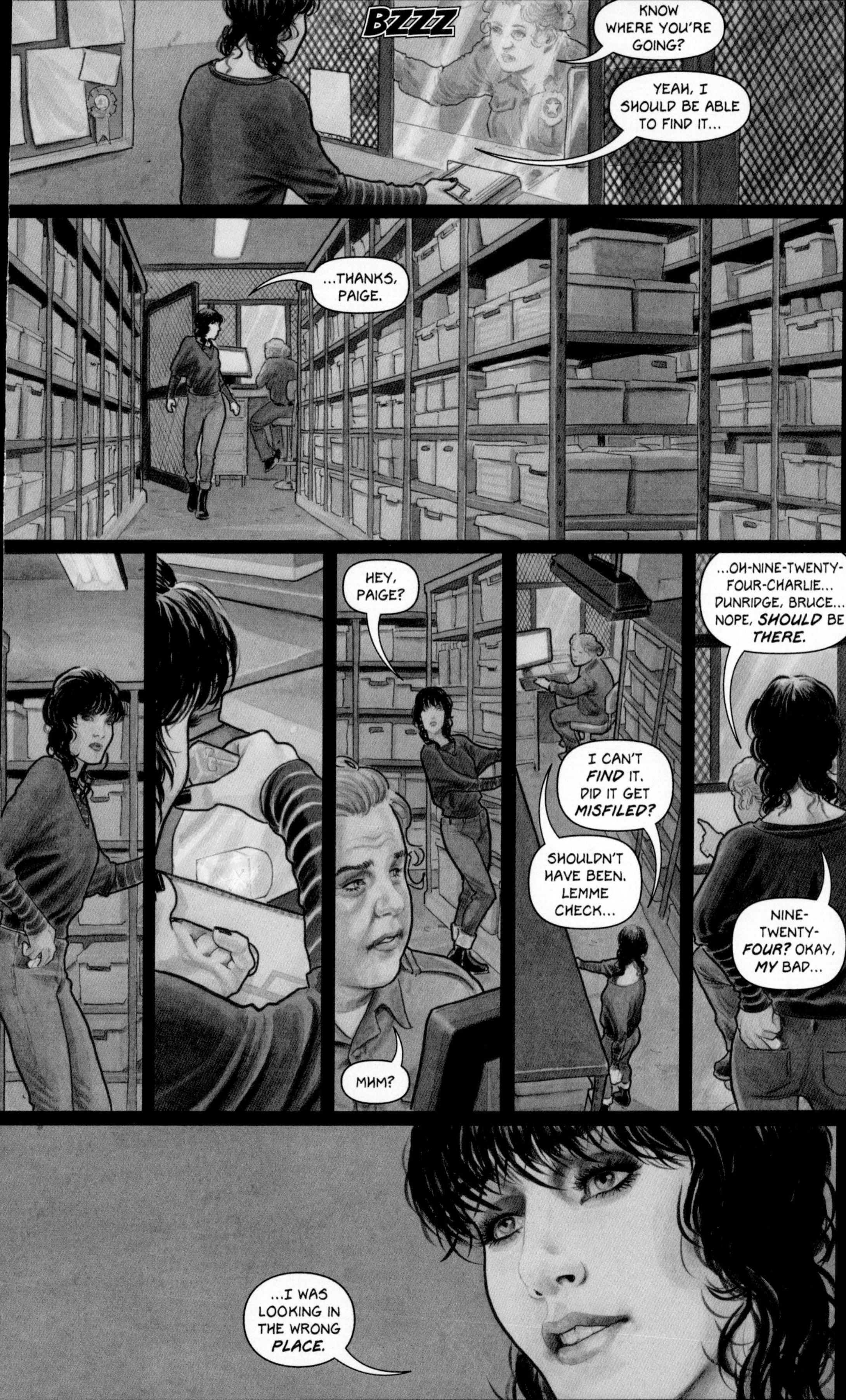
BZZZ
KNOW WHERE YOU'RE GOING?
YEAH, I SHOULD BE ABLE TO FIND IT...
...THANKS, PAIGE.
HEY, PAIGE?
MHM?
I CAN'T FIND IT. DID IT GET MISFILED?
SHOULDN'T HAVE BEEN. LEMME CHECK...
...OH-NINE-TWENTY-FOUR-CHARLIE... DUNRIDGE, BRUCE... NOPE, SHOULD BE THERE.
NINE-TWENTY-FOUR? OKAY, MY BAD...
...I WAS LOOKING IN THE WRONG PLACE.

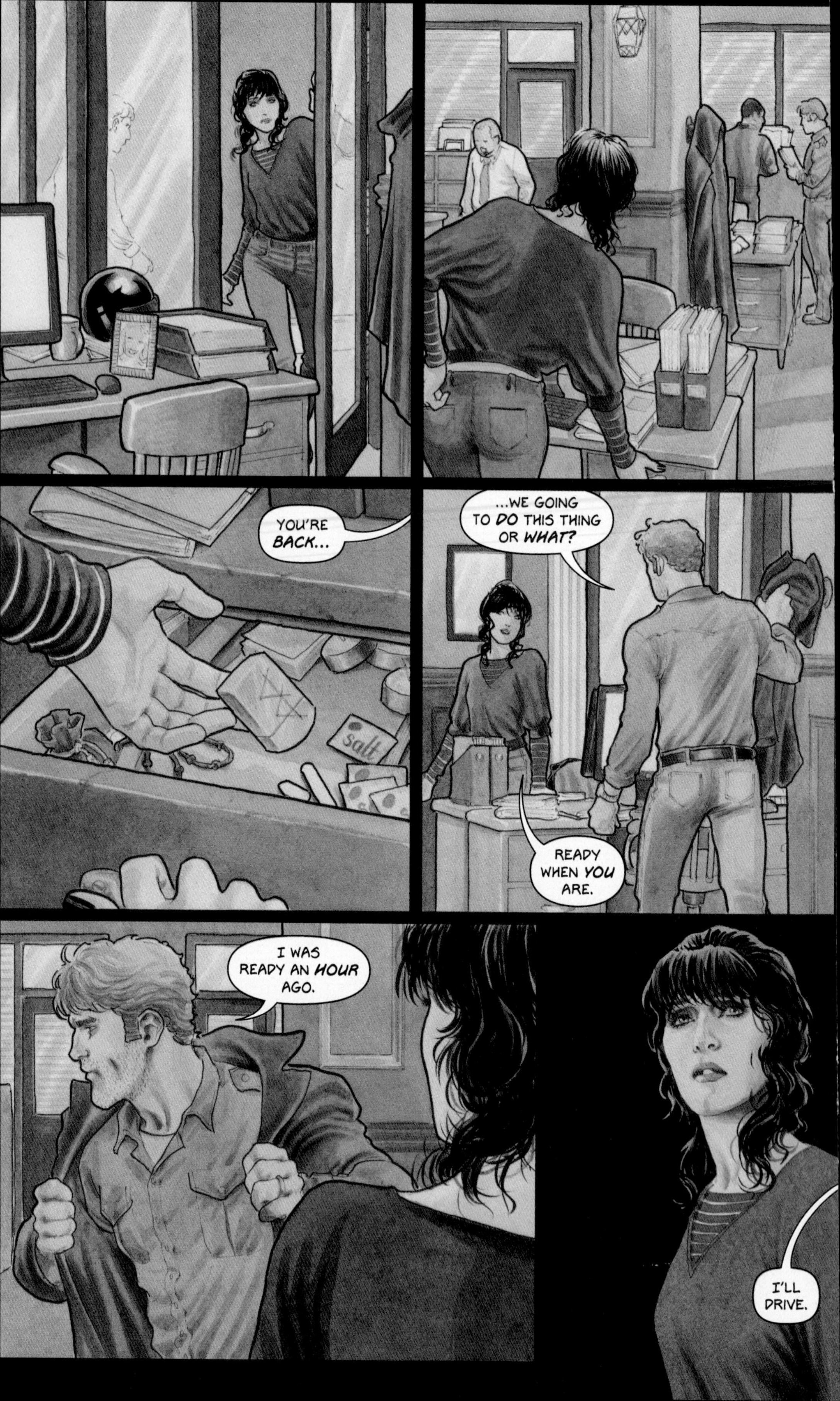
YOU'RE BACK...
...WE GOING TO DO THIS THING OR WHAT?
READY WHEN YOU ARE.
I WAS READY AN HOUR AGO.
I'LL DRIVE.
salt

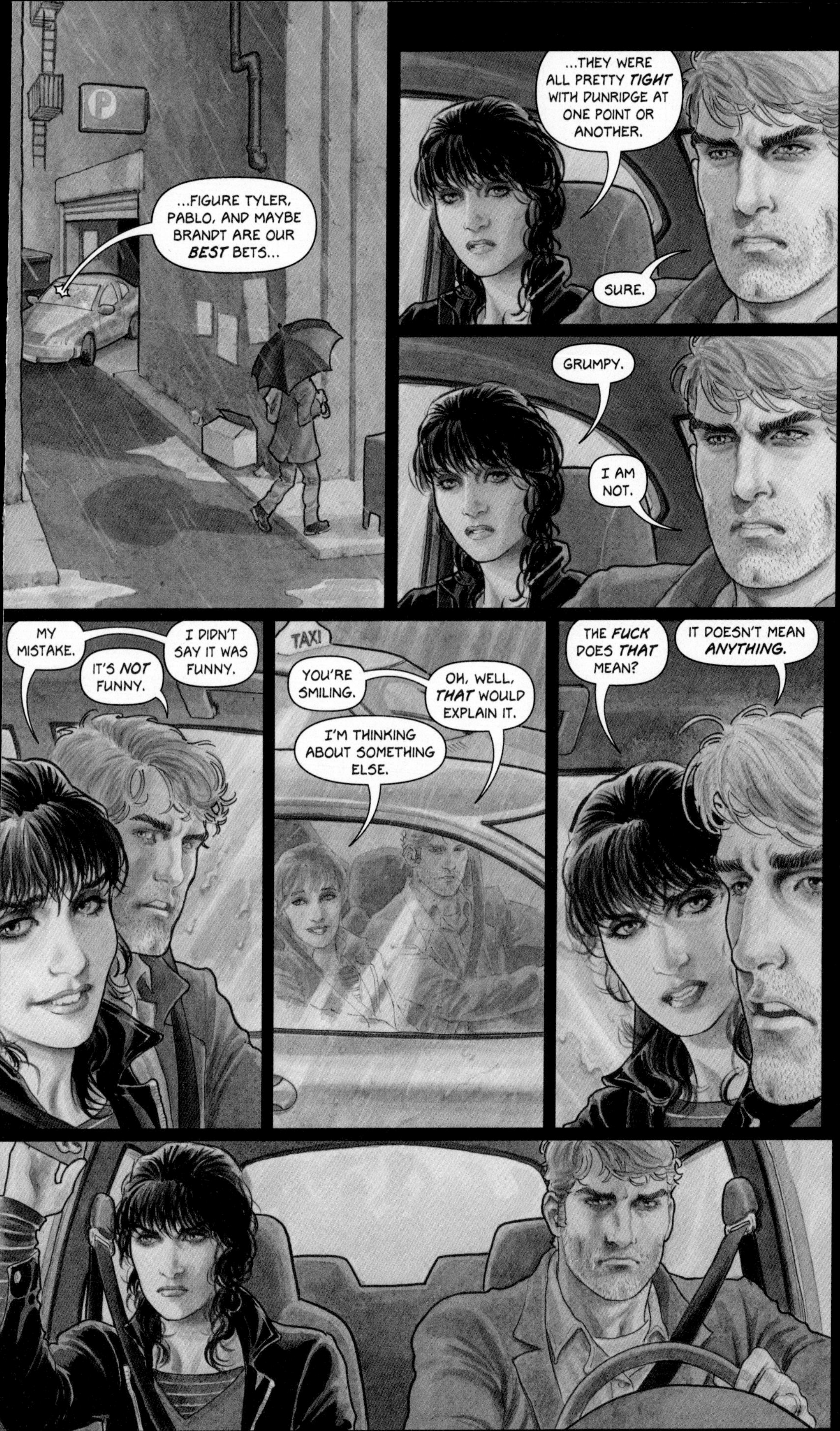

...FIGURE TYLER, PABLO, AND MAYBE BRANDT ARE OUR *BEST* BETS...
...THEY WERE ALL PRETTY *TIGHT* WITH DUNRIDGE AT ONE POINT OR ANOTHER.
SURE.
GRUMPY.
I AM NOT.
MY MISTAKE.
IT'S *NOT* FUNNY.
I DIDN'T SAY IT WAS FUNNY.
TAXI
YOU'RE SMILING.
I'M THINKING ABOUT SOMETHING ELSE.
OH, WELL, *THAT* WOULD EXPLAIN IT.
THE *FUCK* DOES *THAT* MEAN?
IT DOESN'T MEAN *ANYTHING*.

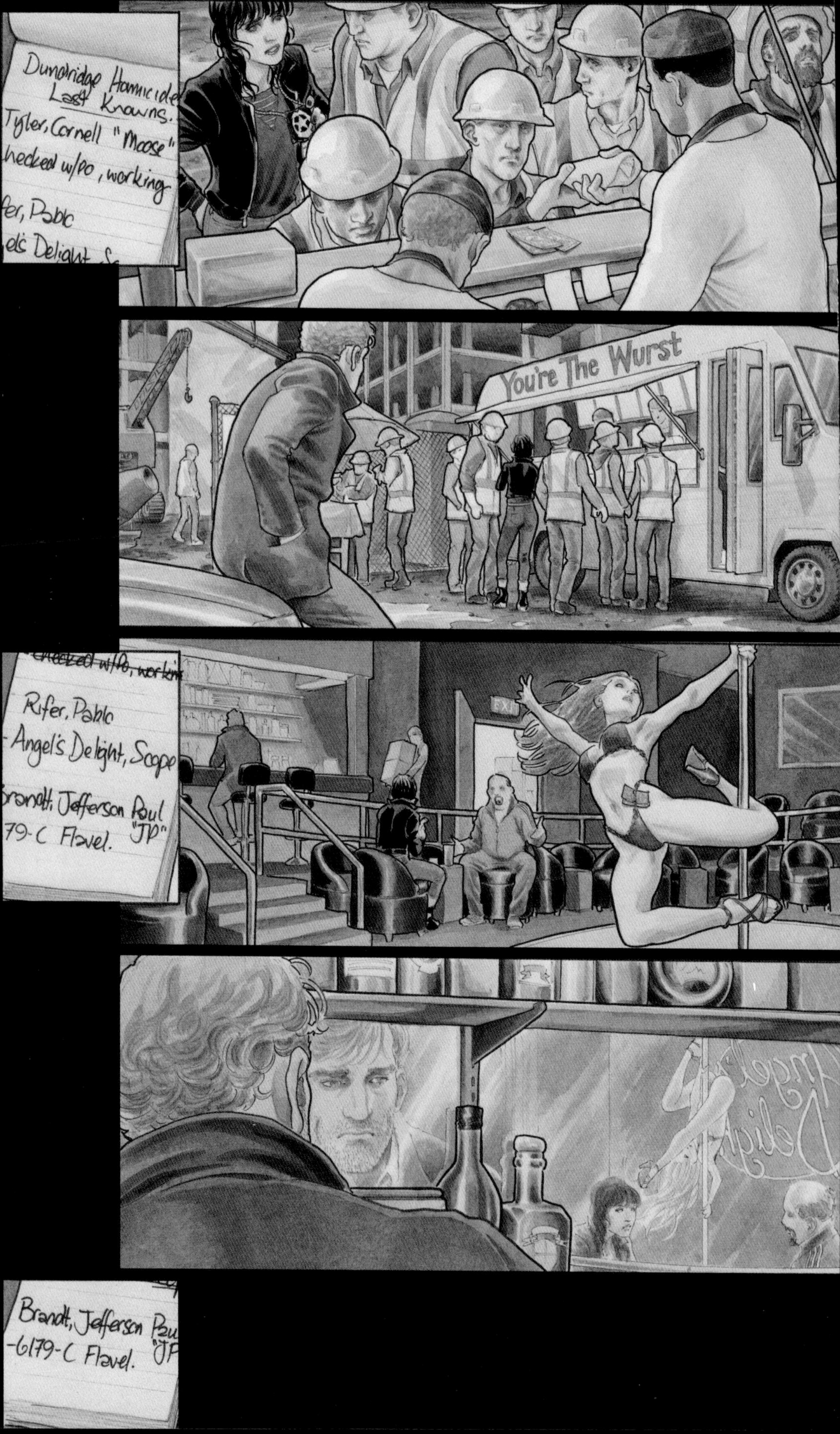

Dundridge Homicide
Last Knowns.
Tyler, Cornell "Moose"
hecked w/po, working
fer, Pablo
el's Delight
You're The Wurst
Rifer, Pablo
- Angel's Delight, Scope
Brandt, Jefferson Paul "JP"
79-C Flavel.
EXIT
Brandt, Jefferson Pau "JP"
-6179-C Flavel.

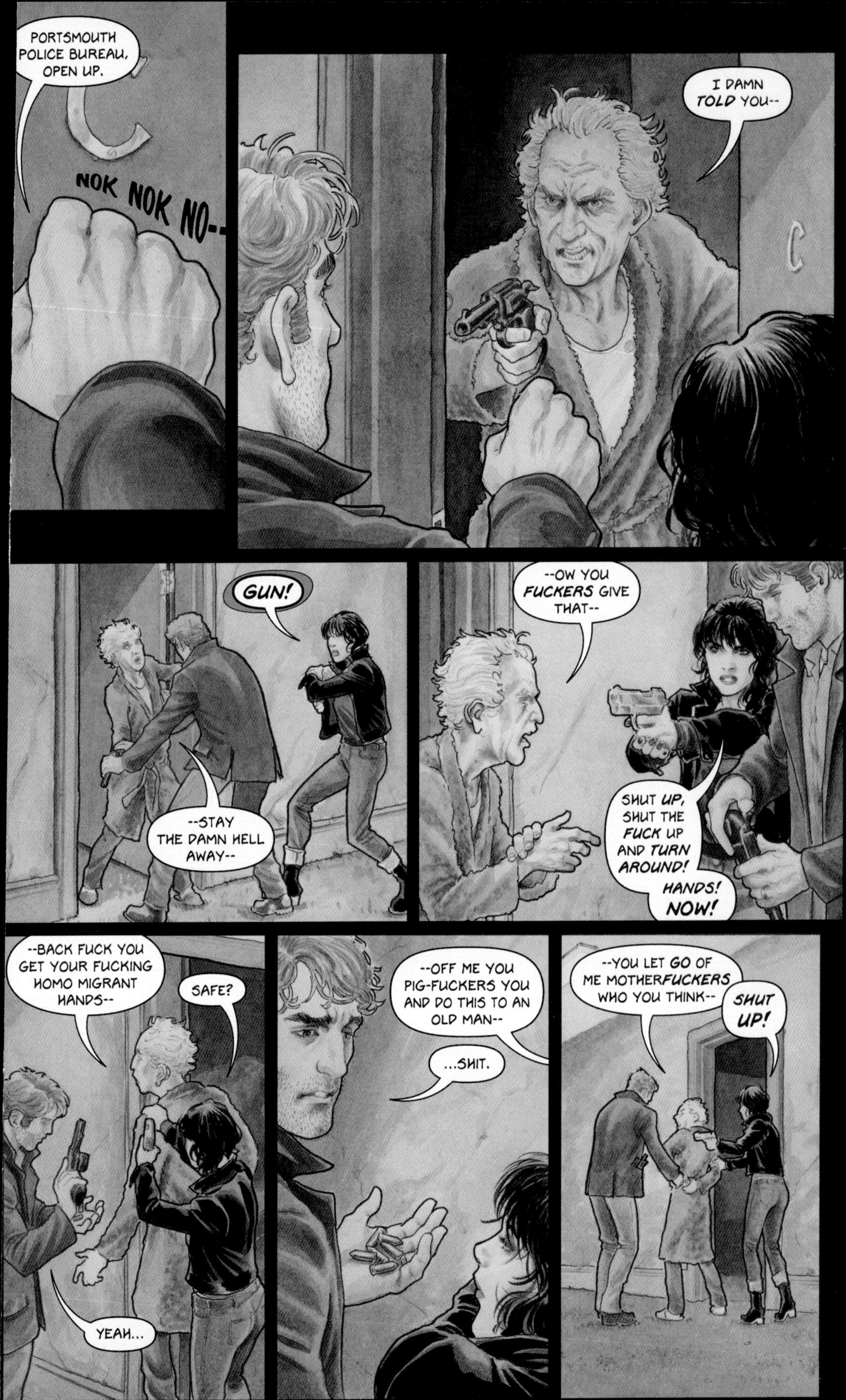
PORTSMOUTH POLICE BUREAU, OPEN UP.
NOK NOK NO--
I DAMN TOLD YOU--
GUN!
--STAY THE DAMN HELL AWAY--
--OW YOU FUCKERS GIVE THAT--
SHUT UP, SHUT THE FUCK UP AND TURN AROUND!
HANDS! NOW!
--BACK FUCK YOU GET YOUR FUCKING HOMO MIGRANT HANDS--
SAFE?
YEAH...
--OFF ME YOU PIG-FUCKERS YOU AND DO THIS TO AN OLD MAN--
...SHIT.
--YOU LET GO OF ME MOTHERFUCKERS WHO YOU THINK--
SHUT UP!

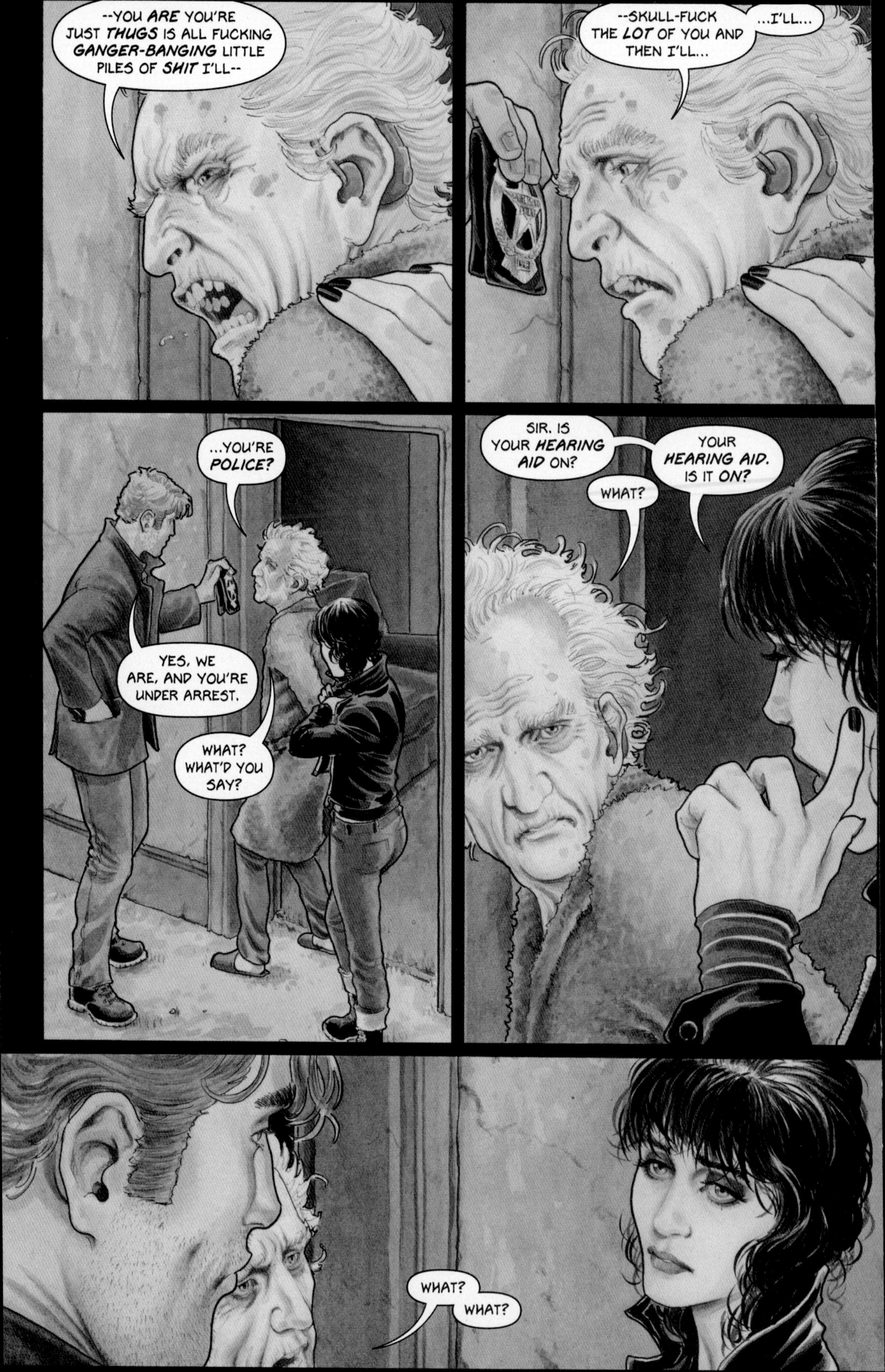
--YOU ARE YOU'RE JUST THUGS IS ALL FUCKING GANGER-BANGING LITTLE PILES OF SHIT I'LL--
--SKULL-FUCK THE LOT OF YOU AND THEN I'LL...
...I'LL...
...YOU'RE POLICE?
YES, WE ARE, AND YOU'RE UNDER ARREST.
WHAT? WHAT'D YOU SAY?
SIR. IS YOUR HEARING AID ON?
YOUR HEARING AID. IS IT ON?
WHAT?
WHAT?
WHAT?

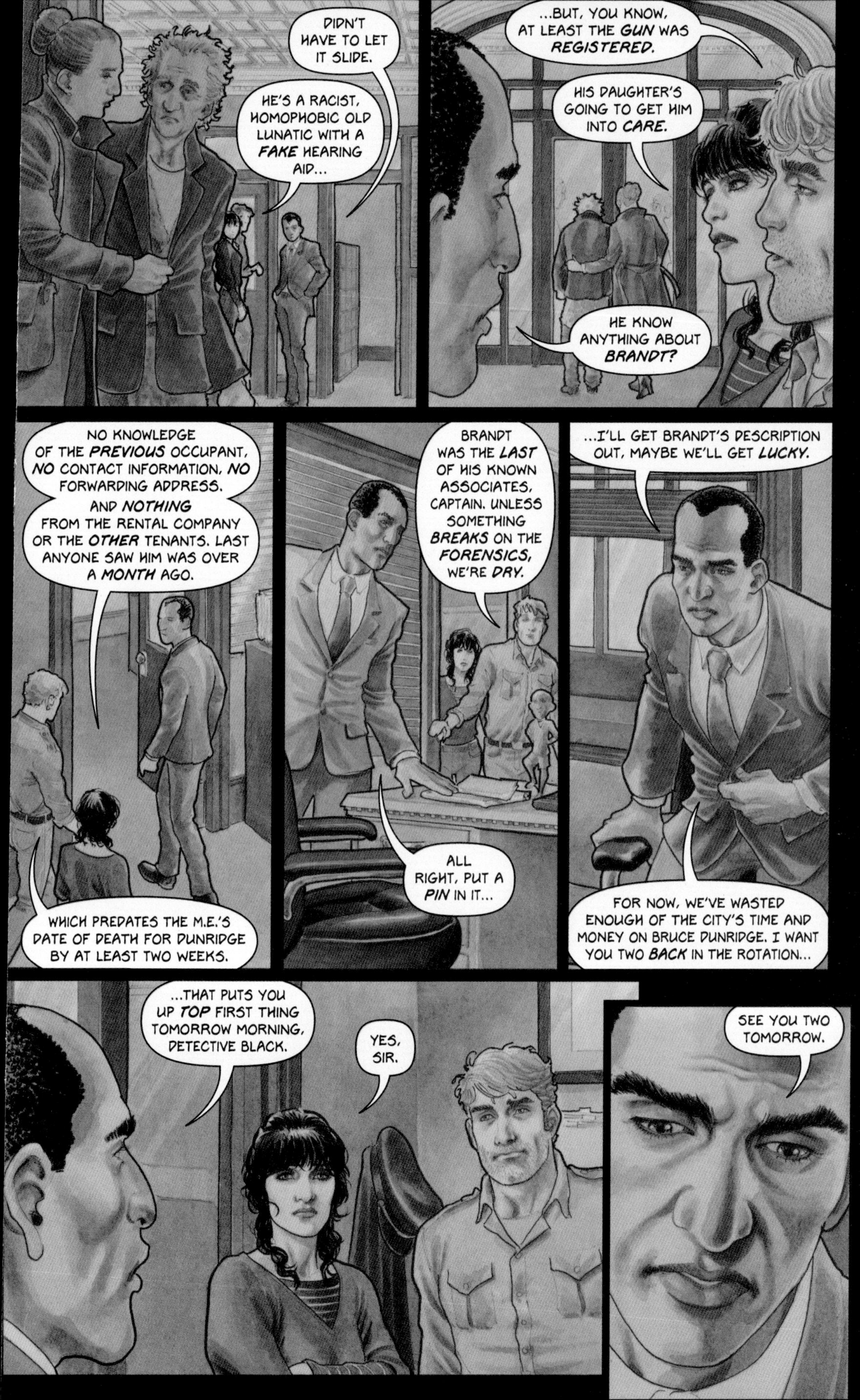
DIDN'T HAVE TO LET IT SLIDE.
HE'S A RACIST, HOMOPHOBIC OLD LUNATIC WITH A FAKE HEARING AID...
...BUT, YOU KNOW, AT LEAST THE GUN WAS REGISTERED.
HIS DAUGHTER'S GOING TO GET HIM INTO CARE.
HE KNOW ANYTHING ABOUT BRANDT?
NO KNOWLEDGE OF THE PREVIOUS OCCUPANT, NO CONTACT INFORMATION, NO FORWARDING ADDRESS.
AND NOTHING FROM THE RENTAL COMPANY OR THE OTHER TENANTS. LAST ANYONE SAW HIM WAS OVER A MONTH AGO.
WHICH PREDATES THE M.E.'S DATE OF DEATH FOR DUNRIDGE BY AT LEAST TWO WEEKS.
BRANDT WAS THE LAST OF HIS KNOWN ASSOCIATES, CAPTAIN. UNLESS SOMETHING BREAKS ON THE FORENSICS, WE'RE DRY.
ALL RIGHT, PUT A PIN IN IT...
...I'LL GET BRANDT'S DESCRIPTION OUT, MAYBE WE'LL GET LUCKY.
FOR NOW, WE'VE WASTED ENOUGH OF THE CITY'S TIME AND MONEY ON BRUCE DUNRIDGE. I WANT YOU TWO BACK IN THE ROTATION...
...THAT PUTS YOU UP TOP FIRST THING TOMORROW MORNING, DETECTIVE BLACK.
YES, SIR.
SEE YOU TWO TOMORROW.

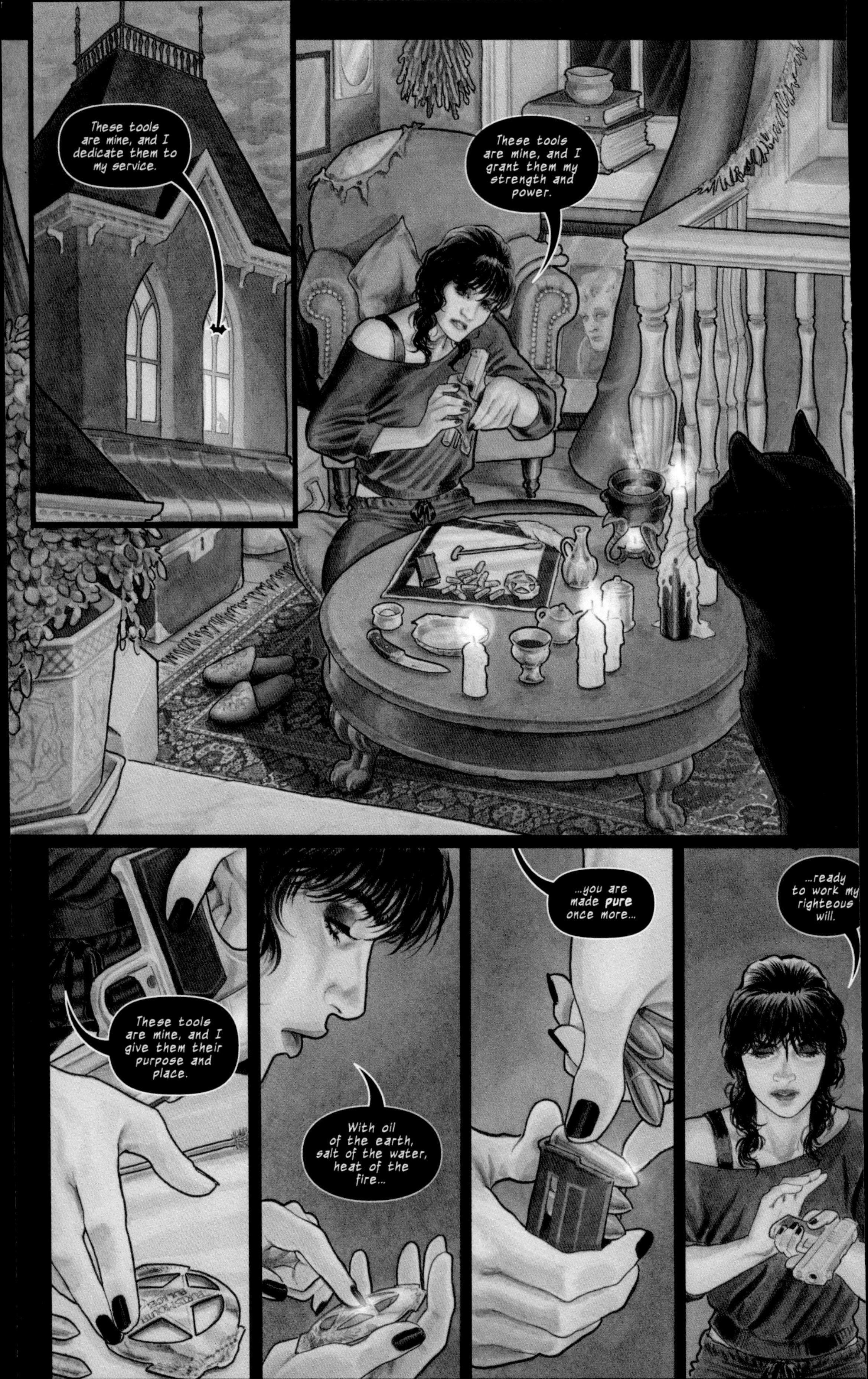
These tools are mine, and I dedicate them to my service.
These tools are mine, and I grant them my strength and power.
These tools are mine, and I give them their purpose and place.
With oil of the earth, salt of the water, heat of the fire...
...you are made **pure** once more...
...ready to work my righteous will.

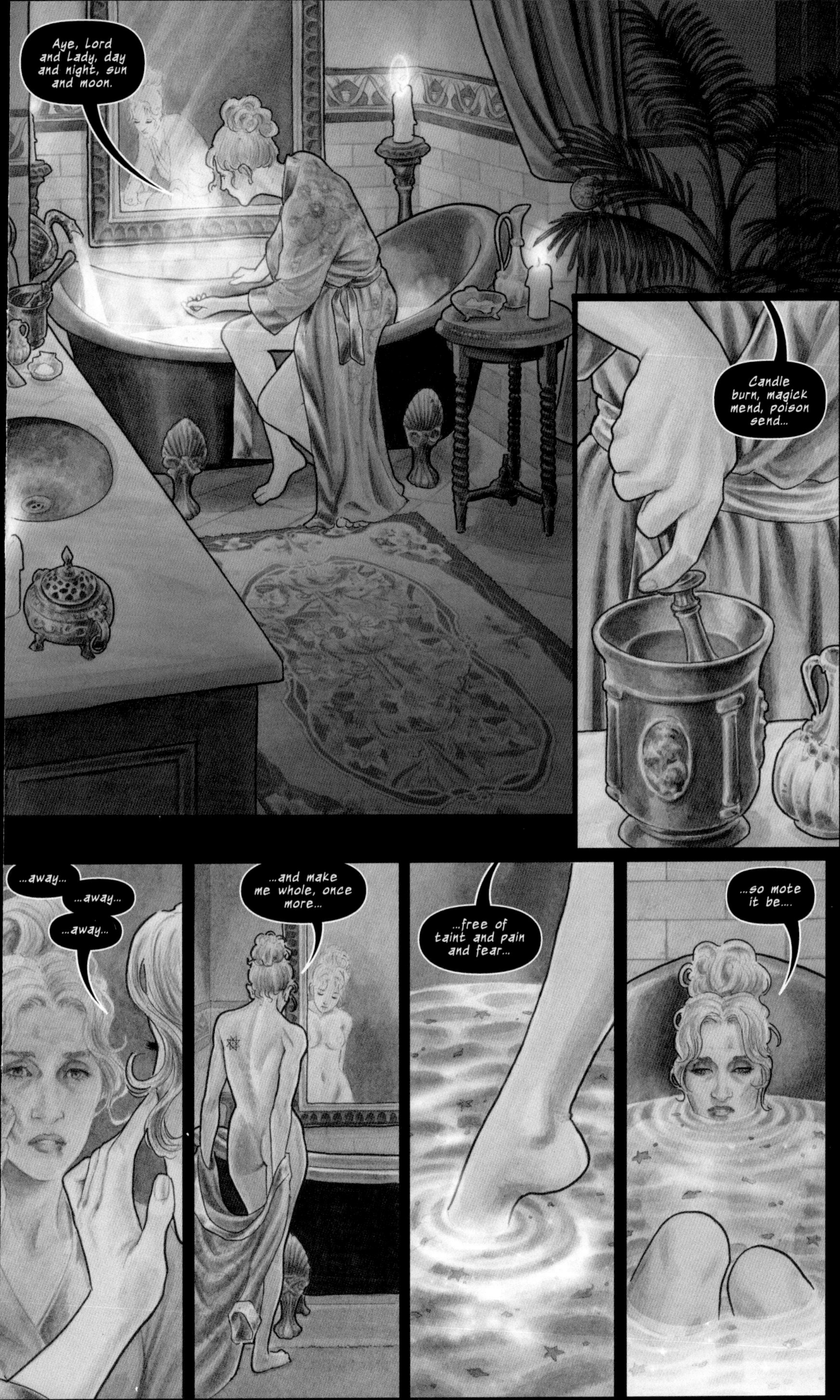
Aye, Lord and Lady, day and night, sun and moon.
Candle burn, magick mend, poison send...
...away...
...away...
...away...
...and make me whole, once more...
...free of taint and pain and fear...
...so mote it be....

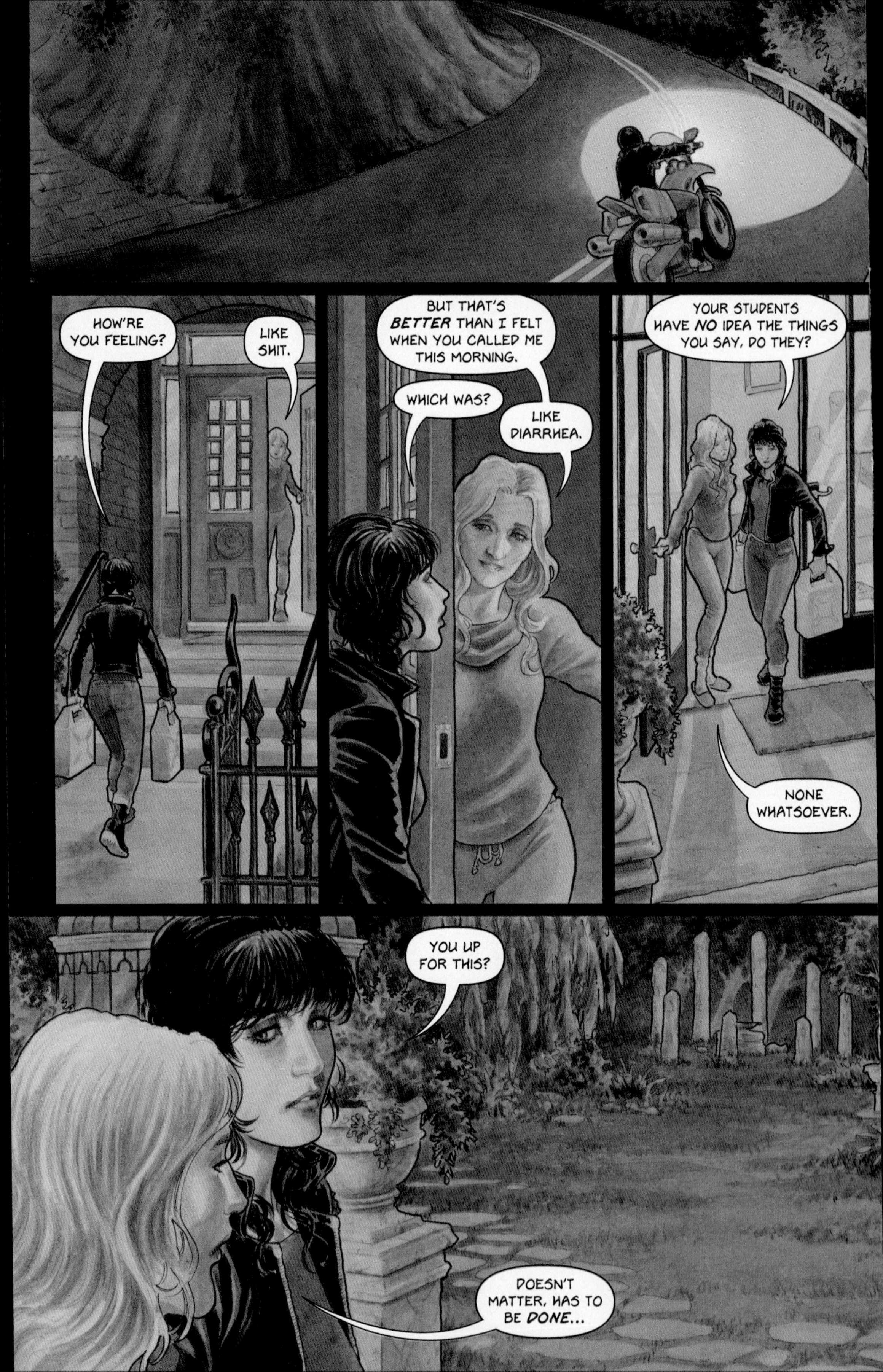
HOW'RE YOU FEELING?
LIKE SHIT.
BUT THAT'S BETTER THAN I FELT WHEN YOU CALLED ME THIS MORNING.
WHICH WAS?
LIKE DIARRHEA.
YOUR STUDENTS HAVE NO IDEA THE THINGS YOU SAY, DO THEY?
NONE WHATSOEVER.
YOU UP FOR THIS?
DOESN'T MATTER, HAS TO BE DONE...

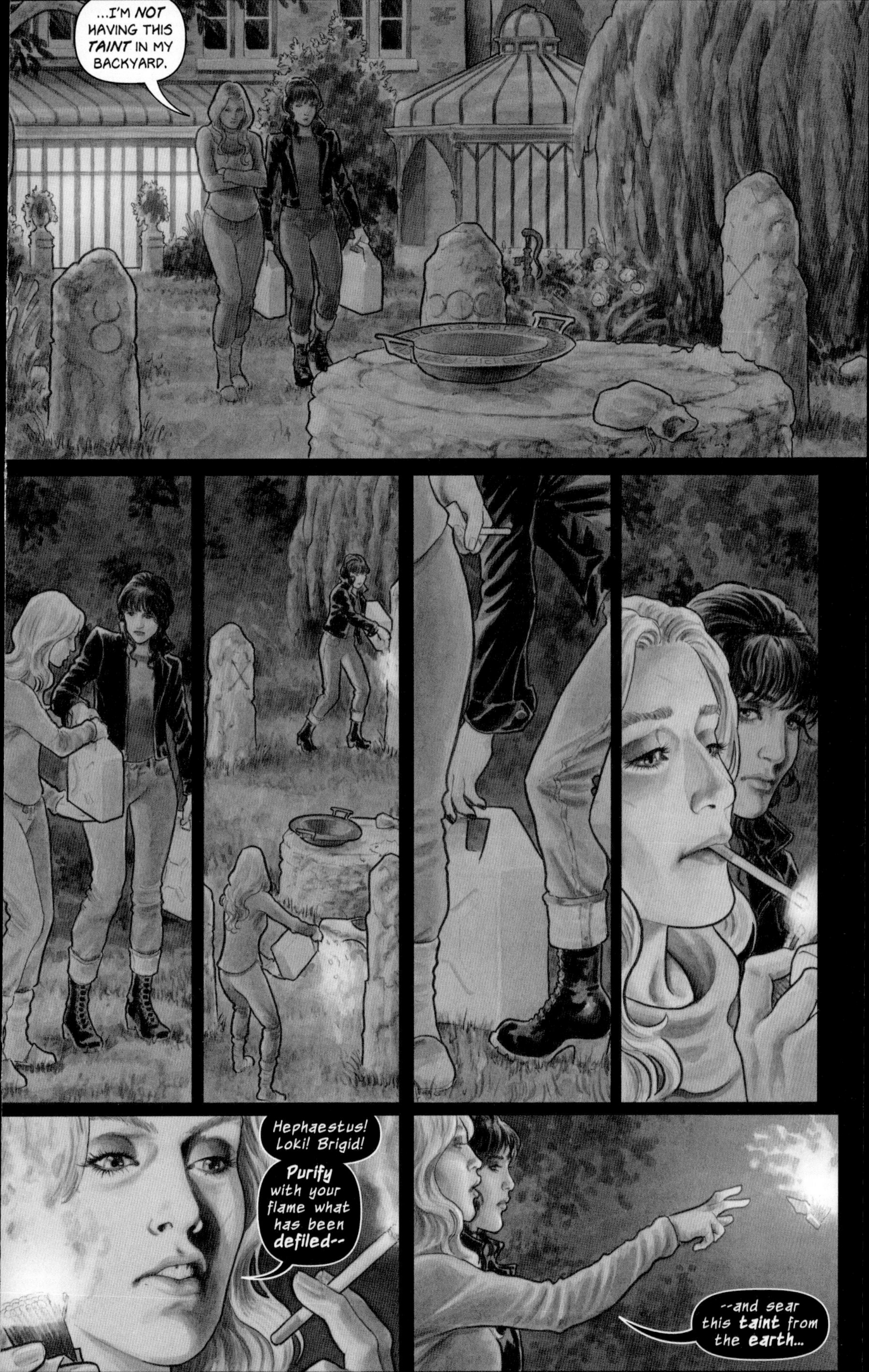
...I'M NOT HAVING THIS TAINT IN MY BACKYARD.
Hephaestus! Loki! Brigid!
Purify with your flame what has been defiled--
--and sear this taint from the earth...

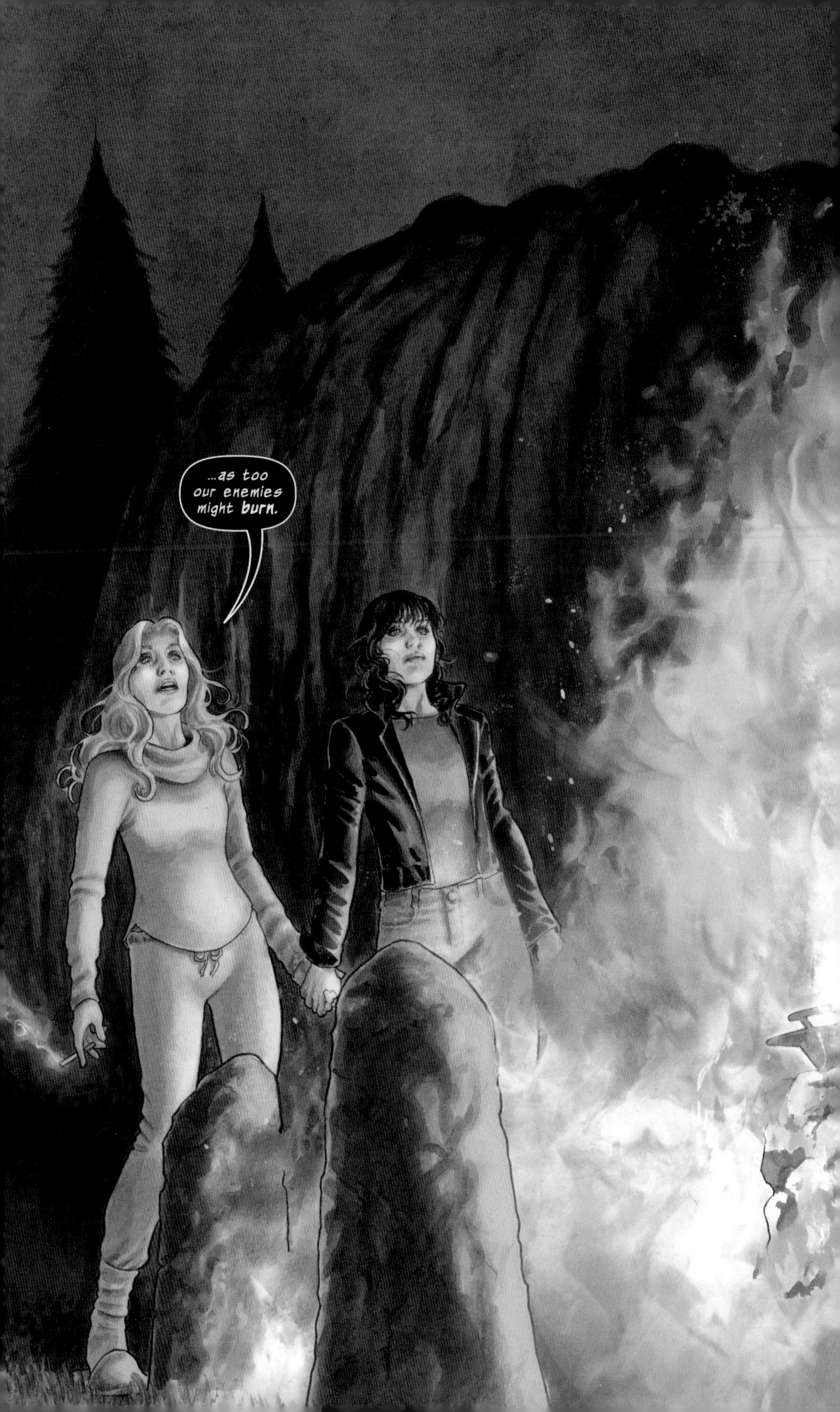
...as too our enemies might **burn**.

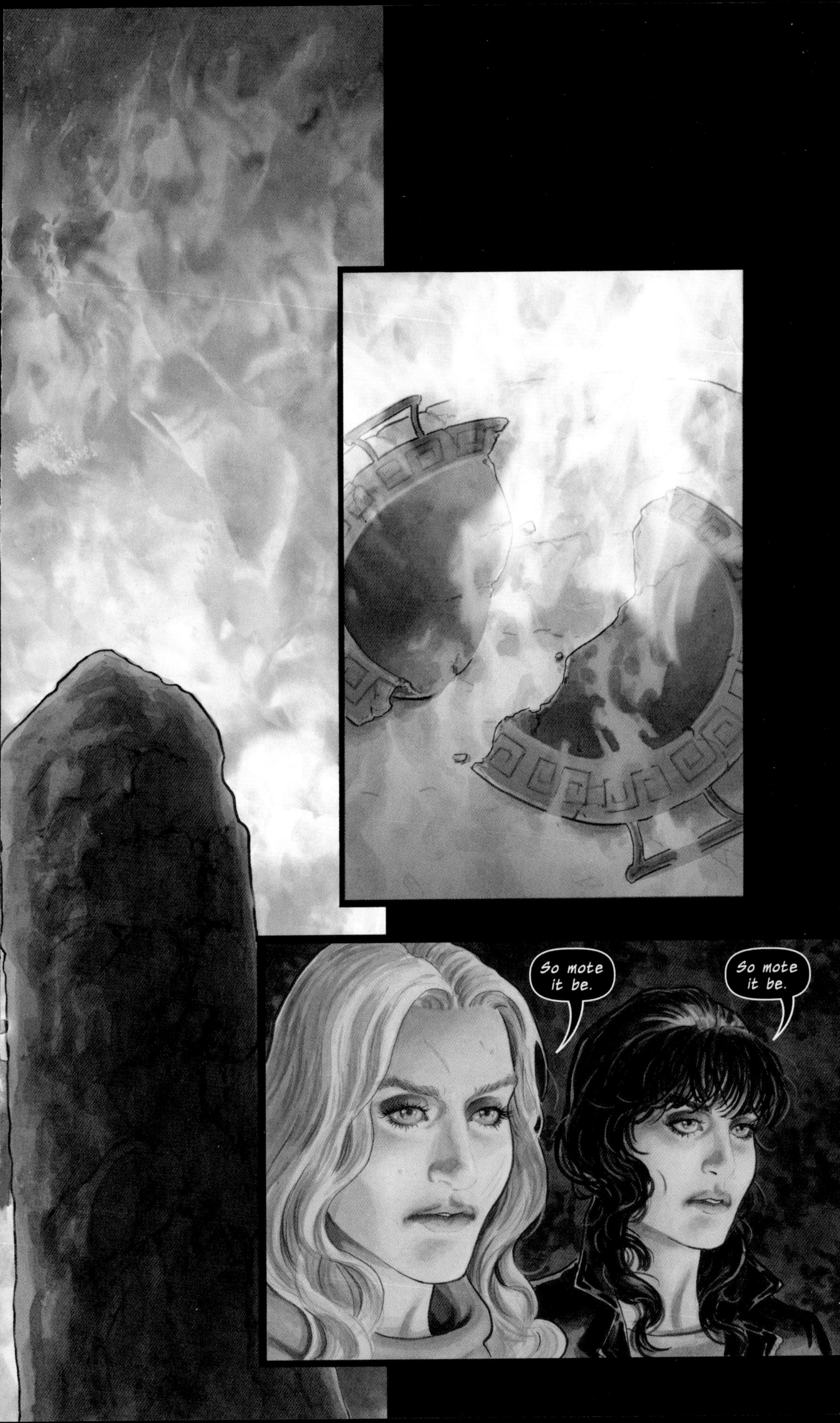
So mote it be.
So mote it be.

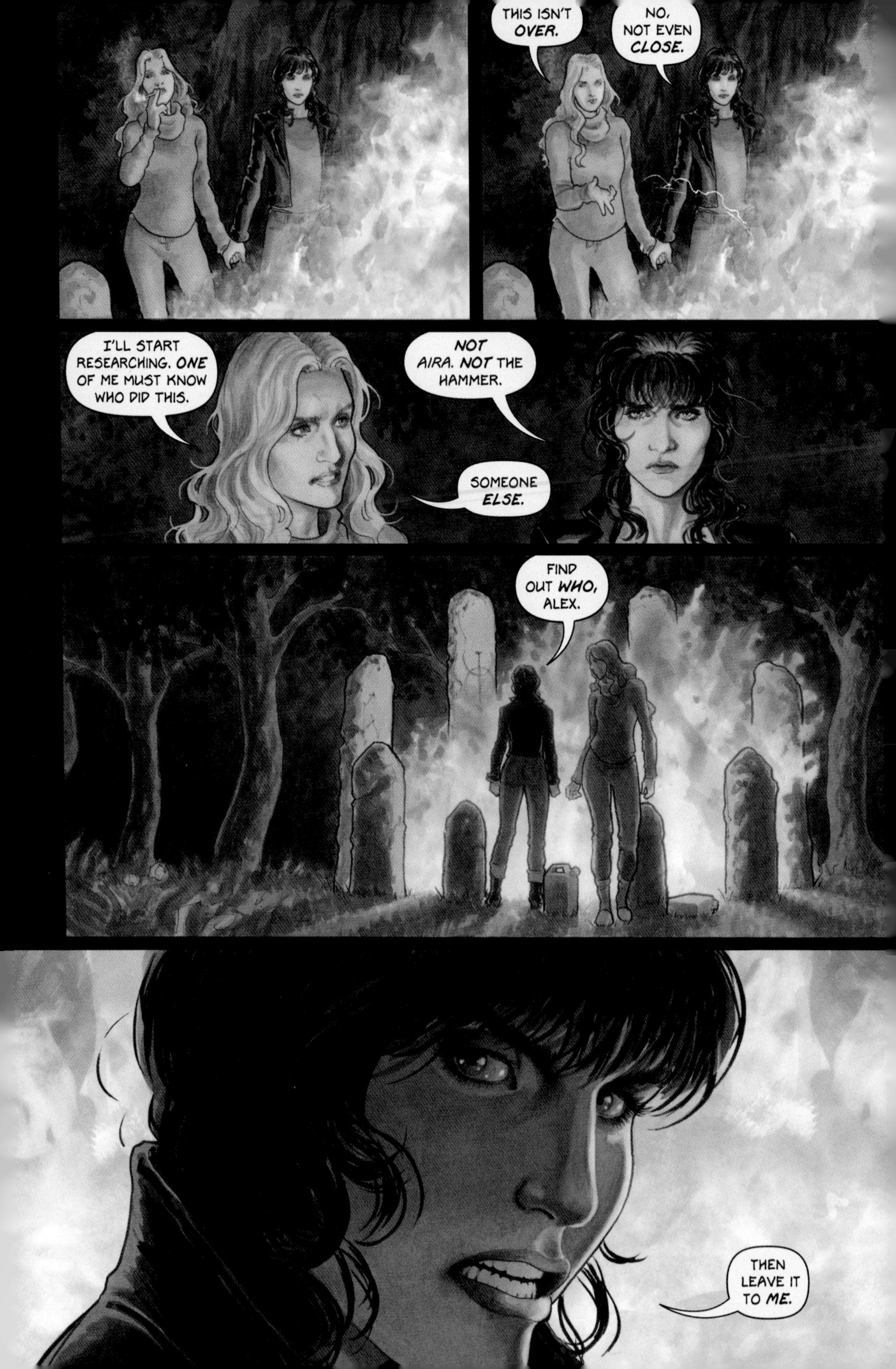
THIS ISN'T *OVER.*
NO, NOT EVEN *CLOSE.*
I'LL START RESEARCHING. *ONE* OF ME MUST KNOW WHO DID THIS.
NOT AIRA. *NOT* THE HAMMER.
SOMEONE *ELSE.*
FIND OUT *WHO,* ALEX.
THEN LEAVE IT TO *ME.*

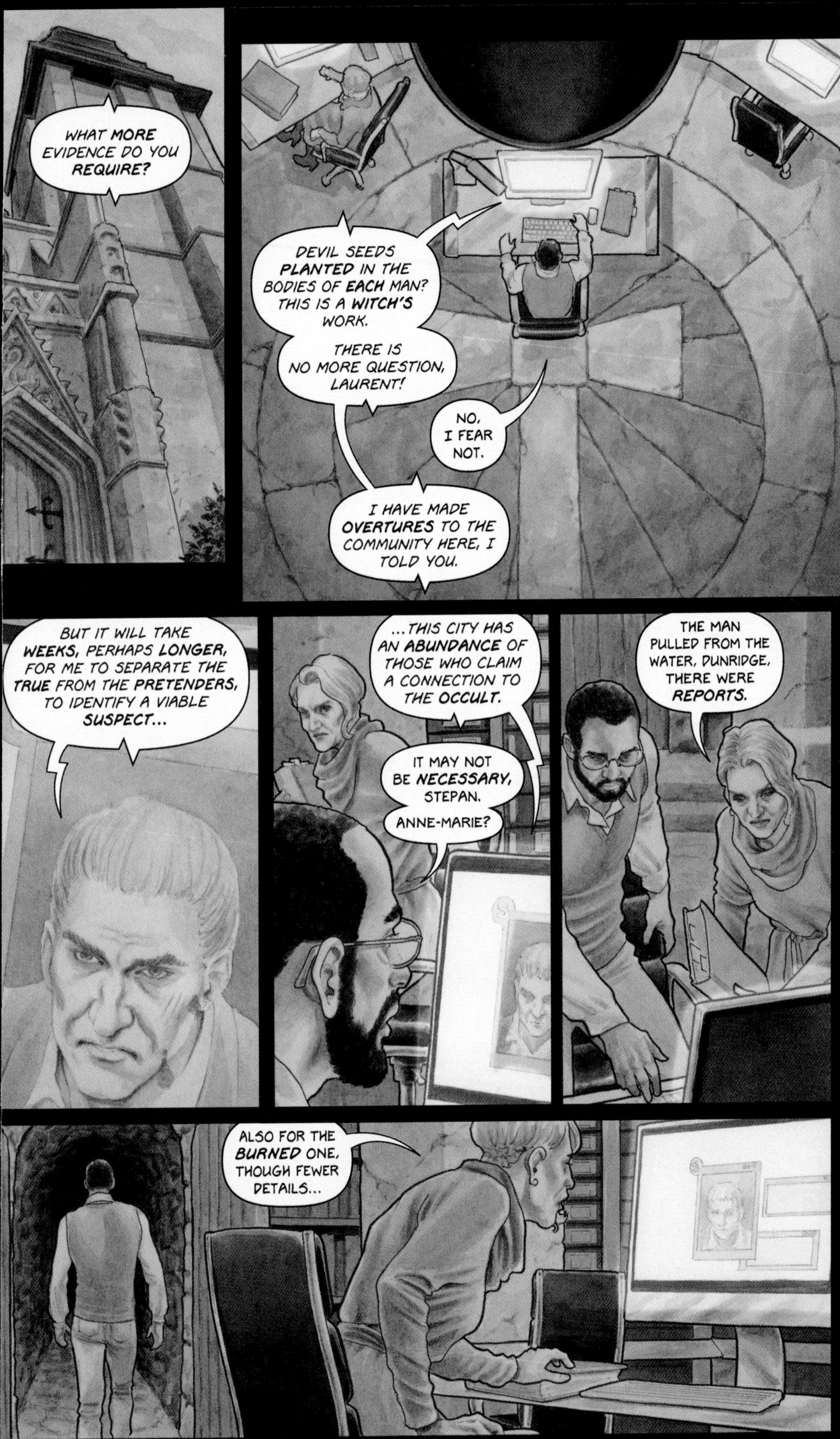
WHAT MORE EVIDENCE DO YOU REQUIRE?
DEVIL SEEDS PLANTED IN THE BODIES OF EACH MAN? THIS IS A WITCH'S WORK.
THERE IS NO MORE QUESTION, LAURENT!
NO, I FEAR NOT.
I HAVE MADE OVERTURES TO THE COMMUNITY HERE, I TOLD YOU.
BUT IT WILL TAKE WEEKS, PERHAPS LONGER, FOR ME TO SEPARATE THE TRUE FROM THE PRETENDERS, TO IDENTIFY A VIABLE SUSPECT...
...THIS CITY HAS AN ABUNDANCE OF THOSE WHO CLAIM A CONNECTION TO THE OCCULT.
IT MAY NOT BE NECESSARY, STEPAN.
ANNE-MARIE?
THE MAN PULLED FROM THE WATER, DUNRIDGE, THERE WERE REPORTS.
ALSO FOR THE BURNED ONE, THOUGH FEWER DETAILS...

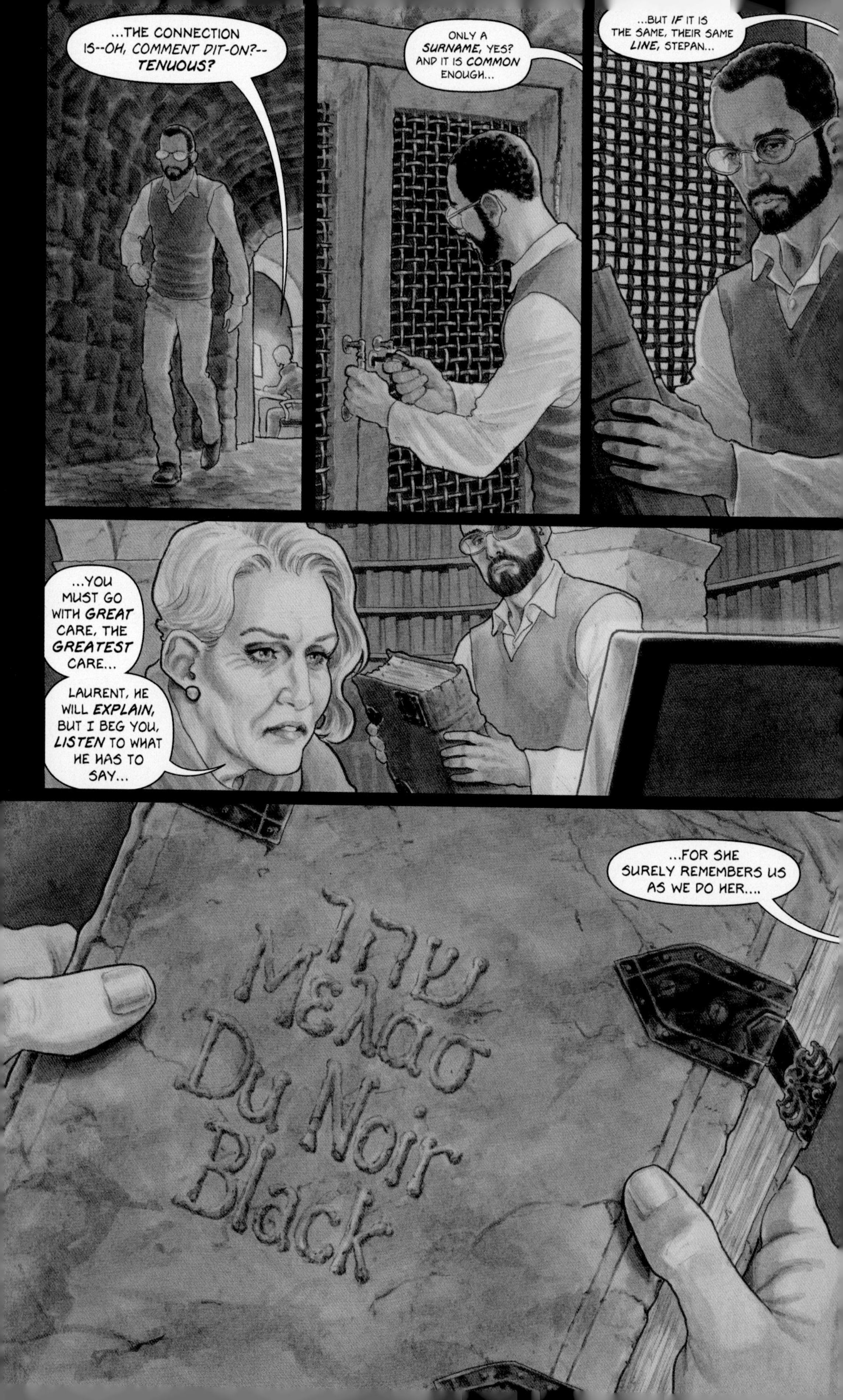

...THE CONNECTION IS--OH, COMMENT DIT-ON?-- TENUOUS?
ONLY A SURNAME, YES? AND IT IS COMMON ENOUGH...
...BUT IF IT IS THE SAME, THEIR SAME LINE, STEPAN...
...YOU MUST GO WITH GREAT CARE, THE GREATEST CARE...
LAURENT, HE WILL EXPLAIN, BUT I BEG YOU, LISTEN TO WHAT HE HAS TO SAY...
...FOR SHE SURELY REMEMBERS US AS WE DO HER....
Du Noir
Black

...ARTMENT   CITY OF PORTSMOU...

...ED	FIRST NAME	MIDDLE NAME	RACE	SEX	AGE	RESIDENCE OF PERSON KILLED		OFFENSE SERIAL NO
		TITLE OR RELATIONSHIP	RACE	SEX	AGE	ADDRESS OF PERSON KILLED ...E		PHONE OF PERSON

...ME)   AFTER INVESTIGATION CHANGED TO

...STREET AND NUMBER OR INTERSECTION	DIVISION	PLATOON	BEAT	OFFICERS MAKING REPORT	I.D. NO	NAME
...OCCURENCE	TIME OF DAY	DATE REPORTED	...E REPORTED	REPORT RECEIVED BY		RECEIVED — TIME — TYPED

...T	EYES	HAIR	BEARD	...EXION		...RKS, ETC.	CLOTHING

NAME OF CORONER ...E ...ME OF ARRIVAL   A.M   ...CUTOR ATTENDING — TIME OF ARRIVAL
                                                    P.M

...YSICIAN   PERSON WITH WHOM ACCUSE... ...S OR ASSOCIATED

...CIRCUMSTANCES OF OCCURENCE OF OFFEN... ...TS INVESTIGATION)   USE ...ES OF THIS SHEET.

...DY	ADDRESS		...ITNESS TAKEN INTO CUSTODY	ADDRESS

...SSIBLE MOTIVES

	ALIAS	ADDRESS	SEX	...ACE	AGE	HEIGHT	WEIGHT	EYES	HAIR	COMPLEXION
...CUPATION		DRESS AND OTHER MARKS		...FOR SUSPICION						
	ALIAS	ADDRESS	SEX	RACE	AGE	HEIGHT	WEIGHT	EYES	HAIR	COMPLEXION
...CUPATION		DRESS AND OTHER MARKS		CAUSE FOR SUSPICION						

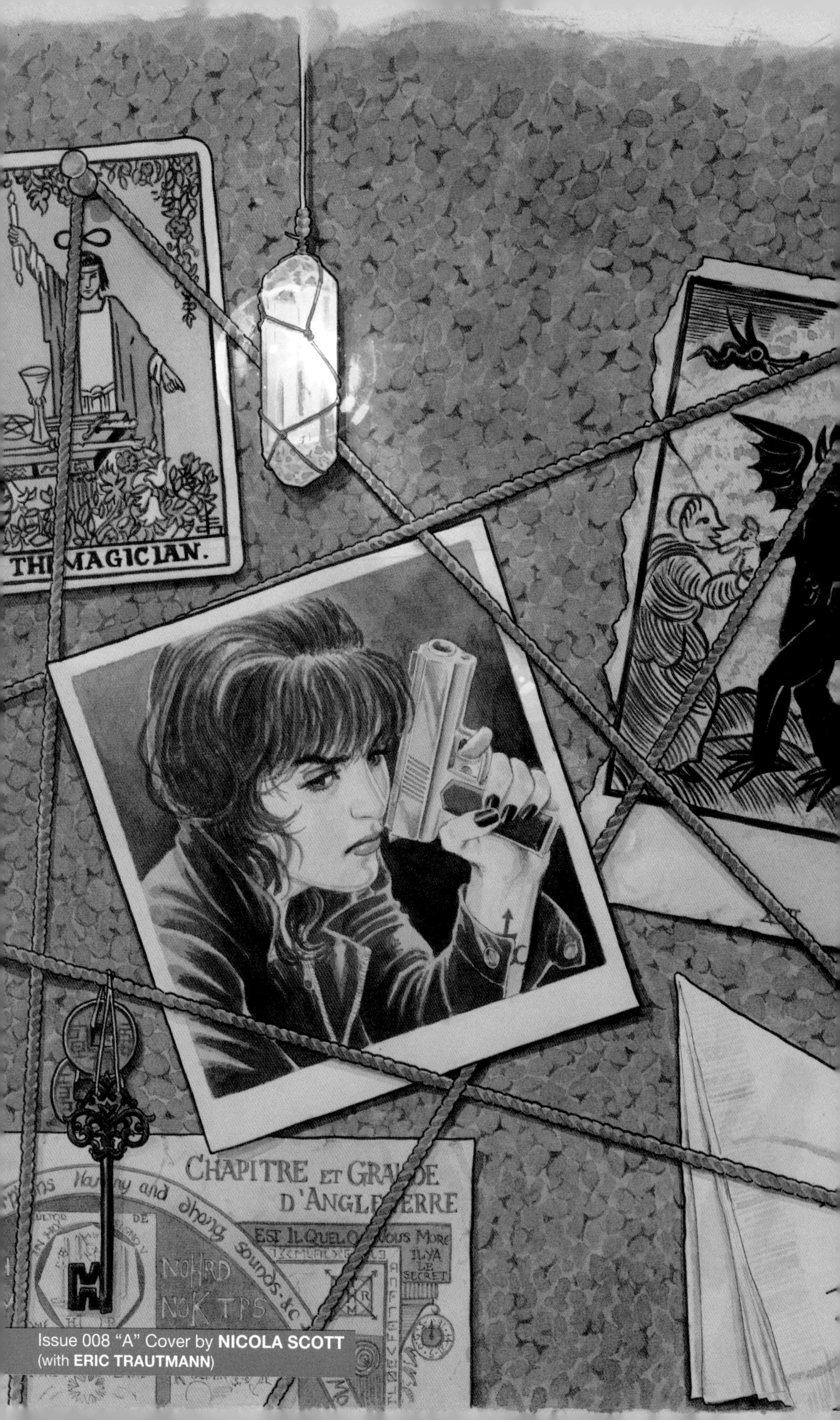
MAGICIAN.
CHAPITRE
ILYA
LE
SECRET

Issue 008 “A” Cover by **NICOLA SCOTT**
(with **ERIC TRAUTMANN**)

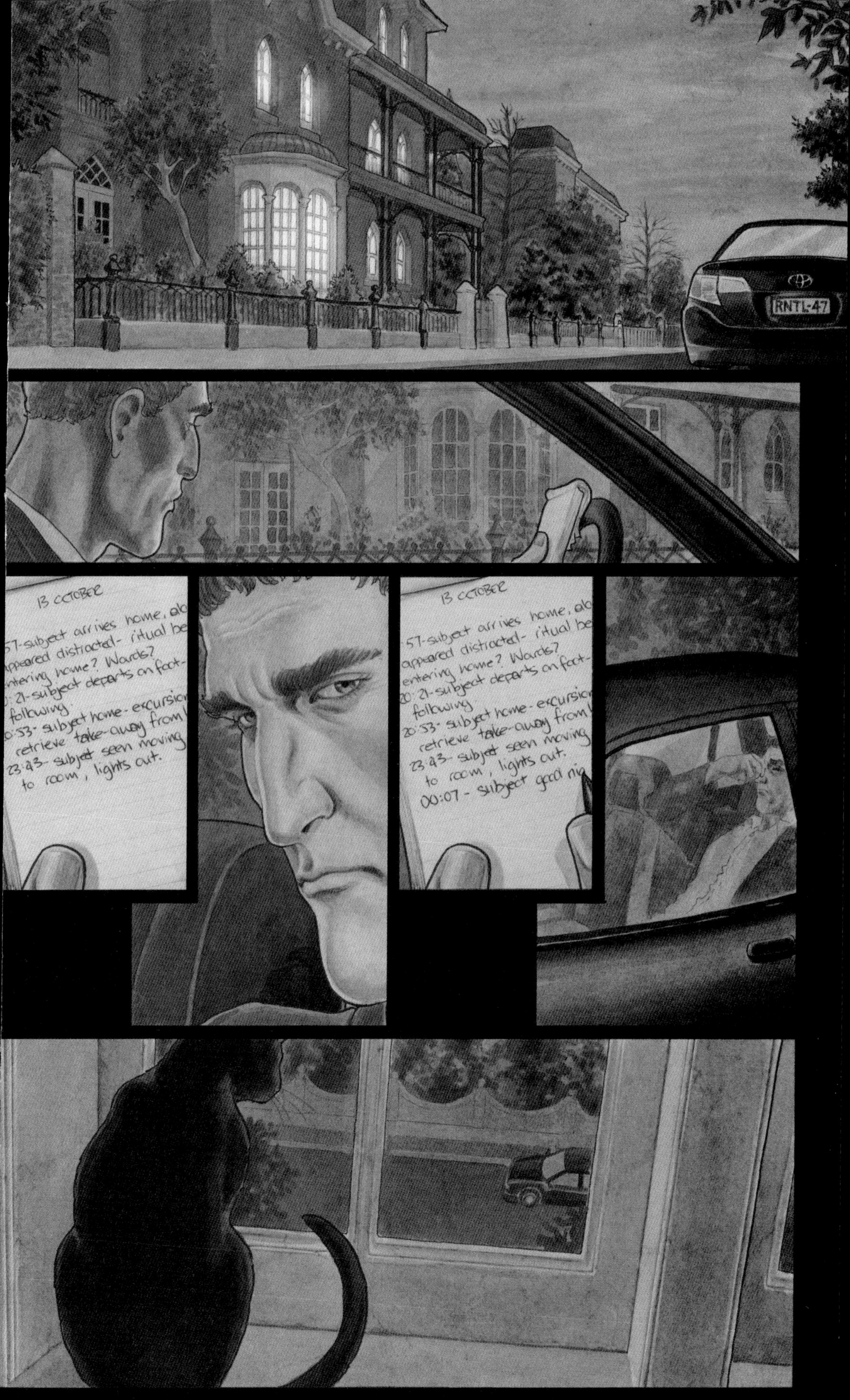
RNTL-47
13 OCTOBER
57-subject arrives home, alo
appeared distracted- ritual be
entering home? Wards?
20:21-subject departs on foot-
following.
20:53- subject home- excursion
retrieve take-away from
23:43- subject seen moving
to room, lights out.
13 OCTOBER
57-subject arrives home, alo
appeared distracted- ritual be
entering home? Wards?
20:21-subject departs on foot-
following.
20:53- subject home- excursion
retrieve take-away from
23:43- subject seen moving
to room, lights out.
00:07 - subject good ni

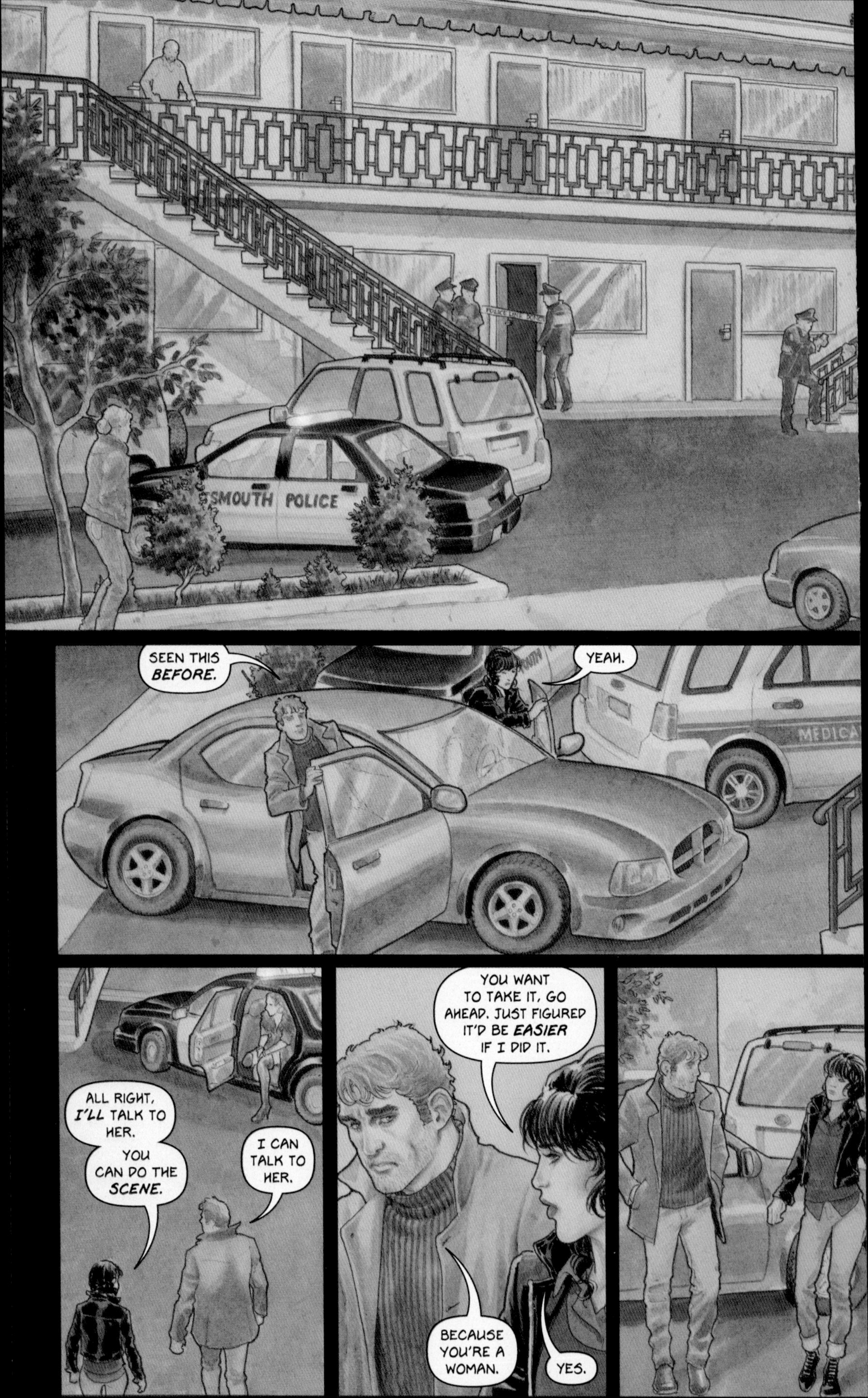
SMOUTH POLICE
SEEN THIS *BEFORE.*
YEAH.
ALL RIGHT, *I'LL* TALK TO HER.
YOU CAN DO THE *SCENE.*
I CAN TALK TO HER.
YOU WANT TO TAKE IT, GO AHEAD. JUST FIGURED IT'D BE *EASIER* IF I DID IT.
BECAUSE YOU'RE A WOMAN.
YES.

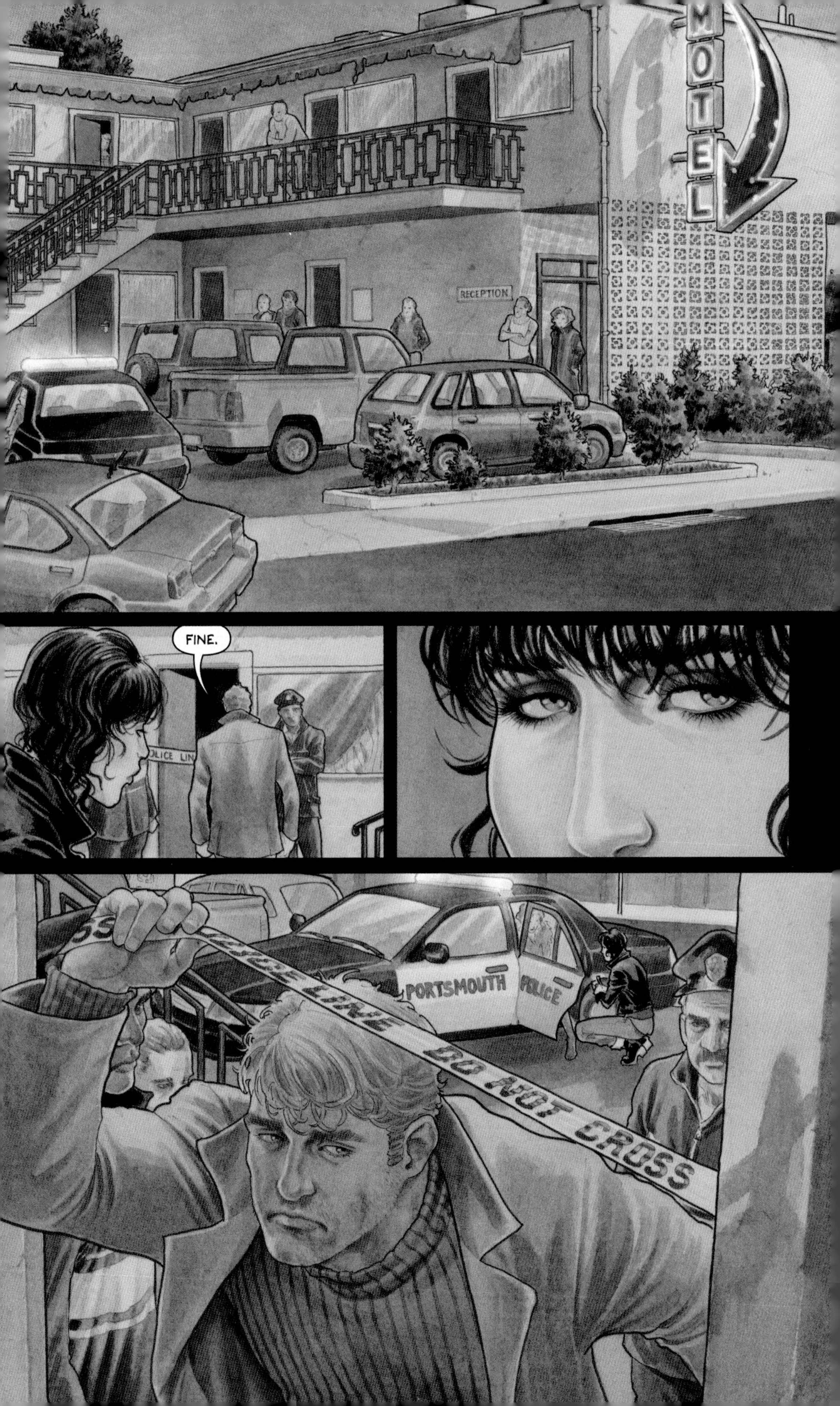
MOTEL
RECEPTION
FINE.
PORTSMOUTH
POLICE
DO NOT CROSS

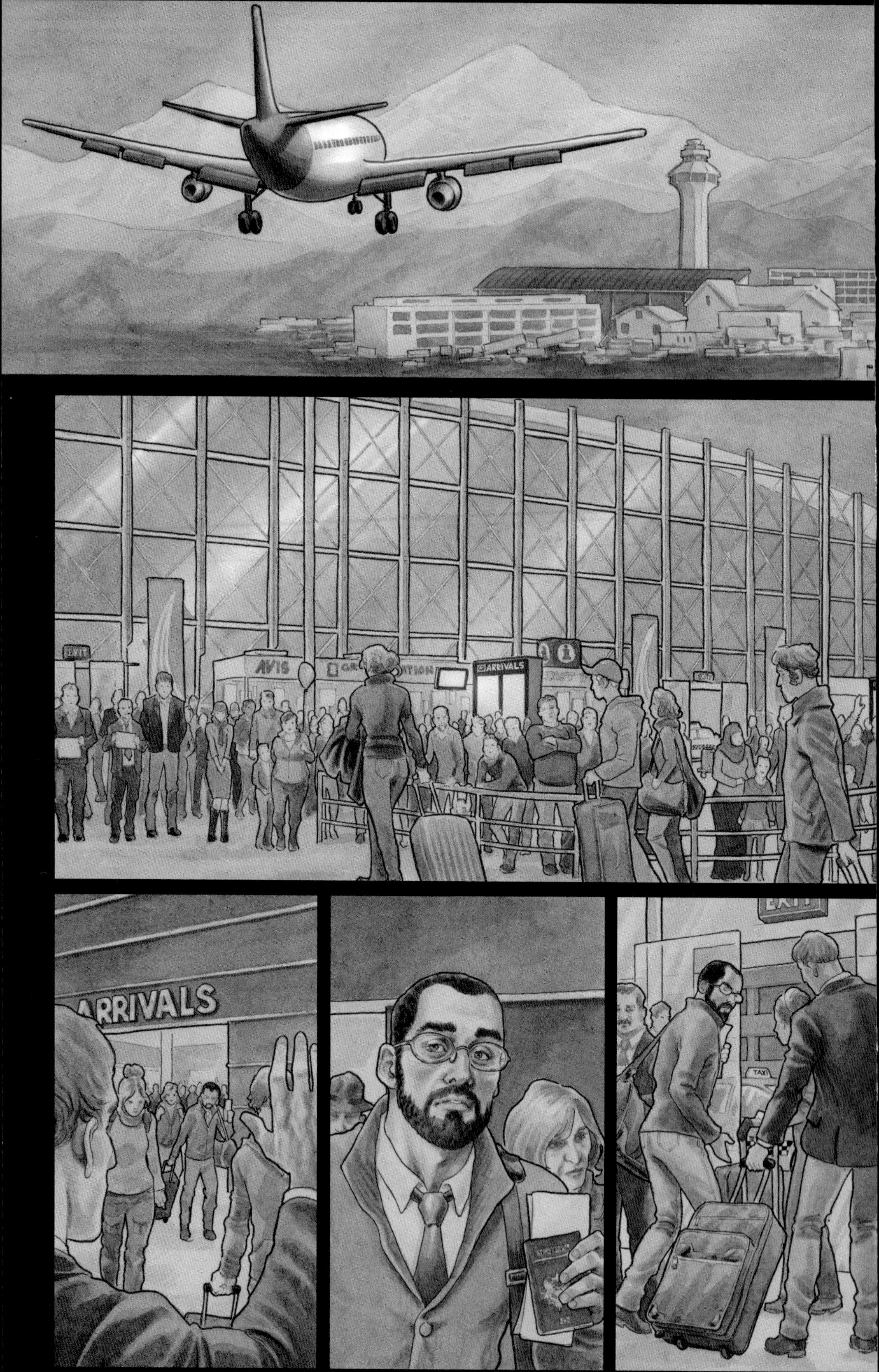
EXIT
AVIS
ARRIVALS
ARRIVALS
TAXI

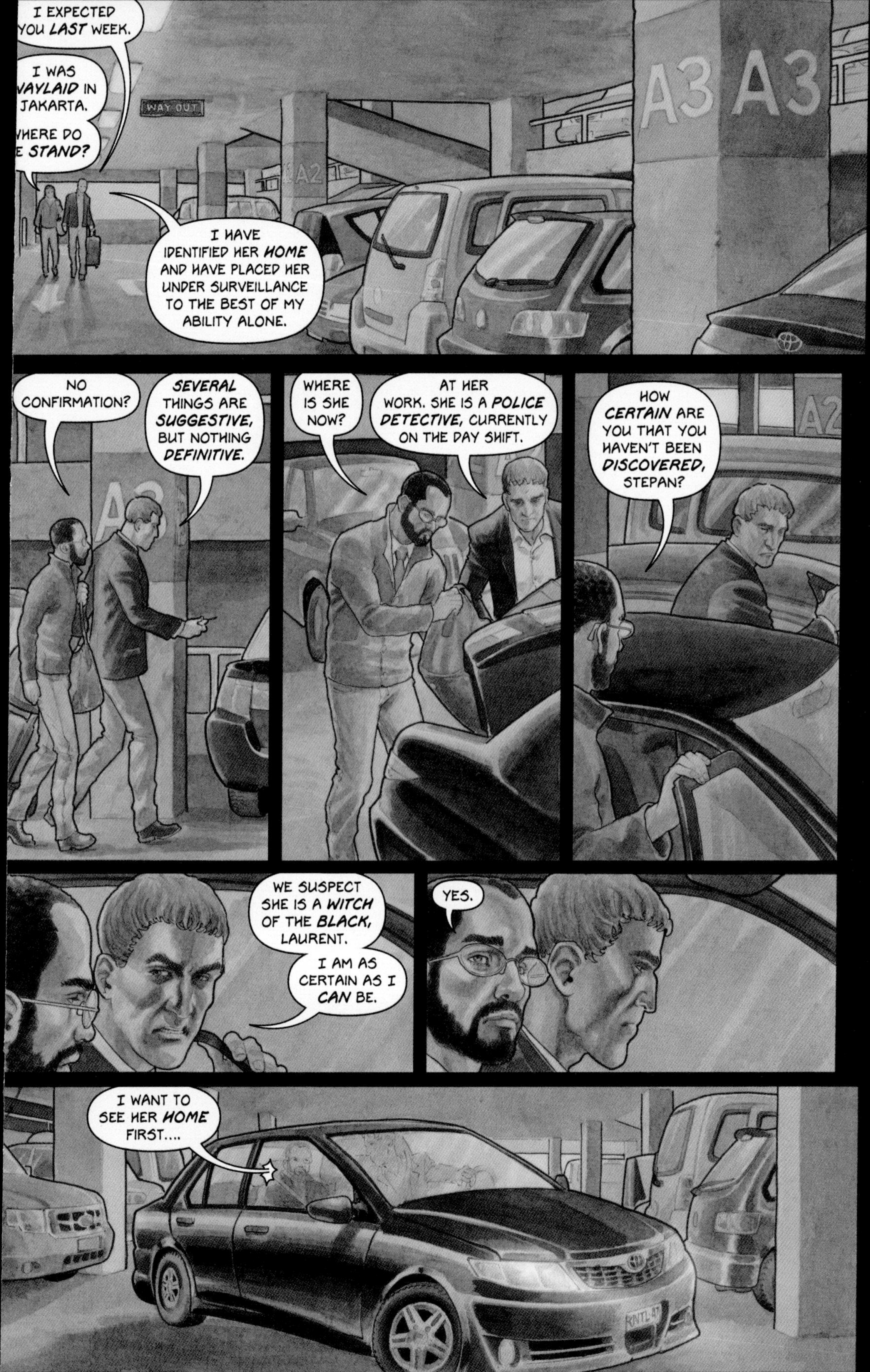
I EXPECTED YOU LAST WEEK.
I WAS WAYLAID IN JAKARTA.
WHERE DO WE STAND?
WAY OUT
A2
A3 A3
I HAVE IDENTIFIED HER HOME AND HAVE PLACED HER UNDER SURVEILLANCE TO THE BEST OF MY ABILITY ALONE.
NO CONFIRMATION?
SEVERAL THINGS ARE SUGGESTIVE, BUT NOTHING DEFINITIVE.
WHERE IS SHE NOW?
AT HER WORK. SHE IS A POLICE DETECTIVE, CURRENTLY ON THE DAY SHIFT.
HOW CERTAIN ARE YOU THAT YOU HAVEN'T BEEN DISCOVERED, STEPAN?
WE SUSPECT SHE IS A WITCH OF THE BLACK, LAURENT.
I AM AS CERTAIN AS I CAN BE.
YES.
I WANT TO SEE HER HOME FIRST....

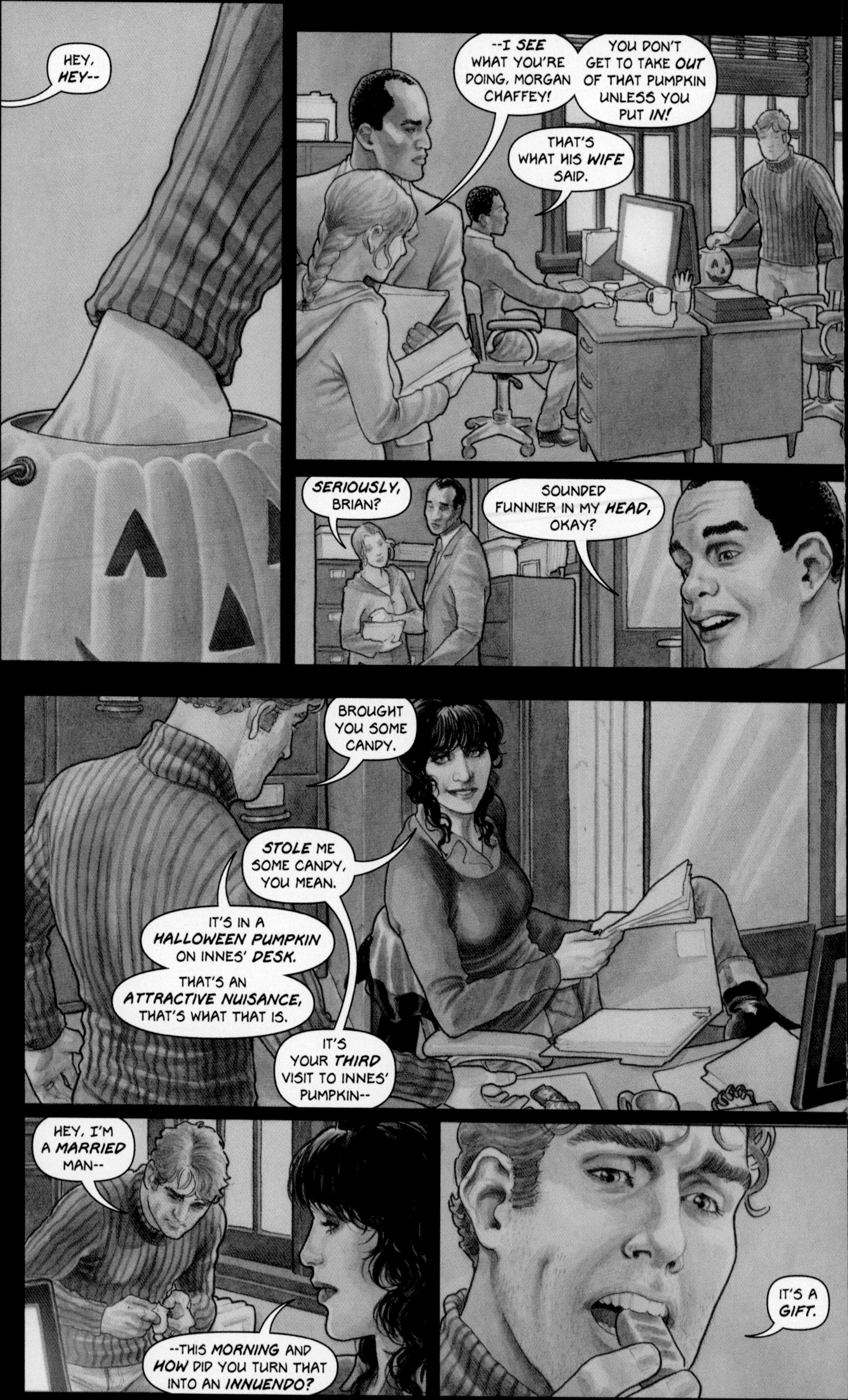
HEY, HEY--
--I SEE WHAT YOU'RE DOING, MORGAN CHAFFEY!
YOU DON'T GET TO TAKE OUT OF THAT PUMPKIN UNLESS YOU PUT IN!
THAT'S WHAT HIS WIFE SAID.
SERIOUSLY, BRIAN?
SOUNDED FUNNIER IN MY HEAD, OKAY?
BROUGHT YOU SOME CANDY.
STOLE ME SOME CANDY, YOU MEAN.
IT'S IN A HALLOWEEN PUMPKIN ON INNES' DESK.
THAT'S AN ATTRACTIVE NUISANCE, THAT'S WHAT THAT IS.
IT'S YOUR THIRD VISIT TO INNES' PUMPKIN--
HEY, I'M A MARRIED MAN--
--THIS MORNING AND HOW DID YOU TURN THAT INTO AN INNUENDO?
IT'S A GIFT.

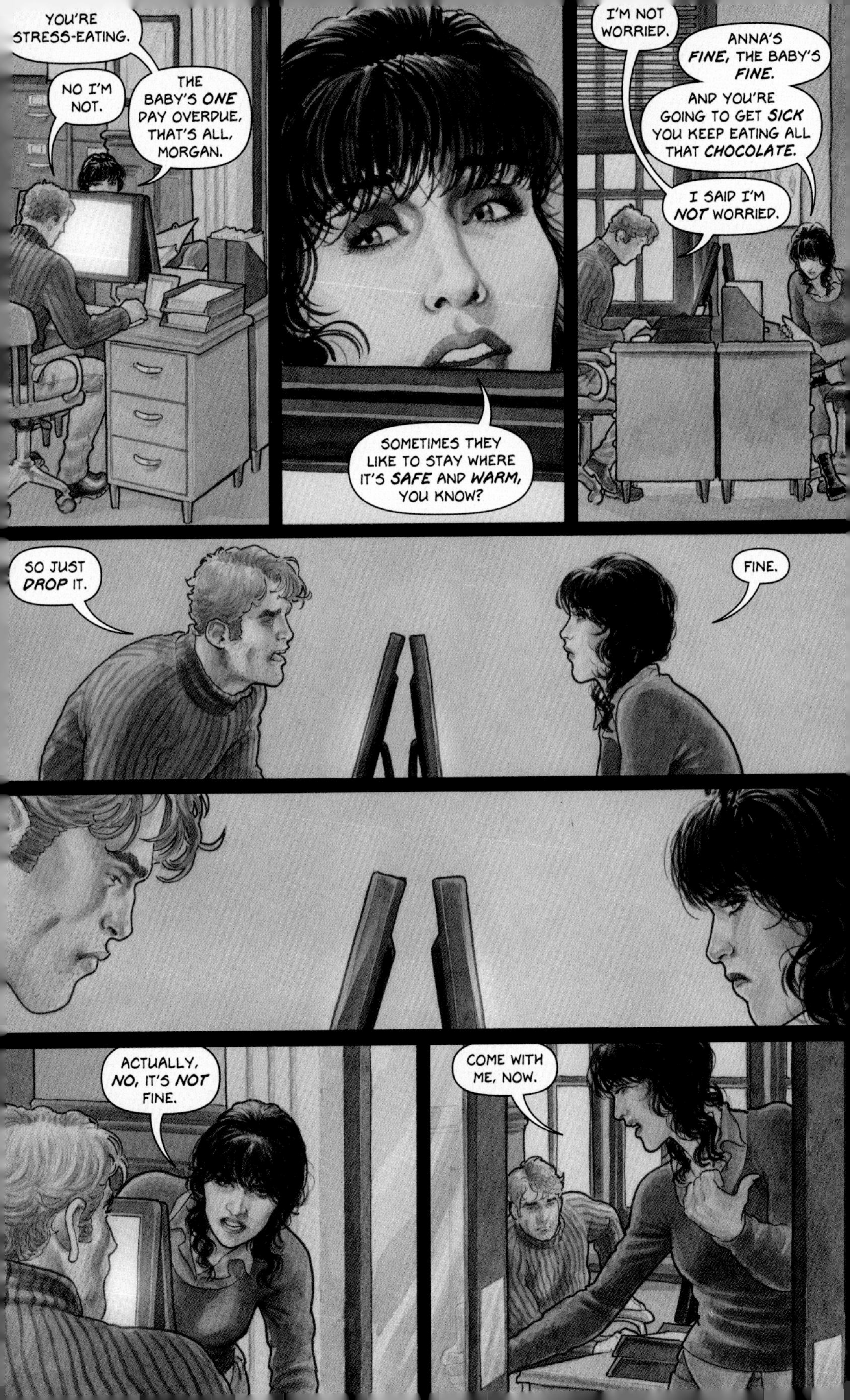

YOU'RE STRESS-EATING.
NO I'M NOT.
THE BABY'S *ONE* DAY OVERDUE, THAT'S ALL, MORGAN.
SOMETIMES THEY LIKE TO STAY WHERE IT'S *SAFE* AND *WARM*, YOU KNOW?
I'M NOT WORRIED.
ANNA'S *FINE*, THE BABY'S *FINE*.
AND YOU'RE GOING TO GET *SICK* YOU KEEP EATING ALL THAT *CHOCOLATE*.
I SAID I'M *NOT* WORRIED.
SO JUST *DROP* IT.
FINE.
ACTUALLY, *NO*, IT'S *NOT* FINE.
COME WITH ME, NOW.

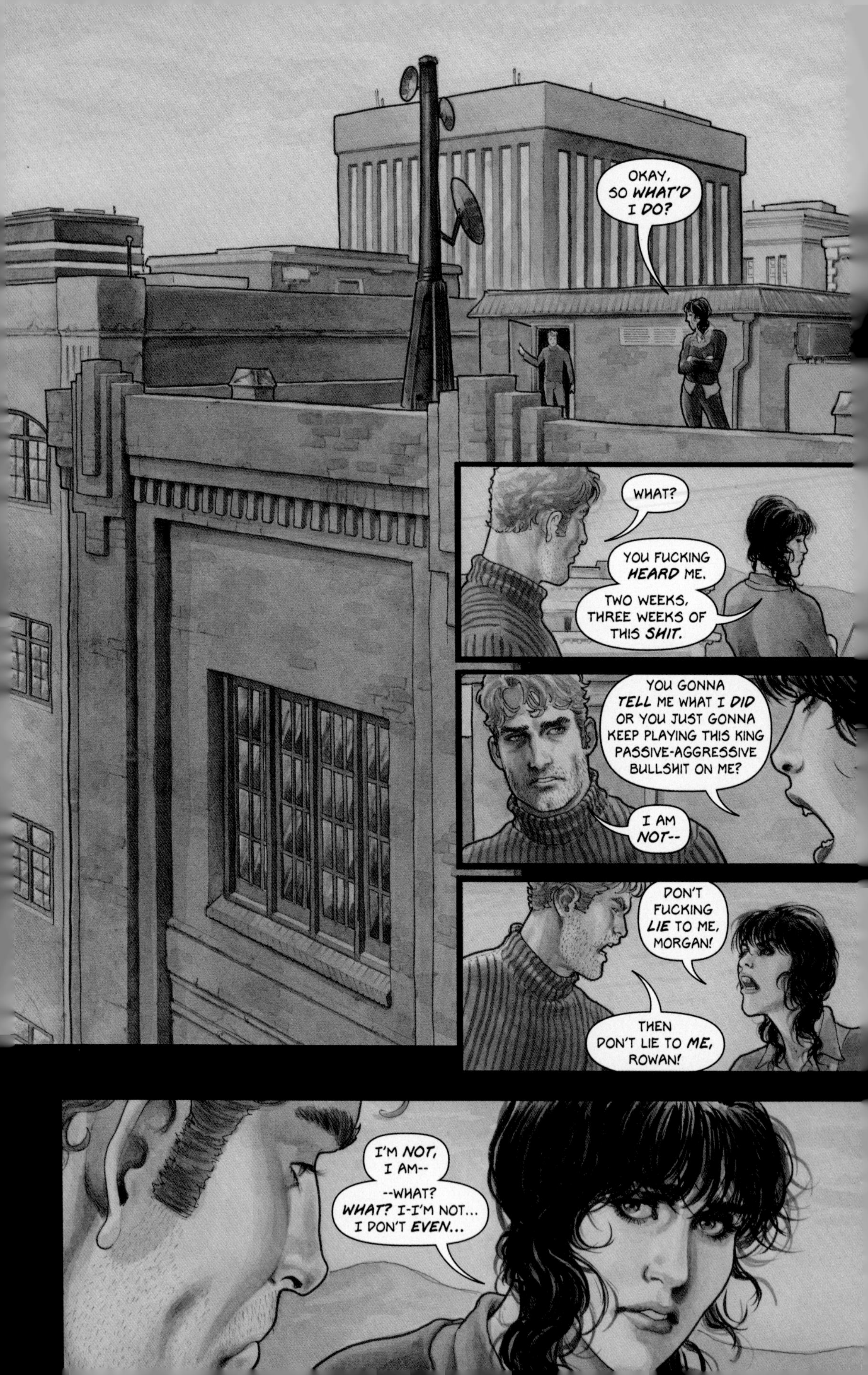
OKAY, SO WHAT'D I DO?
WHAT?
YOU FUCKING HEARD ME.
TWO WEEKS, THREE WEEKS OF THIS SHIT.
YOU GONNA TELL ME WHAT I DID OR YOU JUST GONNA KEEP PLAYING THIS KING PASSIVE-AGGRESSIVE BULLSHIT ON ME?
I AM NOT--
DON'T FUCKING LIE TO ME, MORGAN!
THEN DON'T LIE TO ME, ROWAN!
I'M NOT, I AM--
--WHAT? WHAT? I-I'M NOT... I DON'T EVEN...

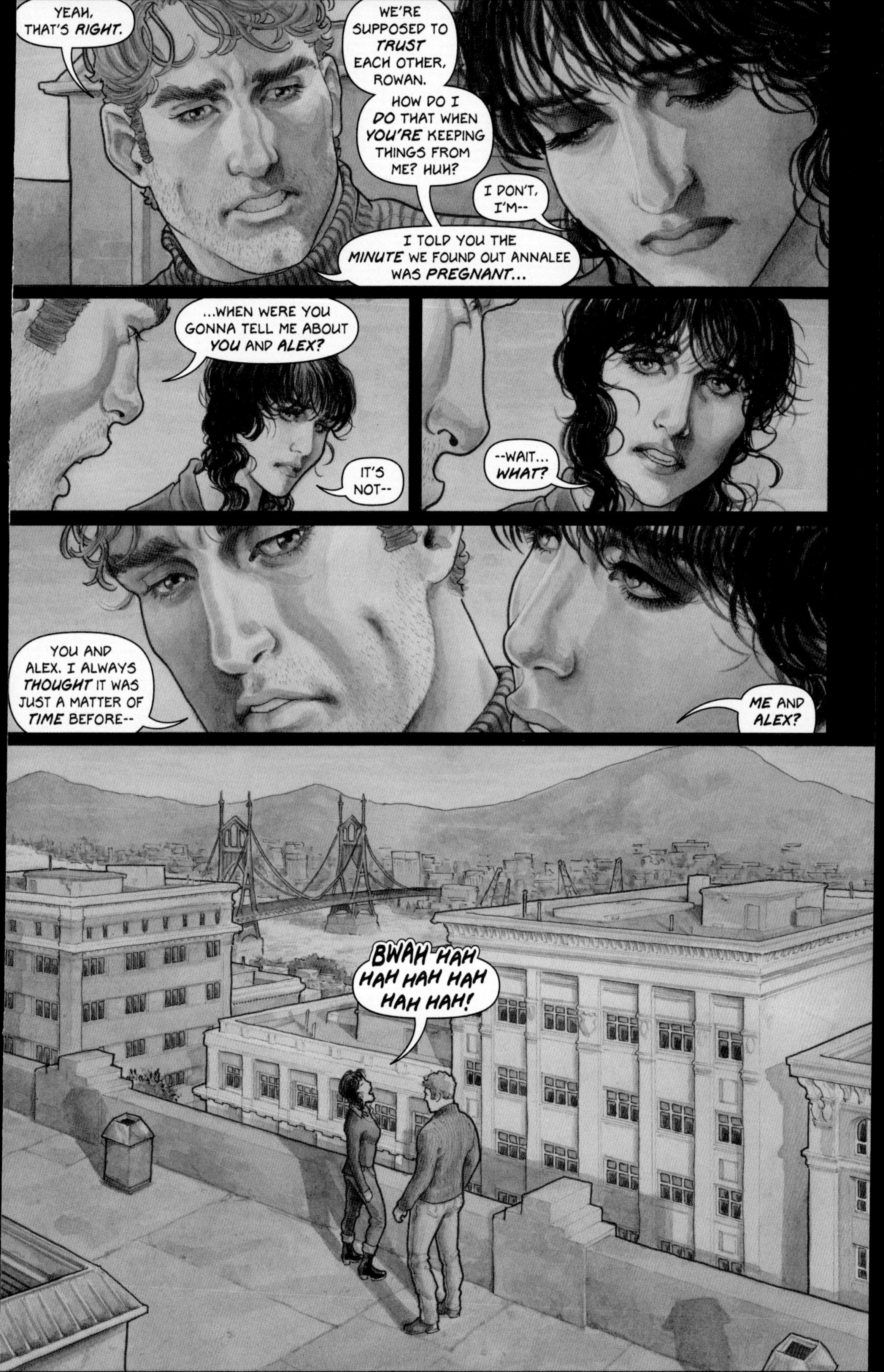
YEAH, THAT'S RIGHT.
WE'RE SUPPOSED TO TRUST EACH OTHER, ROWAN.
HOW DO I DO THAT WHEN YOU'RE KEEPING THINGS FROM ME? HUH?
I DON'T, I'M--
I TOLD YOU THE MINUTE WE FOUND OUT ANNALEE WAS PREGNANT...
...WHEN WERE YOU GONNA TELL ME ABOUT YOU AND ALEX?
IT'S NOT--
--WAIT... WHAT?
YOU AND ALEX. I ALWAYS THOUGHT IT WAS JUST A MATTER OF TIME BEFORE--
ME AND ALEX?
BWAH HAH HAH HAH HAH HAH HAH!

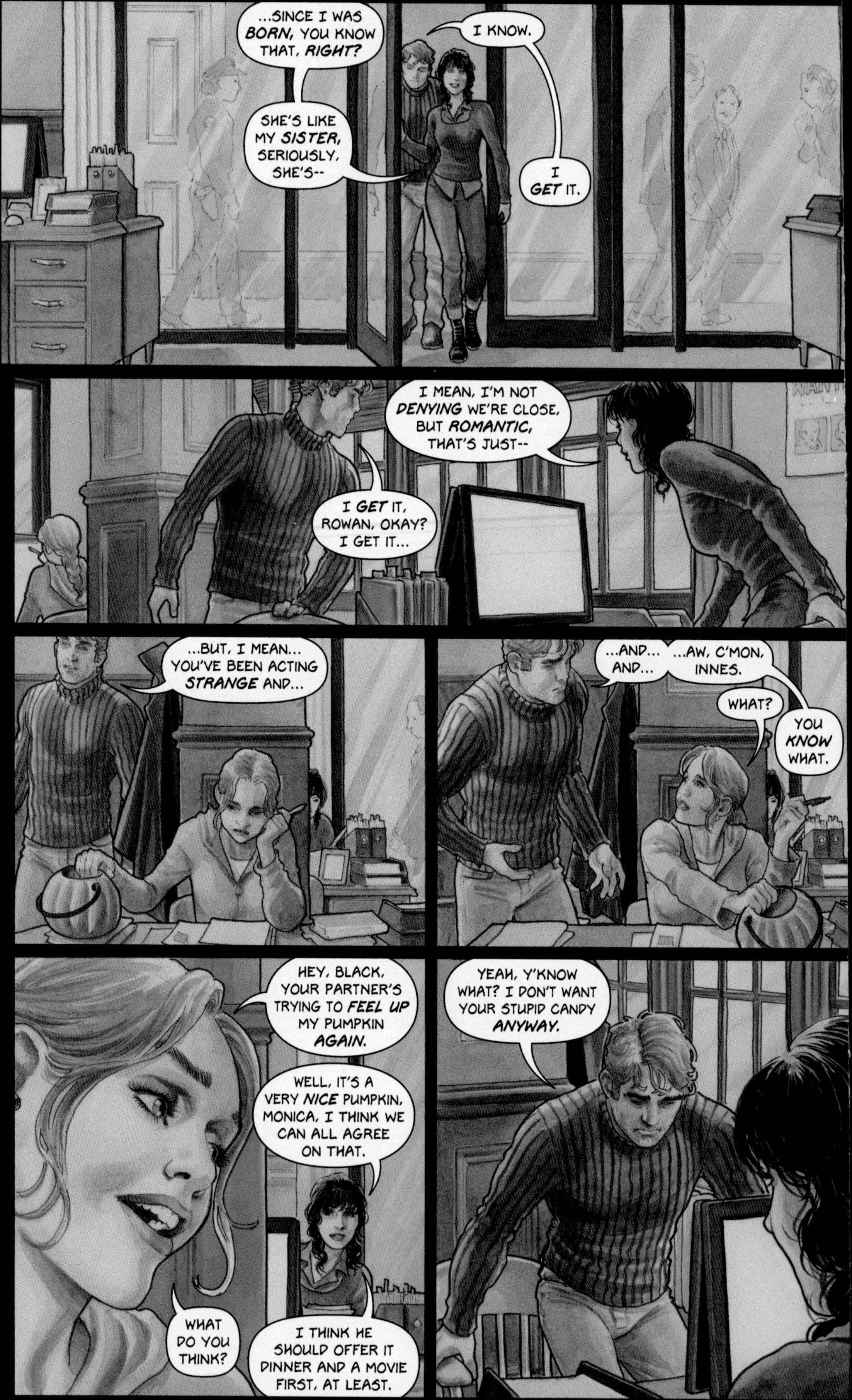
...SINCE I WAS BORN, YOU KNOW THAT, RIGHT?
I KNOW.
SHE'S LIKE MY SISTER, SERIOUSLY, SHE'S--
I GET IT.
I MEAN, I'M NOT DENYING WE'RE CLOSE, BUT ROMANTIC, THAT'S JUST--
I GET IT, ROWAN, OKAY? I GET IT...
...BUT, I MEAN... YOU'VE BEEN ACTING STRANGE AND...
...AND... AND...
...AW, C'MON, INNES.
WHAT?
YOU KNOW WHAT.
HEY, BLACK, YOUR PARTNER'S TRYING TO FEEL UP MY PUMPKIN AGAIN.
WELL, IT'S A VERY NICE PUMPKIN, MONICA, I THINK WE CAN ALL AGREE ON THAT.
WHAT DO YOU THINK?
I THINK HE SHOULD OFFER IT DINNER AND A MOVIE FIRST, AT LEAST.
YEAH, Y'KNOW WHAT? I DON'T WANT YOUR STUPID CANDY ANYWAY.

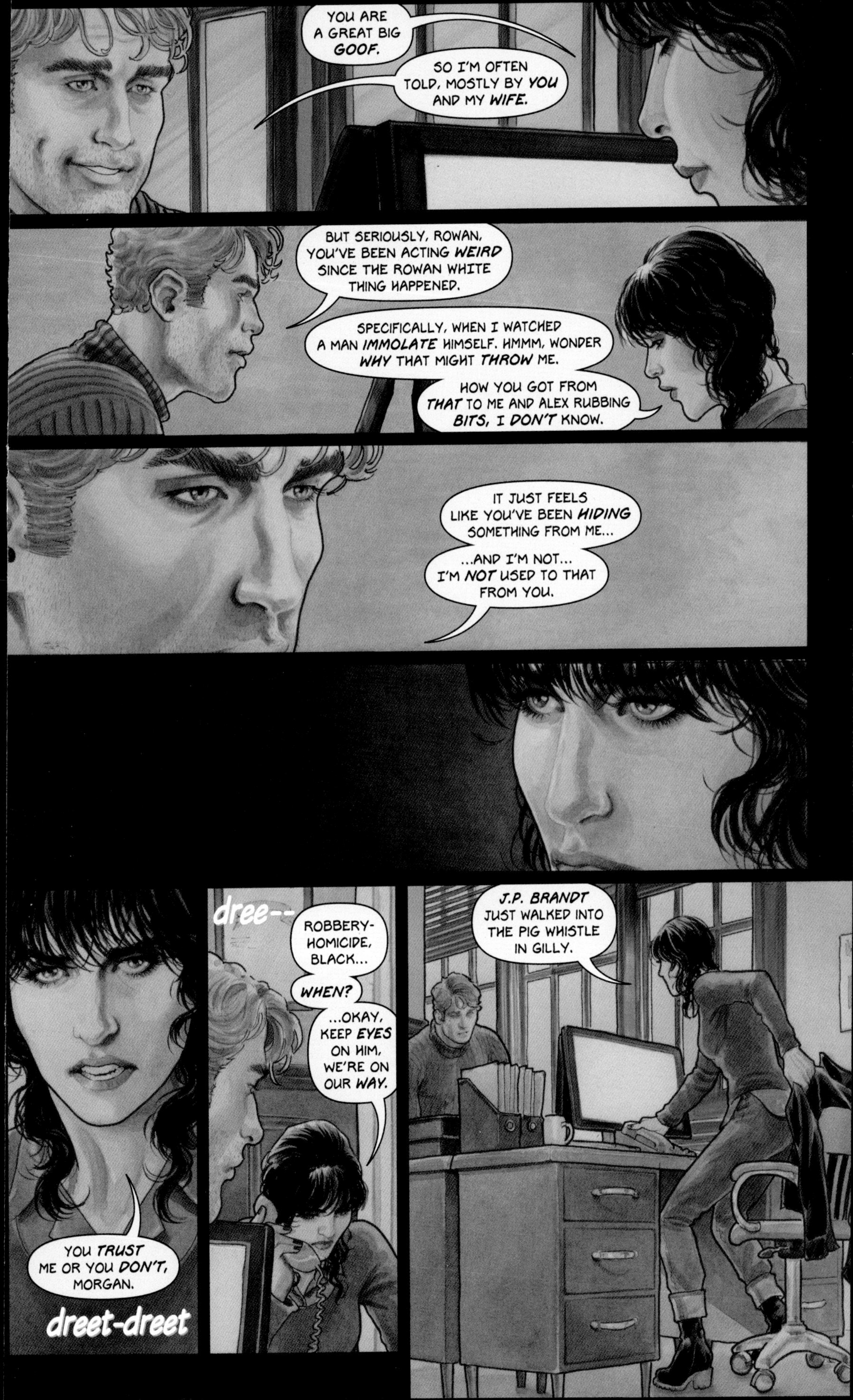
YOU ARE A GREAT BIG GOOF.
SO I'M OFTEN TOLD, MOSTLY BY YOU AND MY WIFE.
BUT SERIOUSLY, ROWAN, YOU'VE BEEN ACTING WEIRD SINCE THE ROWAN WHITE THING HAPPENED.
SPECIFICALLY, WHEN I WATCHED A MAN IMMOLATE HIMSELF. HMMM, WONDER WHY THAT MIGHT THROW ME.
HOW YOU GOT FROM THAT TO ME AND ALEX RUBBING BITS, I DON'T KNOW.
IT JUST FEELS LIKE YOU'VE BEEN HIDING SOMETHING FROM ME...
...AND I'M NOT... I'M NOT USED TO THAT FROM YOU.
YOU TRUST ME OR YOU DON'T, MORGAN.
dreet-dreet
dree--
ROBBERY-HOMICIDE, BLACK...
WHEN?
...OKAY, KEEP EYES ON HIM, WE'RE ON OUR WAY.
J.P. BRANDT JUST WALKED INTO THE PIG WHISTLE IN GILLY.

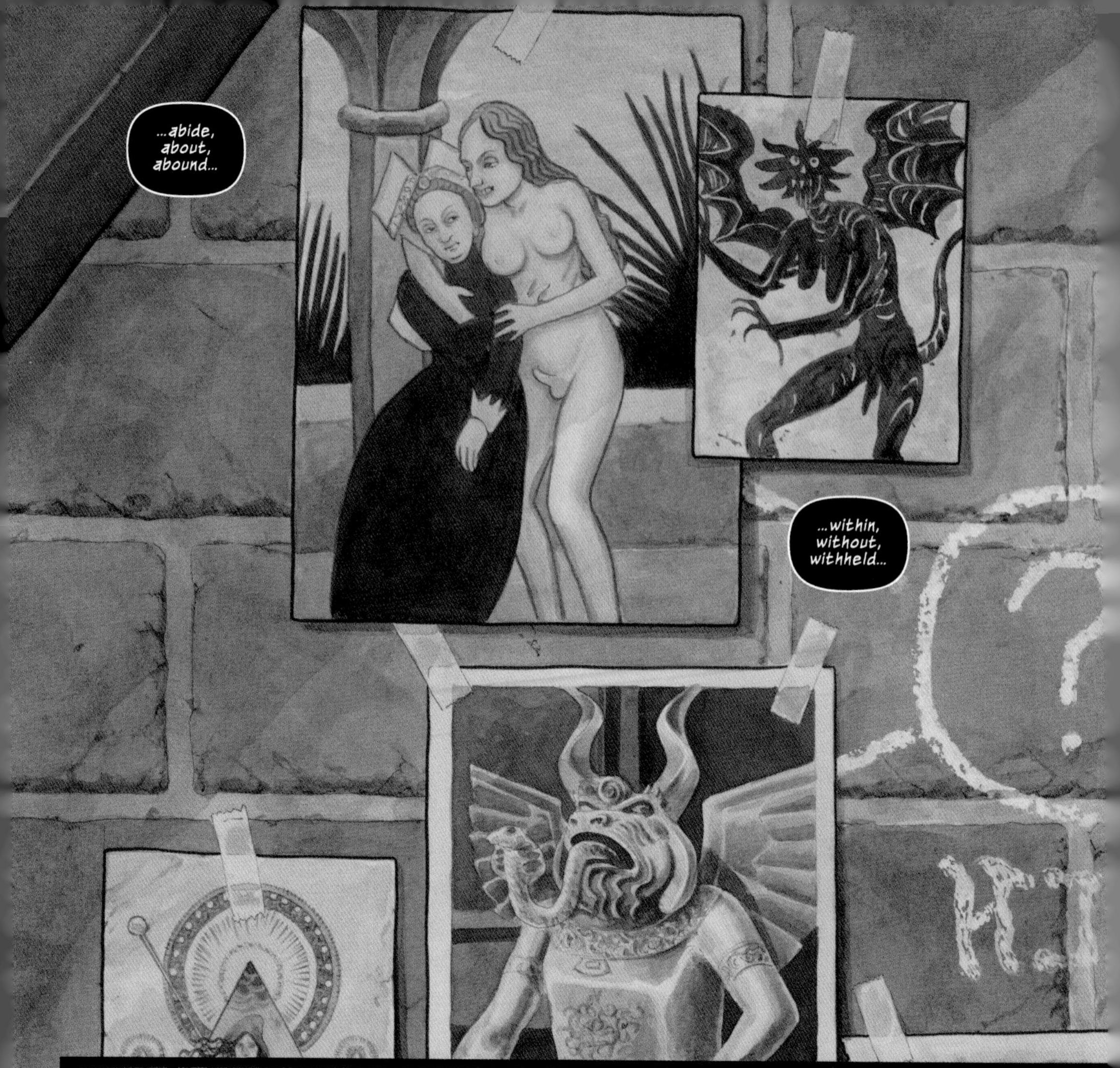
...abide, about, abound...
...within, without, withheld...

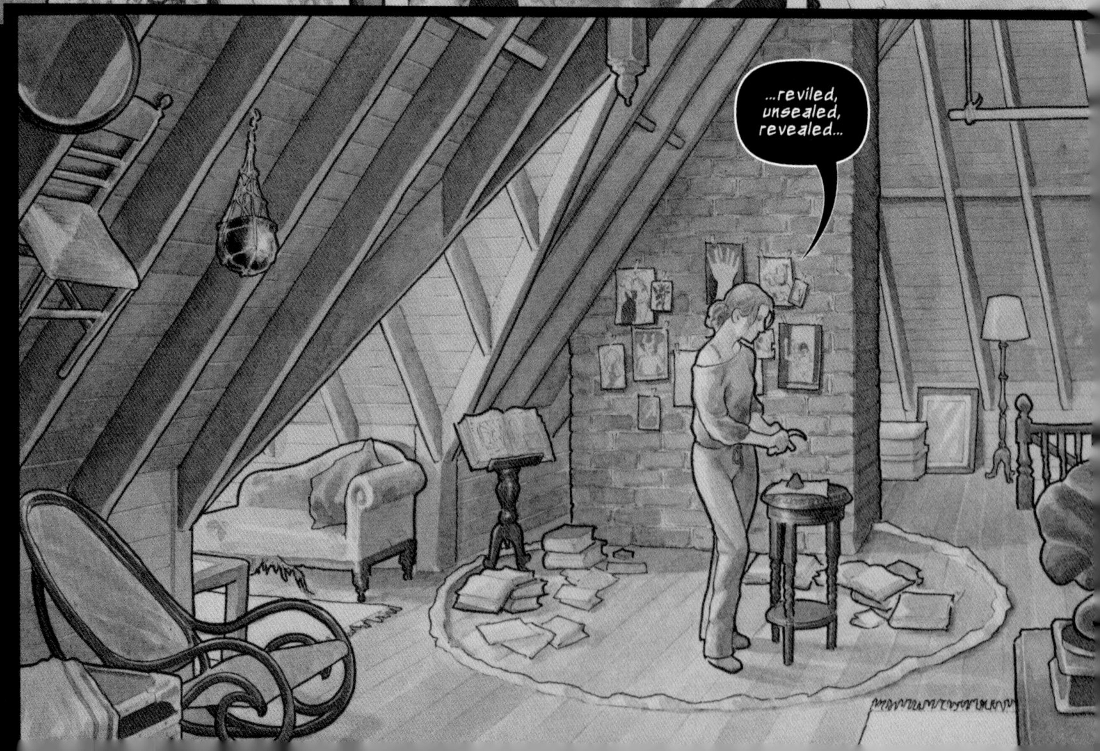
...reviled, unsealed, revealed...

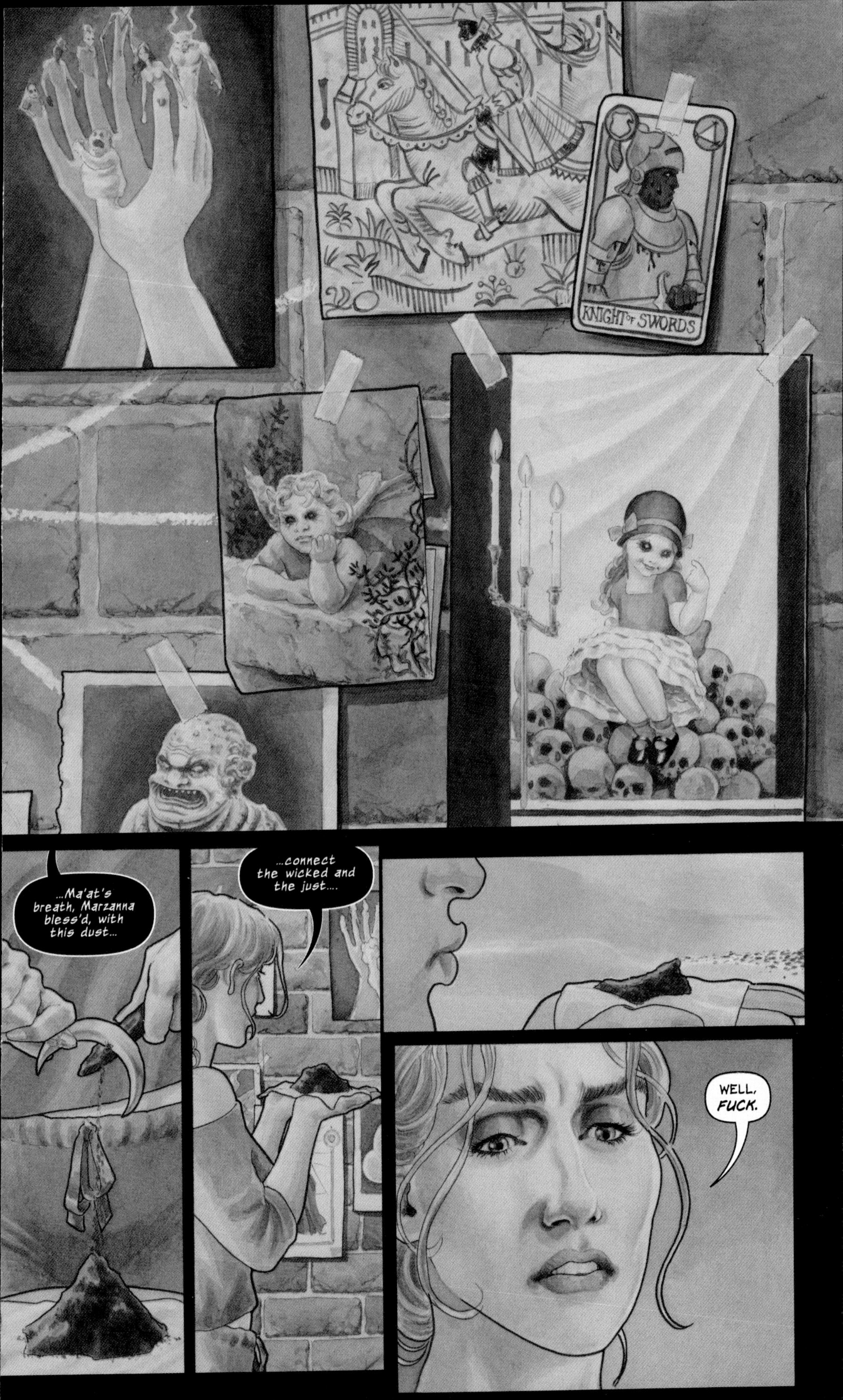
KNIGHT OF SWORDS
...Ma'at's breath, Marzanna bless'd, with this dust...
...connect the wicked and the just....
WELL, FUCK.

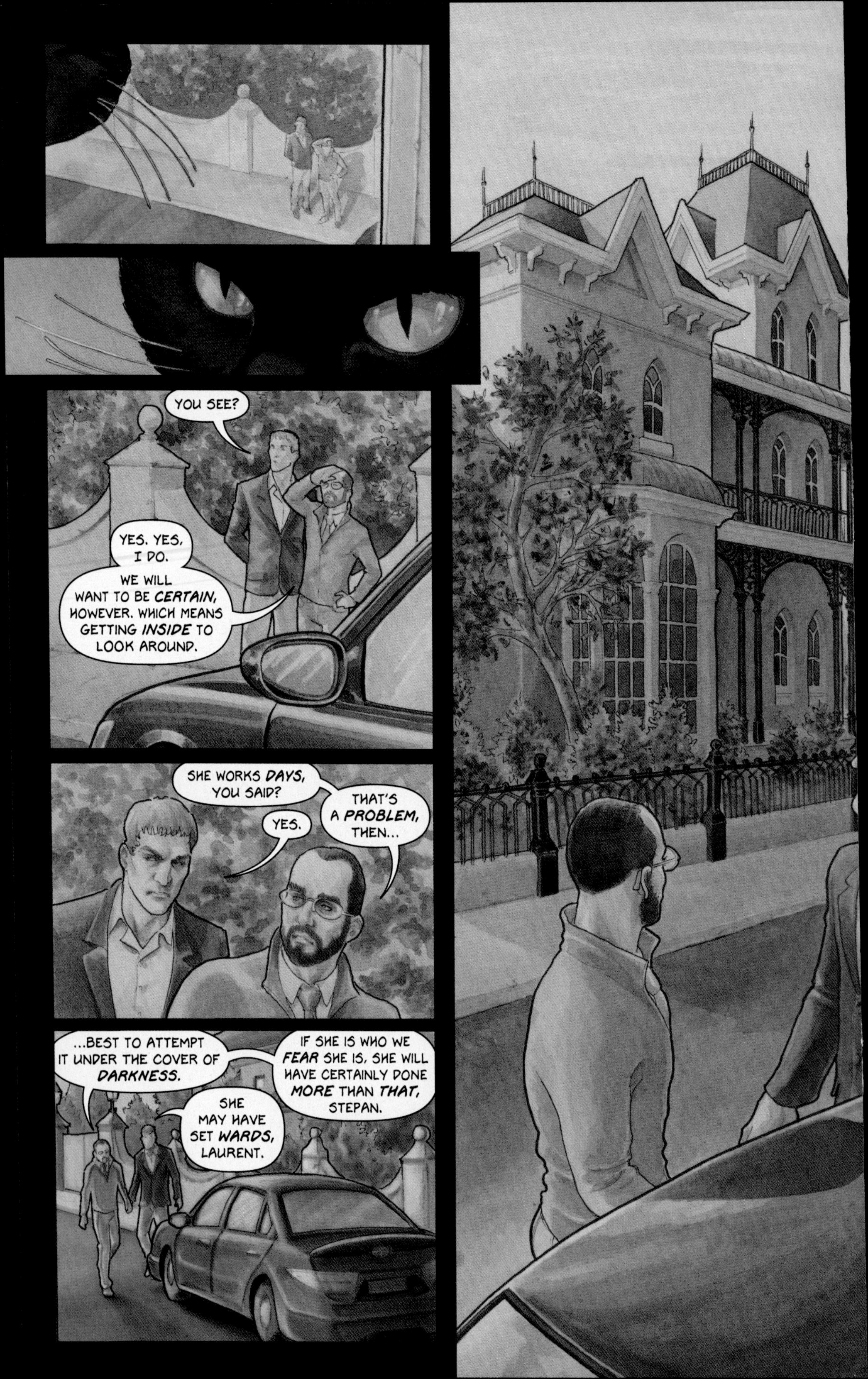
YOU SEE?
YES. YES, I DO.
WE WILL WANT TO BE CERTAIN, HOWEVER. WHICH MEANS GETTING INSIDE TO LOOK AROUND.
SHE WORKS DAYS, YOU SAID?
YES.
THAT'S A PROBLEM, THEN...
...BEST TO ATTEMPT IT UNDER THE COVER OF DARKNESS.
SHE MAY HAVE SET WARDS, LAURENT.
IF SHE IS WHO WE FEAR SHE IS, SHE WILL HAVE CERTAINLY DONE MORE THAN THAT, STEPAN.

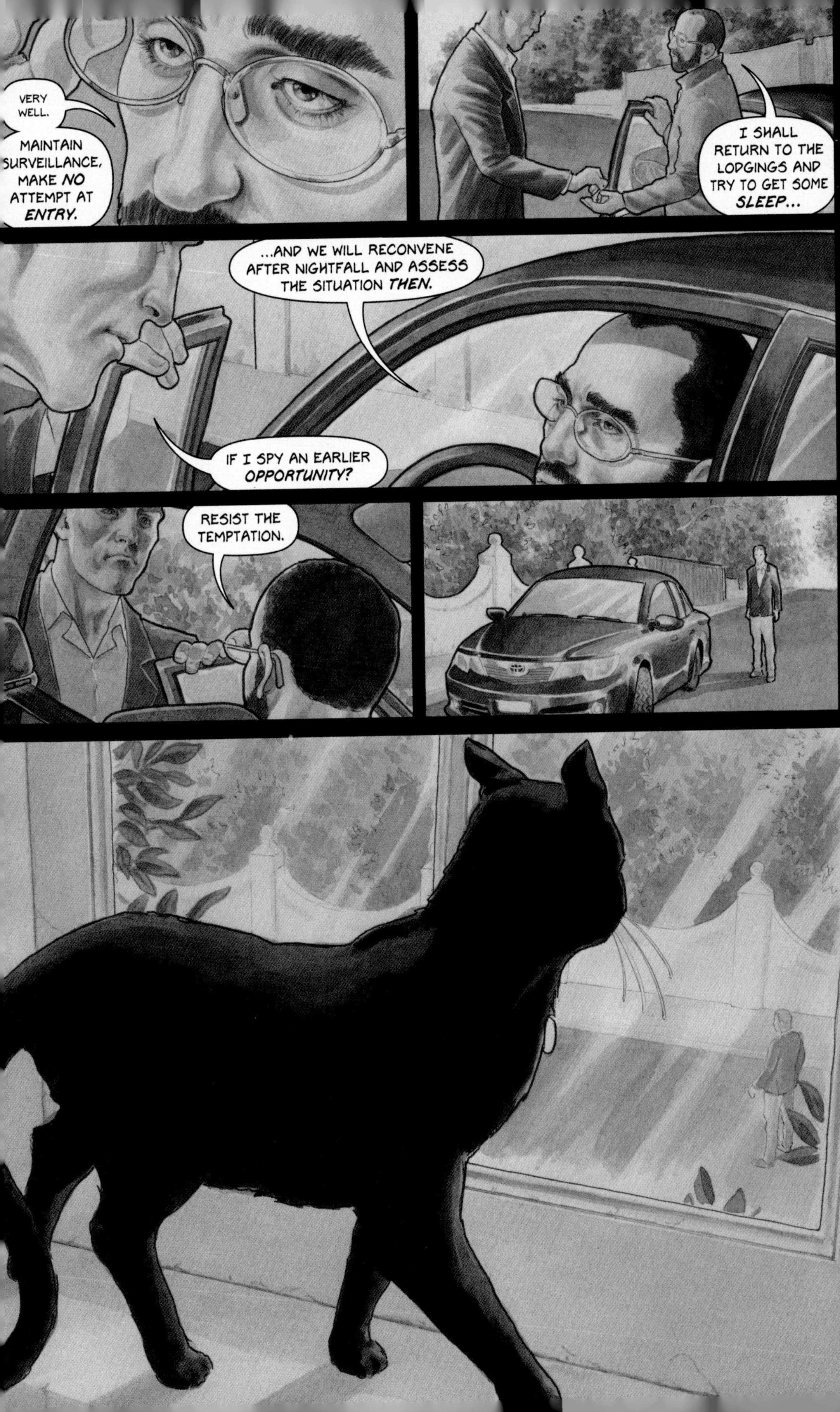
VERY WELL.
MAINTAIN SURVEILLANCE, MAKE *NO* ATTEMPT AT *ENTRY*.
I SHALL RETURN TO THE LODGINGS AND TRY TO GET SOME *SLEEP*...
...AND WE WILL RECONVENE AFTER NIGHTFALL AND ASSESS THE SITUATION *THEN*.
IF I SPY AN EARLIER *OPPORTUNITY*?
RESIST THE TEMPTATION.

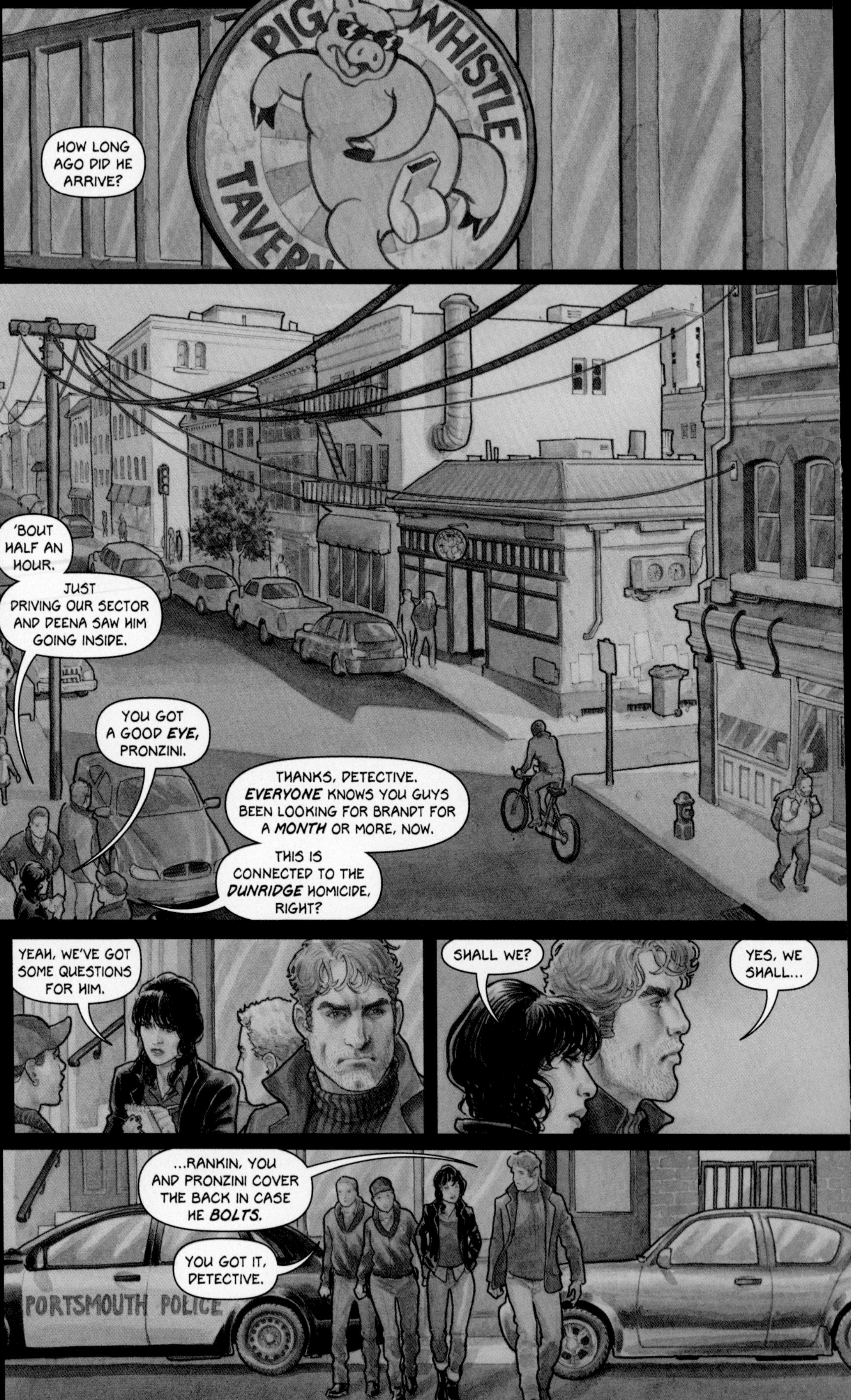
PIG WHISTLE TAVERN
HOW LONG AGO DID HE ARRIVE?
'BOUT HALF AN HOUR.
JUST DRIVING OUR SECTOR AND DEENA SAW HIM GOING INSIDE.
YOU GOT A GOOD EYE, PRONZINI.
THANKS, DETECTIVE. EVERYONE KNOWS YOU GUYS BEEN LOOKING FOR BRANDT FOR A MONTH OR MORE, NOW.
THIS IS CONNECTED TO THE DUNRIDGE HOMICIDE, RIGHT?
YEAH, WE'VE GOT SOME QUESTIONS FOR HIM.
SHALL WE?
YES, WE SHALL...
...RANKIN, YOU AND PRONZINI COVER THE BACK IN CASE HE BOLTS.
YOU GOT IT, DETECTIVE.
PORTSMOUTH POLICE

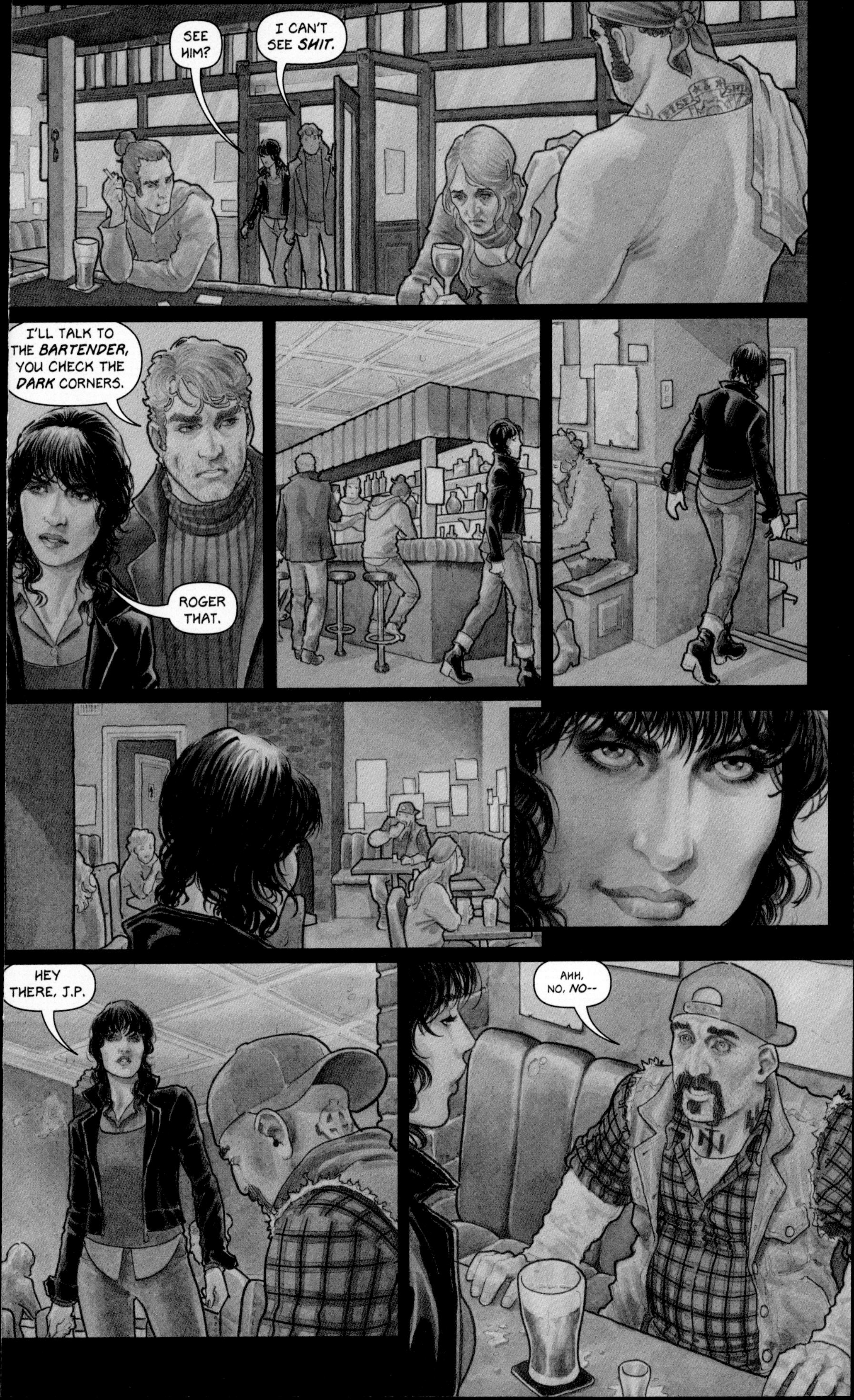
SEE HIM?
I CAN'T SEE *SHIT*.
I'LL TALK TO THE *BARTENDER*, YOU CHECK THE *DARK* CORNERS.
ROGER THAT.
HEY THERE, J.P.
AHH, NO, *NO*--

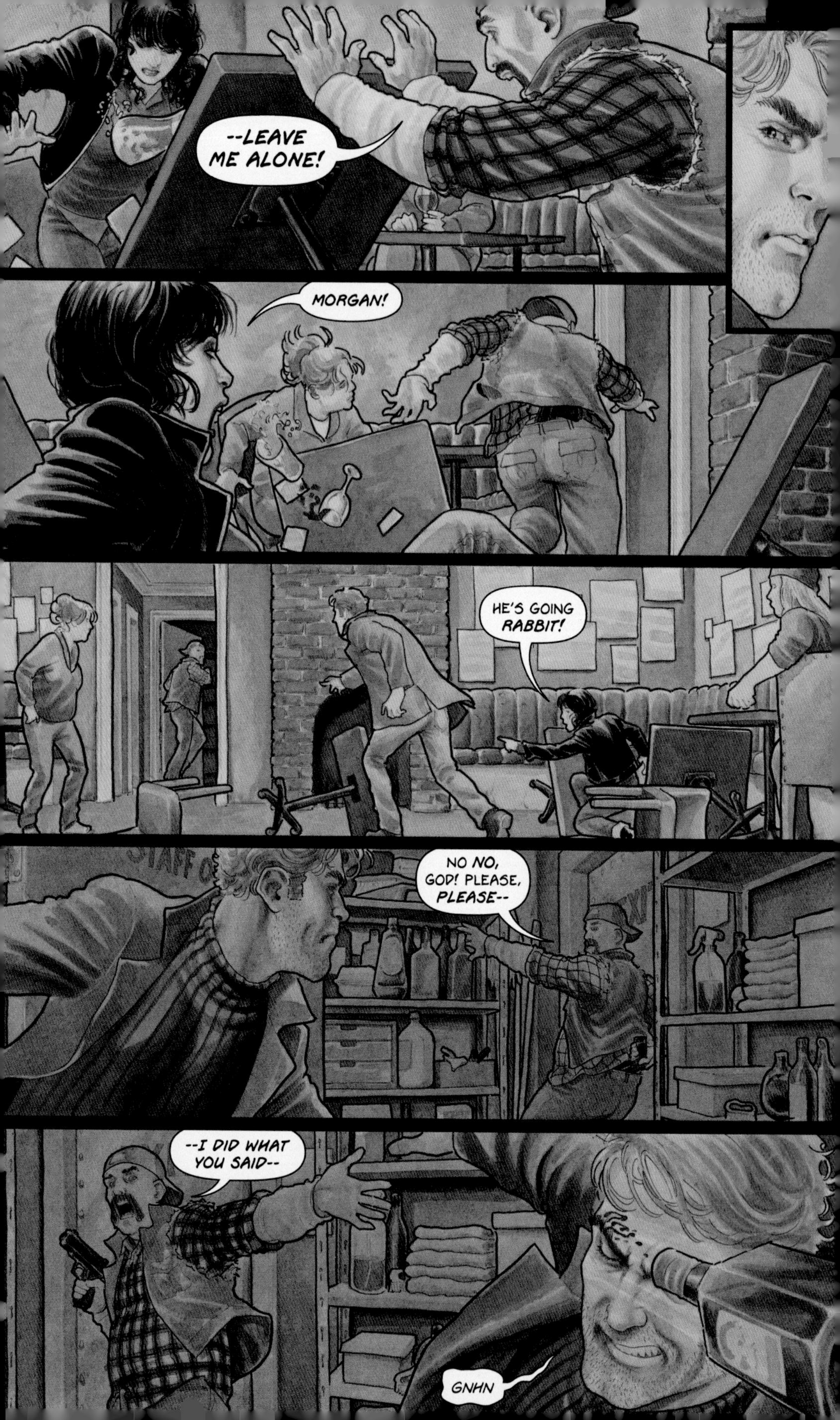
--LEAVE ME ALONE!
MORGAN!
HE'S GOING RABBIT!
NO NO, GOD! PLEASE, PLEASE--
--I DID WHAT YOU SAID--
GNHN

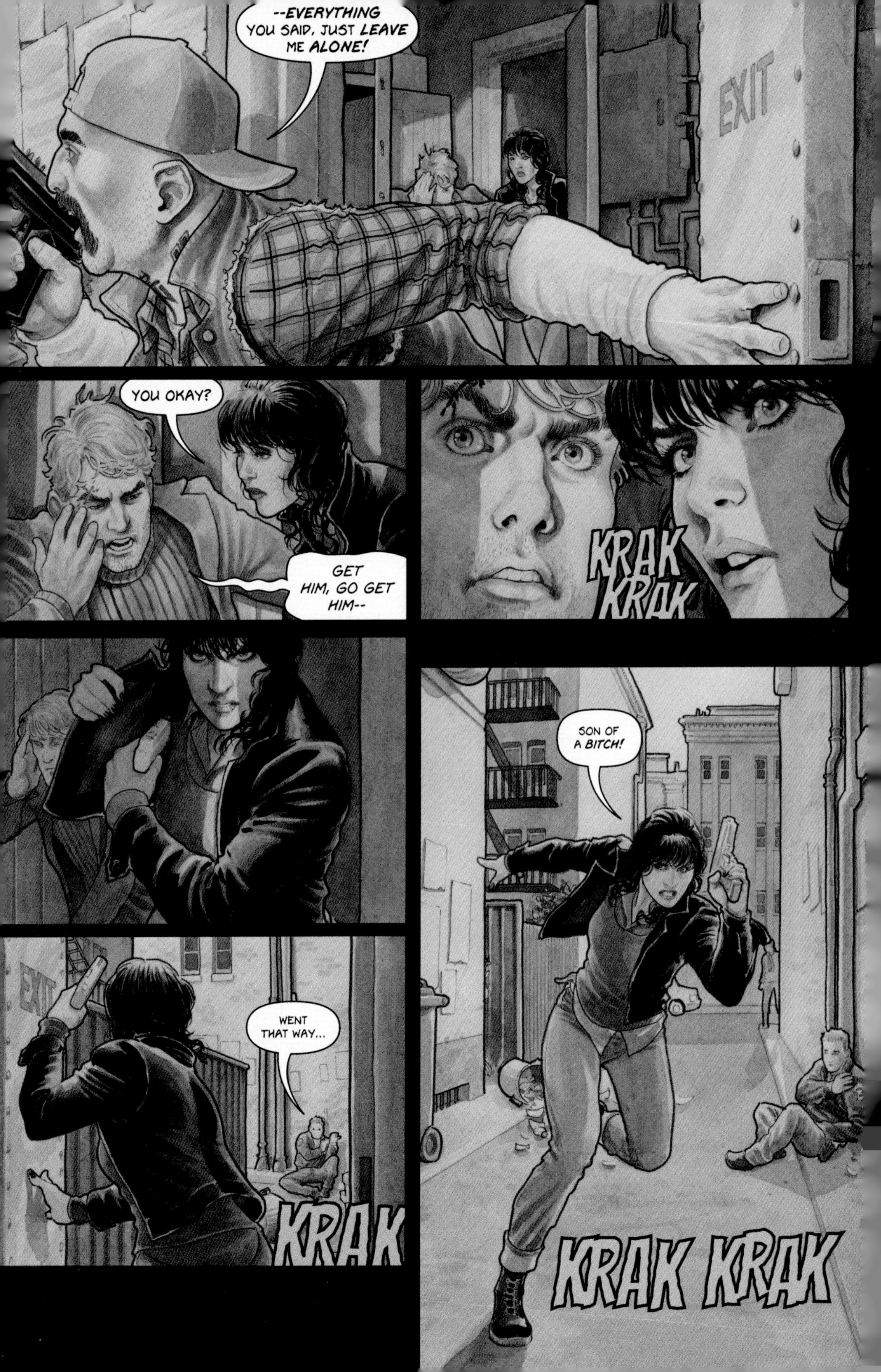
--EVERYTHING YOU SAID, JUST LEAVE ME ALONE!
EXIT
YOU OKAY?
GET HIM, GO GET HIM--
KRAK KRAK
SON OF A BITCH!
EXIT
WENT THAT WAY...
KRAK
KRAK KRAK

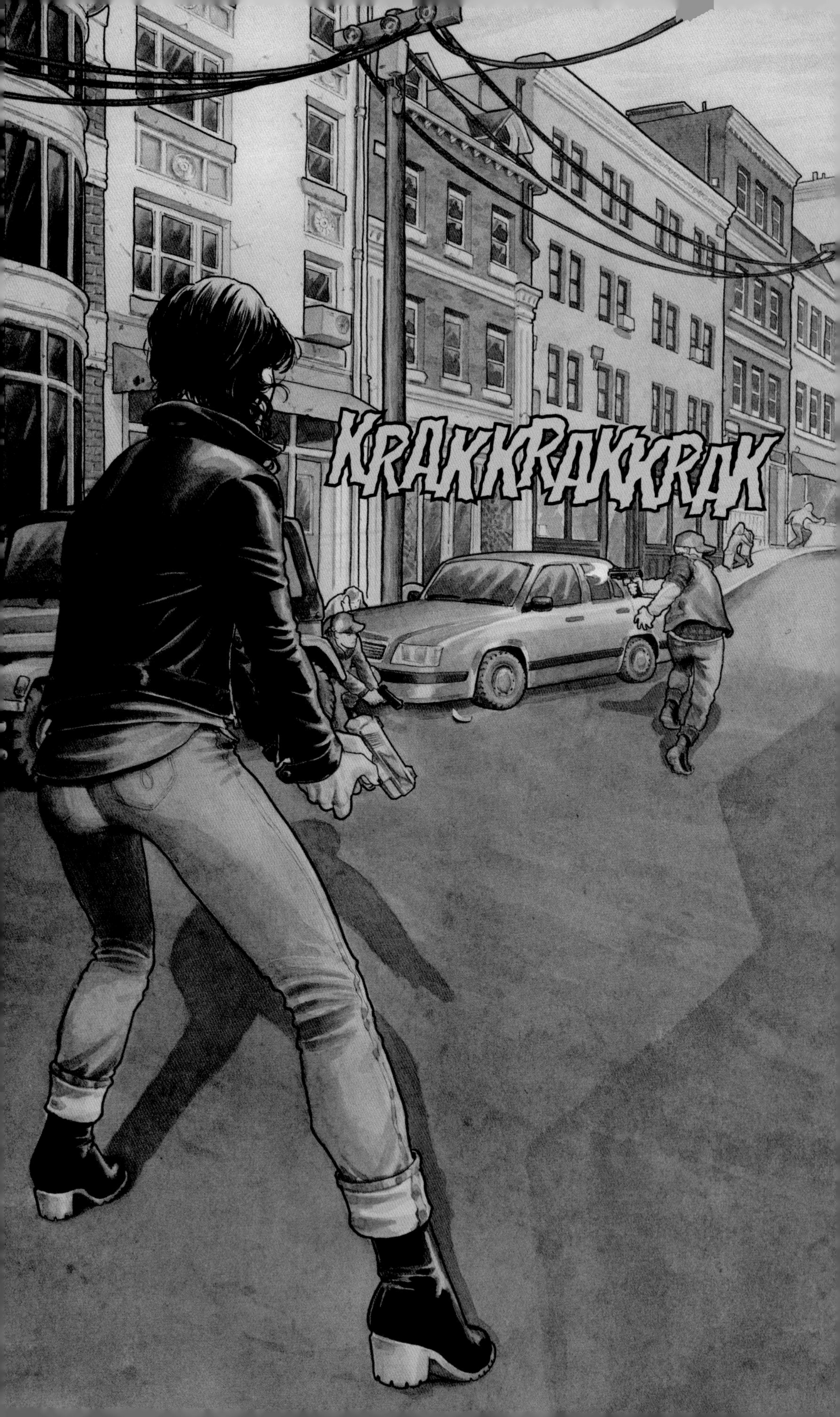
KRAKKRAKKRAK

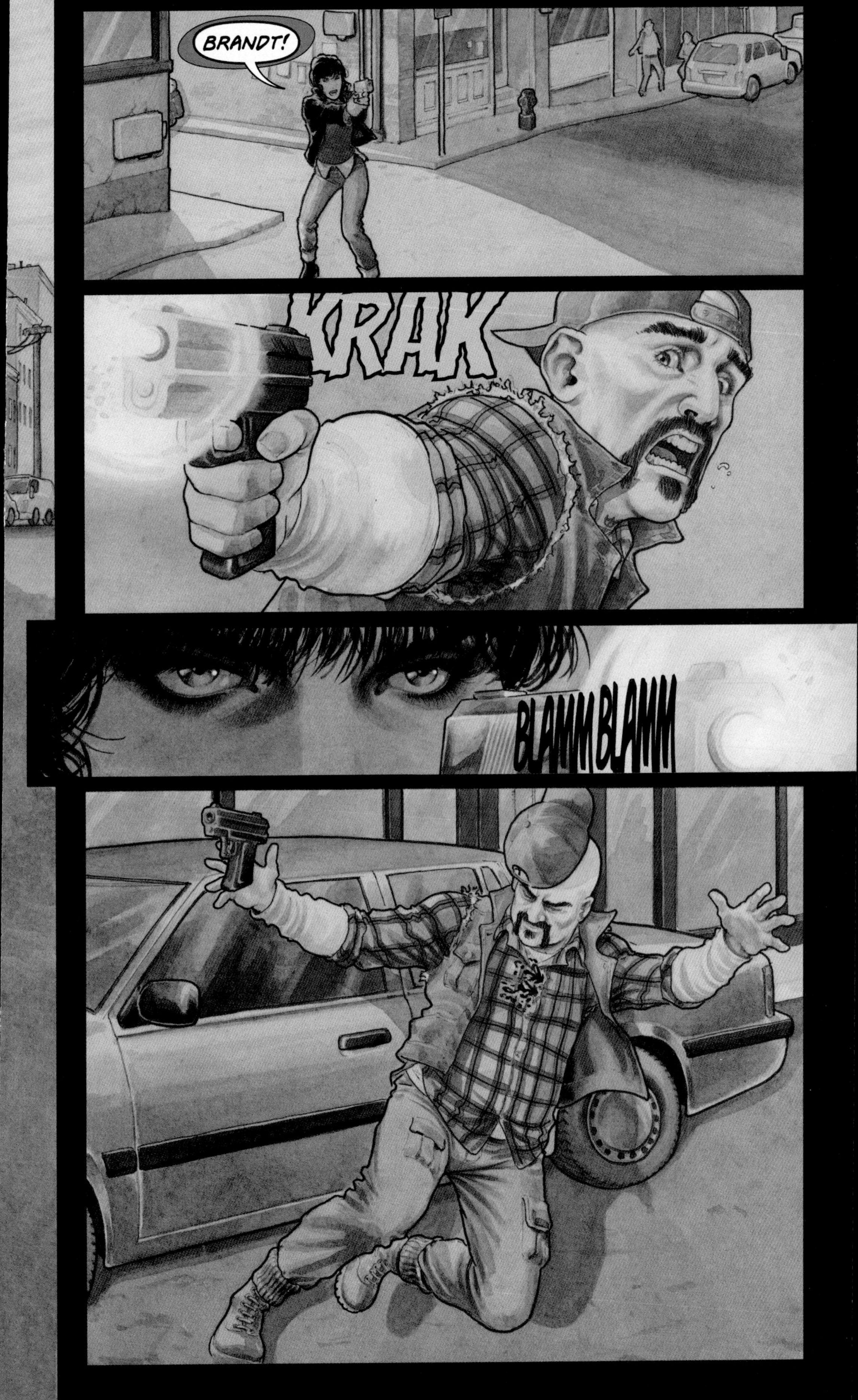

BRANDT!
KRAK
BLAMM BLAMM

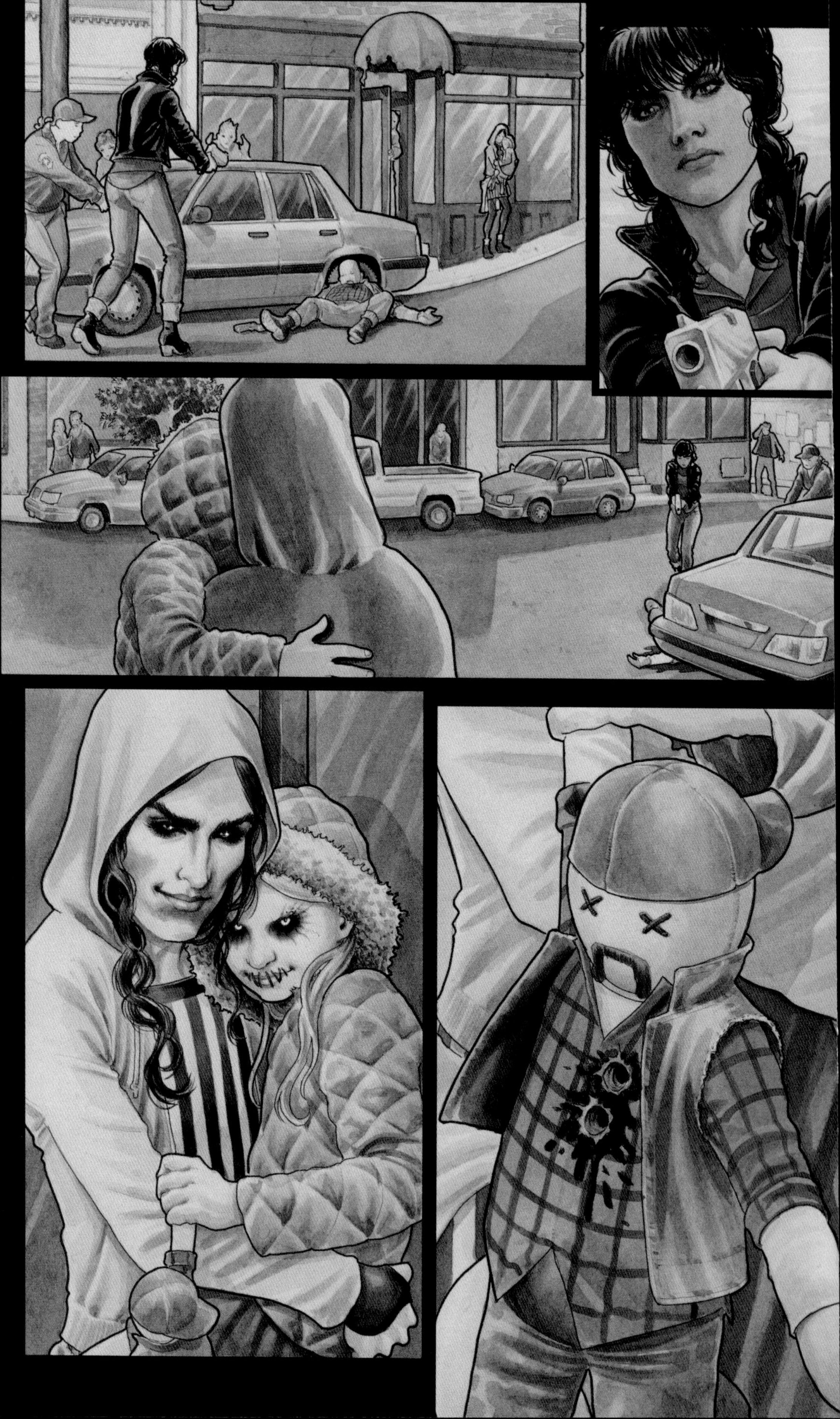

CITY OF PORTSMO

| ...ED | FIRST NAME | MIDDLE NAME | RACE | SEX | AGE | RESIDENCE OF PERSON KILLED | | OFFENSE SERIAL N... |

| | TITLE OR RELATIONSHIP | RACE | SEX | AGE | ADDRESS OF PERSON KILLED... | | PHONE OF PERSON |

...RIME) | AFTER INVESTIGATION CHANGED TO

| STREET AND NUMBER OF INTERSECTION | DIVISION | PLATOON | BEAT | OFFICERS MAKING REPORT | I.D. NO. | NAME |

| OCCURENCE | TIME OF DAY | DATE REPORTED | ...REPORTED | REPORT RECEIVED BY | | RECEIVED — TIME — TYPED |

DESCRIPTION OF DEAD PERSON

| ...HT | EYES | HAIR | BEARD | ...PLEXION | ...MARKS, ETC. | CLOTHING |

NAME OF CORONER... ...TIME OF ARRIVAL   A.M. P.M.   ...CUTOR ATTENDING—TIME OF ARRIVAL

...HYSICIAN | PERSON WITH WHOM ACCUSE... ...OR ASSOCIATED

...E CIRCUMSTANCES OF OCCURENCE OF OFFEN... ...TS INVESTIGATION) | USE ...IDES OF THIS SHEET.

| ...TODY | ADDRESS | ...WITNESS TAKEN INTO CUSTODY | ADDRESS |

...OSSIBLE MOTIVES

DESCRIPTION OF SUSPECTS OR PERSONS WANTED

| | ALIAS | ADDRESS | SEX | RACE | AGE | HEIGHT | WEIGHT | EYES | HAIR | COMPLEXION |

| OCCUPATION | | DRESS AND OTHER MARKS | ...E FOR SUSPICION |

| | ALIAS | ADDRESS | SEX | RACE | AGE | HEIGHT | WEIGHT | EYES | HAIR | COMPLEXION |

| OCCUPATION | | DRESS AND OTHER MARKS | CAUSE FOR SUSPICION |

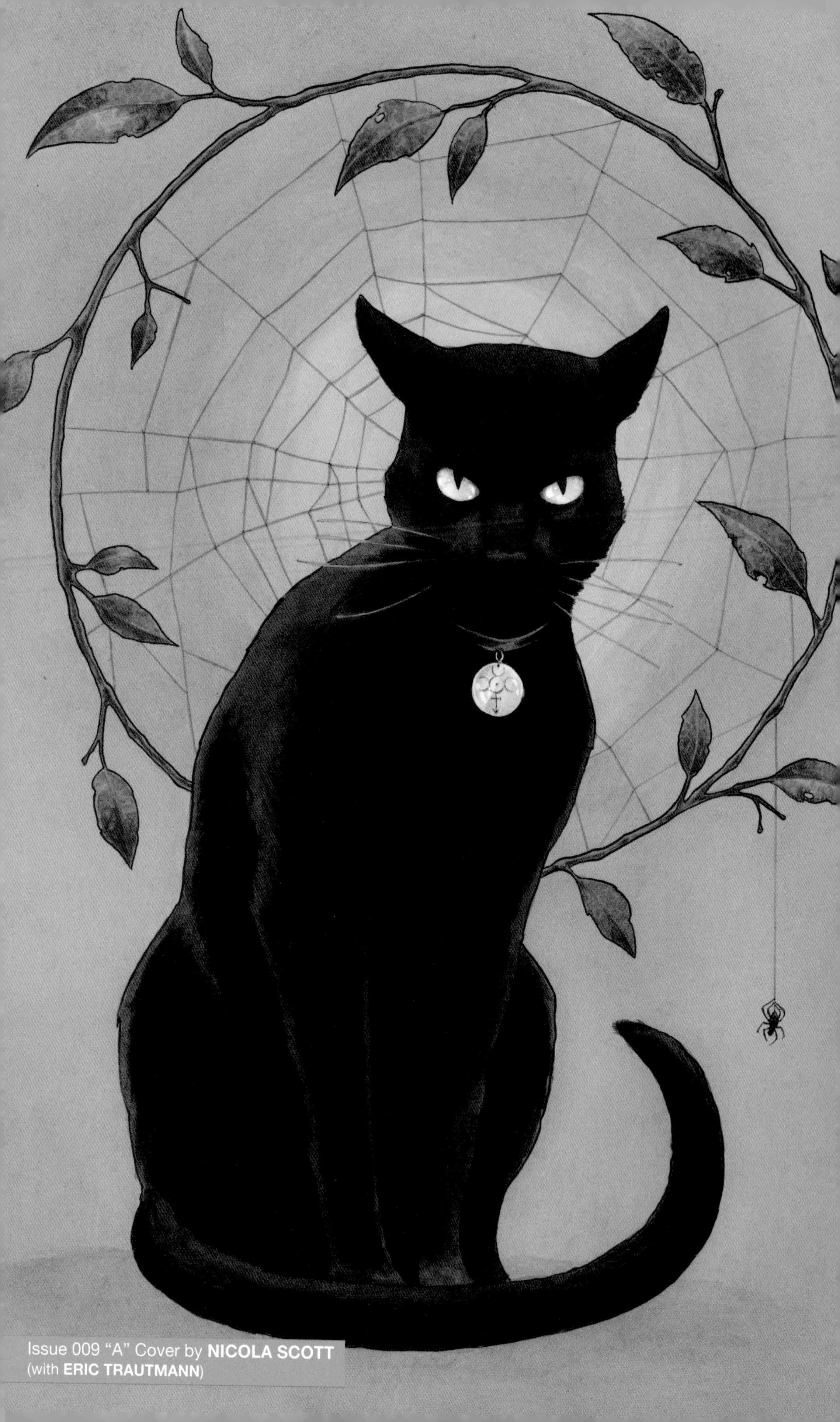

Issue 009 “A” Cover by **NICOLA SCOTT**
(with **ERIC TRAUTMANN**)

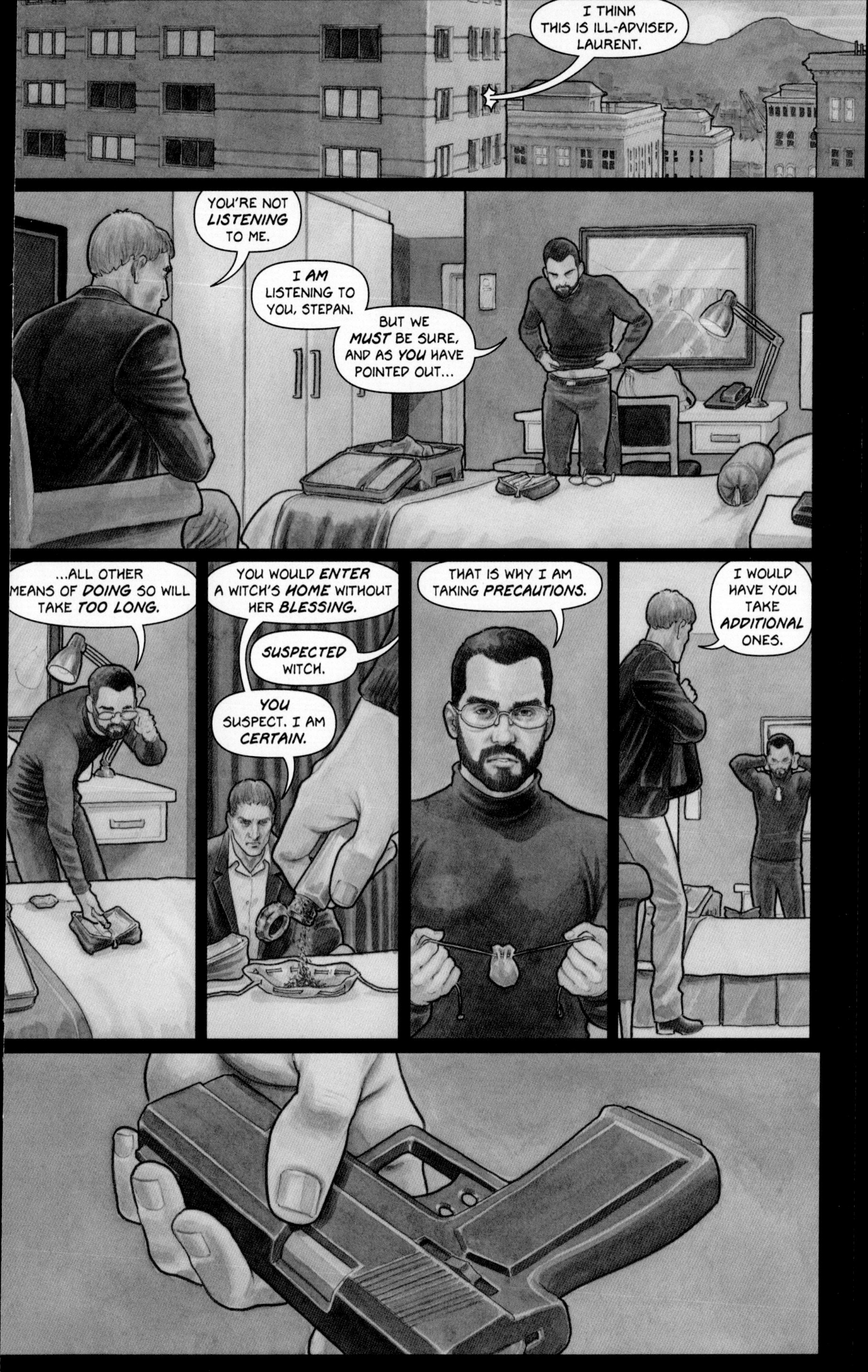
I THINK THIS IS ILL-ADVISED, LAURENT.
YOU'RE NOT LISTENING TO ME.
I AM LISTENING TO YOU, STEPAN.
BUT WE MUST BE SURE, AND AS YOU HAVE POINTED OUT...
...ALL OTHER MEANS OF DOING SO WILL TAKE TOO LONG.
YOU WOULD ENTER A WITCH'S HOME WITHOUT HER BLESSING.
SUSPECTED WITCH.
YOU SUSPECT. I AM CERTAIN.
THAT IS WHY I AM TAKING PRECAUTIONS.
I WOULD HAVE YOU TAKE ADDITIONAL ONES.

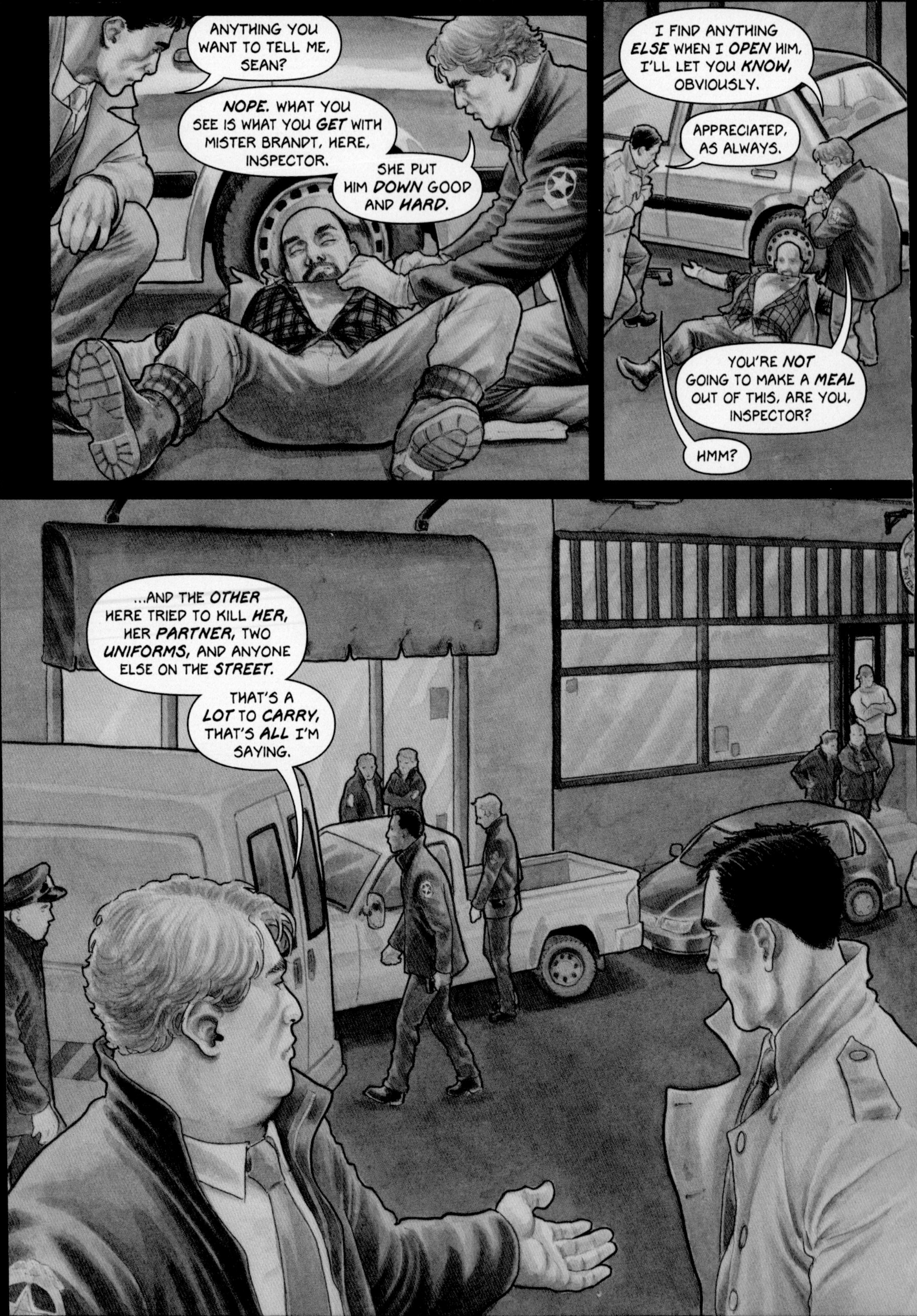
ANYTHING YOU WANT TO TELL ME, SEAN?
NOPE. WHAT YOU SEE IS WHAT YOU GET WITH MISTER BRANDT, HERE, INSPECTOR.
SHE PUT HIM DOWN GOOD AND HARD.
I FIND ANYTHING ELSE WHEN I OPEN HIM, I'LL LET YOU KNOW, OBVIOUSLY.
APPRECIATED, AS ALWAYS.
YOU'RE NOT GOING TO MAKE A MEAL OUT OF THIS, ARE YOU, INSPECTOR?
HMM?
...AND THE OTHER HERE TRIED TO KILL HER, HER PARTNER, TWO UNIFORMS, AND ANYONE ELSE ON THE STREET.
THAT'S A LOT TO CARRY, THAT'S ALL I'M SAYING.

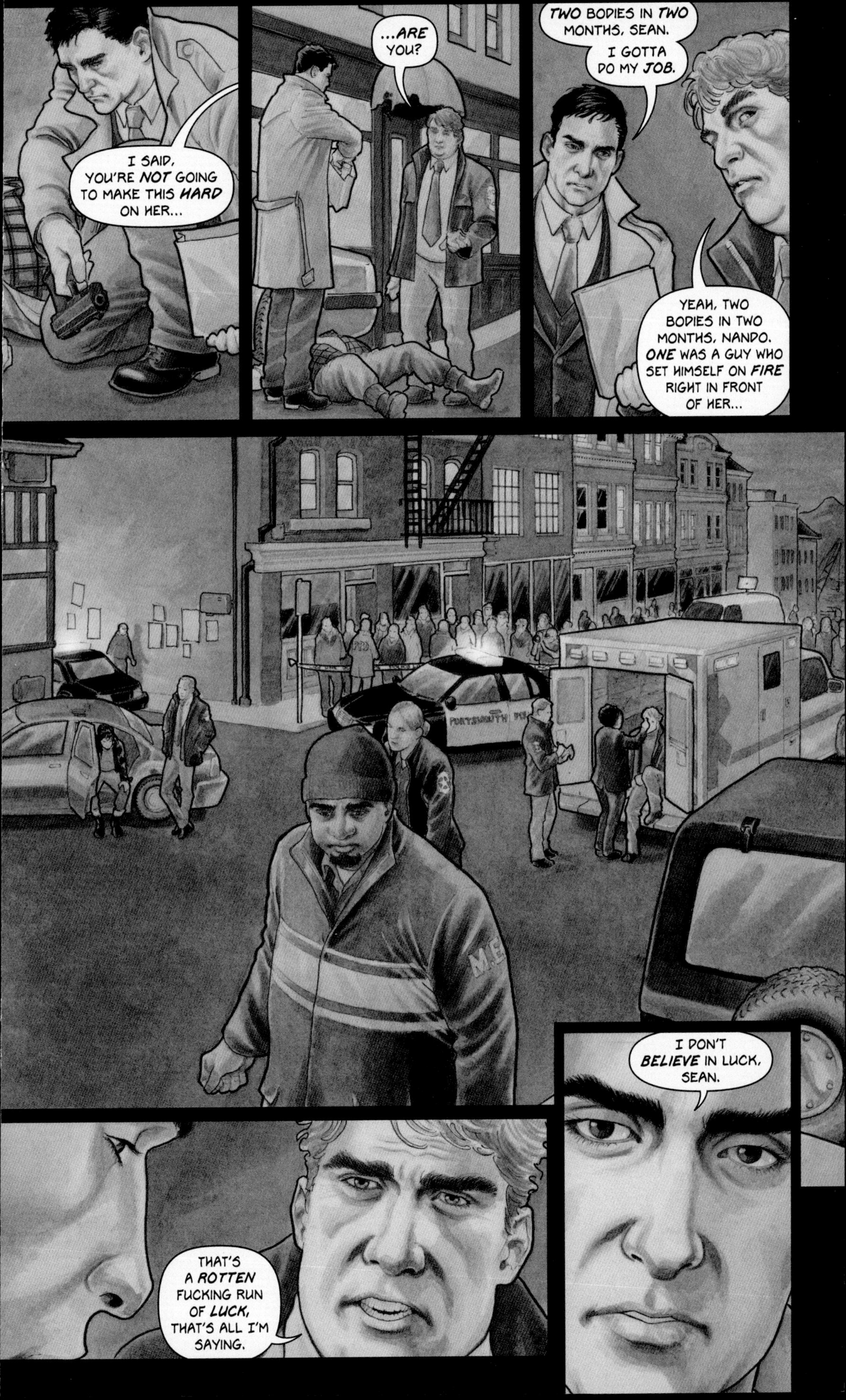
I SAID, YOU'RE NOT GOING TO MAKE THIS HARD ON HER...
...ARE YOU?
TWO BODIES IN TWO MONTHS, SEAN.
I GOTTA DO MY JOB.
YEAH, TWO BODIES IN TWO MONTHS, NANDO. ONE WAS A GUY WHO SET HIMSELF ON FIRE RIGHT IN FRONT OF HER...
PORTSMOUTH
THAT'S A ROTTEN FUCKING RUN OF LUCK, THAT'S ALL I'M SAYING.
I DON'T BELIEVE IN LUCK, SEAN.

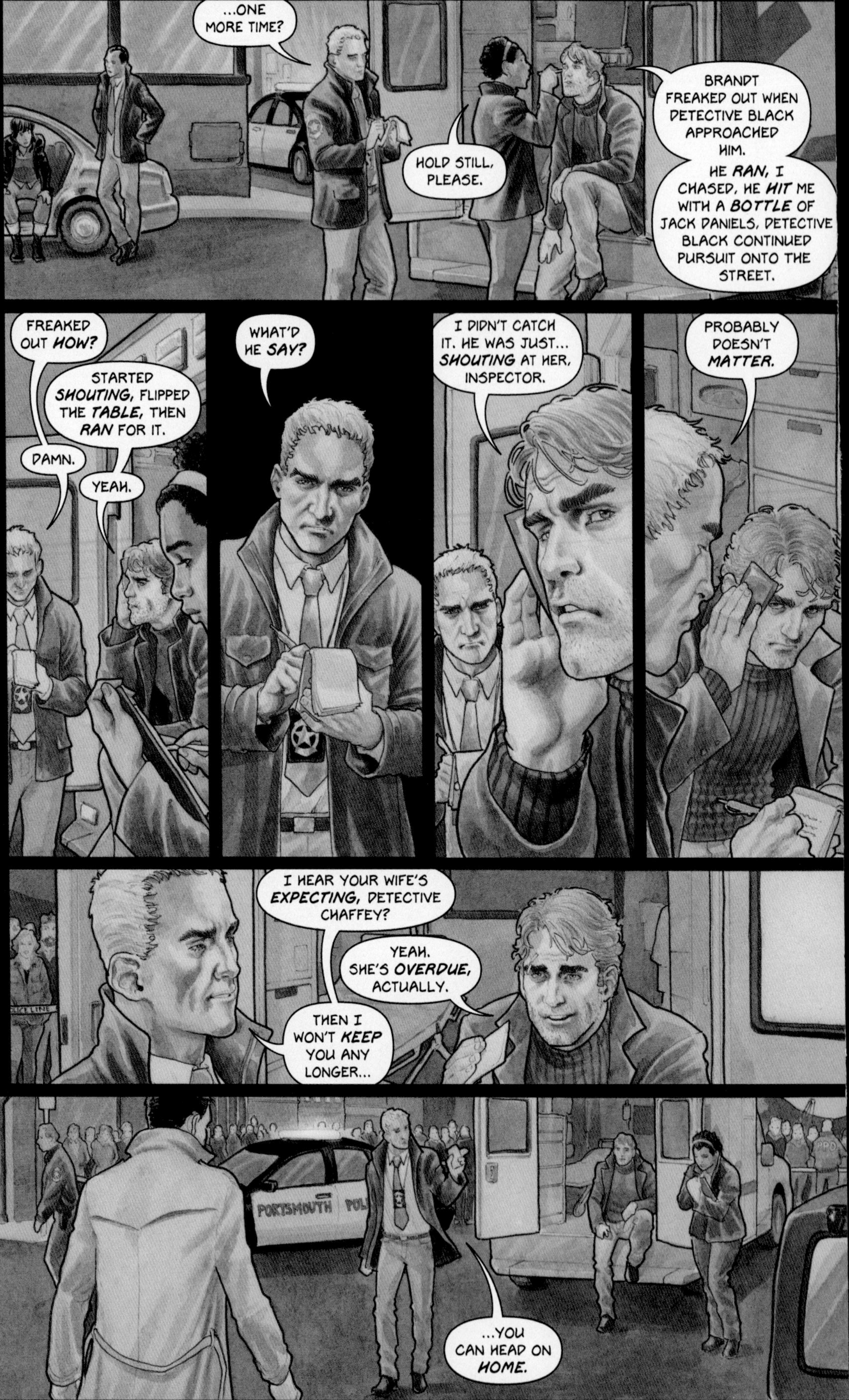
...ONE MORE TIME?
BRANDT FREAKED OUT WHEN DETECTIVE BLACK APPROACHED HIM.
HE RAN, I CHASED, HE HIT ME WITH A BOTTLE OF JACK DANIELS, DETECTIVE BLACK CONTINUED PURSUIT ONTO THE STREET.
HOLD STILL, PLEASE.
FREAKED OUT HOW?
STARTED SHOUTING, FLIPPED THE TABLE, THEN RAN FOR IT.
DAMN.
YEAH.
WHAT'D HE SAY?
I DIDN'T CATCH IT. HE WAS JUST... SHOUTING AT HER, INSPECTOR.
PROBABLY DOESN'T MATTER.
I HEAR YOUR WIFE'S EXPECTING, DETECTIVE CHAFFEY?
YEAH. SHE'S OVERDUE, ACTUALLY.
THEN I WON'T KEEP YOU ANY LONGER...
PORTSMOUTH POL
...YOU CAN HEAD ON HOME.

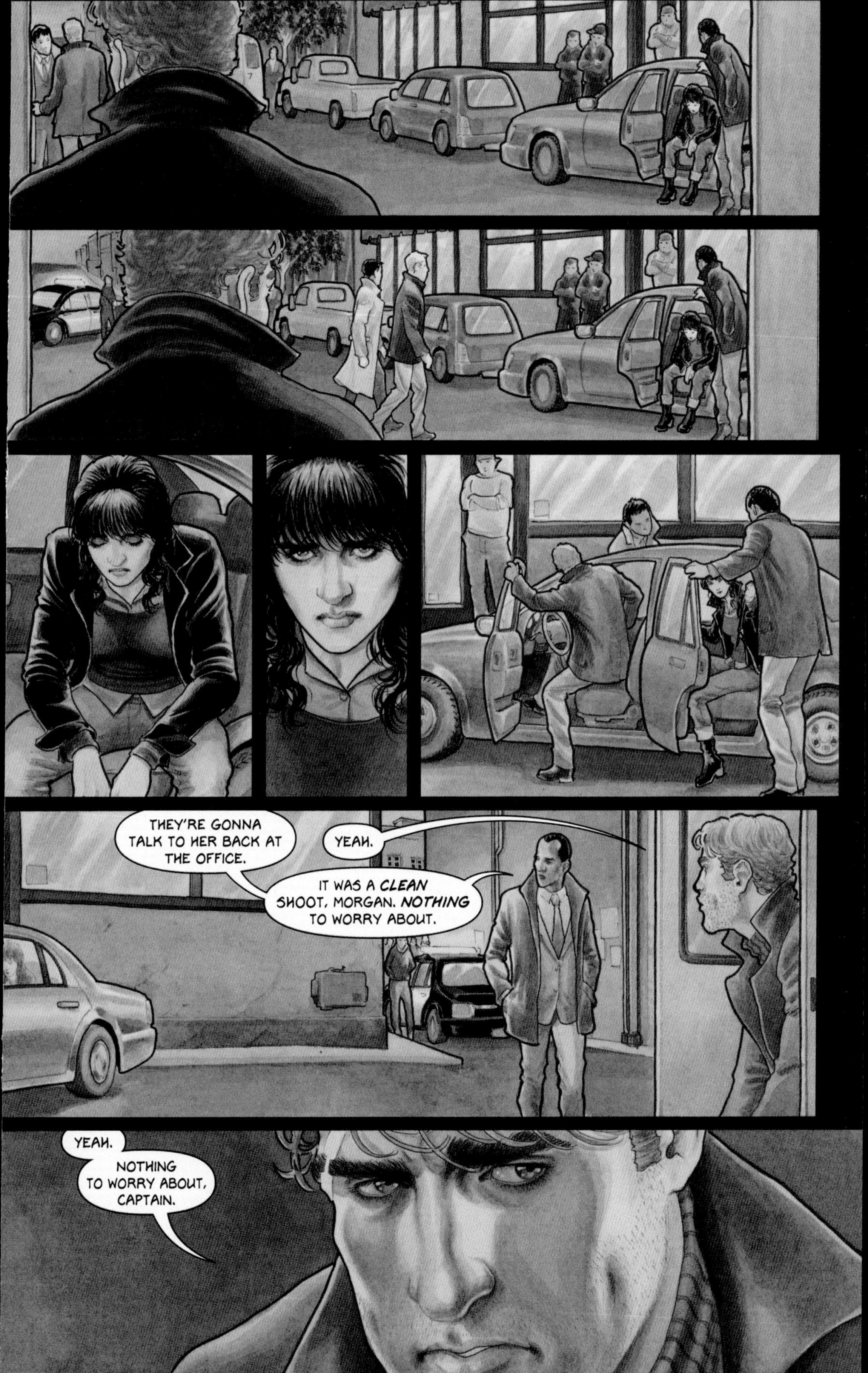
THEY'RE GONNA TALK TO HER BACK AT THE OFFICE.
YEAH.
IT WAS A *CLEAN* SHOOT, MORGAN. *NOTHING* TO WORRY ABOUT.
YEAH.
NOTHING TO WORRY ABOUT, CAPTAIN.

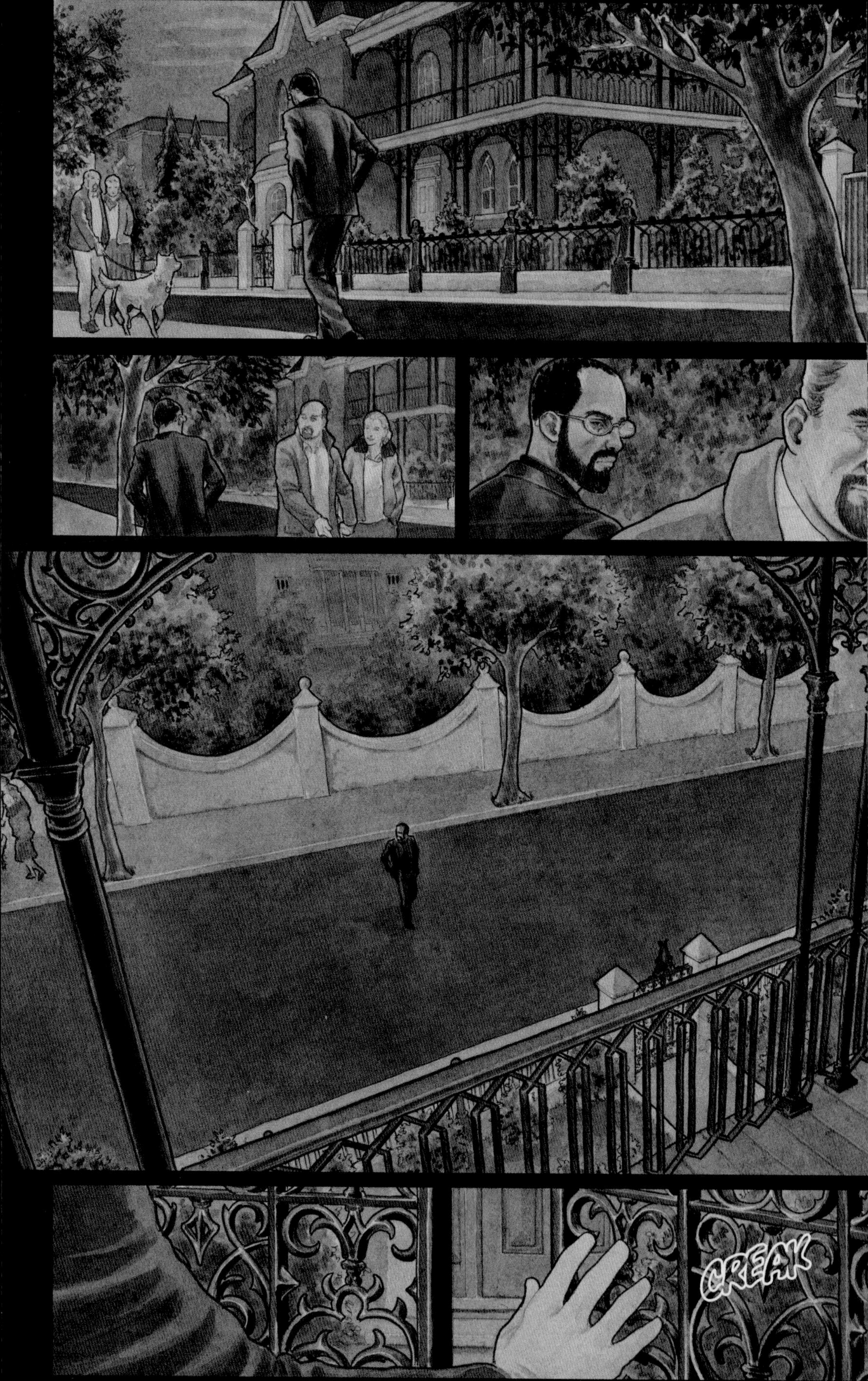
CREAK

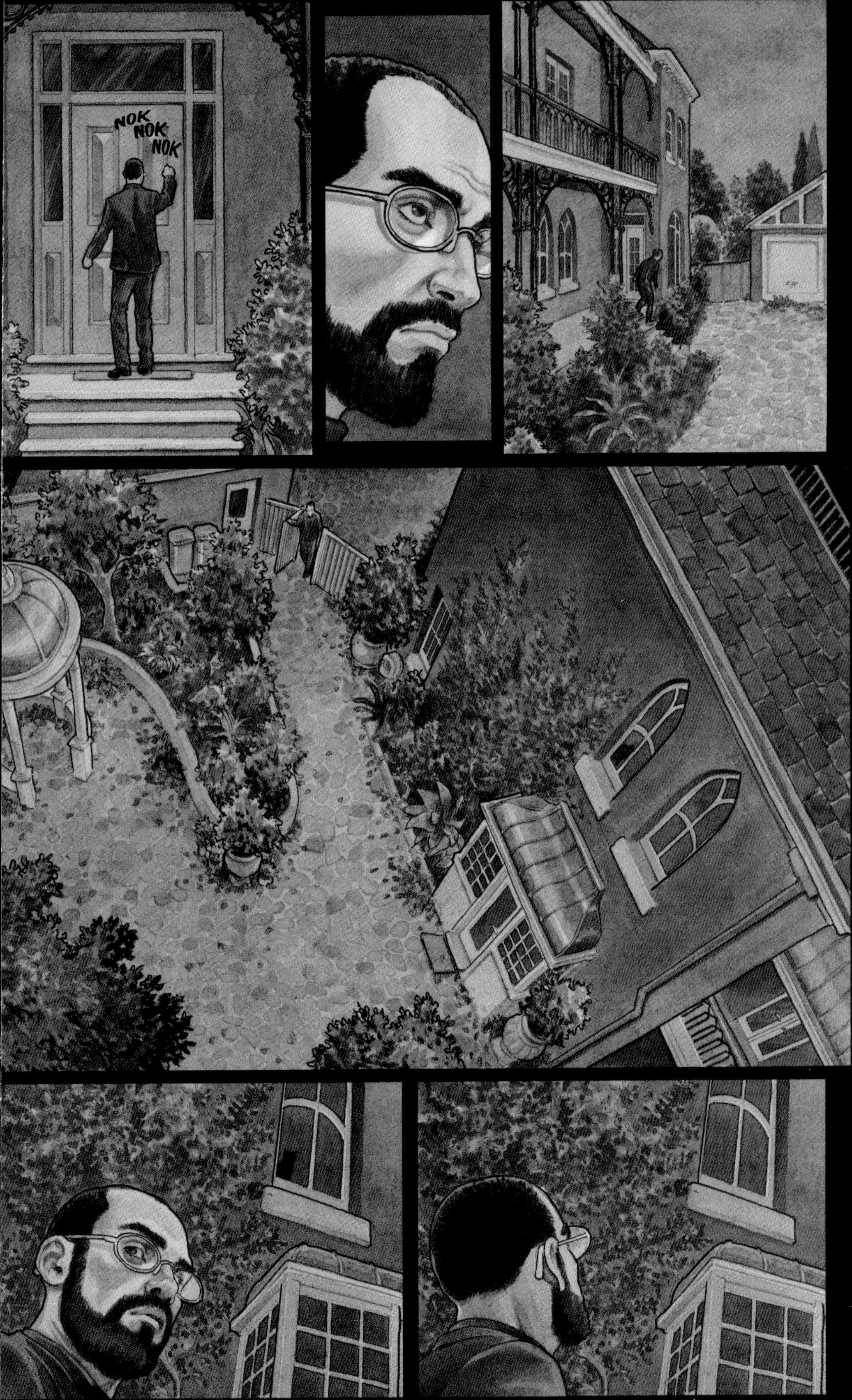
NOK
NOK
NOK

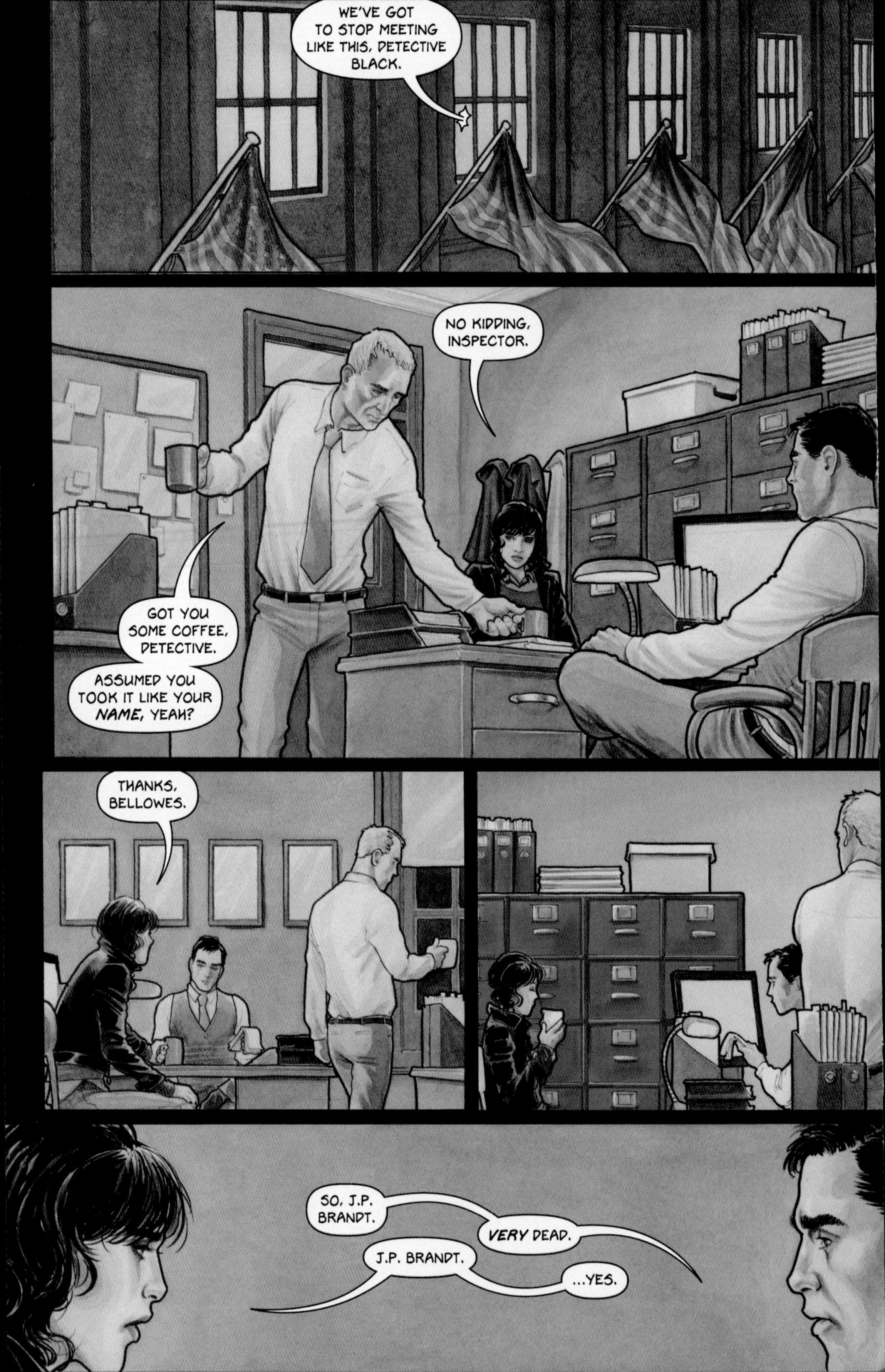
WE'VE GOT TO STOP MEETING LIKE THIS, DETECTIVE BLACK.
NO KIDDING, INSPECTOR.
GOT YOU SOME COFFEE, DETECTIVE.
ASSUMED YOU TOOK IT LIKE YOUR *NAME*, YEAH?
THANKS, BELLOWES.
SO, J.P. BRANDT.
VERY DEAD.
J.P. BRANDT.
...YES.

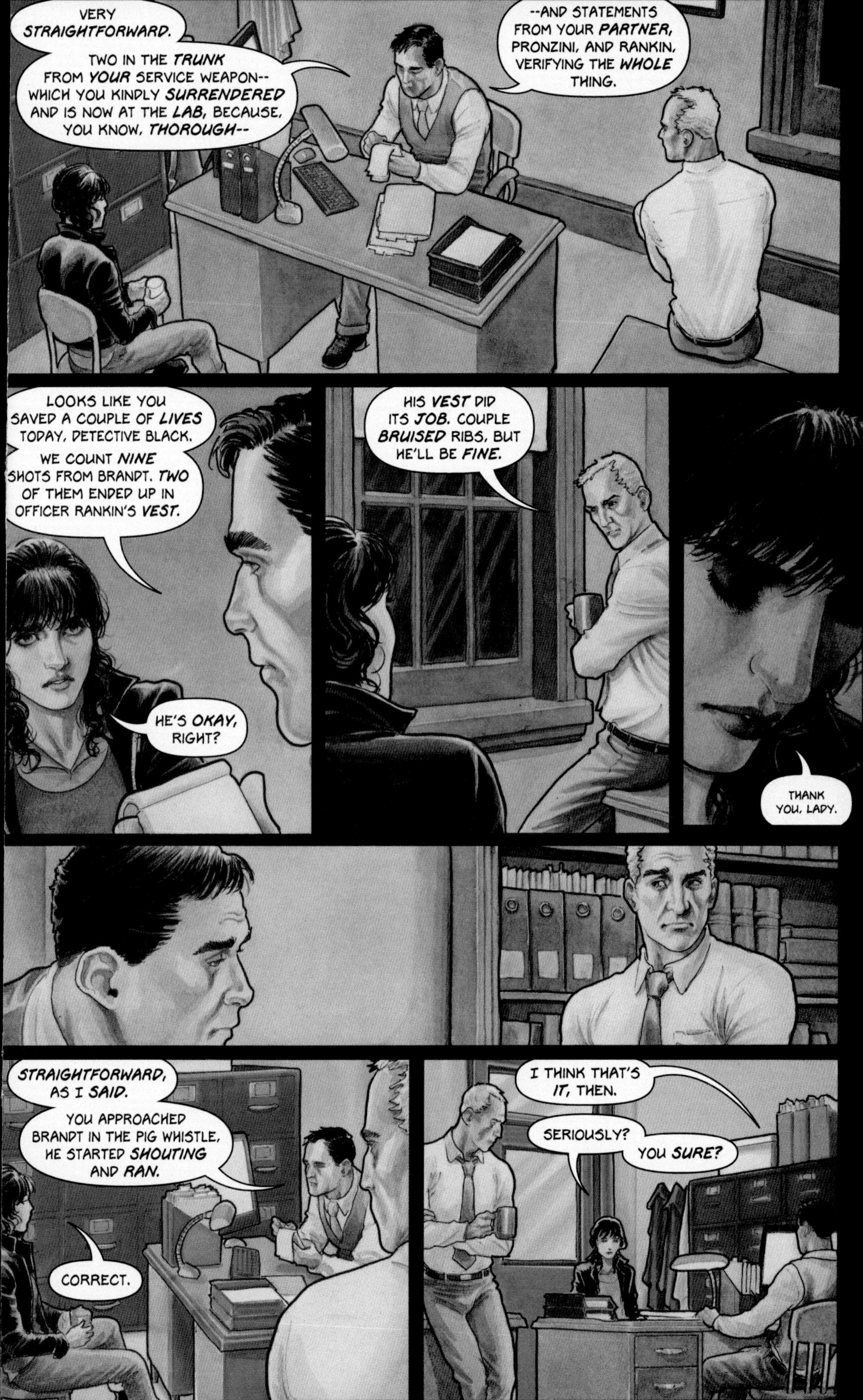
VERY STRAIGHTFORWARD.
TWO IN THE TRUNK FROM YOUR SERVICE WEAPON-- WHICH YOU KINDLY SURRENDERED AND IS NOW AT THE LAB, BECAUSE, YOU KNOW, THOROUGH--
--AND STATEMENTS FROM YOUR PARTNER, PRONZINI, AND RANKIN, VERIFYING THE WHOLE THING.
LOOKS LIKE YOU SAVED A COUPLE OF LIVES TODAY, DETECTIVE BLACK.
WE COUNT NINE SHOTS FROM BRANDT. TWO OF THEM ENDED UP IN OFFICER RANKIN'S VEST.
HE'S OKAY, RIGHT?
HIS VEST DID ITS JOB. COUPLE BRUISED RIBS, BUT HE'LL BE FINE.
THANK YOU, LADY.
STRAIGHTFORWARD, AS I SAID.
YOU APPROACHED BRANDT IN THE PIG WHISTLE, HE STARTED SHOUTING AND RAN.
CORRECT.
I THINK THAT'S IT, THEN.
SERIOUSLY?
YOU SURE?

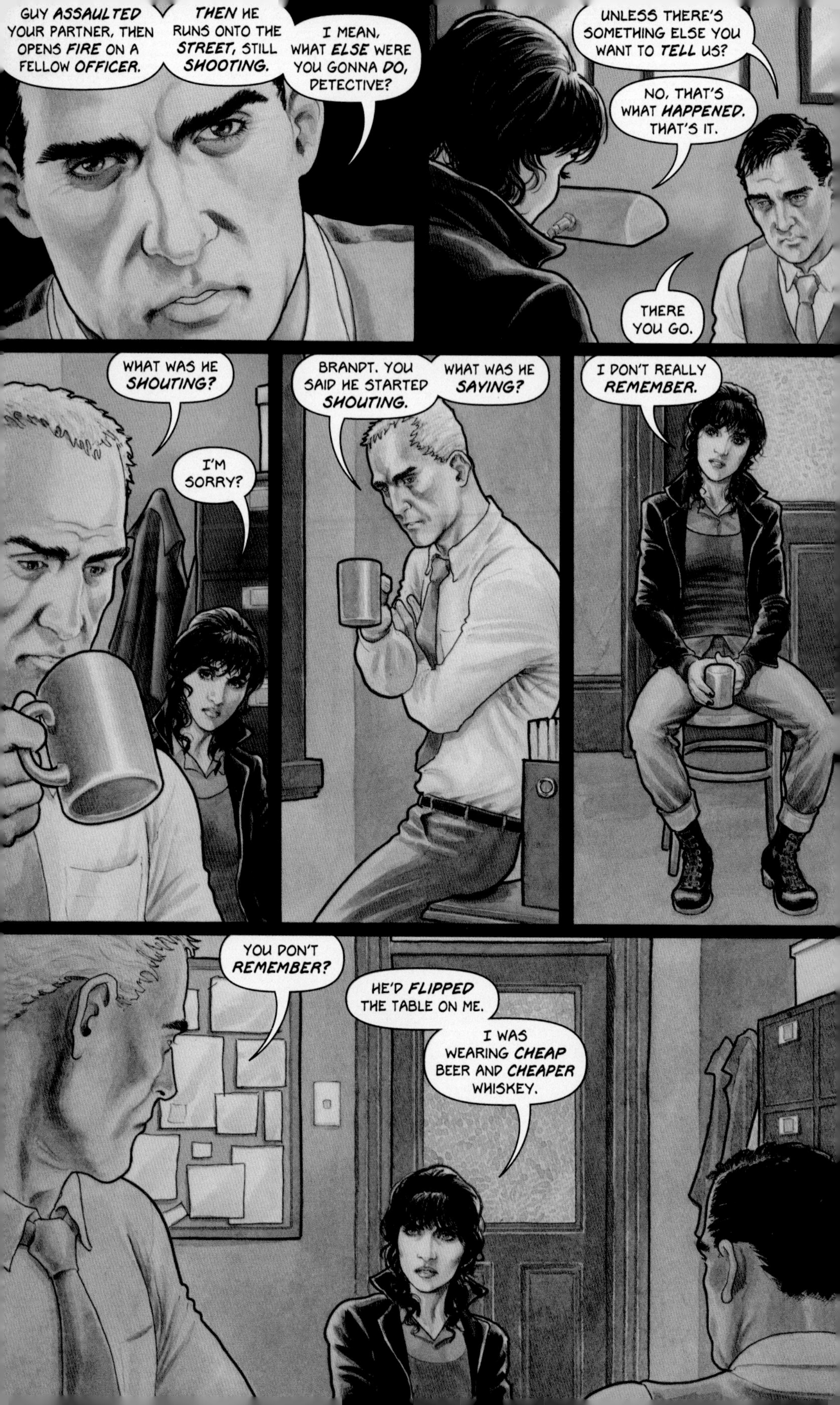
GUY ASSAULTED YOUR PARTNER, THEN OPENS FIRE ON A FELLOW OFFICER.
THEN HE RUNS ONTO THE STREET, STILL SHOOTING.
I MEAN, WHAT ELSE WERE YOU GONNA DO, DETECTIVE?
UNLESS THERE'S SOMETHING ELSE YOU WANT TO TELL US?
NO, THAT'S WHAT HAPPENED. THAT'S IT.
THERE YOU GO.
WHAT WAS HE SHOUTING?
I'M SORRY?
BRANDT. YOU SAID HE STARTED SHOUTING.
WHAT WAS HE SAYING?
I DON'T REALLY REMEMBER.
YOU DON'T REMEMBER?
HE'D FLIPPED THE TABLE ON ME.
I WAS WEARING CHEAP BEER AND CHEAPER WHISKEY.

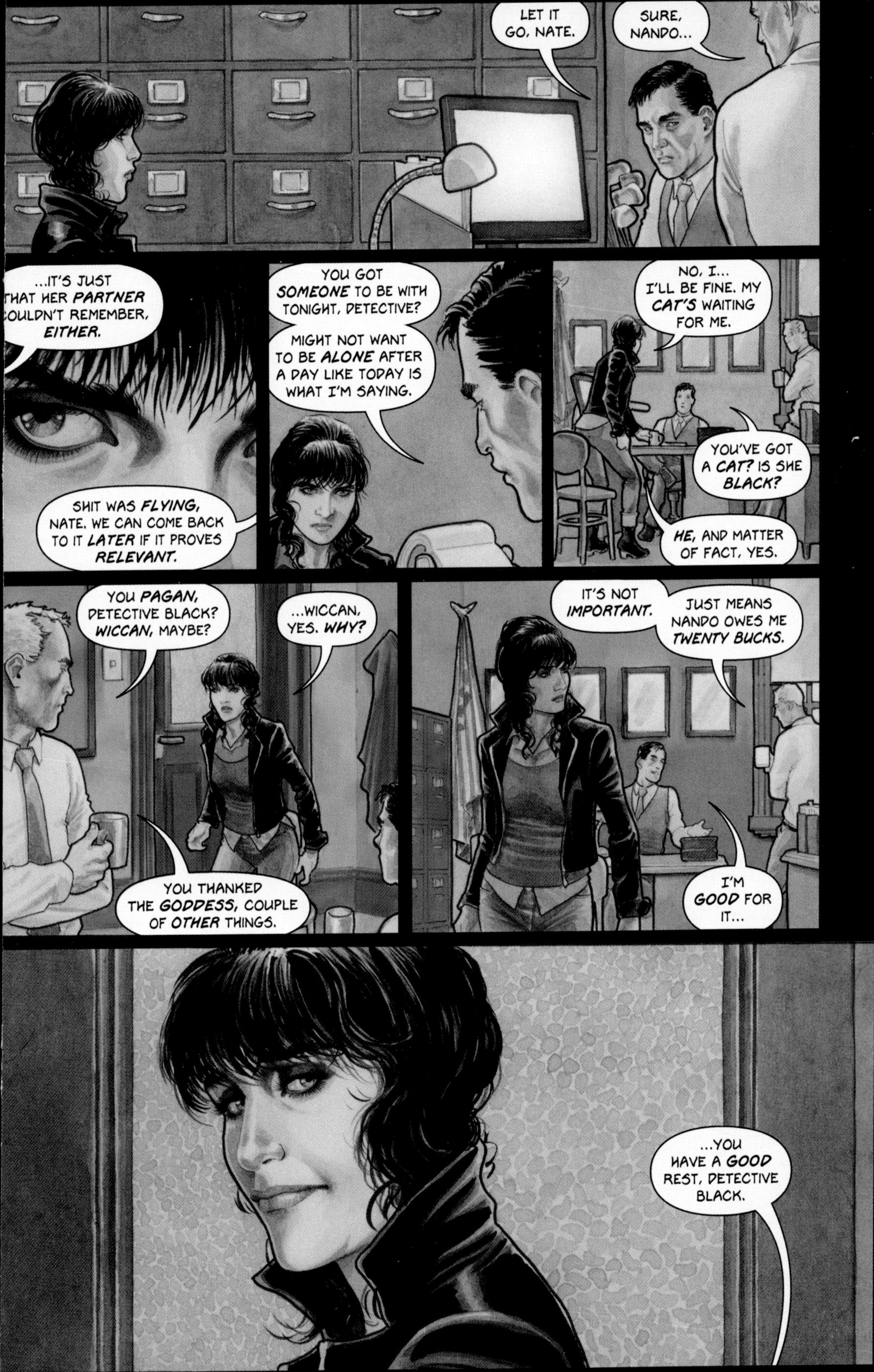
LET IT GO, NATE.
SURE, NANDO...
...IT'S JUST THAT HER PARTNER COULDN'T REMEMBER, EITHER.
SHIT WAS FLYING, NATE. WE CAN COME BACK TO IT LATER IF IT PROVES RELEVANT.
YOU GOT SOMEONE TO BE WITH TONIGHT, DETECTIVE?
MIGHT NOT WANT TO BE ALONE AFTER A DAY LIKE TODAY IS WHAT I'M SAYING.
NO, I... I'LL BE FINE. MY CAT'S WAITING FOR ME.
YOU'VE GOT A CAT? IS SHE BLACK?
HE, AND MATTER OF FACT, YES.
YOU PAGAN, DETECTIVE BLACK? WICCAN, MAYBE?
...WICCAN, YES. WHY?
YOU THANKED THE GODDESS, COUPLE OF OTHER THINGS.
IT'S NOT IMPORTANT.
JUST MEANS NANDO OWES ME TWENTY BUCKS.
I'M GOOD FOR IT...
...YOU HAVE A GOOD REST, DETECTIVE BLACK.

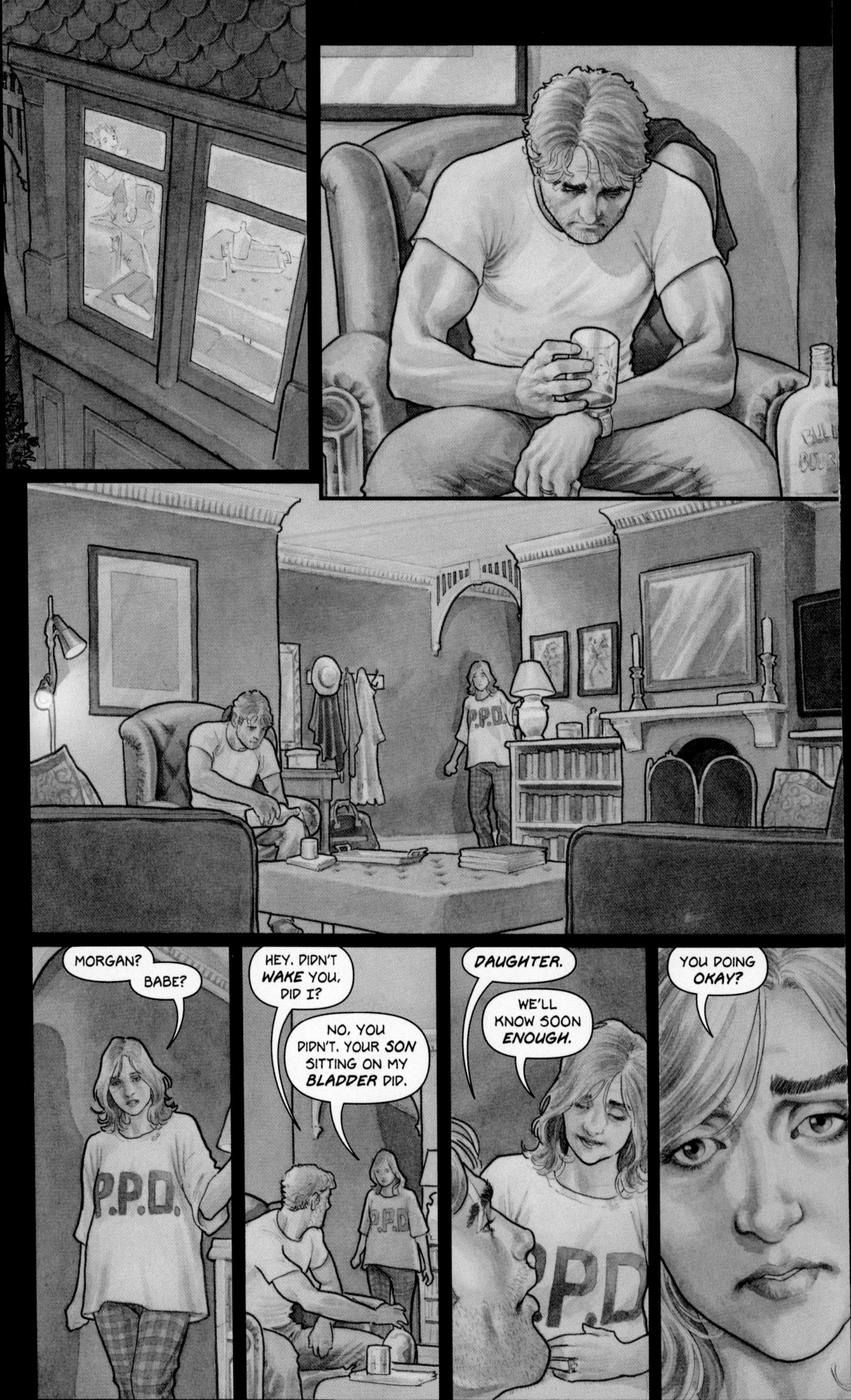

BULL
BURN
MORGAN?
BABE?
HEY. DIDN'T WAKE YOU, DID I?
NO, YOU DIDN'T. YOUR SON SITTING ON MY BLADDER DID.
DAUGHTER.
WE'LL KNOW SOON ENOUGH.
YOU DOING OKAY?

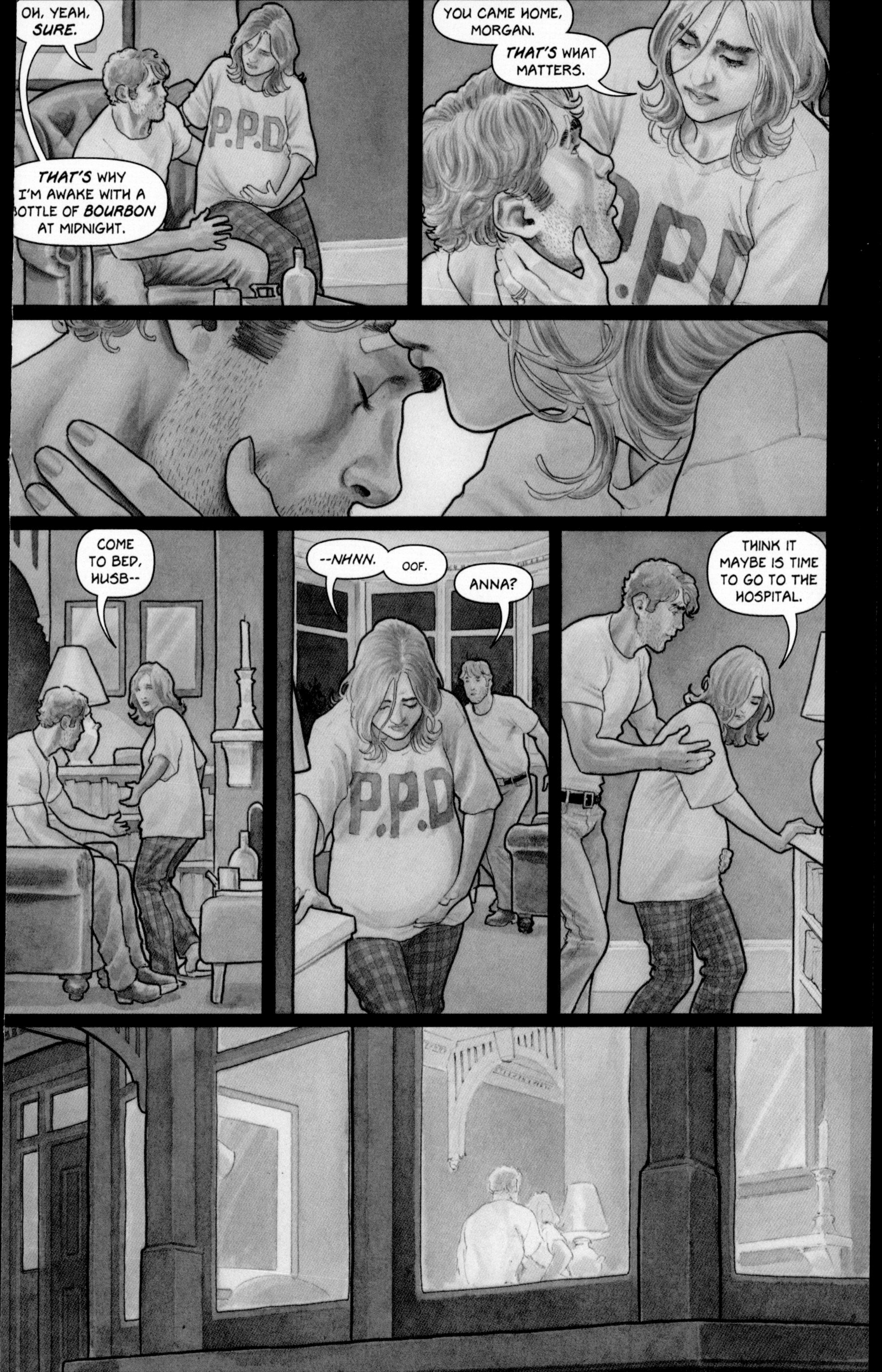
OH, YEAH, SURE.
THAT'S WHY I'M AWAKE WITH A BOTTLE OF BOURBON AT MIDNIGHT.
YOU CAME HOME, MORGAN.
THAT'S WHAT MATTERS.
COME TO BED, HUSB--
--NHNN.
OOF.
ANNA?
THINK IT MAYBE IS TIME TO GO TO THE HOSPITAL.

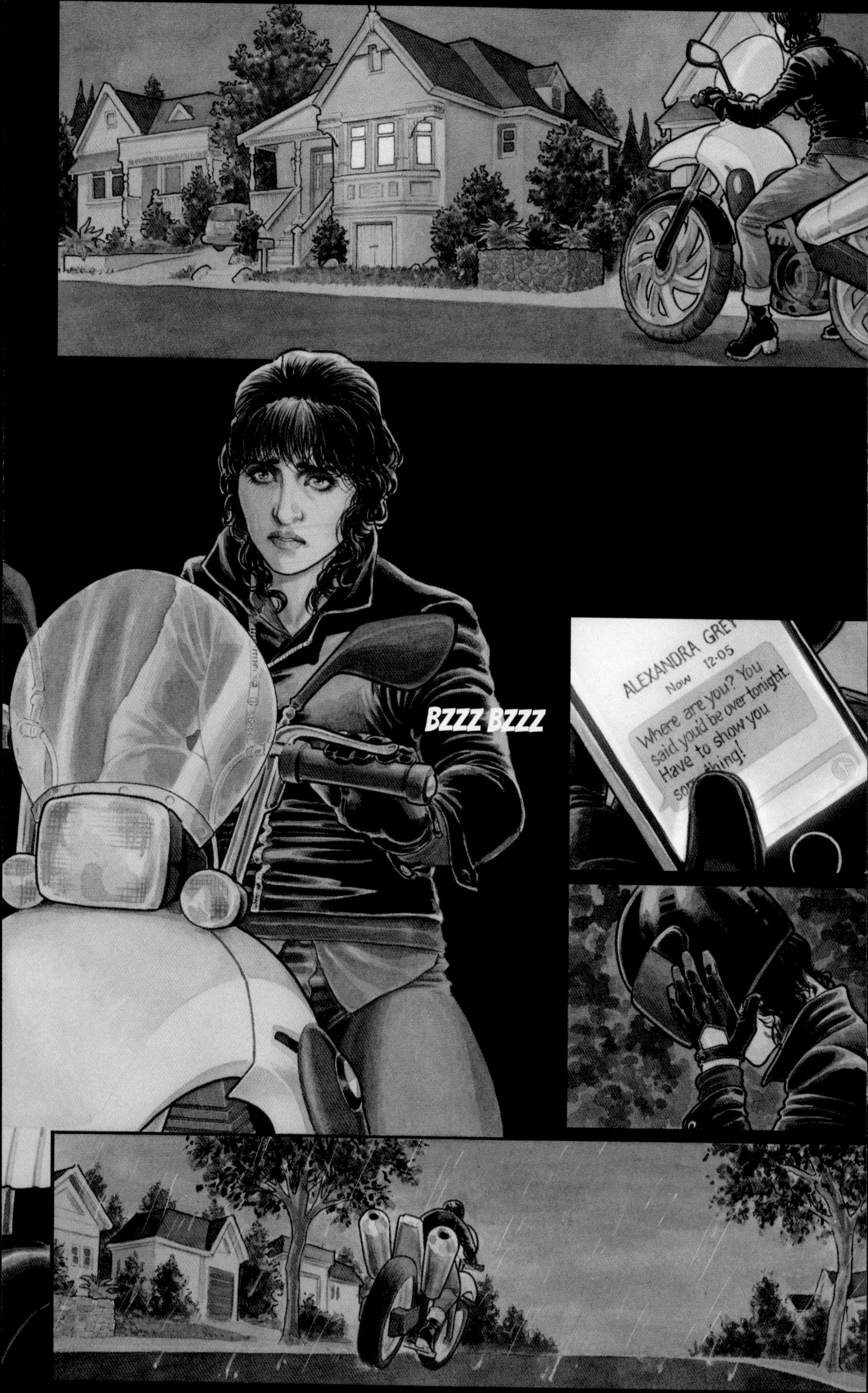
BZZZ BZZZ
ALEXANDRA GRE
Now 12-05
Where are you? You said you'd be over tonight. Have to show you

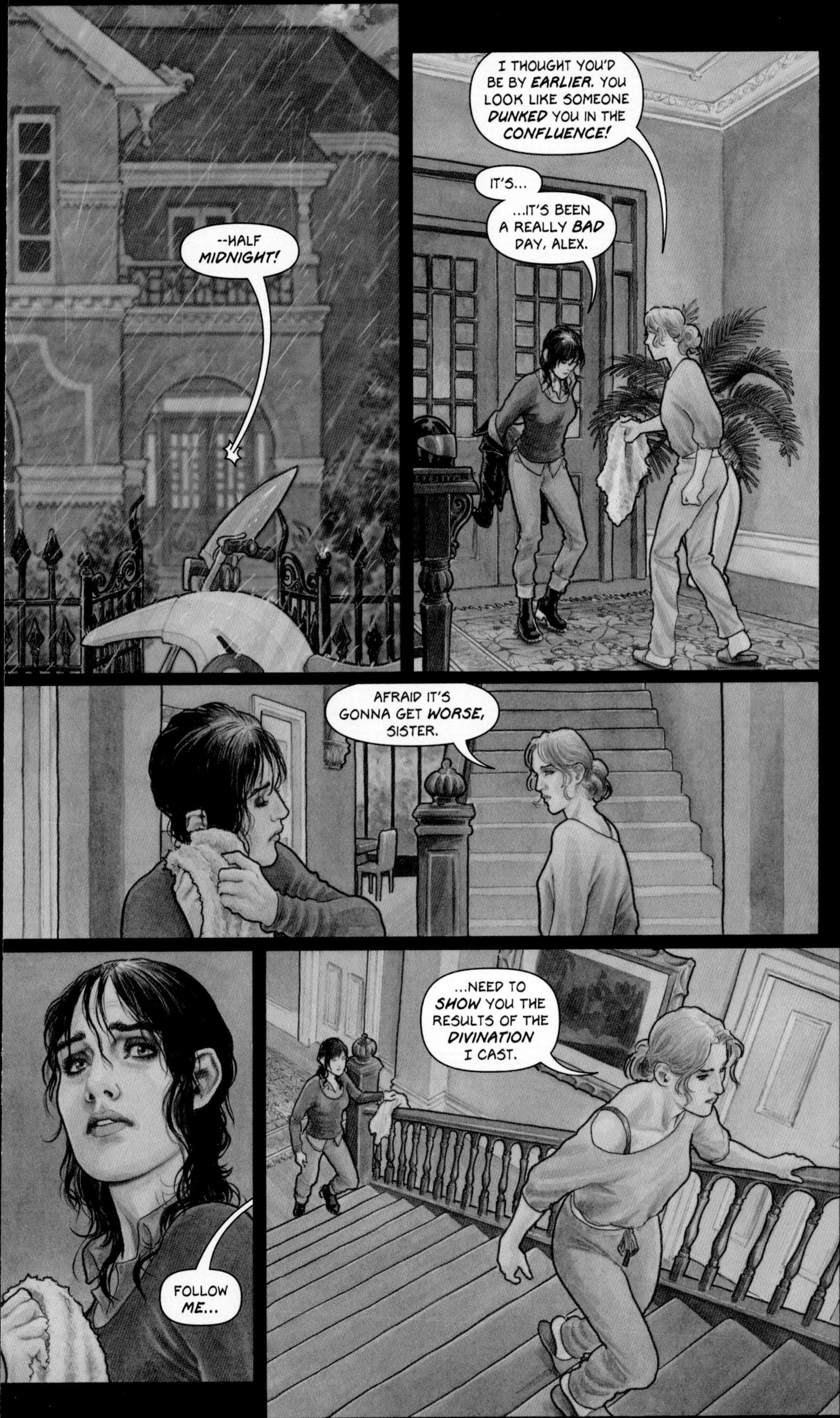
--HALF MIDNIGHT!
I THOUGHT YOU'D BE BY EARLIER. YOU LOOK LIKE SOMEONE DUNKED YOU IN THE CONFLUENCE!
IT'S...
...IT'S BEEN A REALLY BAD DAY, ALEX.
AFRAID IT'S GONNA GET WORSE, SISTER.
...NEED TO SHOW YOU THE RESULTS OF THE DIVINATION I CAST.
FOLLOW ME...

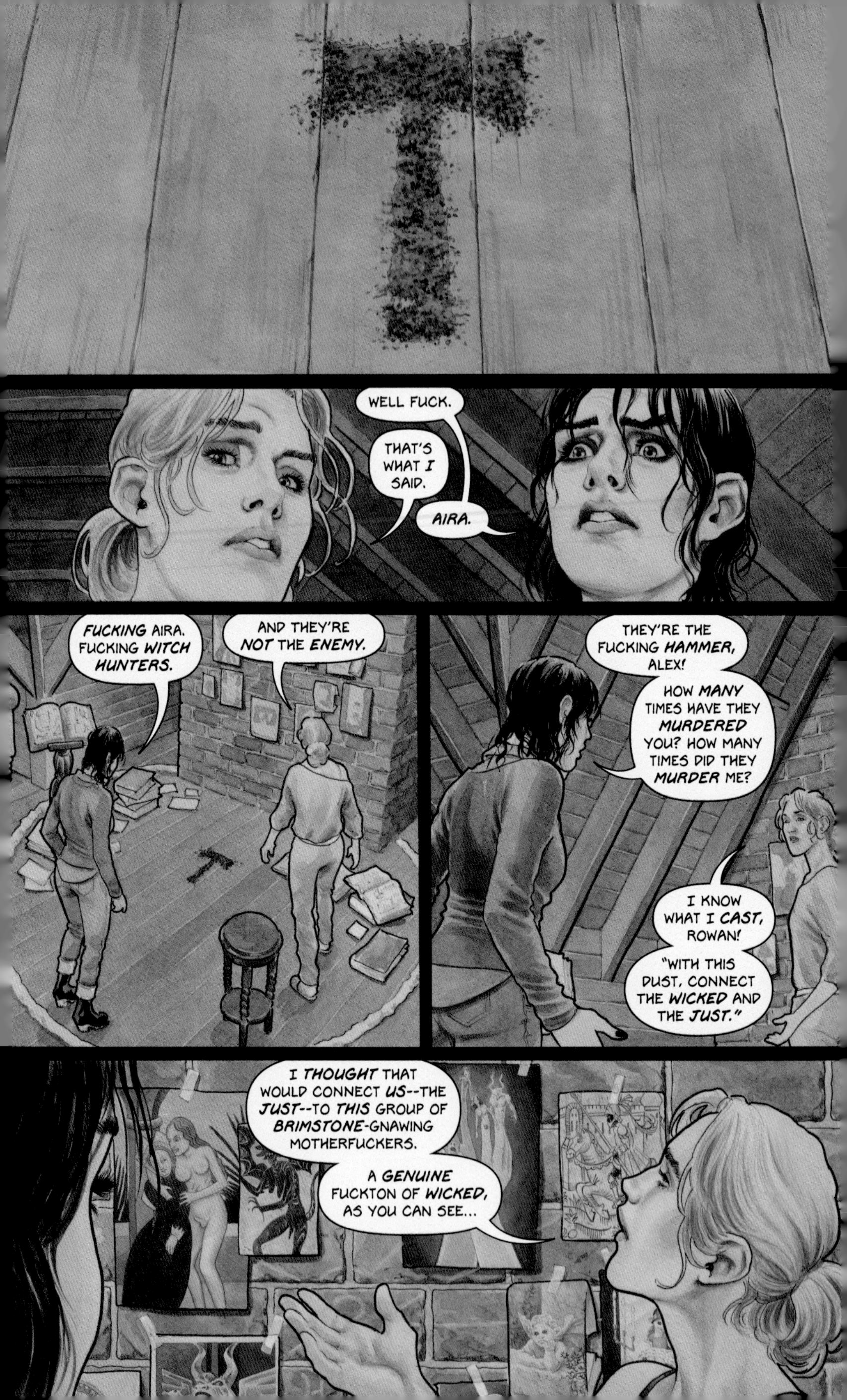
WELL FUCK.
THAT'S WHAT I SAID.
AIRA.
FUCKING AIRA. FUCKING WITCH HUNTERS.
AND THEY'RE NOT THE ENEMY.
THEY'RE THE FUCKING HAMMER, ALEX!
HOW MANY TIMES HAVE THEY MURDERED YOU? HOW MANY TIMES DID THEY MURDER ME?
I KNOW WHAT I CAST, ROWAN!
"WITH THIS DUST, CONNECT THE WICKED AND THE JUST."
I THOUGHT THAT WOULD CONNECT US--THE JUST--TO THIS GROUP OF BRIMSTONE-GNAWING MOTHERFUCKERS.
A GENUINE FUCKTON OF WICKED, AS YOU CAN SEE...

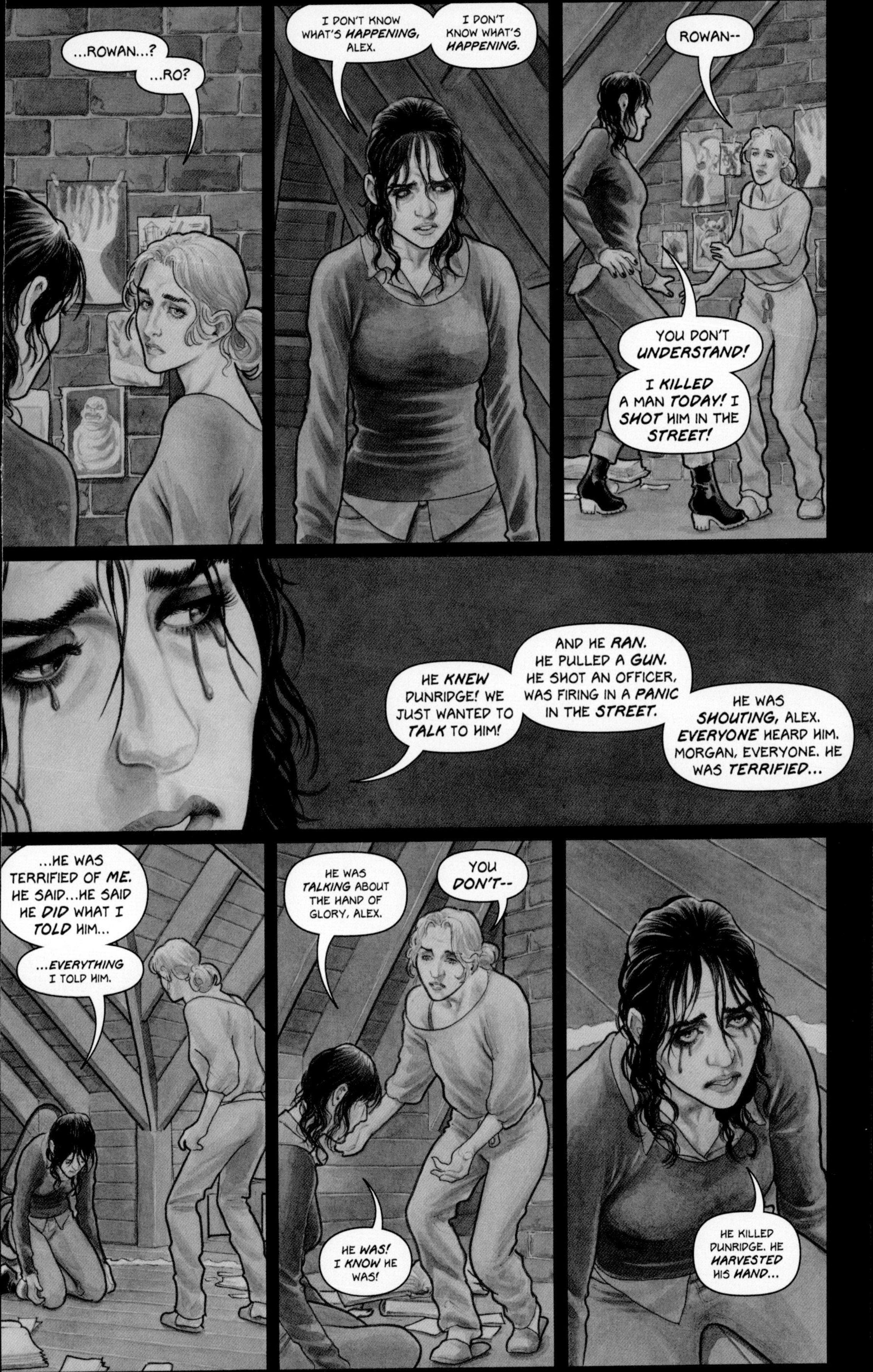
...ROWAN...?
...RO?
I DON'T KNOW WHAT'S HAPPENING, ALEX.
I DON'T KNOW WHAT'S HAPPENING.
ROWAN--
YOU DON'T UNDERSTAND!
I KILLED A MAN TODAY! I SHOT HIM IN THE STREET!
HE KNEW DUNRIDGE! WE JUST WANTED TO TALK TO HIM!
AND HE RAN. HE PULLED A GUN. HE SHOT AN OFFICER, WAS FIRING IN A PANIC IN THE STREET.
HE WAS SHOUTING, ALEX. EVERYONE HEARD HIM. MORGAN, EVERYONE. HE WAS TERRIFIED...
...HE WAS TERRIFIED OF ME. HE SAID...HE SAID HE DID WHAT I TOLD HIM...
...EVERYTHING I TOLD HIM.
HE WAS TALKING ABOUT THE HAND OF GLORY, ALEX.
YOU DON'T--
HE WAS! I KNOW HE WAS!
HE KILLED DUNRIDGE. HE HARVESTED HIS HAND...

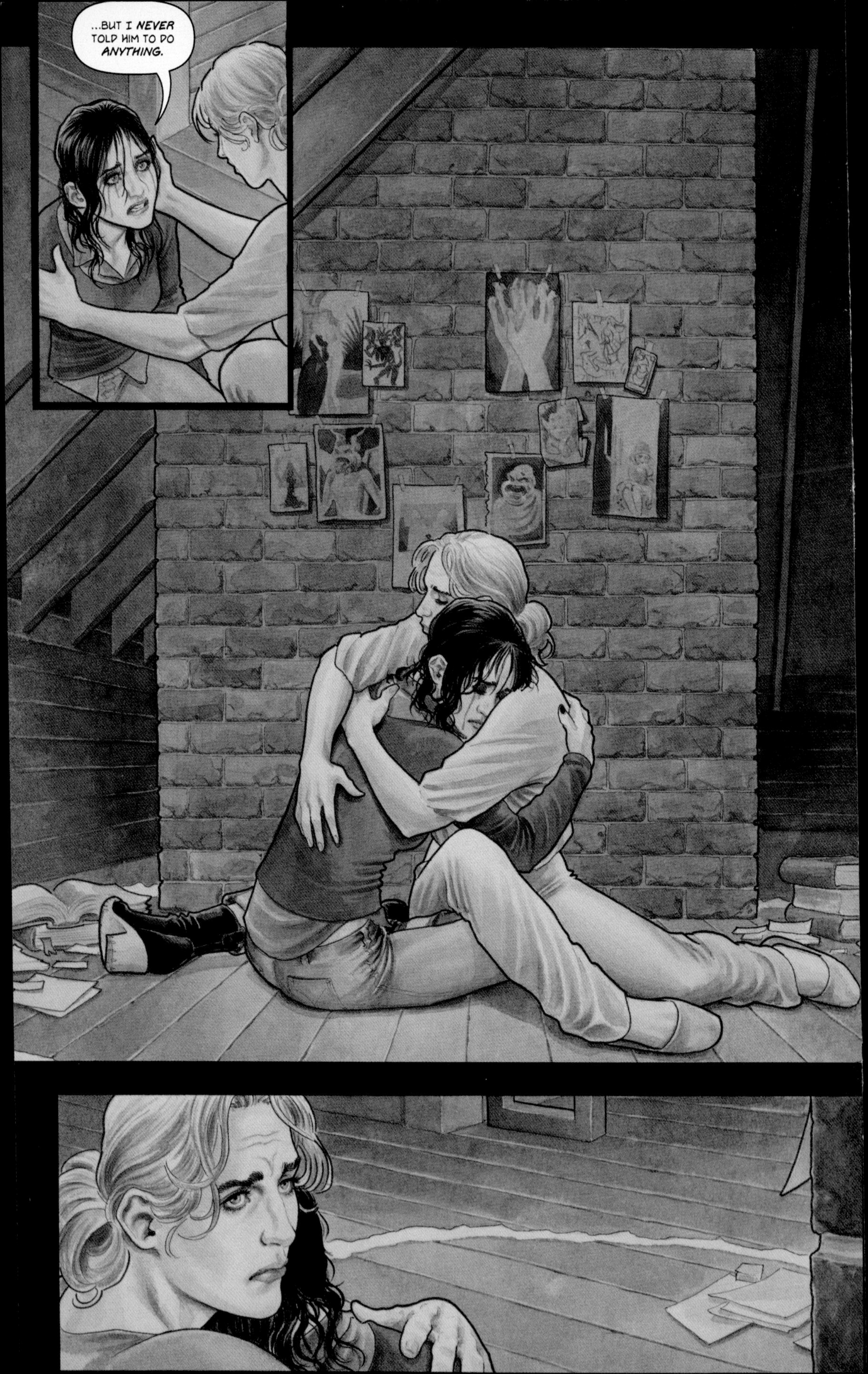
...BUT I *NEVER* TOLD HIM TO DO *ANYTHING.*

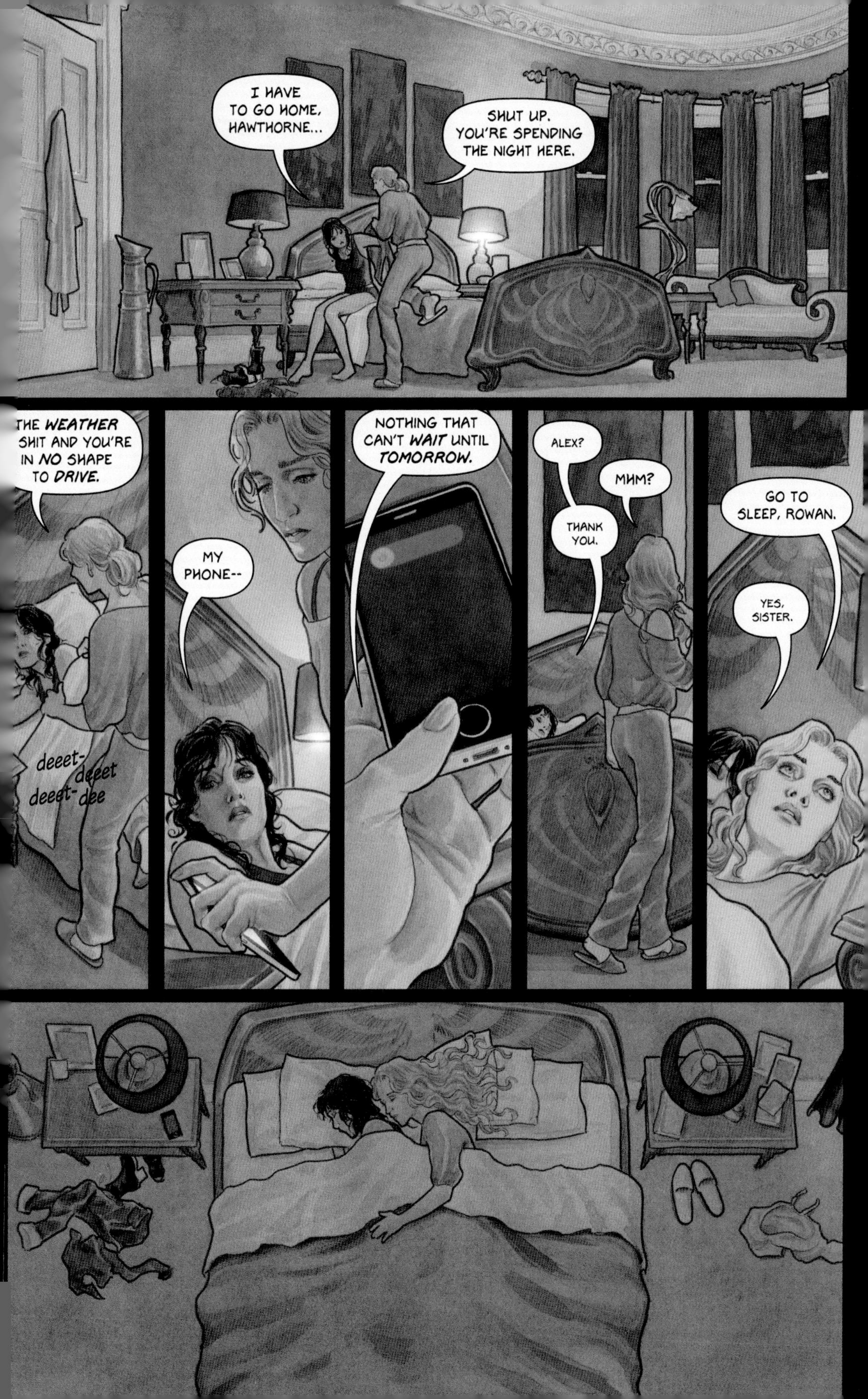
I HAVE TO GO HOME, HAWTHORNE...
SHUT UP. YOU'RE SPENDING THE NIGHT HERE.
THE WEATHER SHIT AND YOU'RE IN NO SHAPE TO DRIVE.
deeet-deeet deeet-dee
MY PHONE--
NOTHING THAT CAN'T WAIT UNTIL TOMORROW.
ALEX?
MHM?
THANK YOU.
GO TO SLEEP, ROWAN.
YES, SISTER.

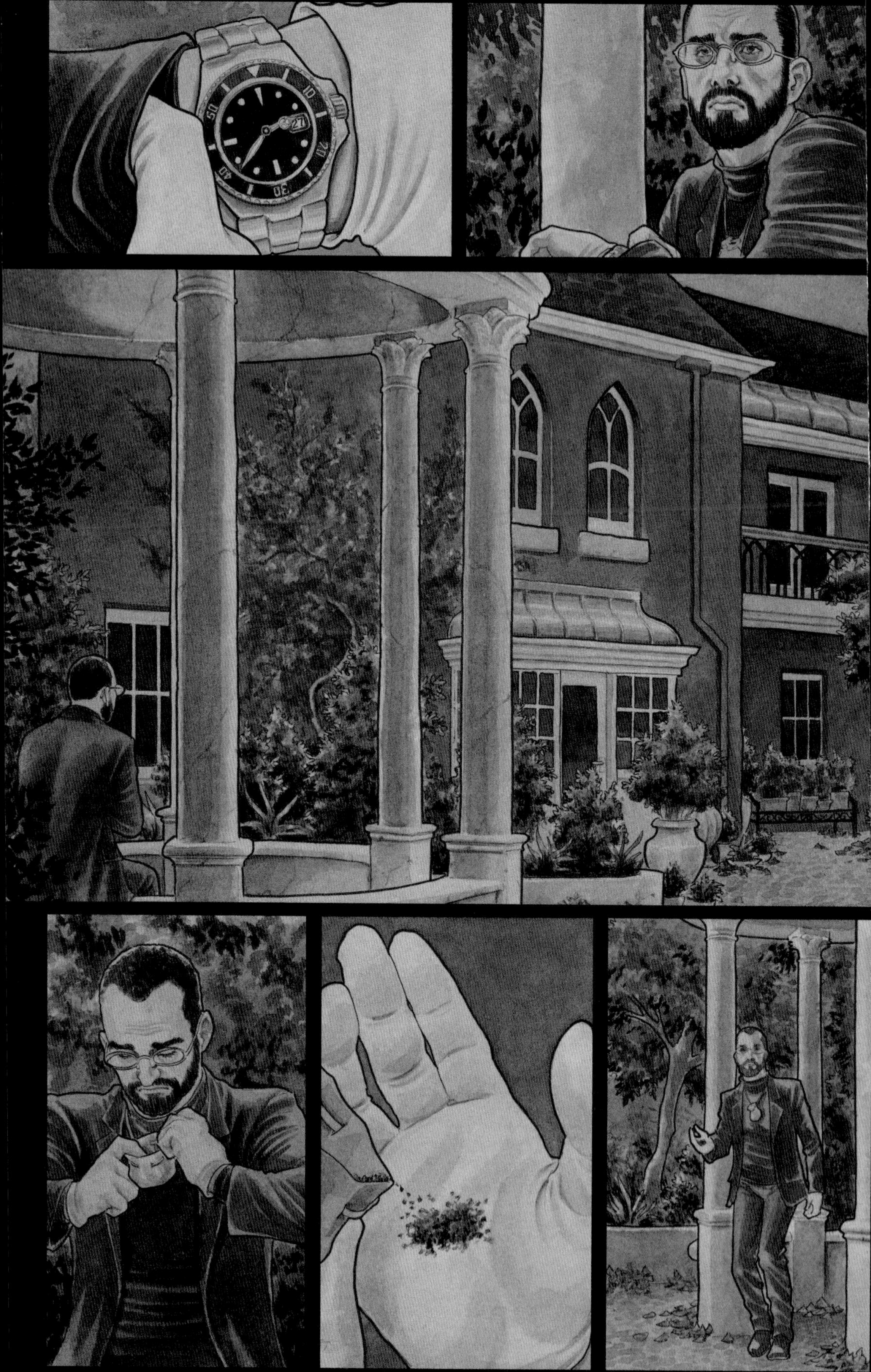

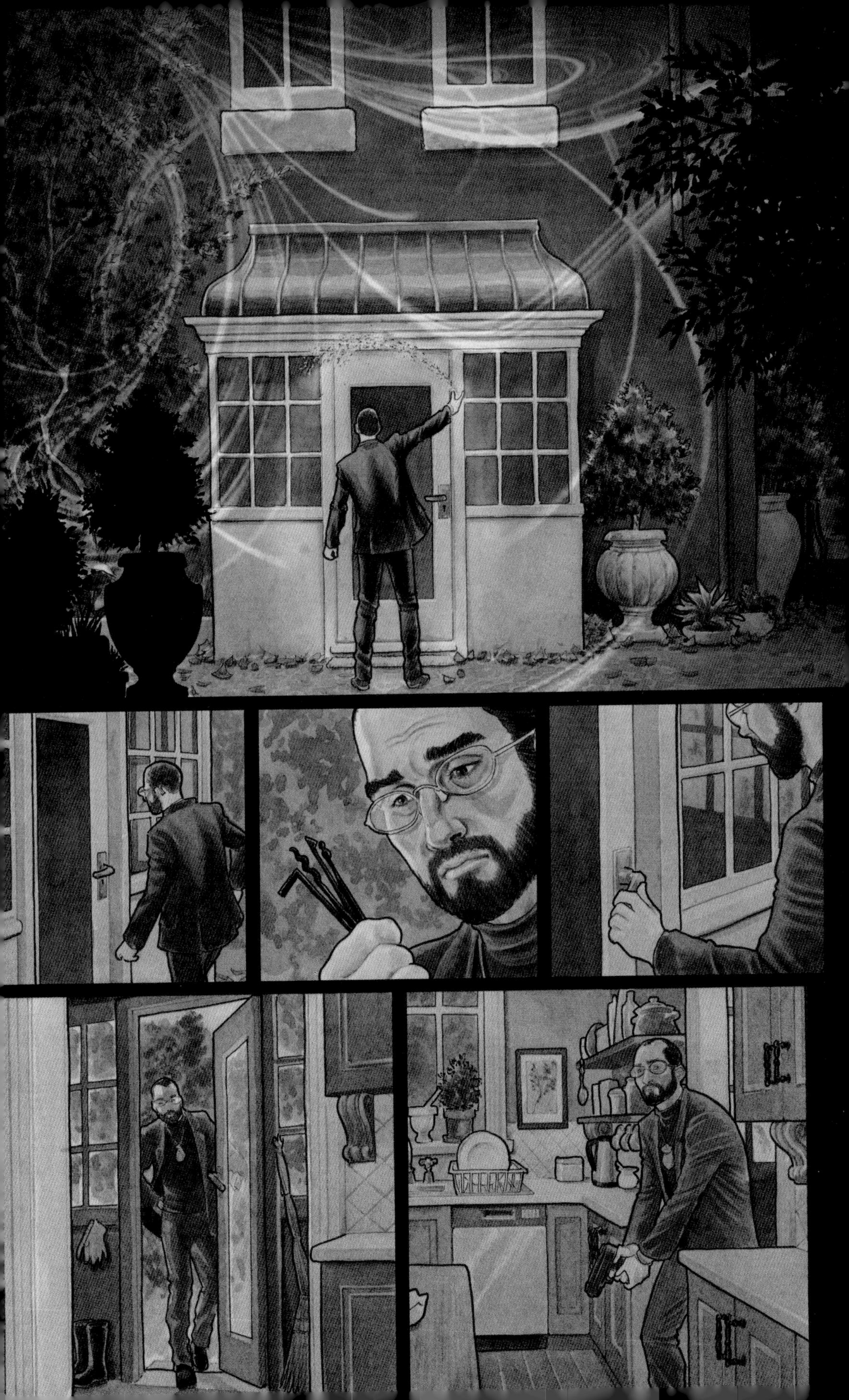

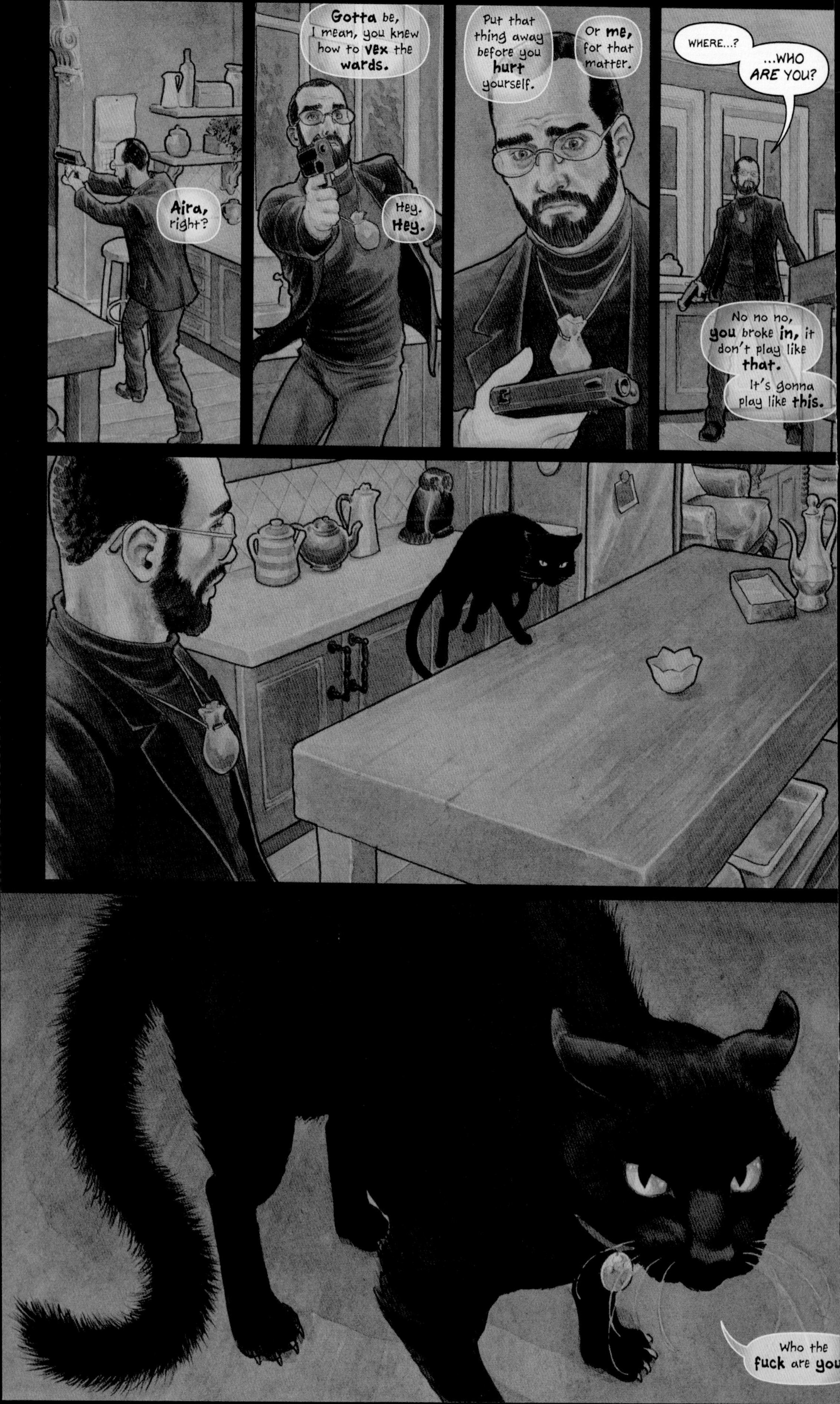

Aira, right?
Gotta be, I mean, you knew how to vex the wards.
Hey. Hey.
Put that thing away before you hurt yourself.
Or me, for that matter.
WHERE...?
...WHO ARE YOU?
No no no, you broke in, it don't play like that.
It's gonna play like this.
Who the fuck are you

ARTMENT · CITY OF PORTSMOU

LED	FIRST NAME		MIDDLE NAME	RACE	SEX	AGE	RESIDENCE OF PERSON KILLED		OFFENSE SERIAL NO
		TITLE OR RELATIONSHIP		RACE	SEX	AGE	ADDRESS OF PERSON KILLED		PHONE OF PERSON

ME) · AFTER INVESTIGATION CHANGED TO

STREET AND NUMBER OR INTERSECTION		DIVISION	PLATOON	BEAT	OFFICERS MAKING REPORT		I.D. NO.		NAME
OCCURRENCE	TIME OF DAY	DATE REPORTED	ME REPORTED	REPORT RECEIVED BY			RECEIVED — TIME — TYPED		

DESCRIPTION OF DEAD PERSON

T	EYES	HAIR	BEARD	LEXION		ARKS. ETC.		CLOTHING
	NAME OF CORONER	ME OF ARRIVAL			A.M. P.M.	CUTOR ATTENDING—TIME OF ARRIVAL		
HYSICIAN			PERSON WITH WHOM ACCUSE			OR ASSOCIATED		

CIRCUMSTANCES OF OCCURENCE OF OFFENSE AND ITS INVESTIGATION) · USE ATH SIDES OF THIS SHEET.

ODY	ADDRESS		WITNESS TAKEN INTO CUSTODY		ADDRESS

OSSIBLE MOTIVES

DESCRIPTION OF SUSPECTS OR PERSONS WANTED

	ALIAS	ADDRESS		SEX	RACE	AGE	HEIGHT	WEIGHT	EYES	HAIR	COMPLEXION
OCCUPATION		DRESS AND OTHER MARKS			SE FOR SUSPICION						
	ALIAS	ADDRESS		SEX	RACE	AGE	HEIGHT	WEIGHT	EYES	HAIR	COMPLEXION
OCCUPATION		DRESS AND OTHER MARKS			CAUSE FOR SUSPICION						

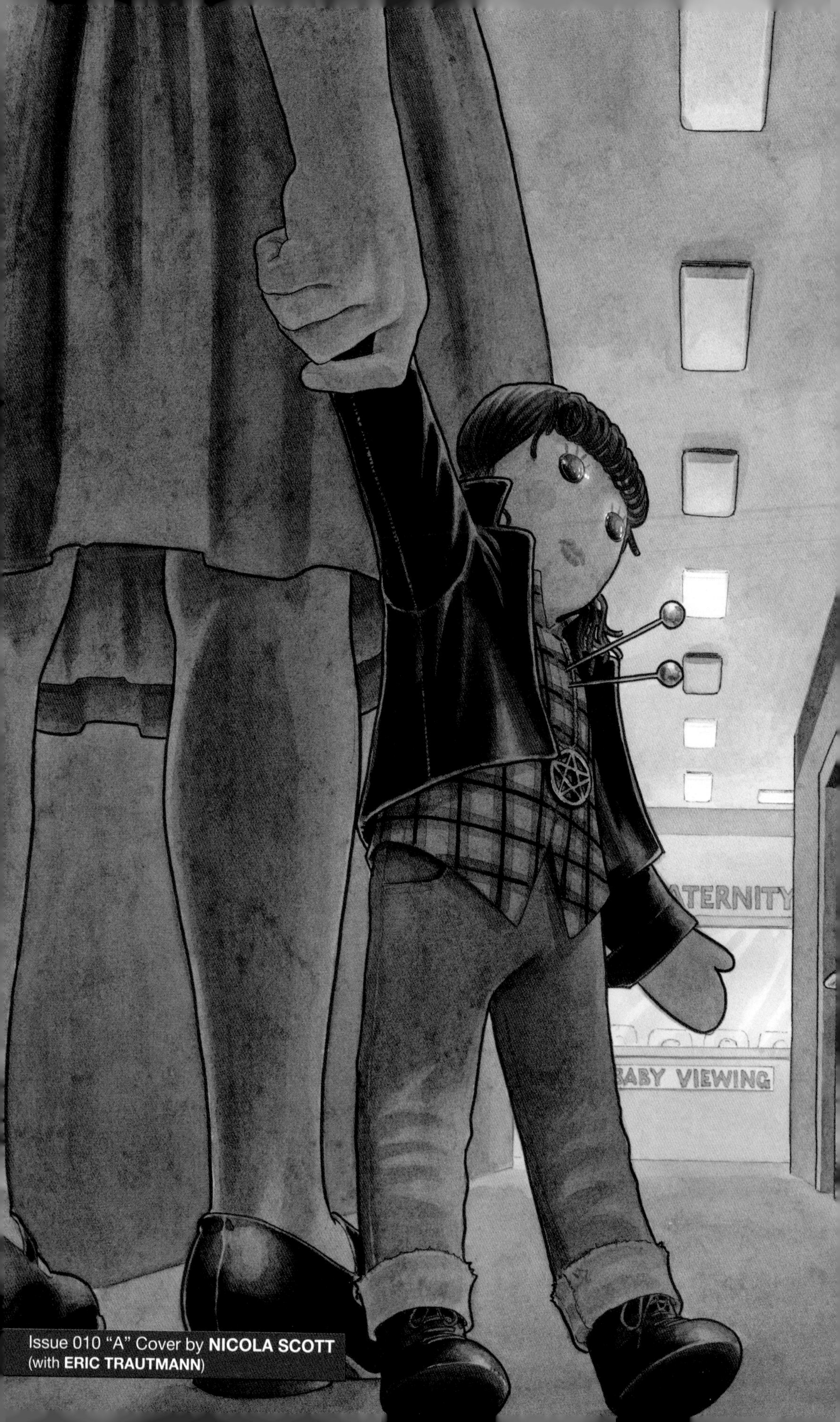
ATERNITY
BABY VIEWING
Issue 010 "A" Cover by **NICOLA SCOTT**
(with **ERIC TRAUTMANN**)

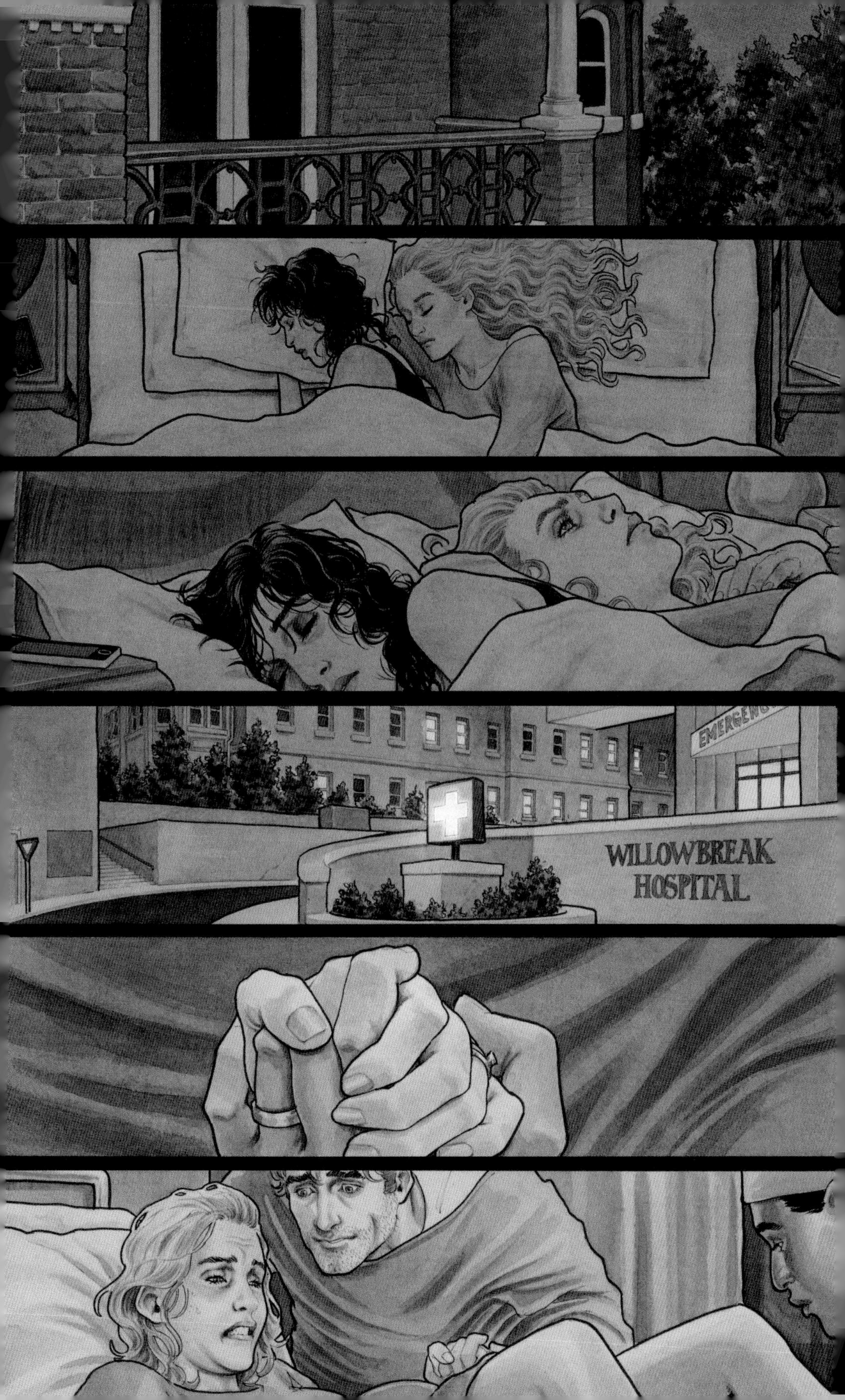
EMERGENC
WILLOWBREAK
HOSPITAL

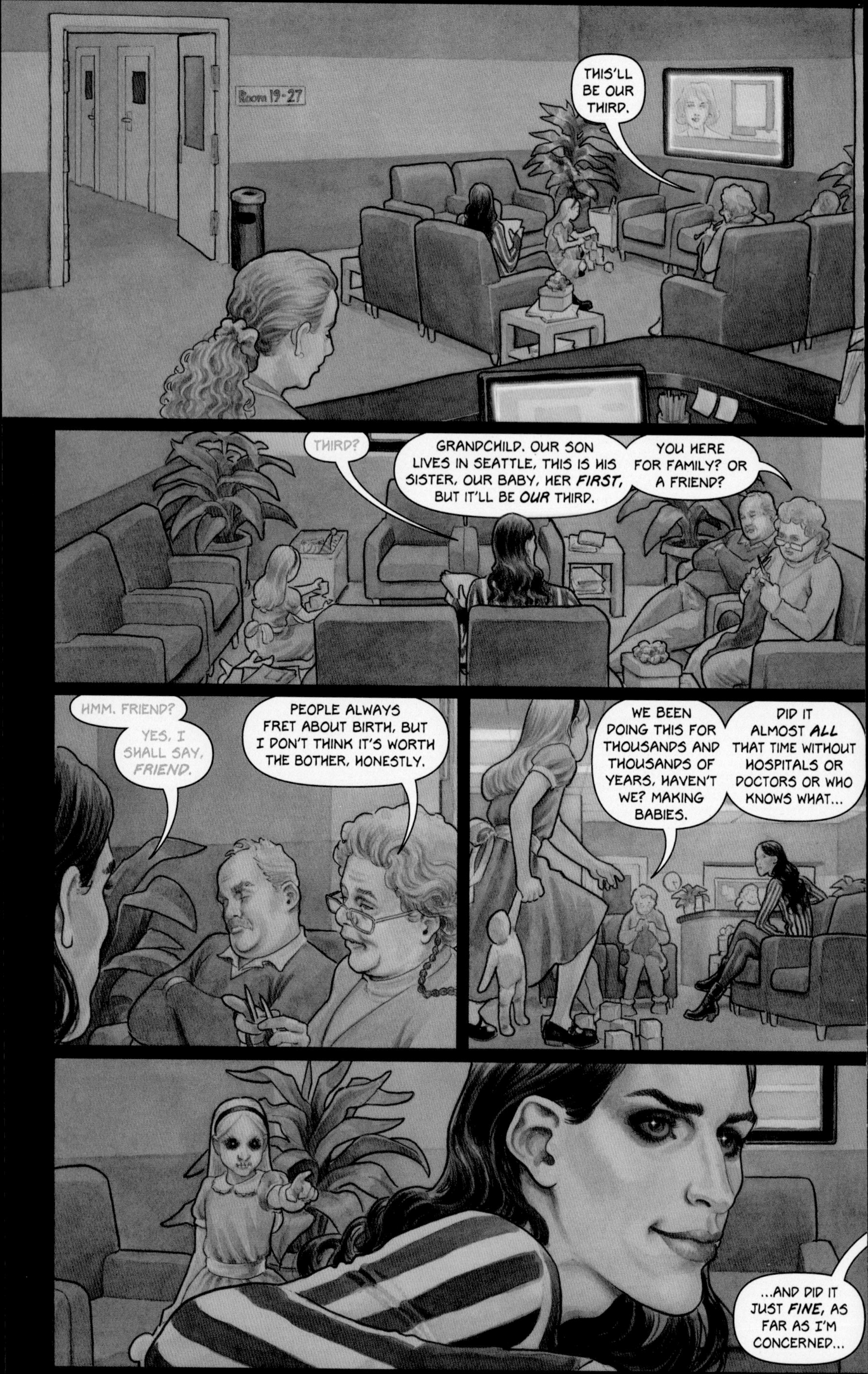

Room 19-27
THIS'LL BE OUR THIRD.
THIRD?
GRANDCHILD. OUR SON LIVES IN SEATTLE, THIS IS HIS SISTER, OUR BABY, HER *FIRST*, BUT IT'LL BE *OUR* THIRD.
YOU HERE FOR FAMILY? OR A FRIEND?
HMM. FRIEND?
YES. I SHALL SAY, *FRIEND*.
PEOPLE ALWAYS FRET ABOUT BIRTH, BUT I DON'T THINK IT'S WORTH THE BOTHER, HONESTLY.
WE BEEN DOING THIS FOR THOUSANDS AND THOUSANDS OF YEARS, HAVEN'T WE? MAKING BABIES.
DID IT ALMOST ***ALL*** THAT TIME WITHOUT HOSPITALS OR DOCTORS OR WHO KNOWS WHAT...
...AND DID IT JUST *FINE*, AS FAR AS I'M CONCERNED...

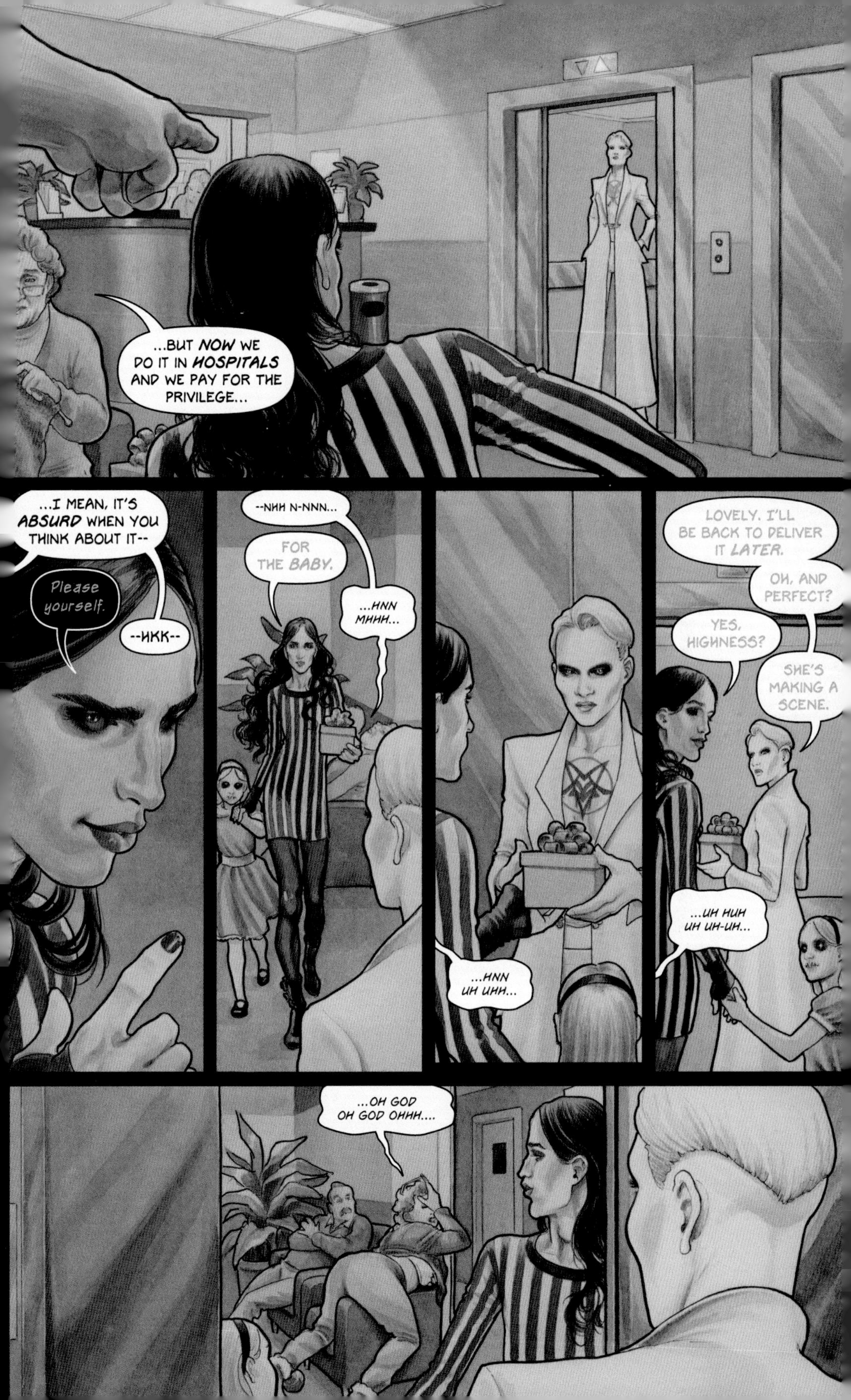

...BUT *NOW* WE DO IT IN *HOSPITALS* AND WE PAY FOR THE PRIVILEGE...
...I MEAN, IT'S *ABSURD* WHEN YOU THINK ABOUT IT--
Please yourself.
--HKK--
--NHH N-NNN...
FOR THE *BABY*.
...HNN MHHH...
...HNN UH UHH...
LOVELY. I'LL BE BACK TO DELIVER IT *LATER*.
OH, AND PERFECT?
YES, HIGHNESS?
SHE'S MAKING A SCENE.
...UH HUH UH UH-UH...
...OH GOD OH GOD OHHH....

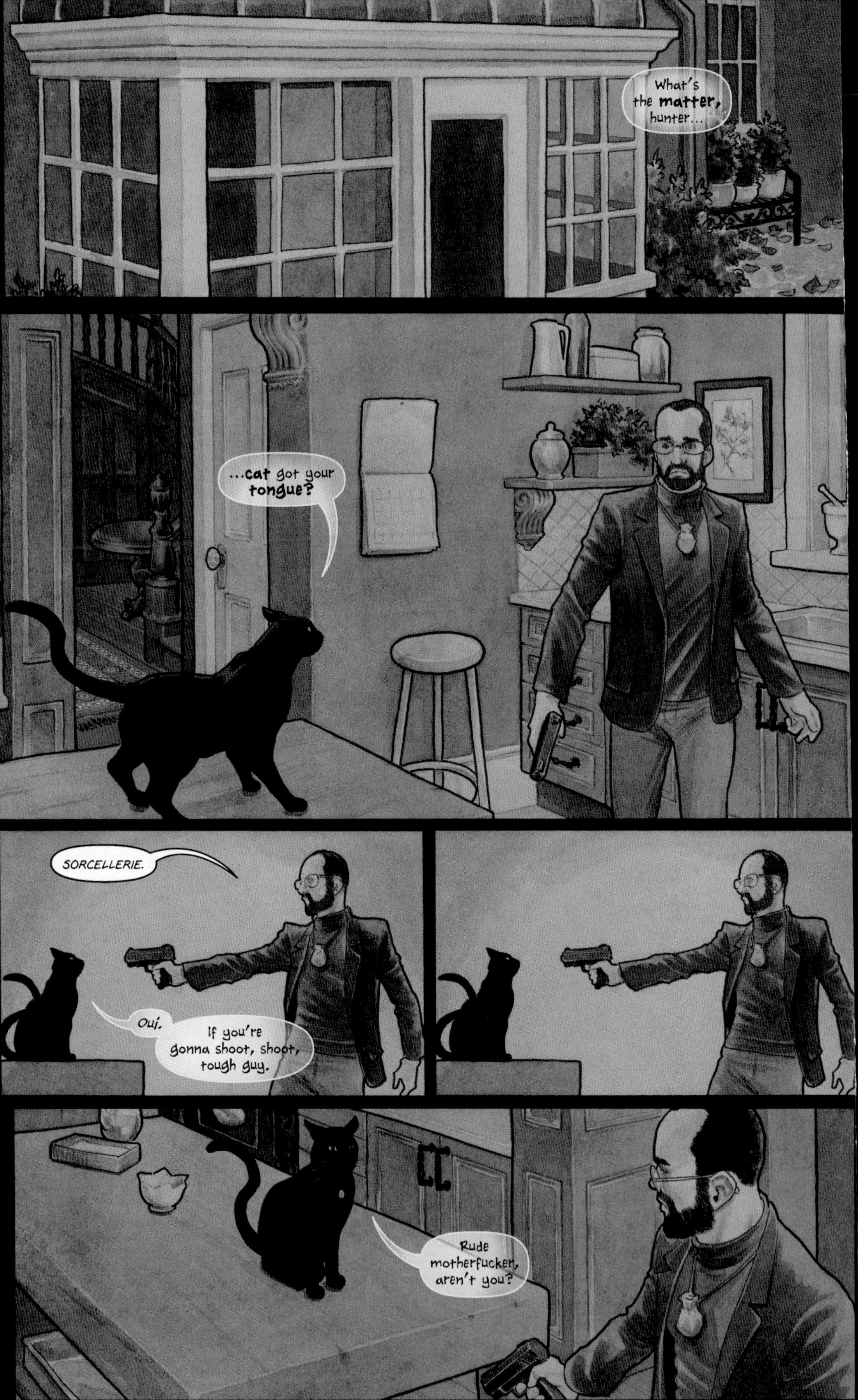
What's the matter, hunter...
...cat got your tongue?
SORCELLERIE.
Oui.
If you're gonna shoot, shoot, tough guy.
Rude motherfucker, aren't you?

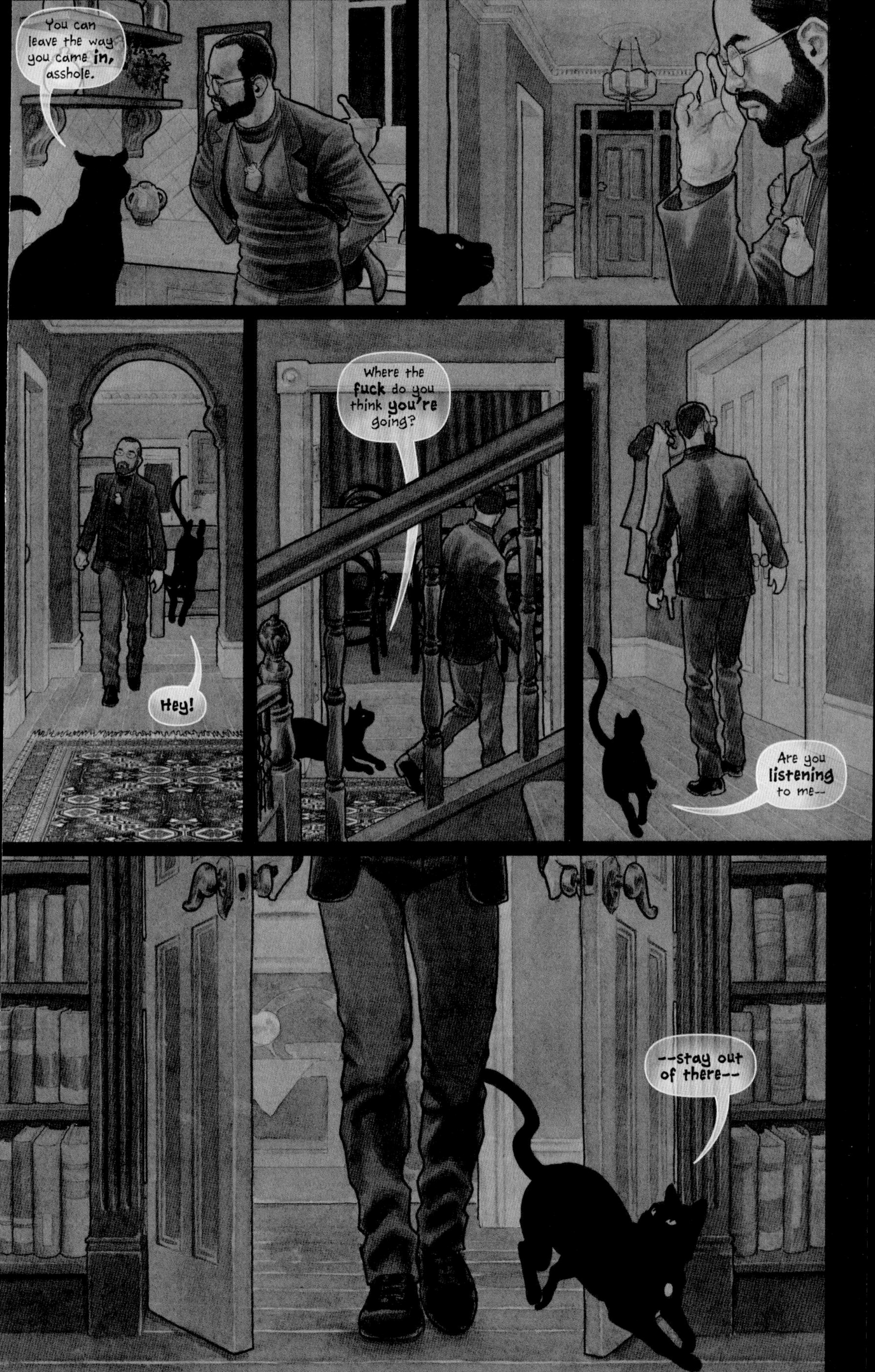
You can leave the way you came in, asshole.
Hey!
Where the fuck do you think you're going?
Are you listening to me--
--stay out of there--

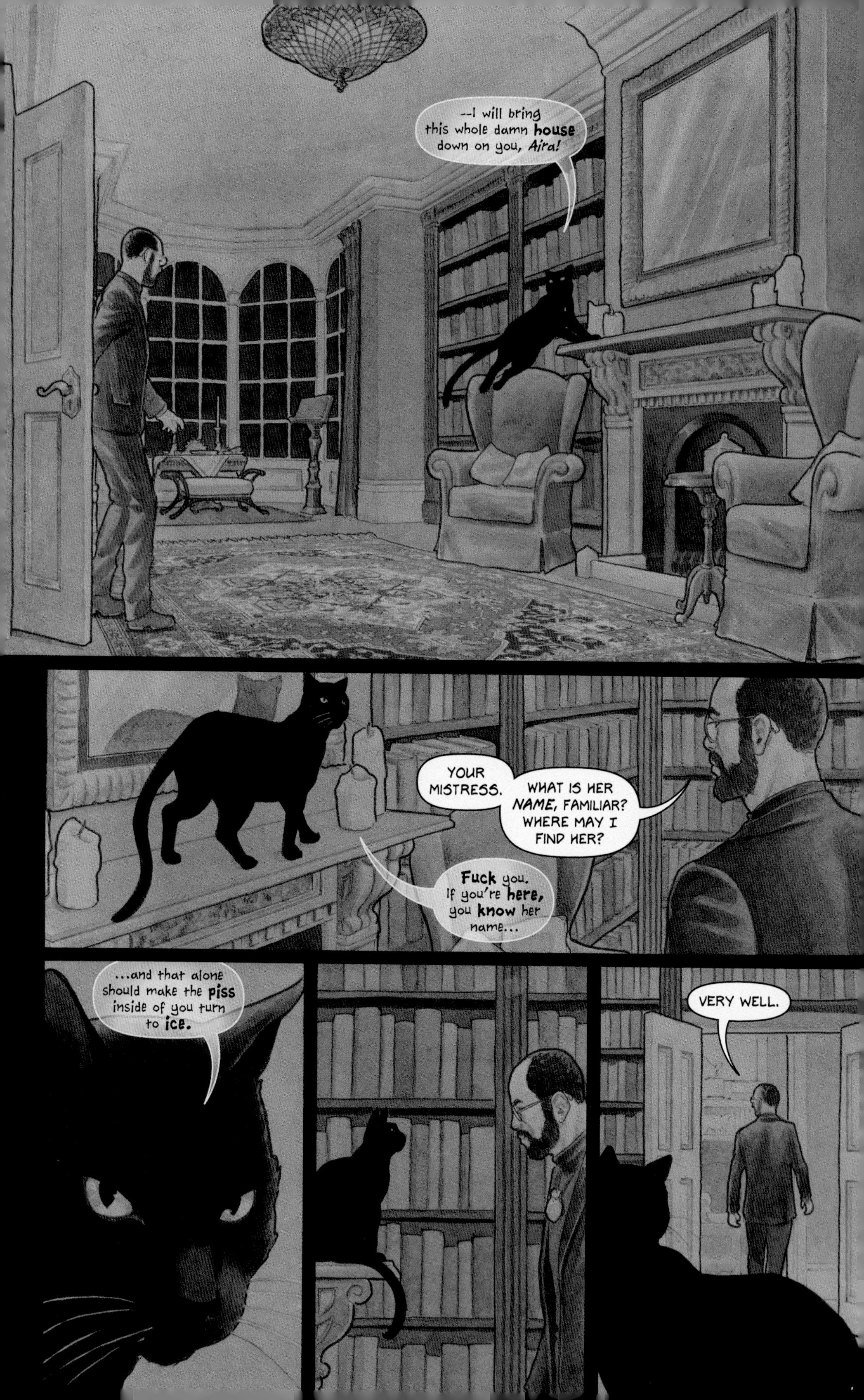
--I will bring this whole damn house down on you, Aira!
YOUR MISTRESS.
WHAT IS HER NAME, FAMILIAR? WHERE MAY I FIND HER?
Fuck you. If you're here, you know her name...
...and that alone should make the piss inside of you turn to ice.
VERY WELL.

I WAS NOT AWARE SHE KEPT A *FAMILIAR*.

HOW LONG HAVE YOU BEEN IN HER SERVICE?

Wow, you just don't **quit**, do you?

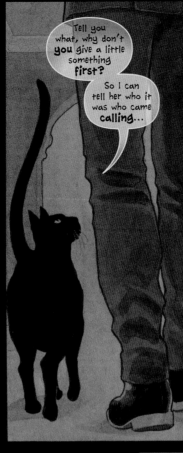

Tell you what, why don't **you** give a little something **first**?

So I can tell her who it was who came **calling**...

...unless you've got a **card** you want to leave on the silver salver before you **fuck off**.

MHM.

TELL MISTRESS BLACK THAT MY NAME IS LAURENT LEVEQUE, OF PONT-L'ÉVÊQUE.

IT IS A *NAME* SHE MAY *REMEMBER*.

YOU DID NOT NEED TO.

I **never** said her **name**.

MY APOLOGIES FOR THE INTRUSION TO YOU **AND** YOUR MISTRESS...

...I WILL SEE MYSELF OUT....

Laurent Leveque
Hotel Marquis
I shall await your call

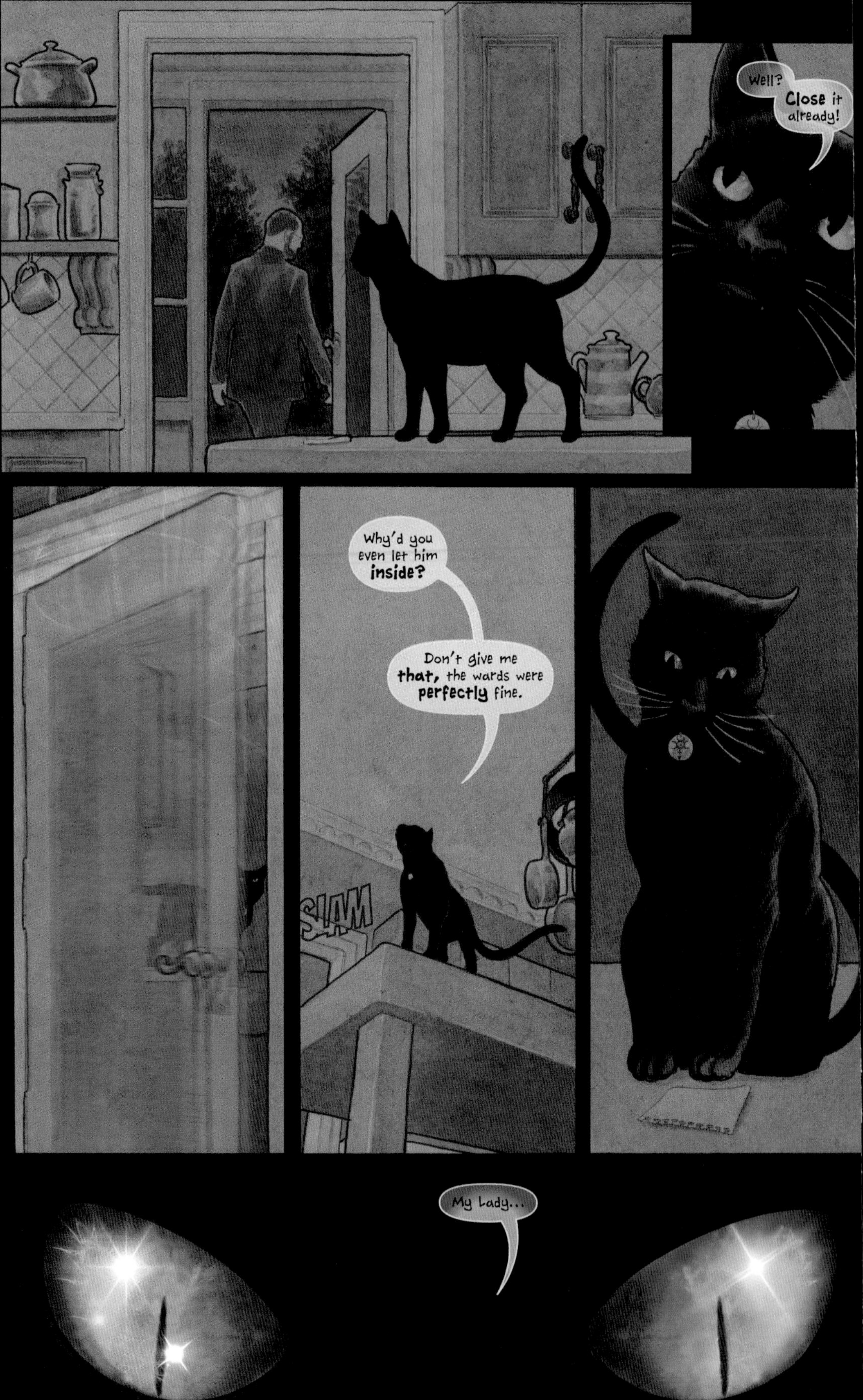
Well?
Close it already!
Why'd you even let him inside?
Don't give me that, the wards were perfectly fine.
SLAM
My Lady...

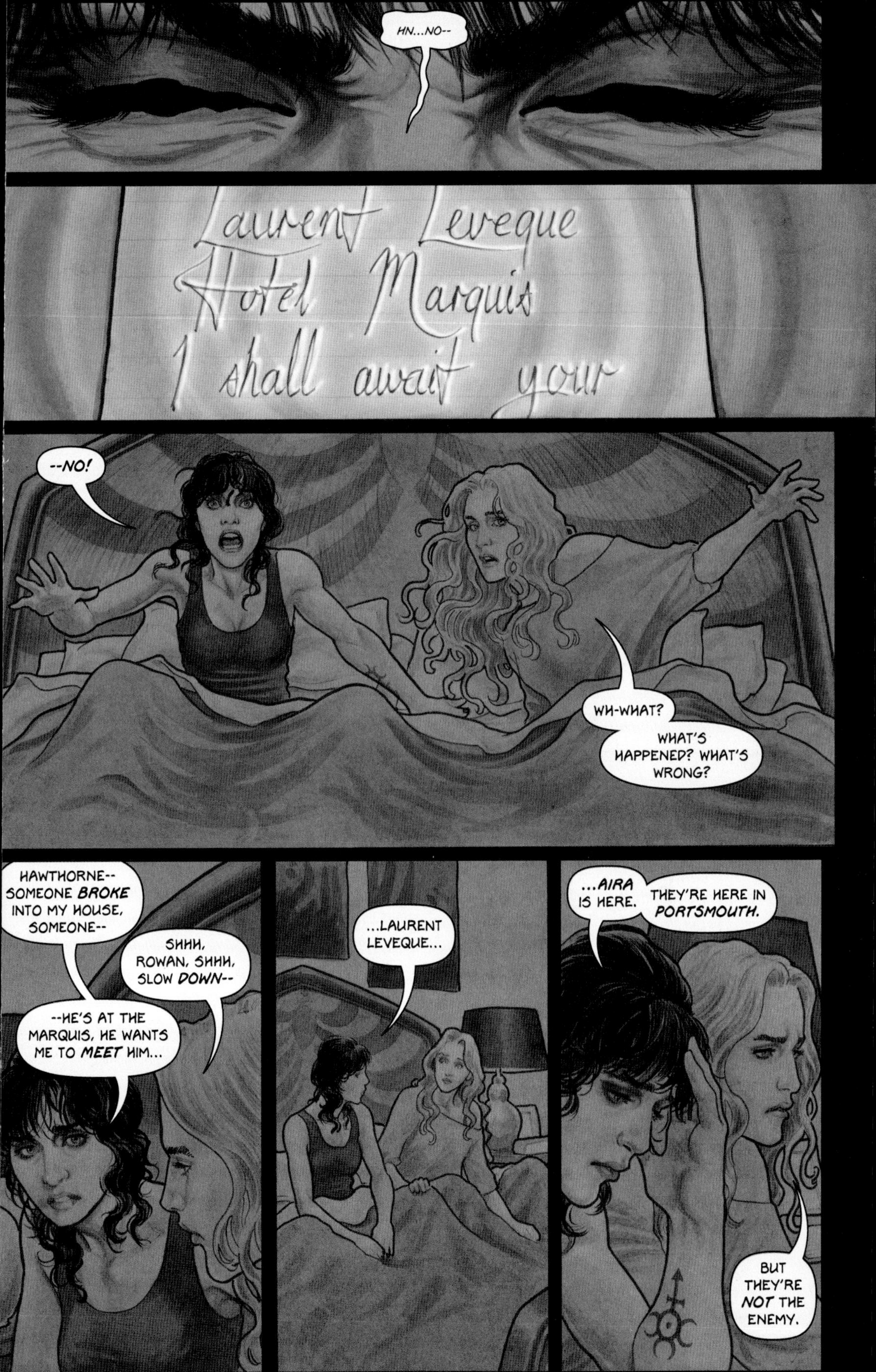
HN...NO--
Laurent Leveque
Hotel Marquis
I shall await your
--NO!
WH-WHAT?
WHAT'S HAPPENED? WHAT'S WRONG?
HAWTHORNE-- SOMEONE BROKE INTO MY HOUSE, SOMEONE--
SHHH, ROWAN, SHHH, SLOW DOWN--
--HE'S AT THE MARQUIS, HE WANTS ME TO MEET HIM...
...LAURENT LEVEQUE...
...AIRA IS HERE.
THEY'RE HERE IN PORTSMOUTH.
BUT THEY'RE NOT THE ENEMY.

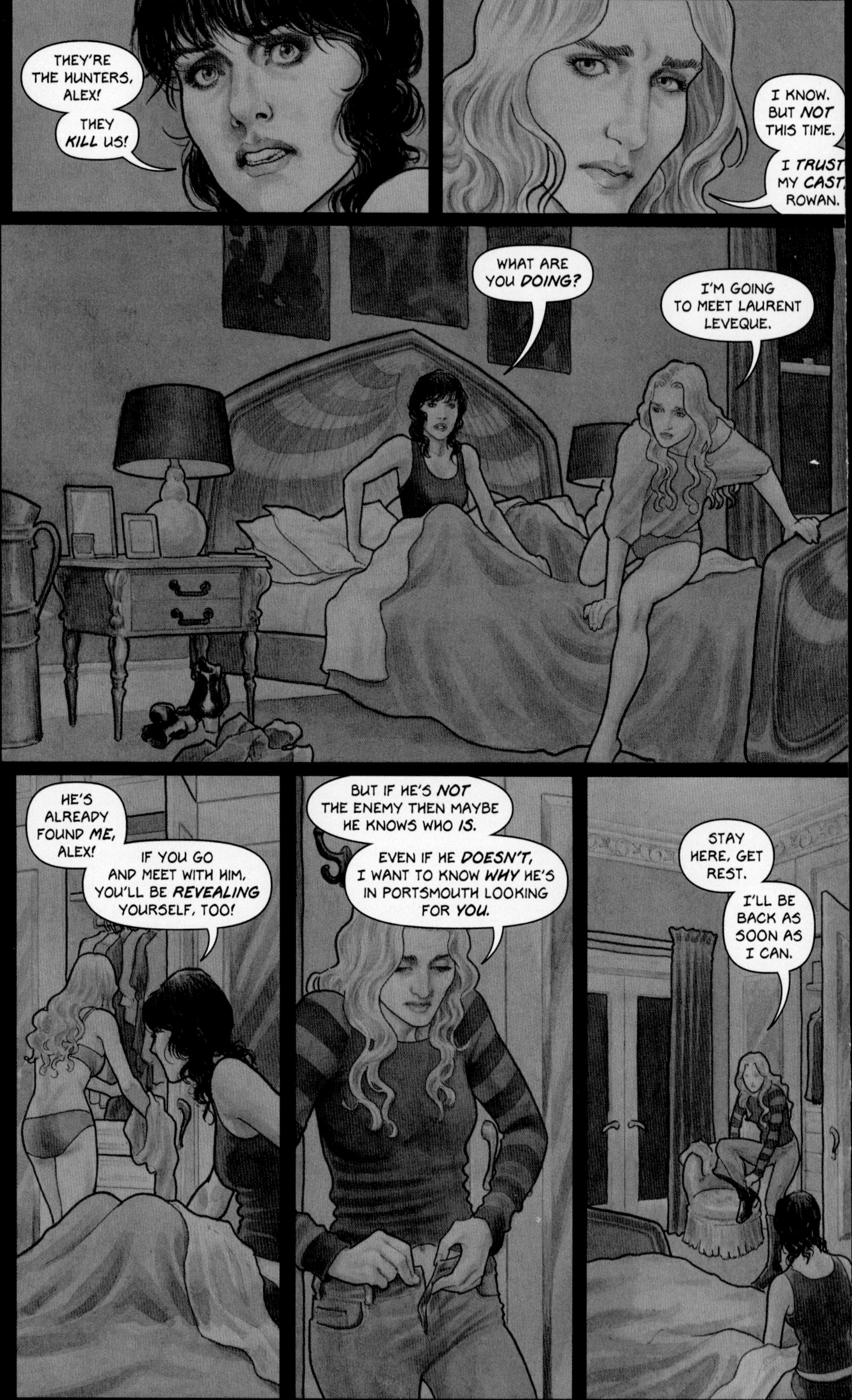
THEY'RE THE HUNTERS, ALEX!
THEY KILL US!
I KNOW. BUT NOT THIS TIME.
I TRUST MY CAST, ROWAN.
WHAT ARE YOU DOING?
I'M GOING TO MEET LAURENT LEVEQUE.
HE'S ALREADY FOUND ME, ALEX!
IF YOU GO AND MEET WITH HIM, YOU'LL BE REVEALING YOURSELF, TOO!
BUT IF HE'S NOT THE ENEMY THEN MAYBE HE KNOWS WHO IS.
EVEN IF HE DOESN'T, I WANT TO KNOW WHY HE'S IN PORTSMOUTH LOOKING FOR YOU.
STAY HERE, GET REST.
I'LL BE BACK AS SOON AS I CAN.

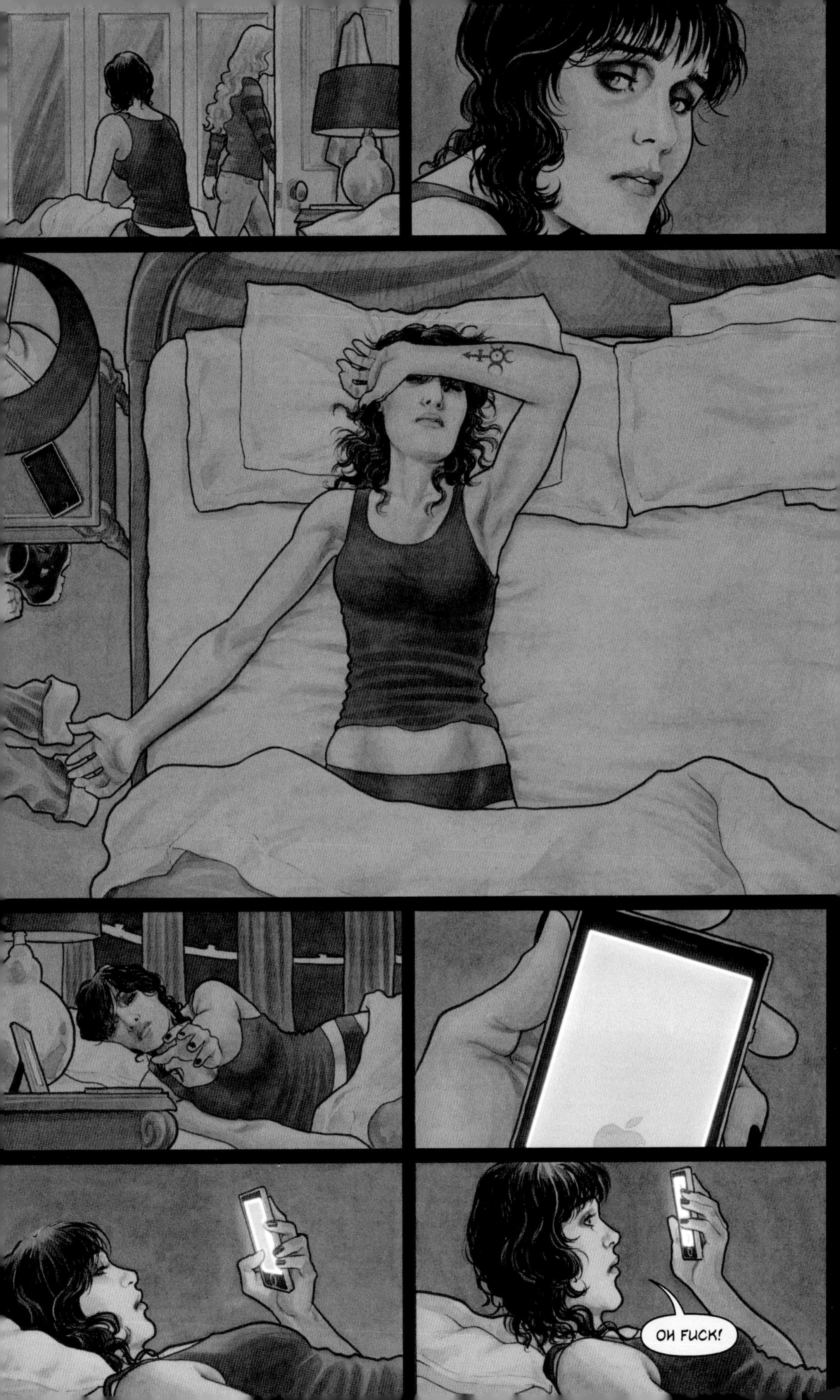
OH FUCK!

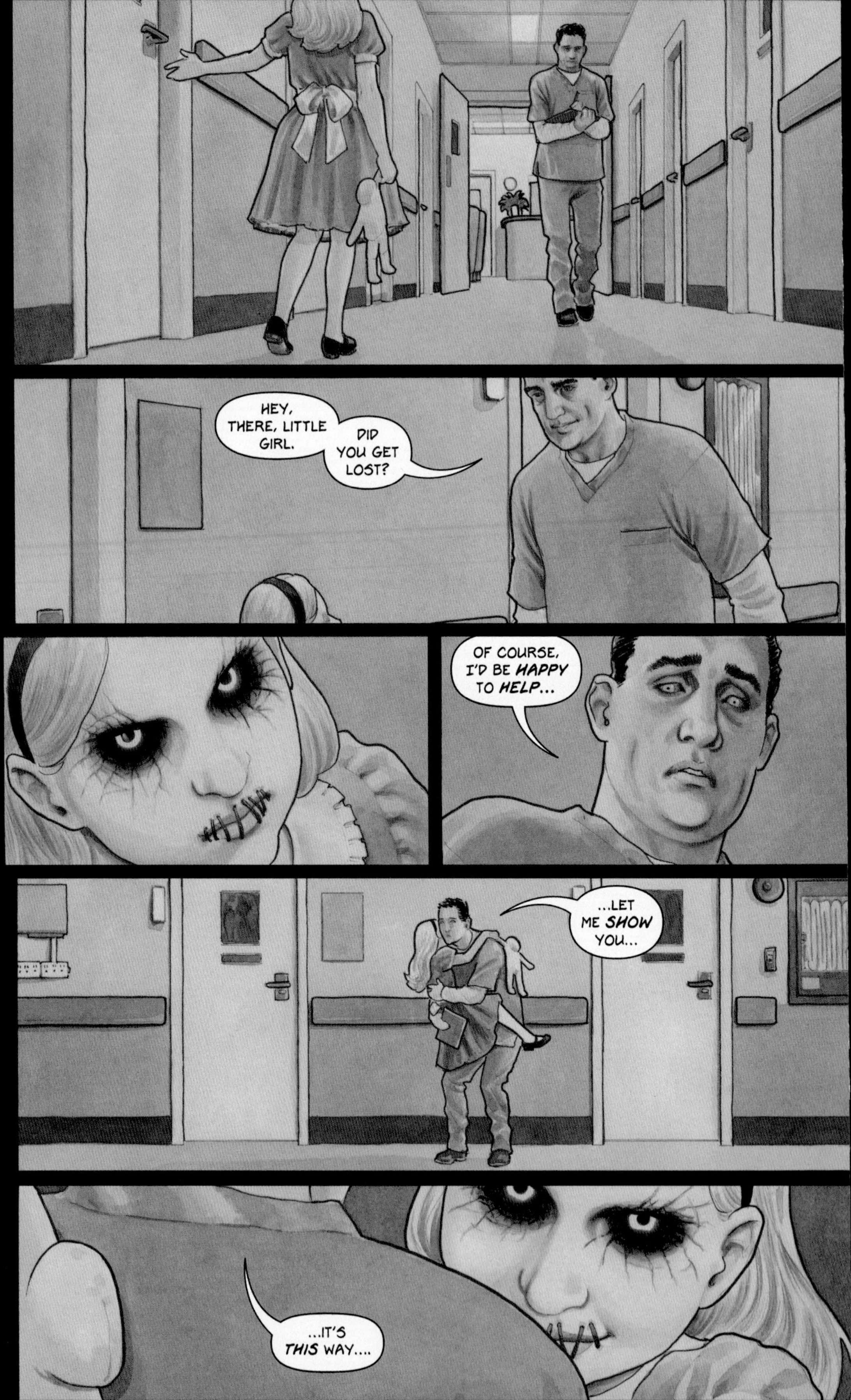
HEY, THERE, LITTLE GIRL.
DID YOU GET LOST?
OF COURSE, I'D BE HAPPY TO HELP...
...LET ME SHOW YOU...
...IT'S THIS WAY....

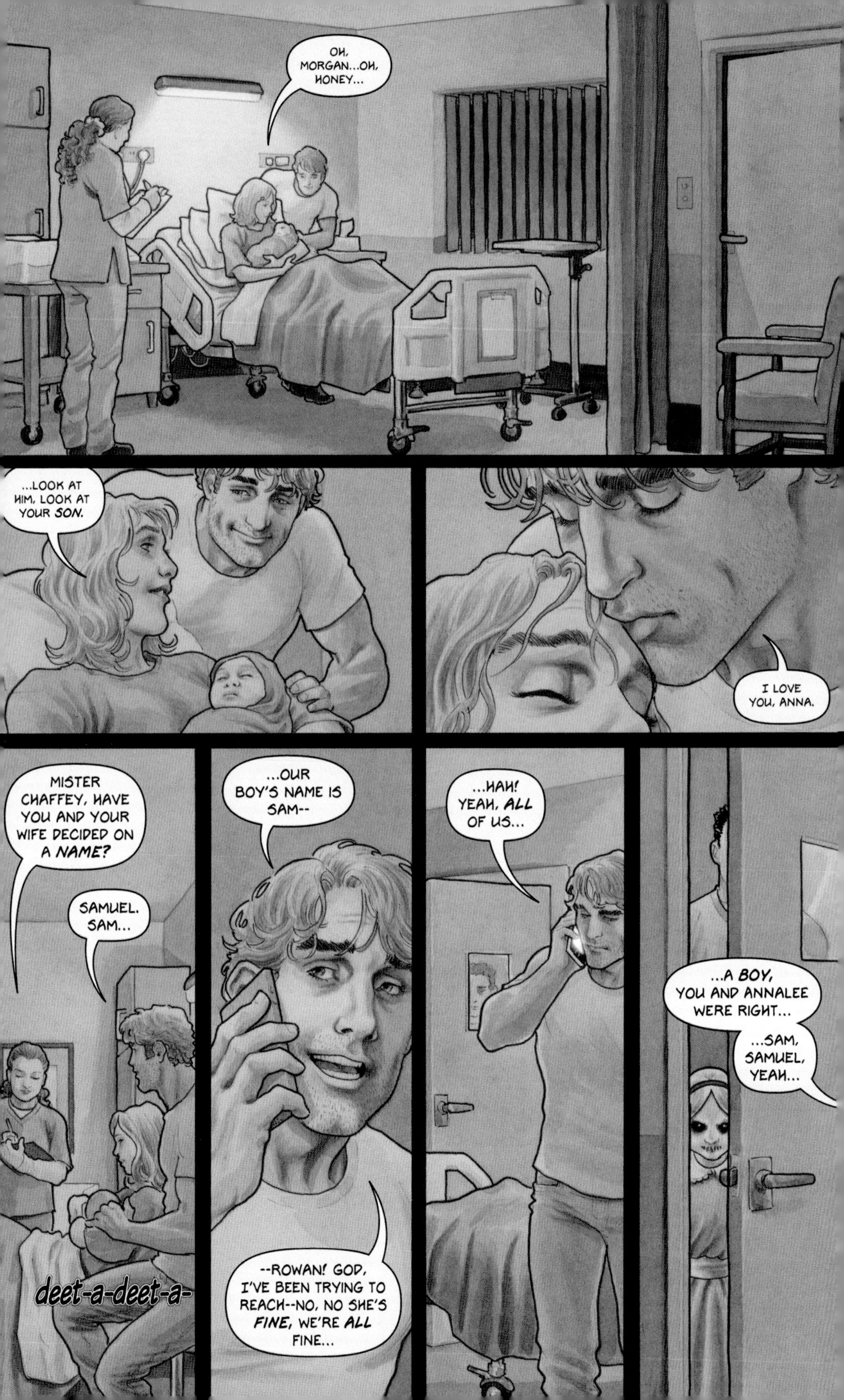
OH, MORGAN...OH, HONEY...
...LOOK AT HIM, LOOK AT YOUR *SON.*
I LOVE YOU, ANNA.
MISTER CHAFFEY, HAVE YOU AND YOUR WIFE DECIDED ON A *NAME?*
SAMUEL. SAM...
deet-a-deet-a-
...OUR BOY'S NAME IS SAM--
--ROWAN! GOD, I'VE BEEN TRYING TO REACH--NO, NO SHE'S *FINE,* WE'RE *ALL* FINE...
...HAH! YEAH, *ALL* OF US...
...A *BOY,* YOU AND ANNALEE WERE RIGHT...
...SAM, SAMUEL, YEAH...

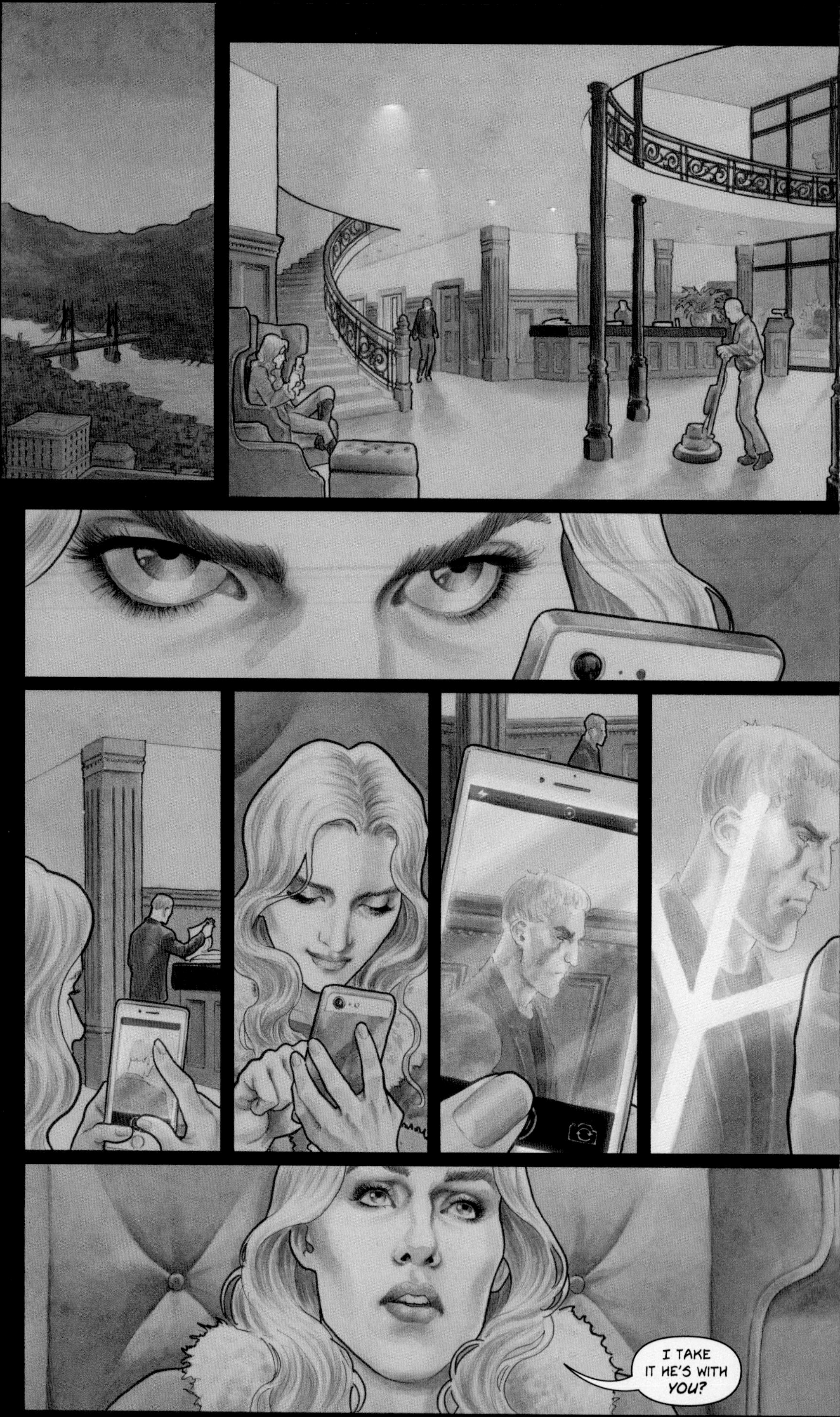
I TAKE IT HE'S WITH YOU?

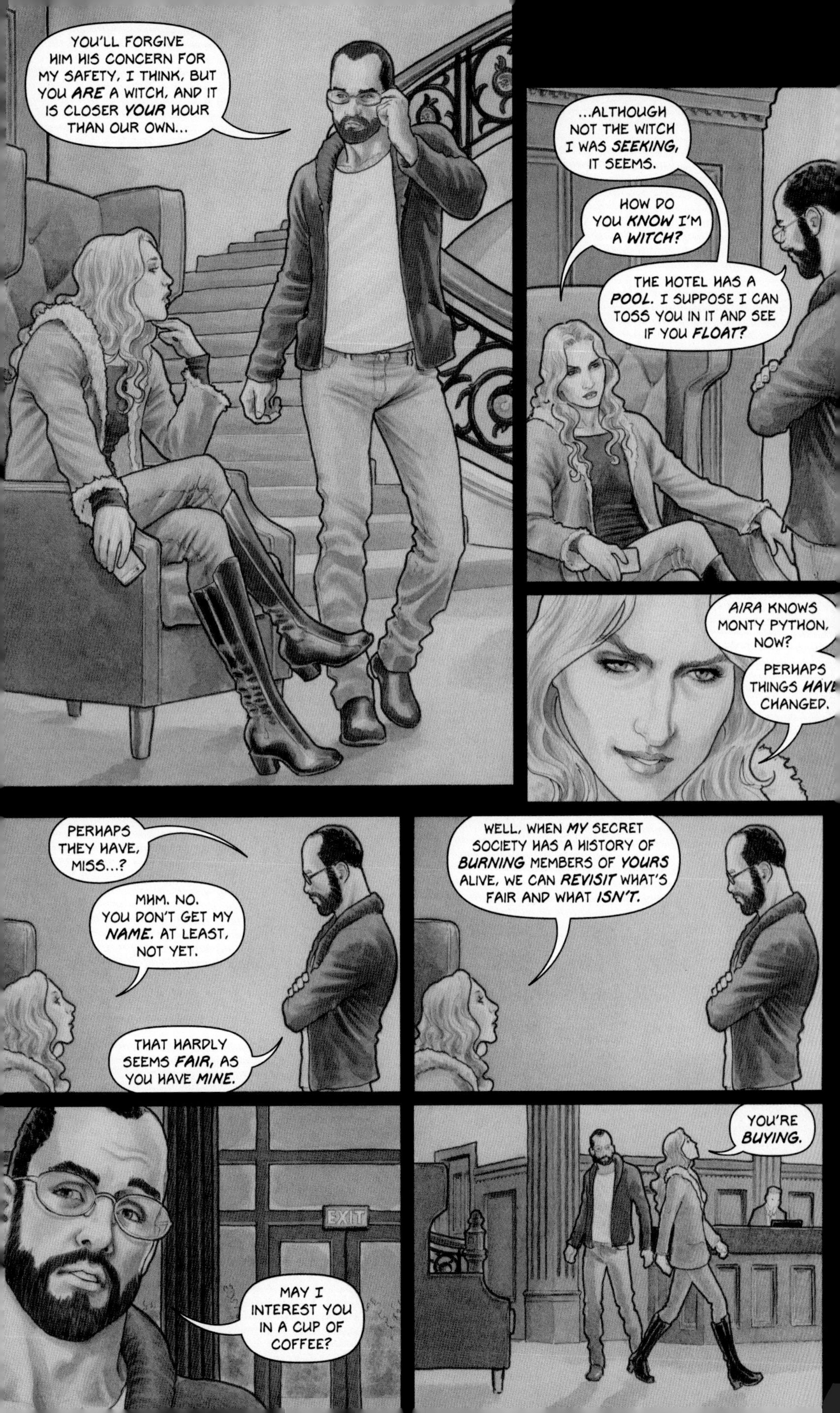
YOU'LL FORGIVE HIM HIS CONCERN FOR MY SAFETY, I THINK, BUT YOU ARE A WITCH, AND IT IS CLOSER YOUR HOUR THAN OUR OWN...
...ALTHOUGH NOT THE WITCH I WAS SEEKING, IT SEEMS.
HOW DO YOU KNOW I'M A WITCH?
THE HOTEL HAS A POOL. I SUPPOSE I CAN TOSS YOU IN IT AND SEE IF YOU FLOAT?
AIRA KNOWS MONTY PYTHON, NOW?
PERHAPS THINGS HAVE CHANGED.
PERHAPS THEY HAVE, MISS...?
MHM. NO. YOU DON'T GET MY NAME. AT LEAST, NOT YET.
THAT HARDLY SEEMS FAIR, AS YOU HAVE MINE.
WELL, WHEN MY SECRET SOCIETY HAS A HISTORY OF BURNING MEMBERS OF YOURS ALIVE, WE CAN REVISIT WHAT'S FAIR AND WHAT ISN'T.
EXIT
MAY I INTEREST YOU IN A CUP OF COFFEE?
YOU'RE BUYING.

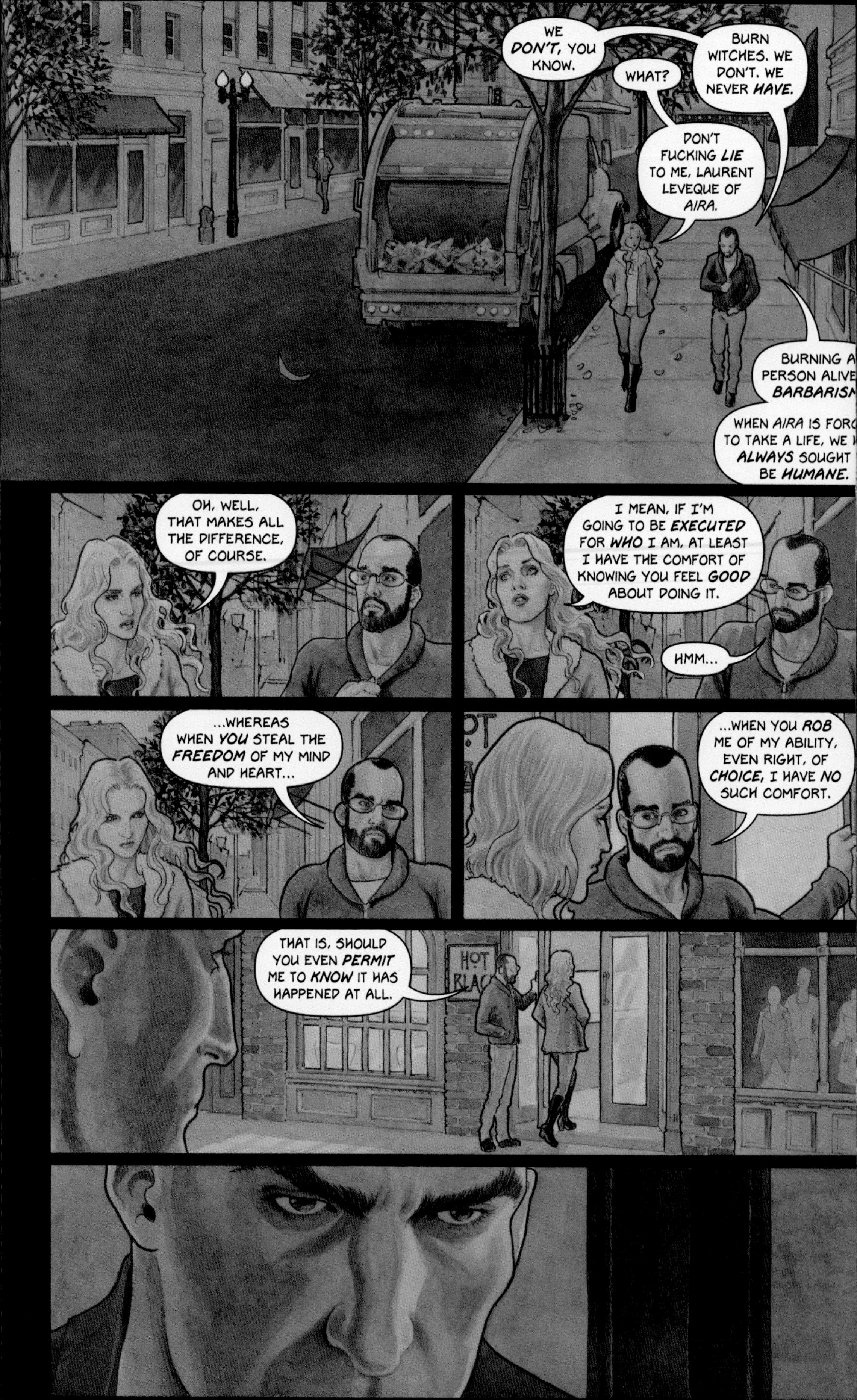
WE DON'T, YOU KNOW.
WHAT?
BURN WITCHES. WE DON'T. WE NEVER HAVE.
DON'T FUCKING LIE TO ME, LAURENT LEVEQUE OF AIRA.
BURNING A PERSON ALIVE BARBARISM
WHEN AIRA IS FORC TO TAKE A LIFE, WE ALWAYS SOUGHT BE HUMANE.
OH, WELL, THAT MAKES ALL THE DIFFERENCE, OF COURSE.
I MEAN, IF I'M GOING TO BE EXECUTED FOR WHO I AM, AT LEAST I HAVE THE COMFORT OF KNOWING YOU FEEL GOOD ABOUT DOING IT.
HMM...
...WHEREAS WHEN YOU STEAL THE FREEDOM OF MY MIND AND HEART...
...WHEN YOU ROB ME OF MY ABILITY, EVEN RIGHT, OF CHOICE, I HAVE NO SUCH COMFORT.
THAT IS, SHOULD YOU EVEN PERMIT ME TO KNOW IT HAS HAPPENED AT ALL.

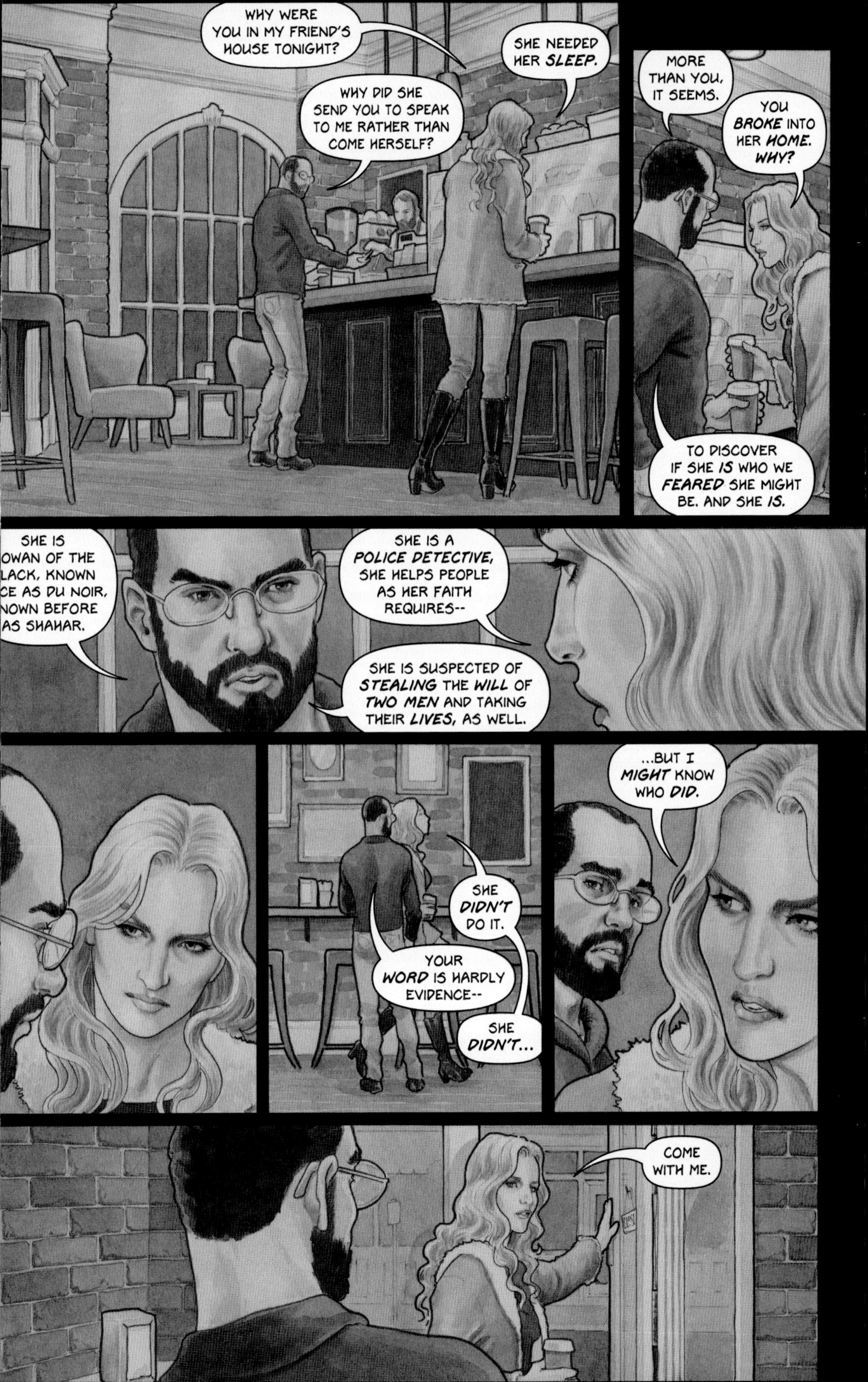

WHY WERE YOU IN MY FRIEND'S HOUSE TONIGHT?
WHY DID SHE SEND YOU TO SPEAK TO ME RATHER THAN COME HERSELF?
SHE NEEDED HER SLEEP.
MORE THAN YOU, IT SEEMS.
YOU BROKE INTO HER HOME. WHY?
TO DISCOVER IF SHE IS WHO WE FEARED SHE MIGHT BE. AND SHE IS.
SHE IS OWAN OF THE LACK, KNOWN CE AS DU NOIR, NOWN BEFORE AS SHAHAR.
SHE IS A POLICE DETECTIVE, SHE HELPS PEOPLE AS HER FAITH REQUIRES--
SHE IS SUSPECTED OF STEALING THE WILL OF TWO MEN AND TAKING THEIR LIVES, AS WELL.
SHE DIDN'T DO IT.
YOUR WORD IS HARDLY EVIDENCE--
SHE DIDN'T...
...BUT I MIGHT KNOW WHO DID.
COME WITH ME.

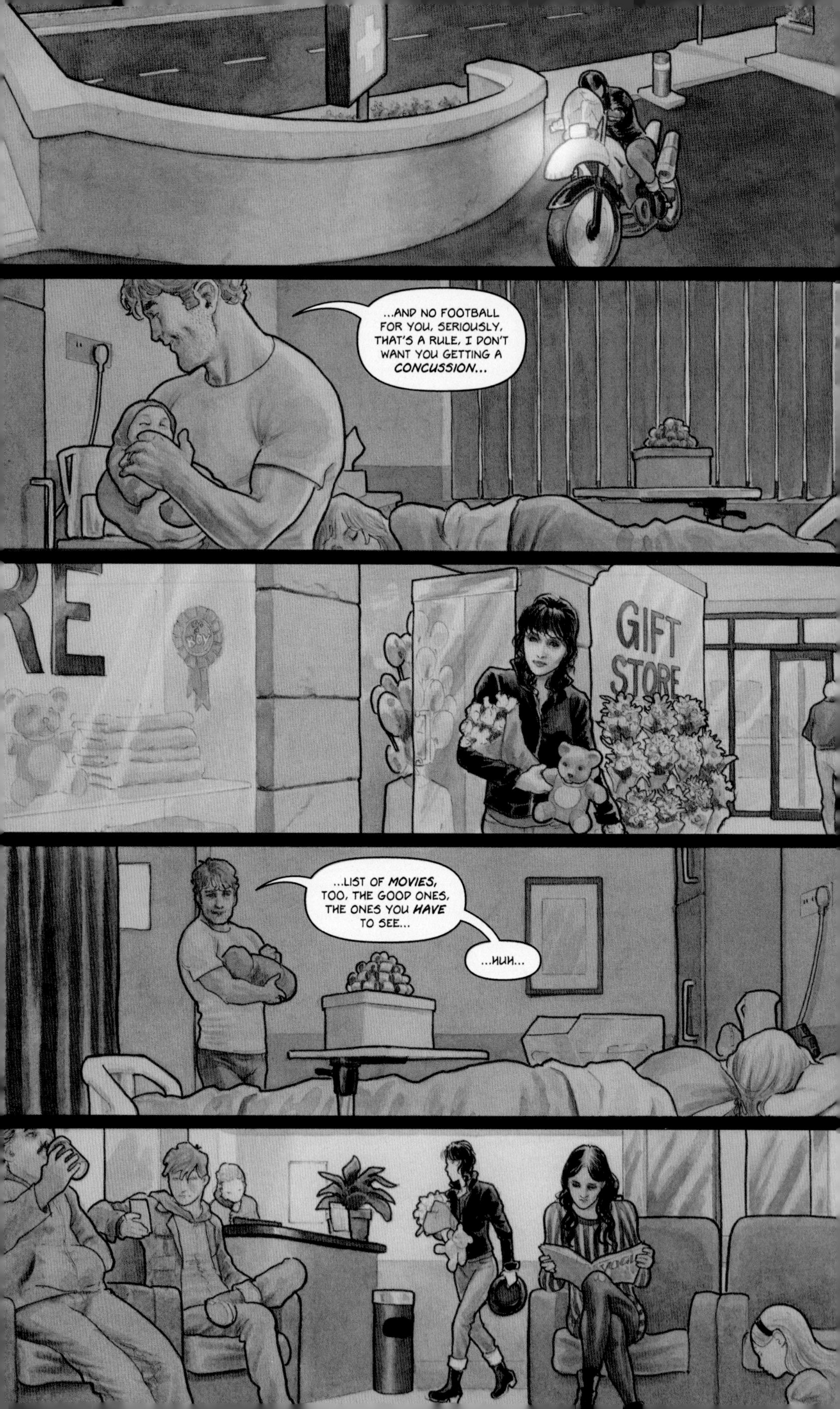

...AND NO FOOTBALL FOR YOU, SERIOUSLY, THAT'S A RULE, I DON'T WANT YOU GETTING A *CONCUSSION*...
GIFT STORE
...LIST OF *MOVIES*, TOO, THE GOOD ONES, THE ONES YOU *HAVE* TO SEE...
...HUH...

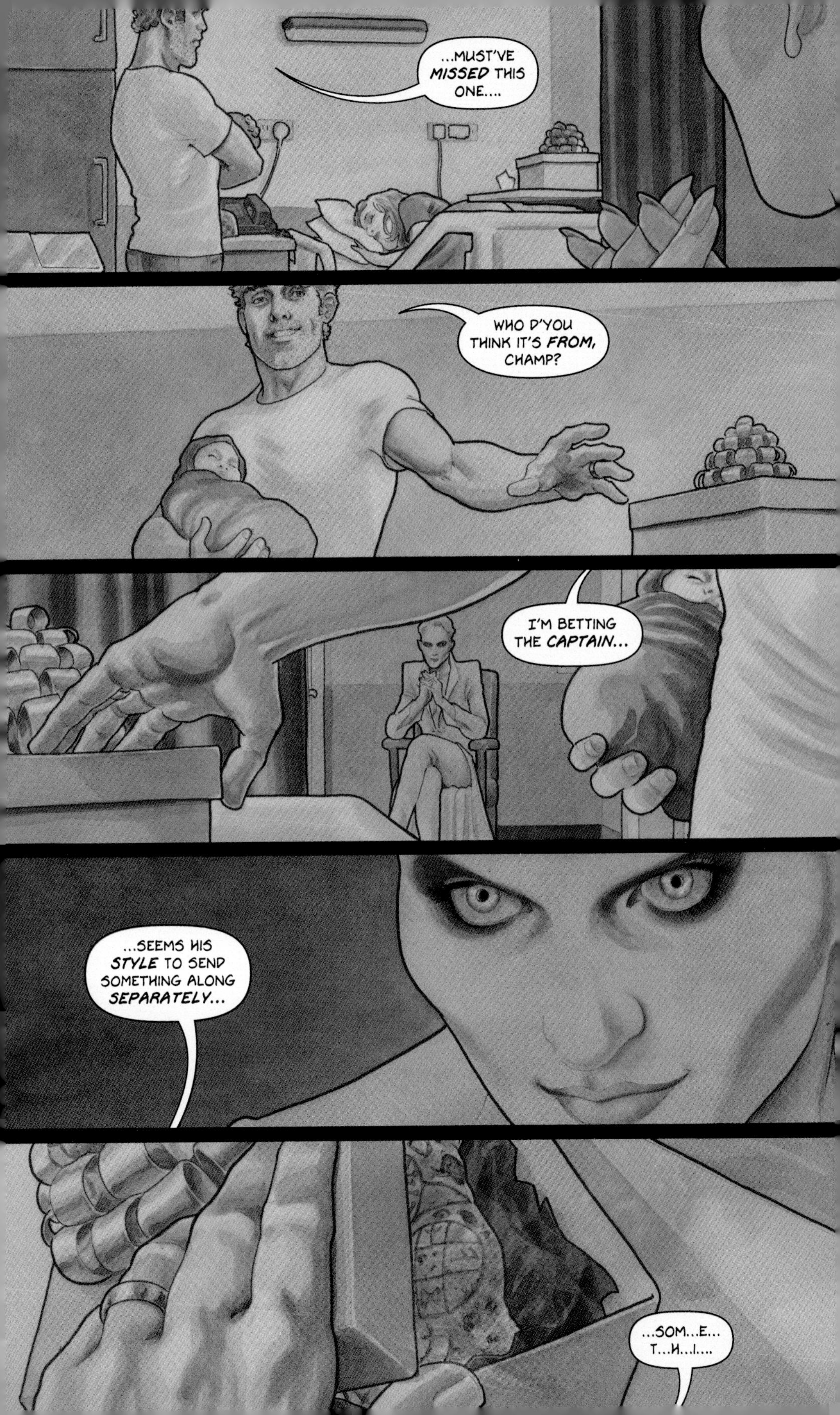
...MUST'VE MISSED THIS ONE....
WHO D'YOU THINK IT'S FROM, CHAMP?
I'M BETTING THE CAPTAIN...
...SEEMS HIS STYLE TO SEND SOMETHING ALONG SEPARATELY...
...SOM...E... T...H...I....

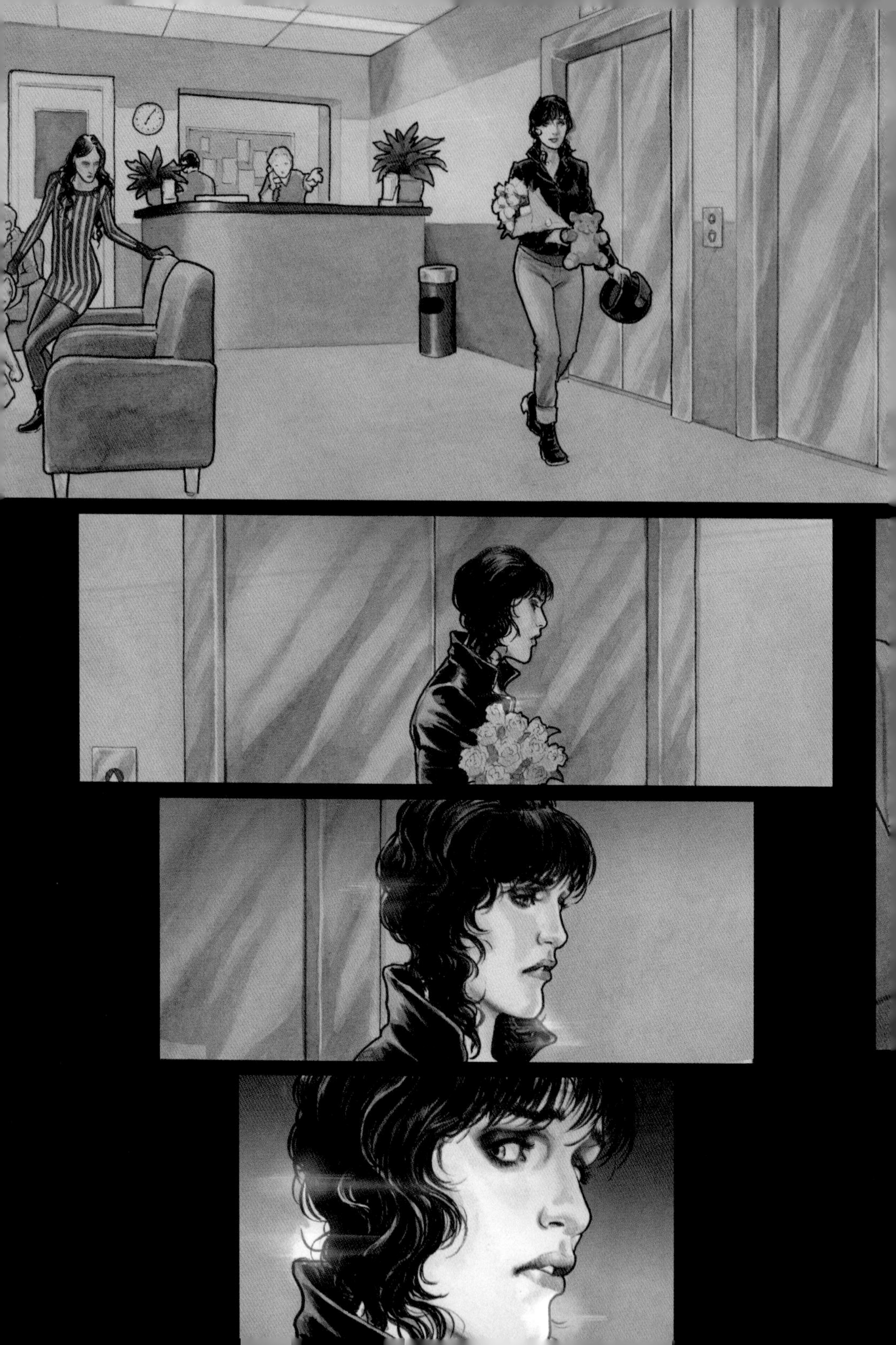

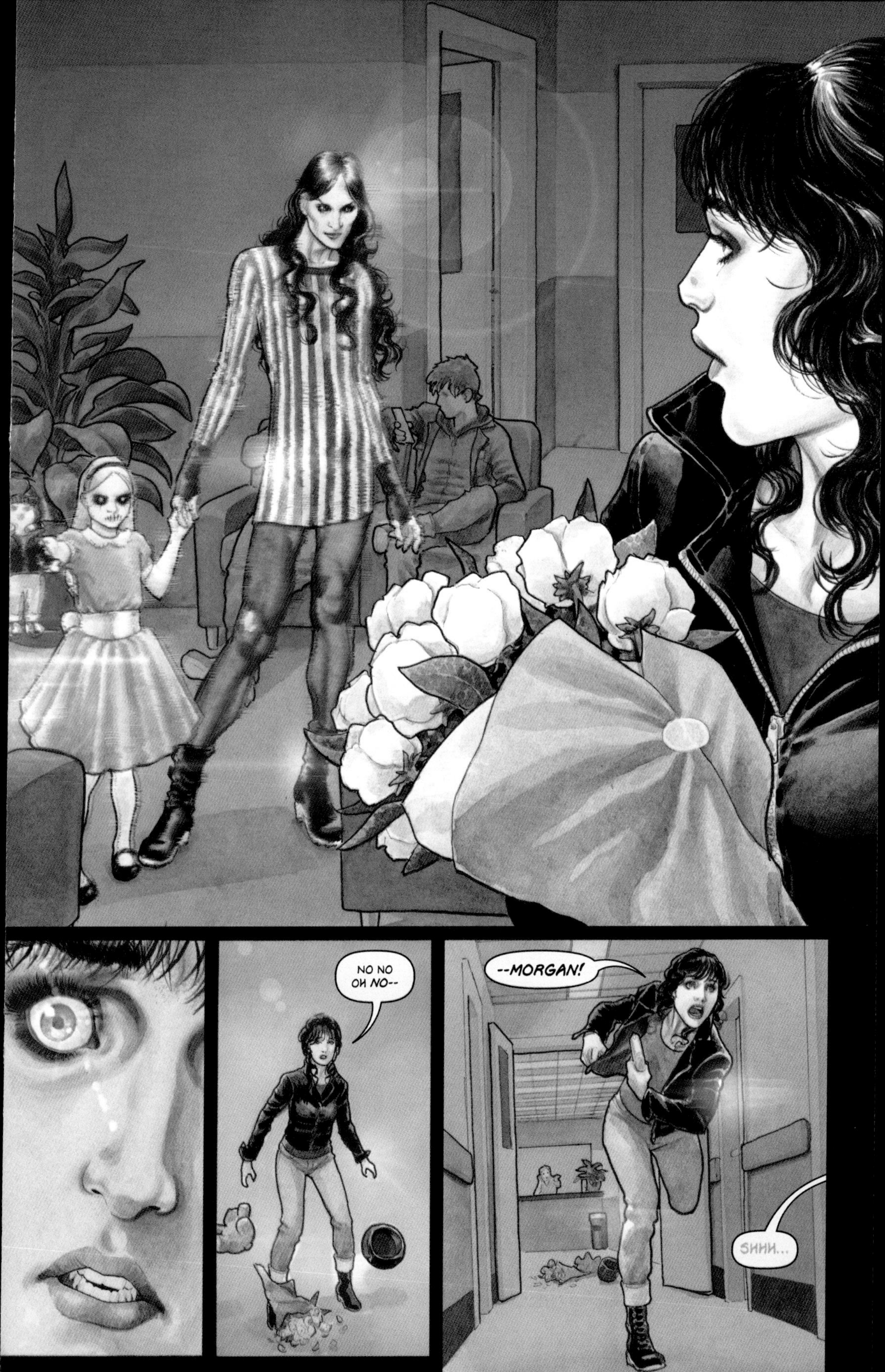
NO NO
OH NO--
--MORGAN!
SHHH...

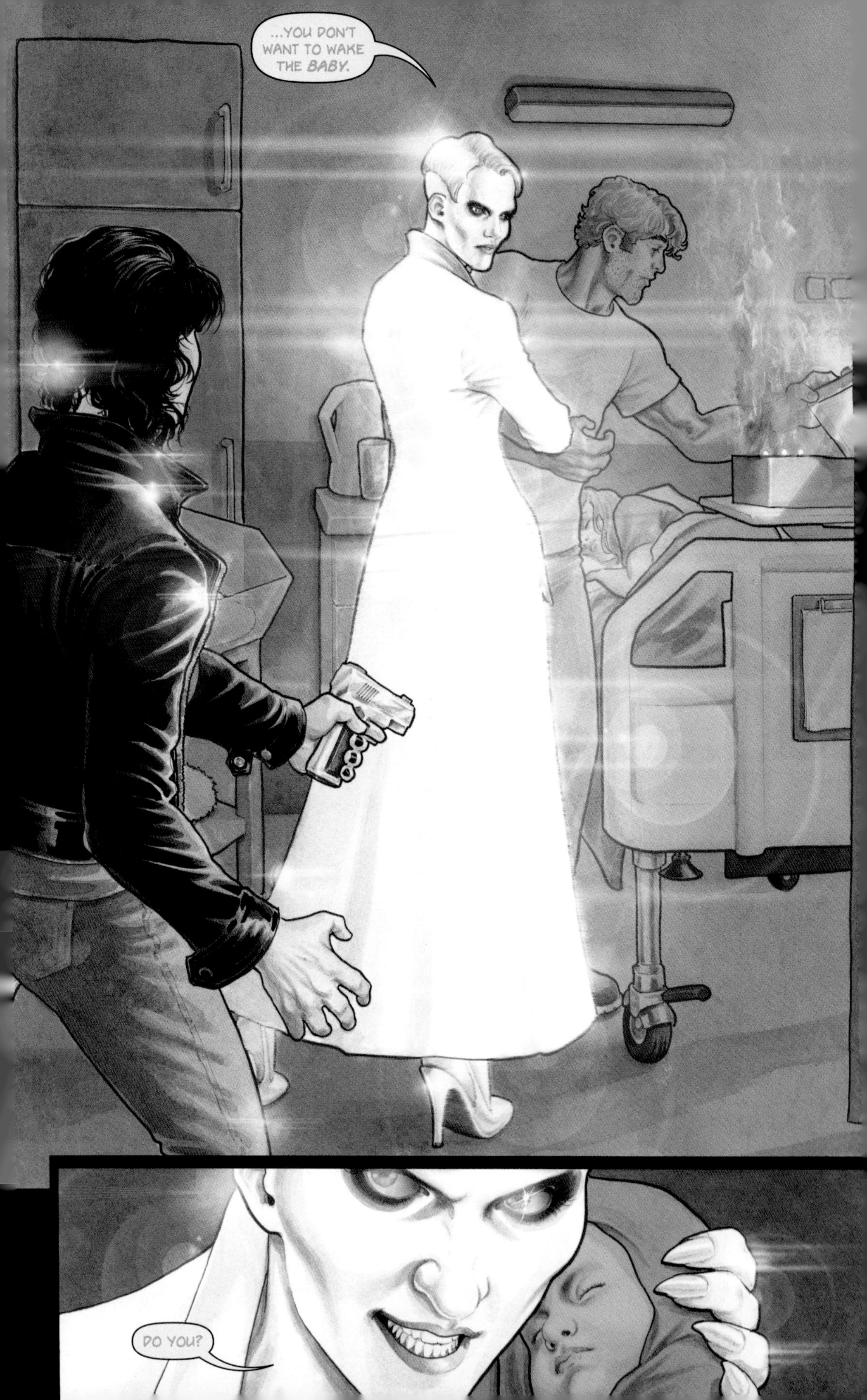
...YOU DON'T WANT TO WAKE THE *BABY*.
DO YOU?

...RTMENT   CITY OF PORTSMOU...

| ...ED | FIRST NAME | | MIDDLE NAME | RACE | SEX | AGE | RESIDENCE OF PERSON KILLED | | OFFENSE SERIAL NO |

| | | TITLE OR RELATIONSHIP | RACE | SEX | AGE | ADDRESS OF PERSON KILLED | | PHONE OF PERSON |

| ...ME) | | | | AFTER INVESTIGATION CHANGED TO |

| STREET AND NUMBER OR INTERSECTION | | DIVISION | PLATOON | BEAT | OFFICERS MAKING REPORT | I.D. NO. | NAME |

| ...OCCURRENCE | TIME OF DAY | DATE REPORTED | ...E REPORTED | REPORT RECEIVED BY | | RECEIVED — TIME — TYPED |

DESCRIPTION OF DEAD PERSON

| ...E | EYES | HAIR | BEARD | ...PLEXION | ...ARKS, ETC. | | CLOTHING |

| | NAME OF CORONER ...TT... TIME OF ARRIVAL | | | A.M. P.M. | ...CUTOR ATTENDING—TIME OF ARRIVAL |

| ...YSICIAN | | | PERSON WITH WHOM ACCUSE... ...ER OR ASSOCIATED |

| CIRCUMSTANCES OF OCCURENCE OF OFFENSE ...TS INVESTIGATION) | | USE ...DES OF THIS SHEET. |

| ...DY | ADDRESS | | WITNESS TAKEN INTO CUSTODY | | ADDRESS |

| ...OSSIBLE MOTIVES |

DESCRIPTION OF SUSPECT ...OR PERSONS WANTED

| | ALIAS | ADDRESS | | SEX | RACE | AGE | HEIGHT | WEIGHT | EYES | HAIR | COMPLEXION |

| ...CCUPATION | | DRESS AND OTHER MARKS | | | ...E FOR SUSPICION |

| | ALIAS | ADDRESS | | SEX | RACE | AGE | HEIGHT | WEIGHT | EYES | HAIR | COMPLEXION |

| ...CCUPATION | | DRESS AND OTHER MARKS | | | CAUSE FOR SUSPICION |

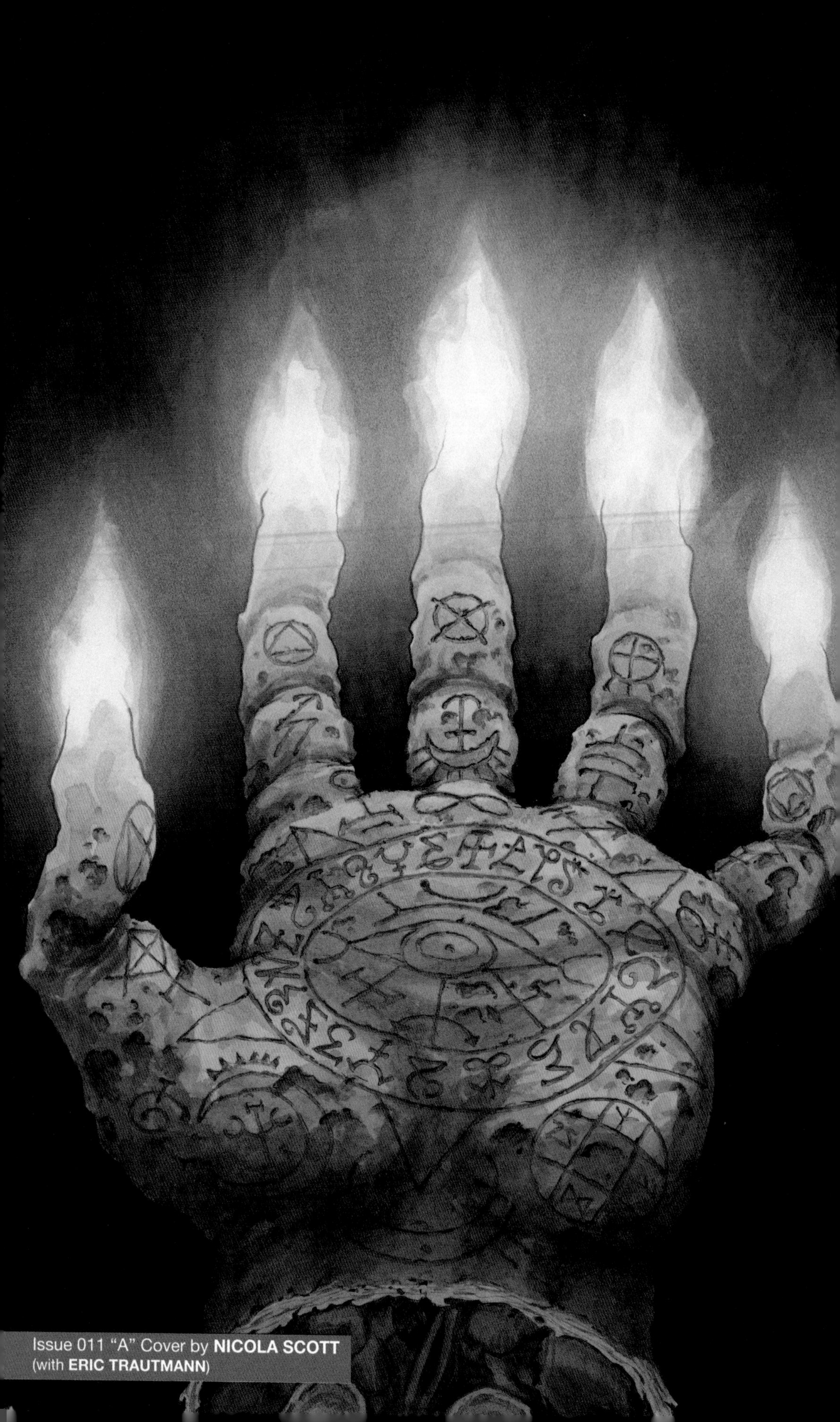

Issue 011 "A" Cover by **NICOLA SCOTT**
(with **ERIC TRAUTMANN**)

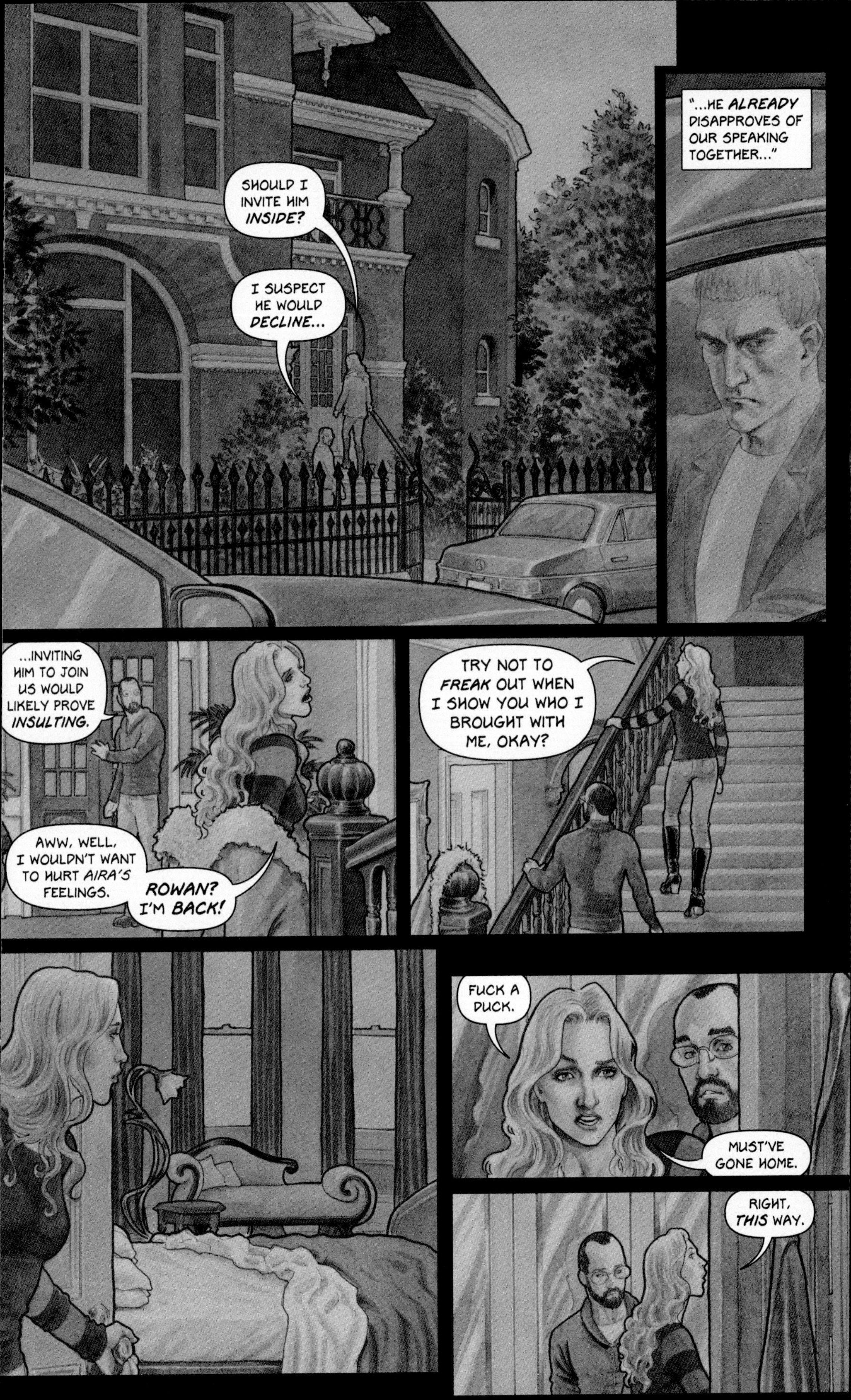
SHOULD I INVITE HIM INSIDE?
I SUSPECT HE WOULD DECLINE...
"...HE ALREADY DISAPPROVES OF OUR SPEAKING TOGETHER..."
...INVITING HIM TO JOIN US WOULD LIKELY PROVE INSULTING.
AWW, WELL, I WOULDN'T WANT TO HURT AIRA'S FEELINGS.
ROWAN? I'M BACK!
TRY NOT TO FREAK OUT WHEN I SHOW YOU WHO I BROUGHT WITH ME, OKAY?
FUCK A DUCK.
MUST'VE GONE HOME.
RIGHT, THIS WAY.

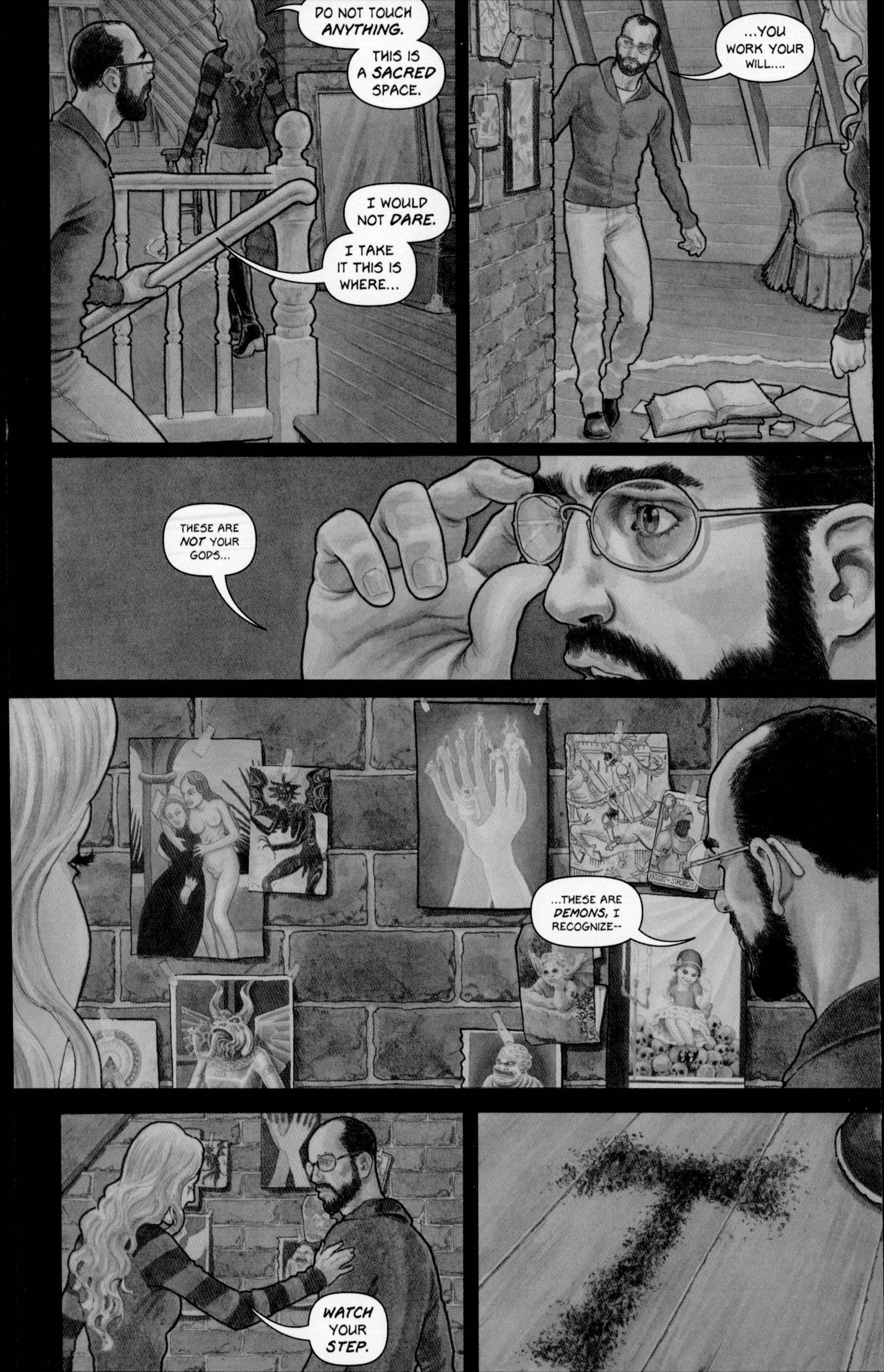
DO NOT TOUCH *ANYTHING.*
THIS IS A *SACRED* SPACE.
I WOULD NOT *DARE.*
I TAKE IT THIS IS WHERE...
...YOU WORK YOUR WILL....
THESE ARE *NOT* YOUR GODS...
KNIGHT of SWORDS
...THESE ARE *DEMONS,* I RECOGNIZE--
WATCH YOUR *STEP.*

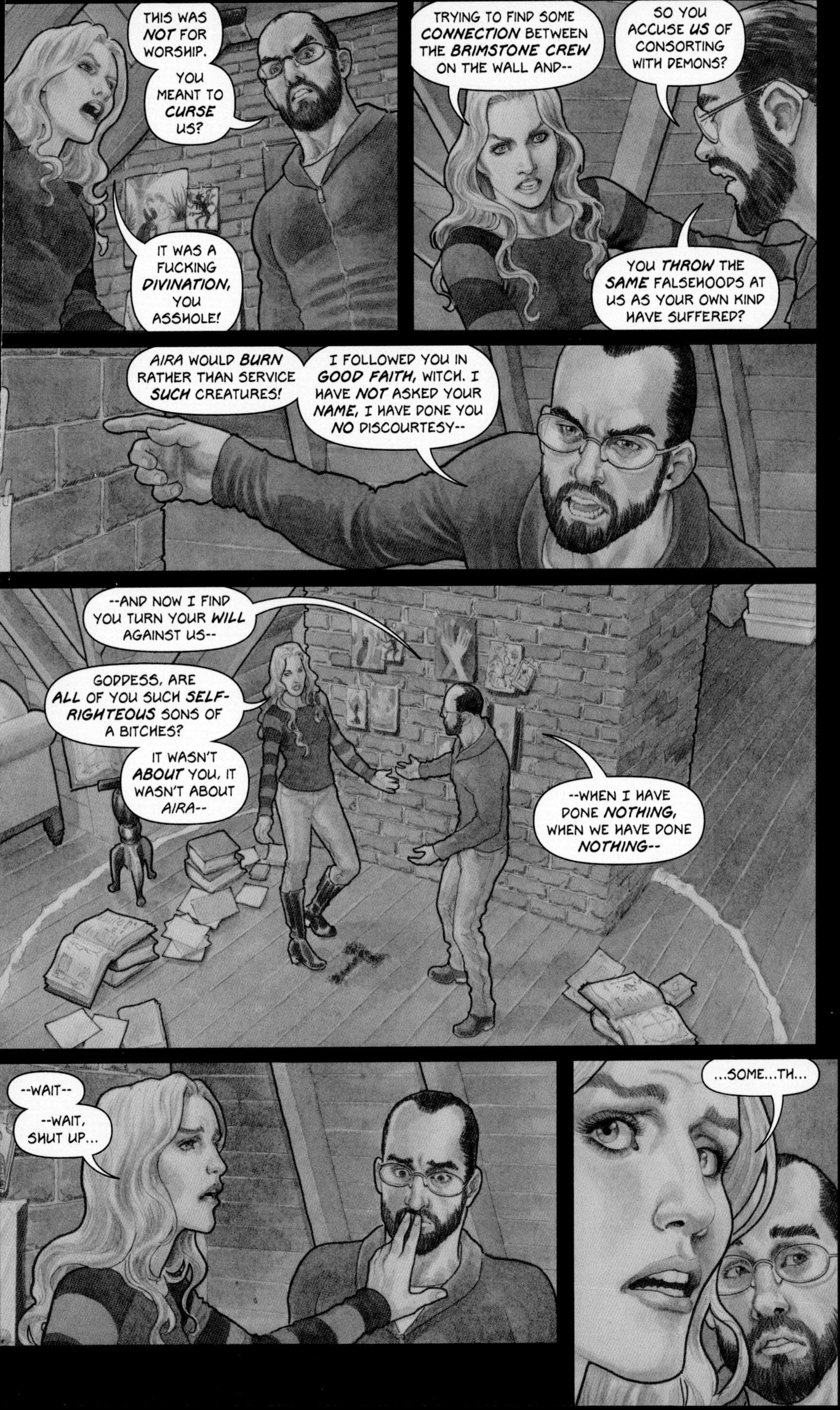
THIS WAS NOT FOR WORSHIP.
YOU MEANT TO CURSE US?
IT WAS A FUCKING DIVINATION, YOU ASSHOLE!
TRYING TO FIND SOME CONNECTION BETWEEN THE BRIMSTONE CREW ON THE WALL AND--
SO YOU ACCUSE US OF CONSORTING WITH DEMONS?
YOU THROW THE SAME FALSEHOODS AT US AS YOUR OWN KIND HAVE SUFFERED?
AIRA WOULD BURN RATHER THAN SERVICE SUCH CREATURES!
I FOLLOWED YOU IN GOOD FAITH, WITCH. I HAVE NOT ASKED YOUR NAME, I HAVE DONE YOU NO DISCOURTESY--
--AND NOW I FIND YOU TURN YOUR WILL AGAINST US--
GODDESS, ARE ALL OF YOU SUCH SELF-RIGHTEOUS SONS OF A BITCHES?
IT WASN'T ABOUT YOU, IT WASN'T ABOUT AIRA--
--WHEN I HAVE DONE NOTHING, WHEN WE HAVE DONE NOTHING--
--WAIT--
--WAIT, SHUT UP...
...SOME...TH...

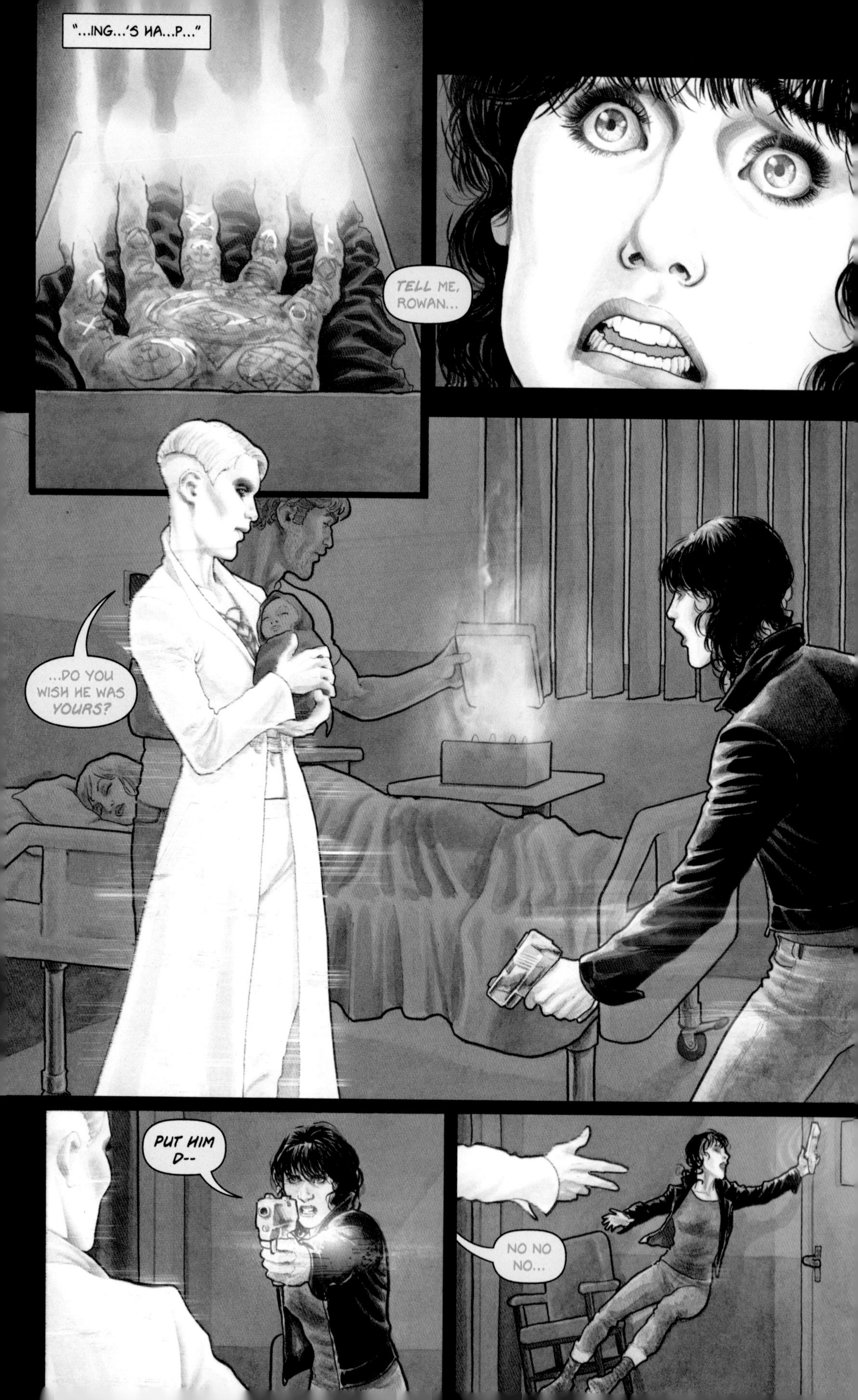
"...ING...'S HA...P..."
TELL ME, ROWAN...
...DO YOU WISH HE WAS YOURS?
PUT HIM D--
NO NO NO...

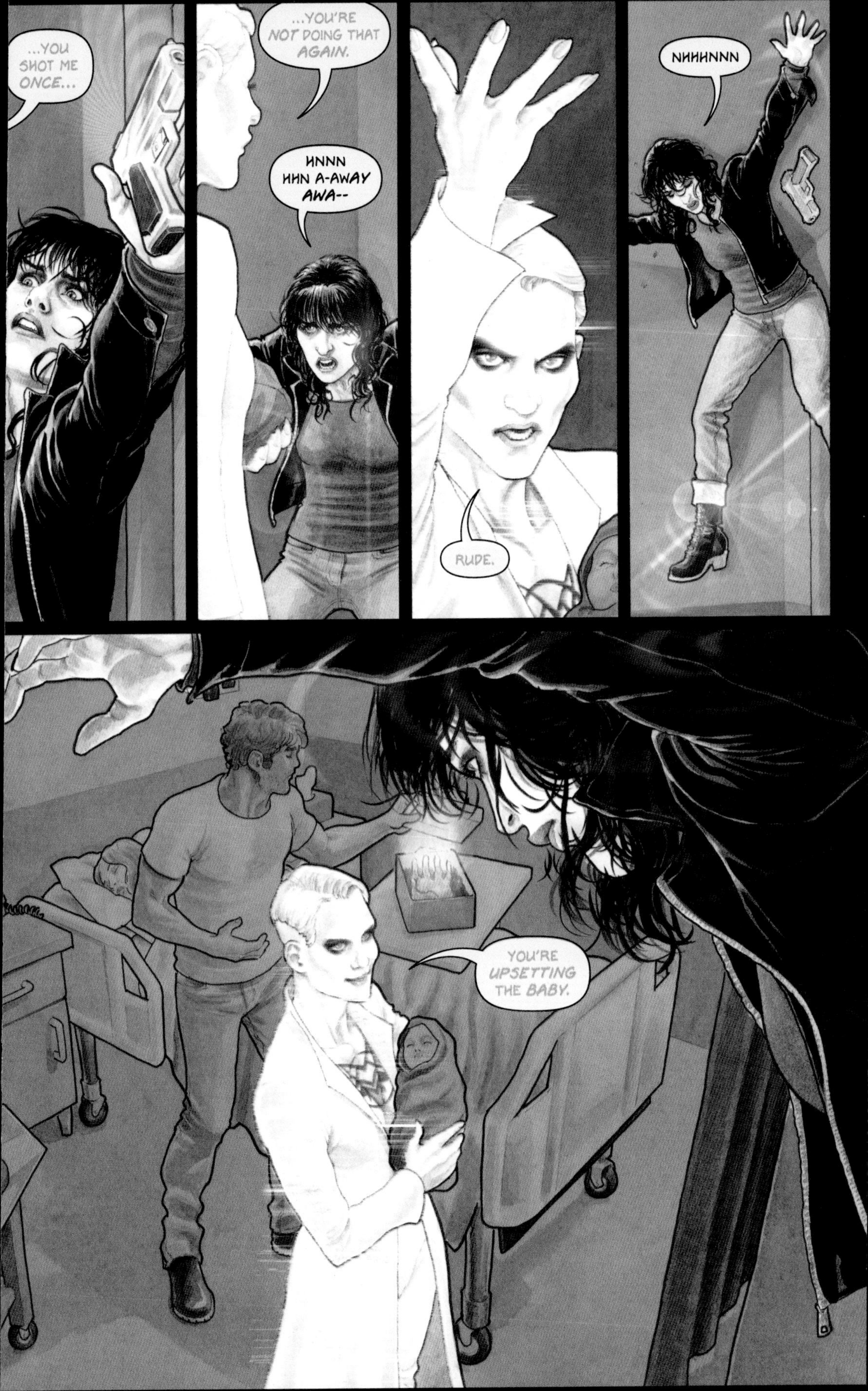
...YOU SHOT ME ONCE...
...YOU'RE NOT DOING THAT AGAIN.
HNNN HHN A-AWAY AWA--
RUDE.
NHHHNNN
YOU'RE UPSETTING THE BABY.

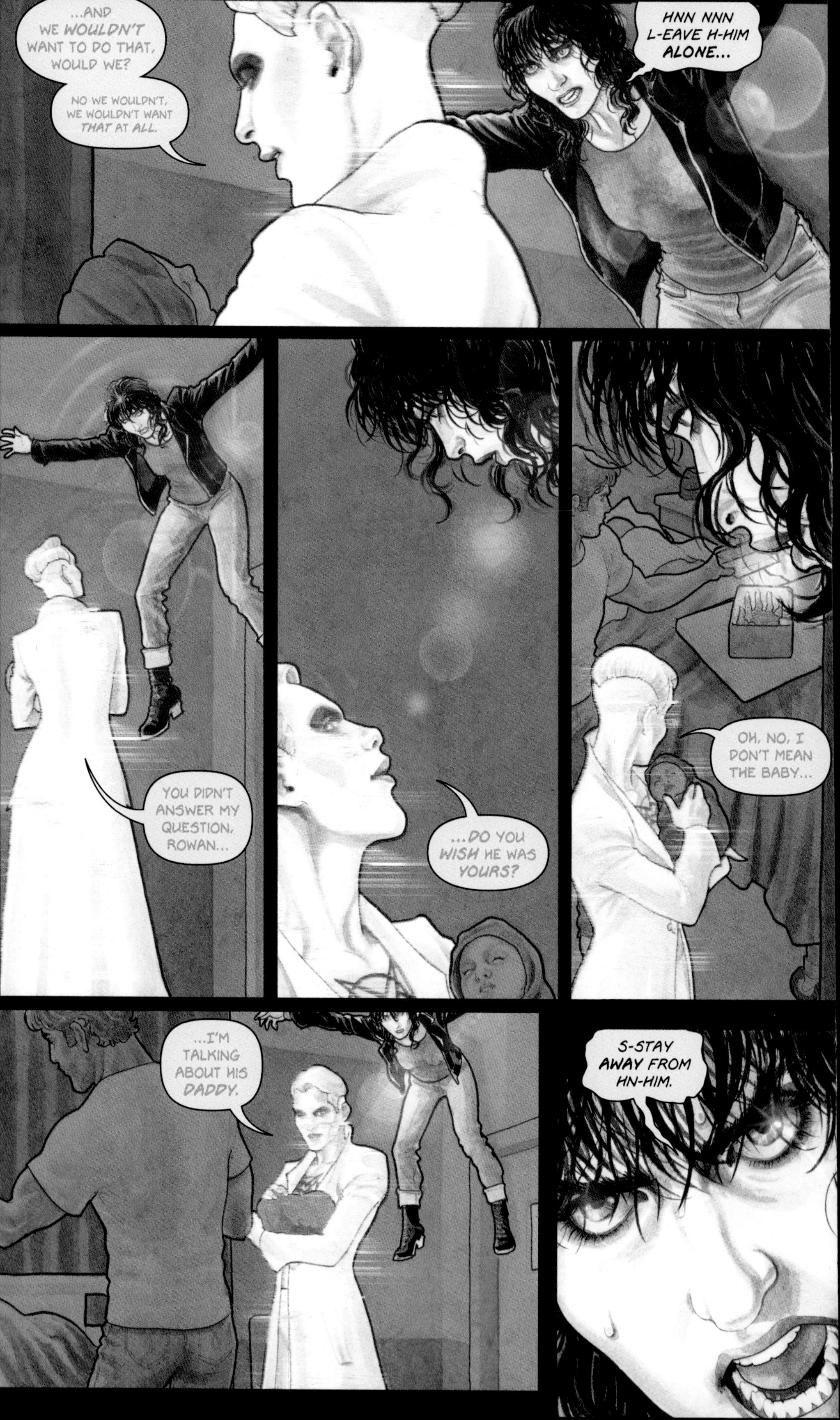
...AND WE WOULDN'T WANT TO DO THAT, WOULD WE?
NO WE WOULDN'T, WE WOULDN'T WANT THAT AT ALL.
HNN NNN L-EAVE H-HIM ALONE...
YOU DIDN'T ANSWER MY QUESTION, ROWAN...
...DO YOU WISH HE WAS YOURS?
OH, NO, I DON'T MEAN THE BABY...
...I'M TALKING ABOUT HIS DADDY.
S-STAY AWAY FROM HN-HIM.

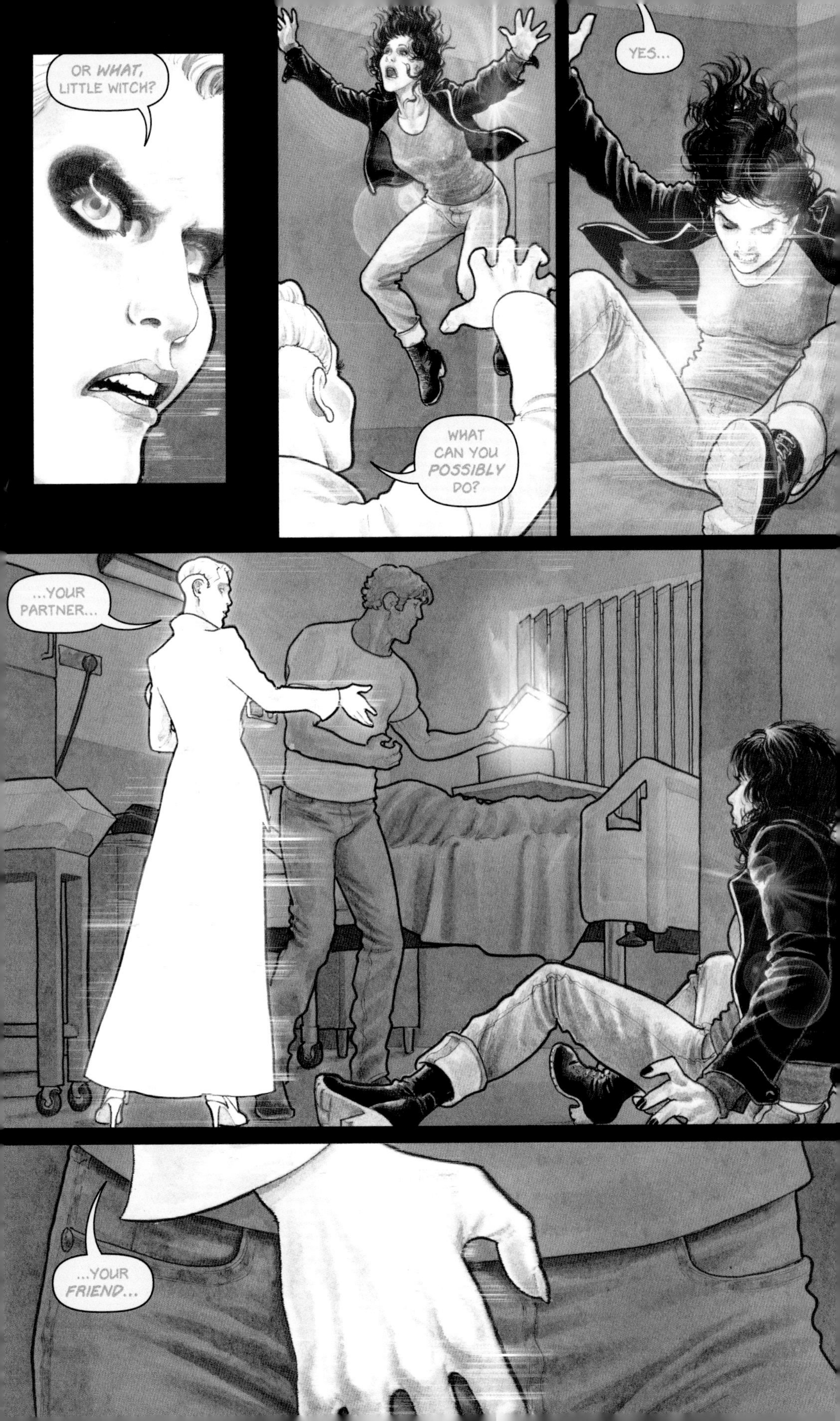
OR *WHAT*, LITTLE WITCH?
WHAT CAN YOU *POSSIBLY* DO?
YES...
...YOUR PARTNER...
...YOUR *FRIEND*...

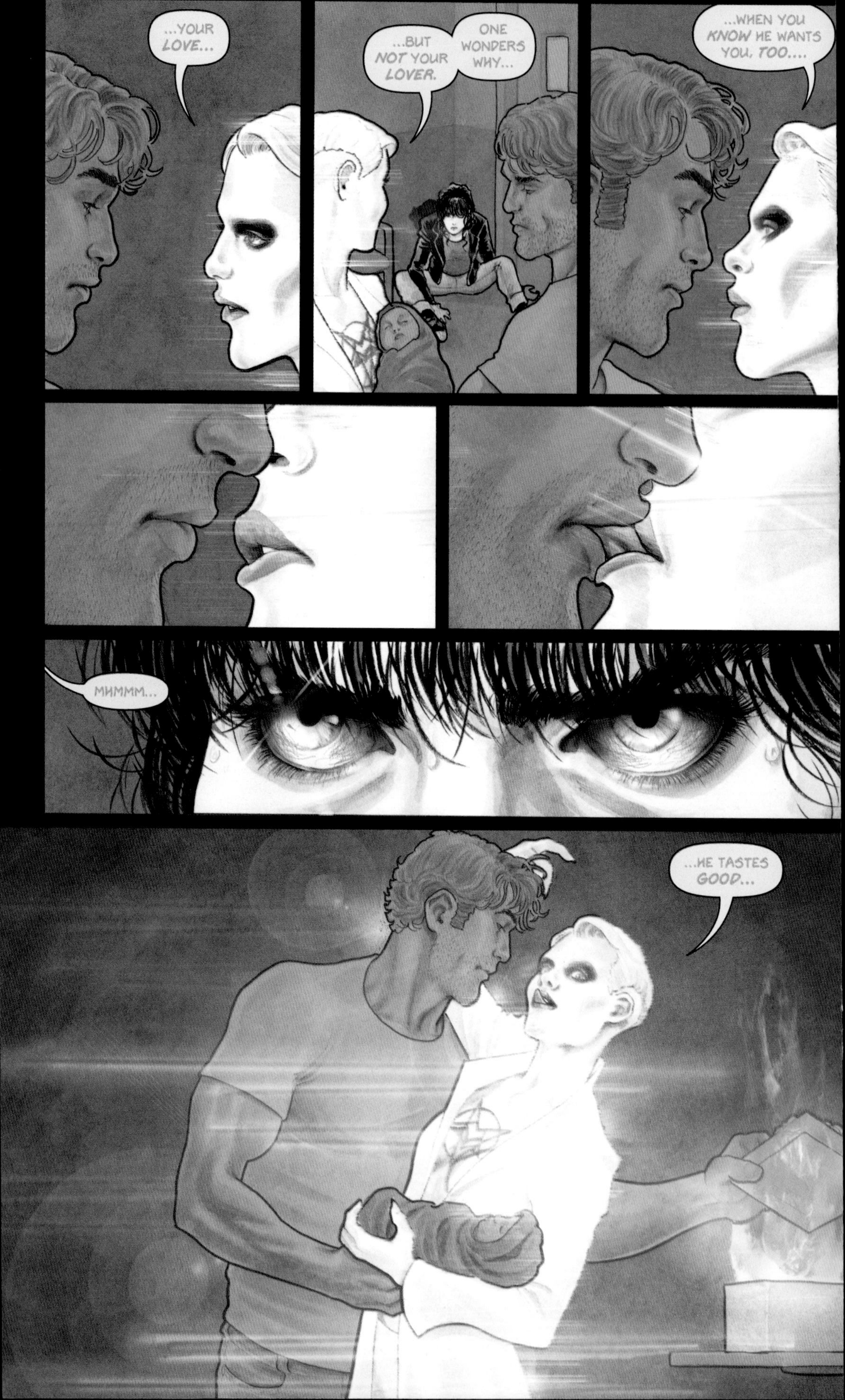
...YOUR LOVE...
...BUT NOT YOUR LOVER.
ONE WONDERS WHY...
...WHEN YOU KNOW HE WANTS YOU, TOO....
MHMMM...
...HE TASTES GOOD...

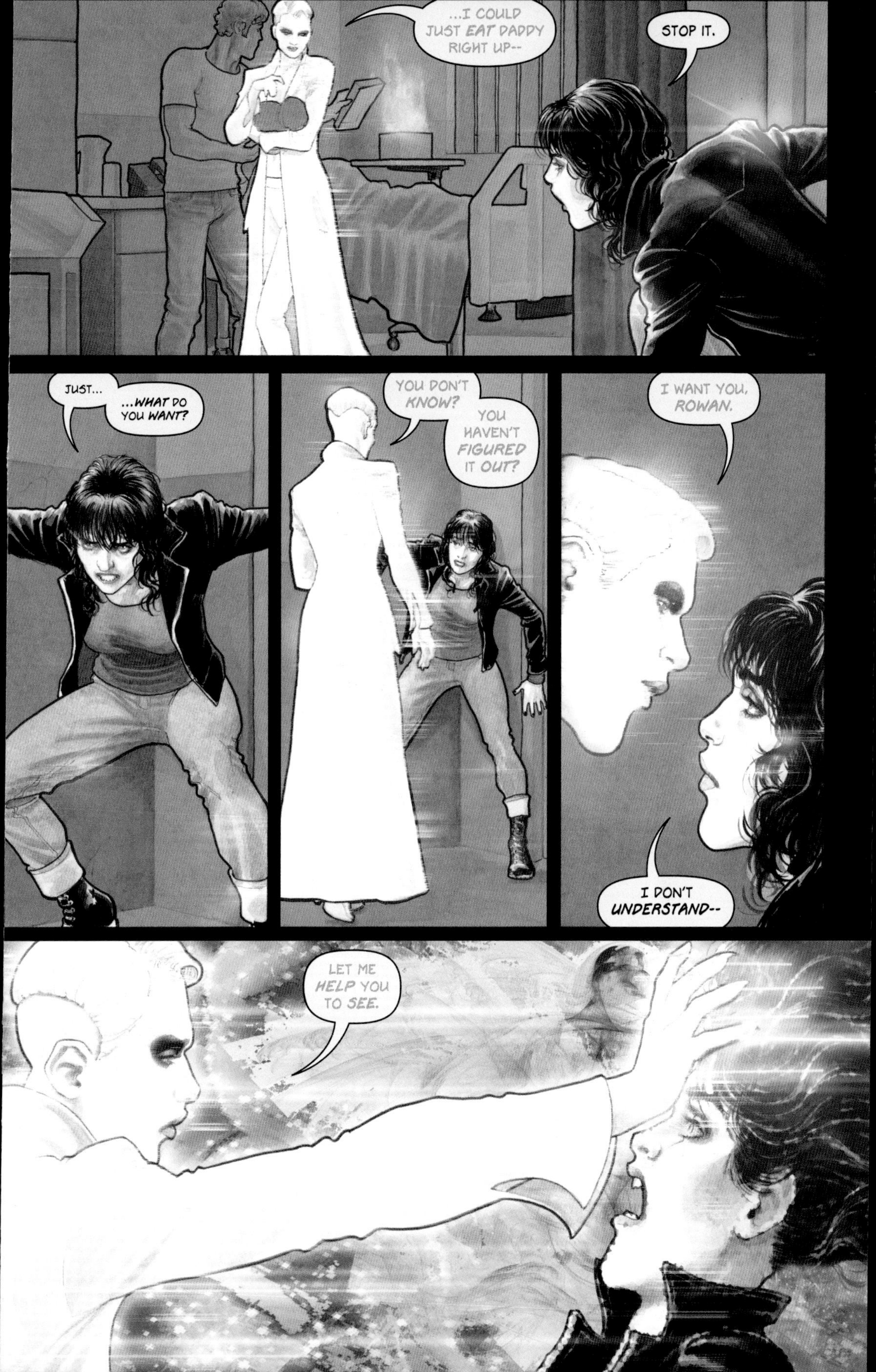
...I COULD JUST EAT DADDY RIGHT UP--
STOP IT.
JUST...
...WHAT DO YOU WANT?
YOU DON'T KNOW?
YOU HAVEN'T FIGURED IT OUT?
I WANT YOU, ROWAN.
I DON'T UNDERSTAND--
LET ME HELP YOU TO SEE.

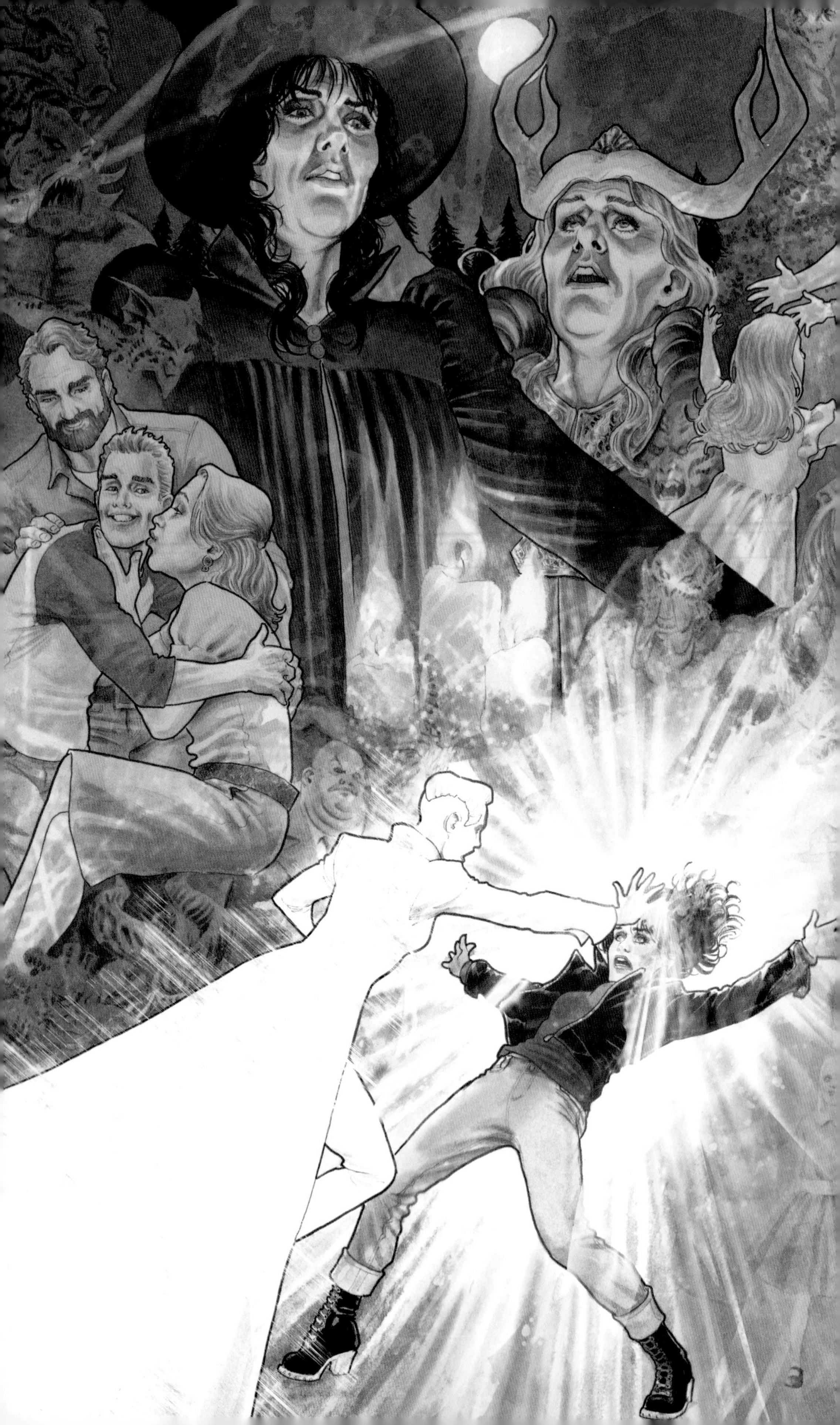

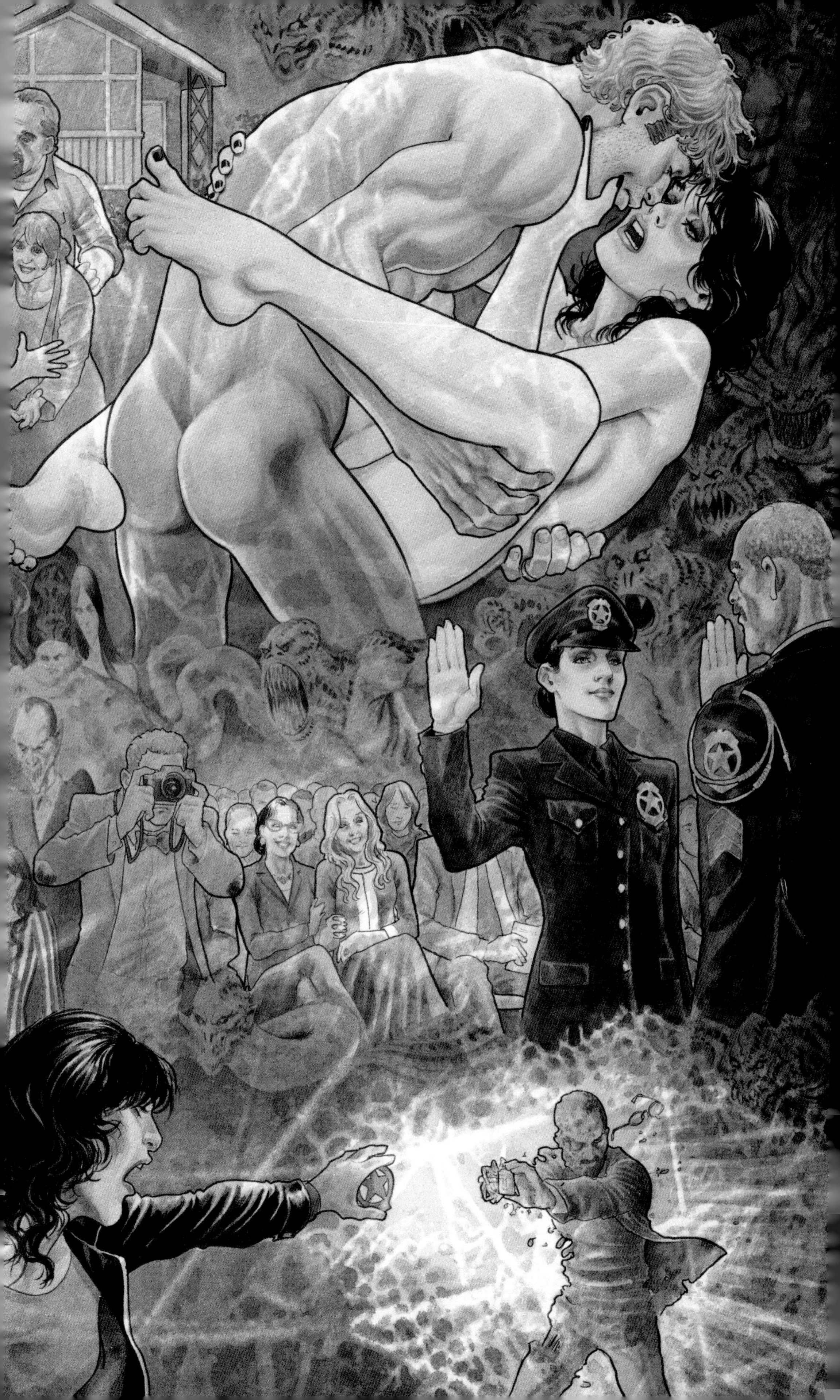

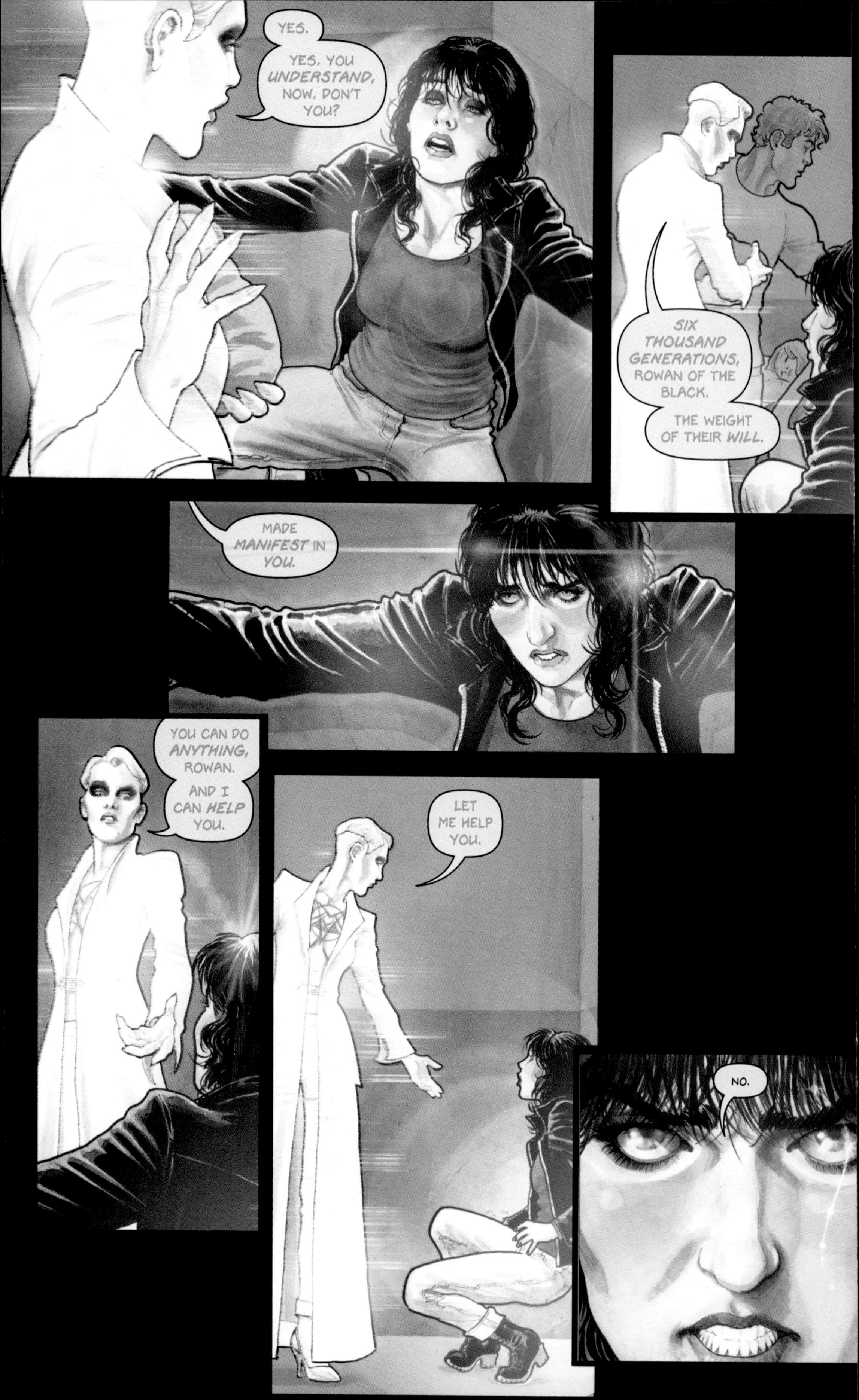
YES.
YES, YOU UNDERSTAND, NOW, DON'T YOU?
SIX THOUSAND GENERATIONS, ROWAN OF THE BLACK.
THE WEIGHT OF THEIR WILL.
MADE MANIFEST IN YOU.
YOU CAN DO ANYTHING, ROWAN.
AND I CAN HELP YOU.
LET ME HELP YOU.
NO.

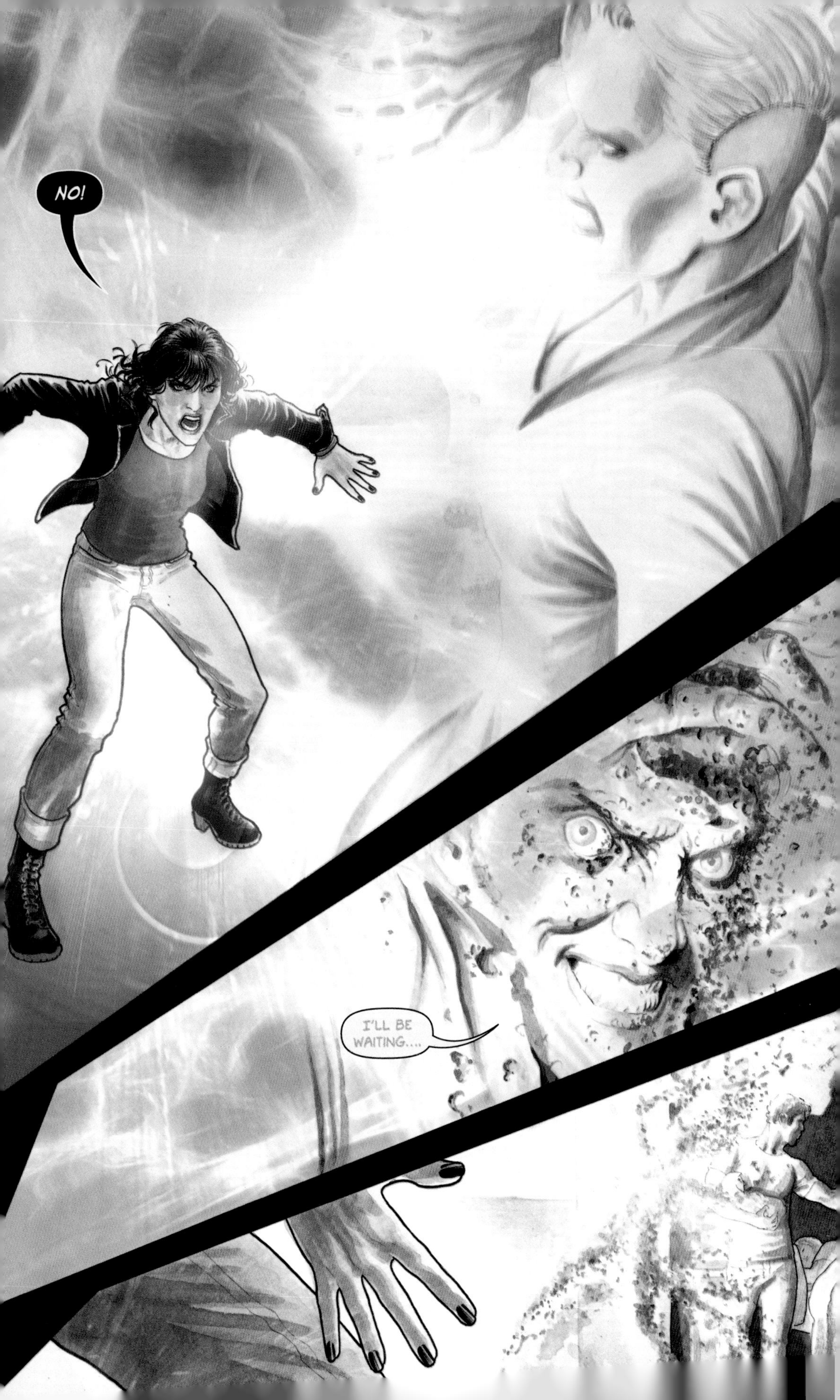
NO!
I'LL BE WAITING....

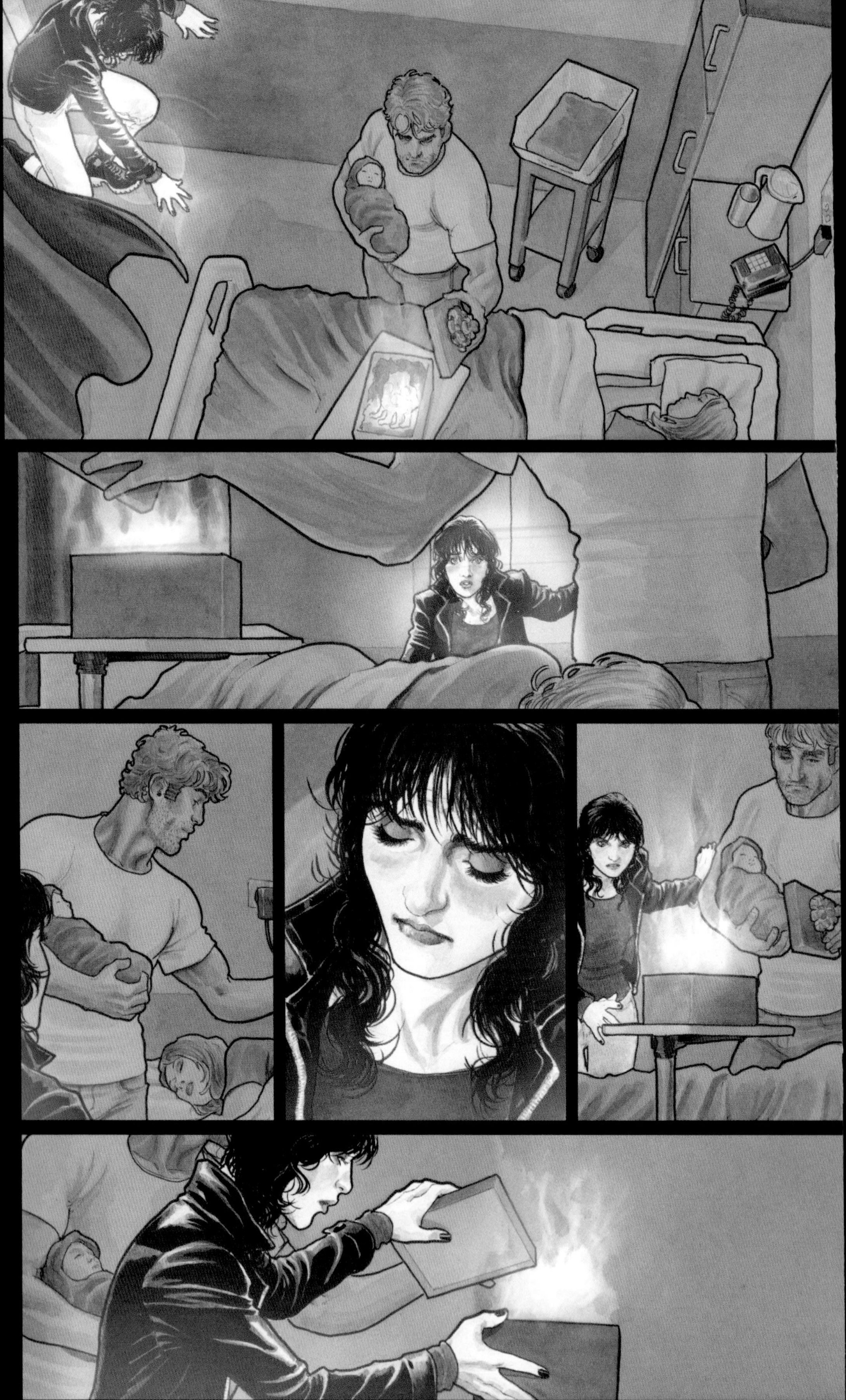

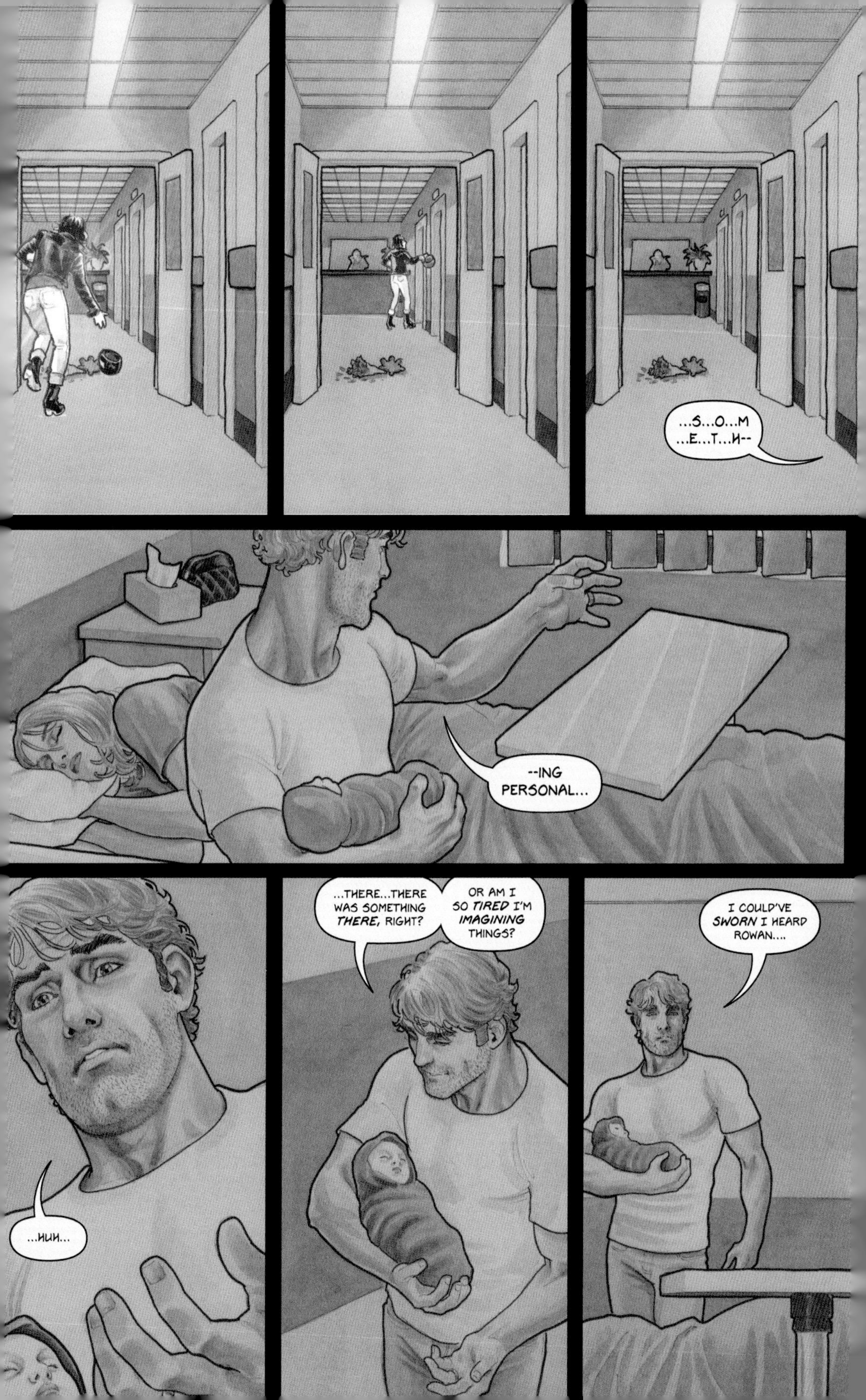
...S...O...M
...E...T...H--
--ING
PERSONAL...
...HUH...
...THERE...THERE WAS SOMETHING THERE, RIGHT?
OR AM I SO TIRED I'M IMAGINING THINGS?
I COULD'VE SWORN I HEARD ROWAN....

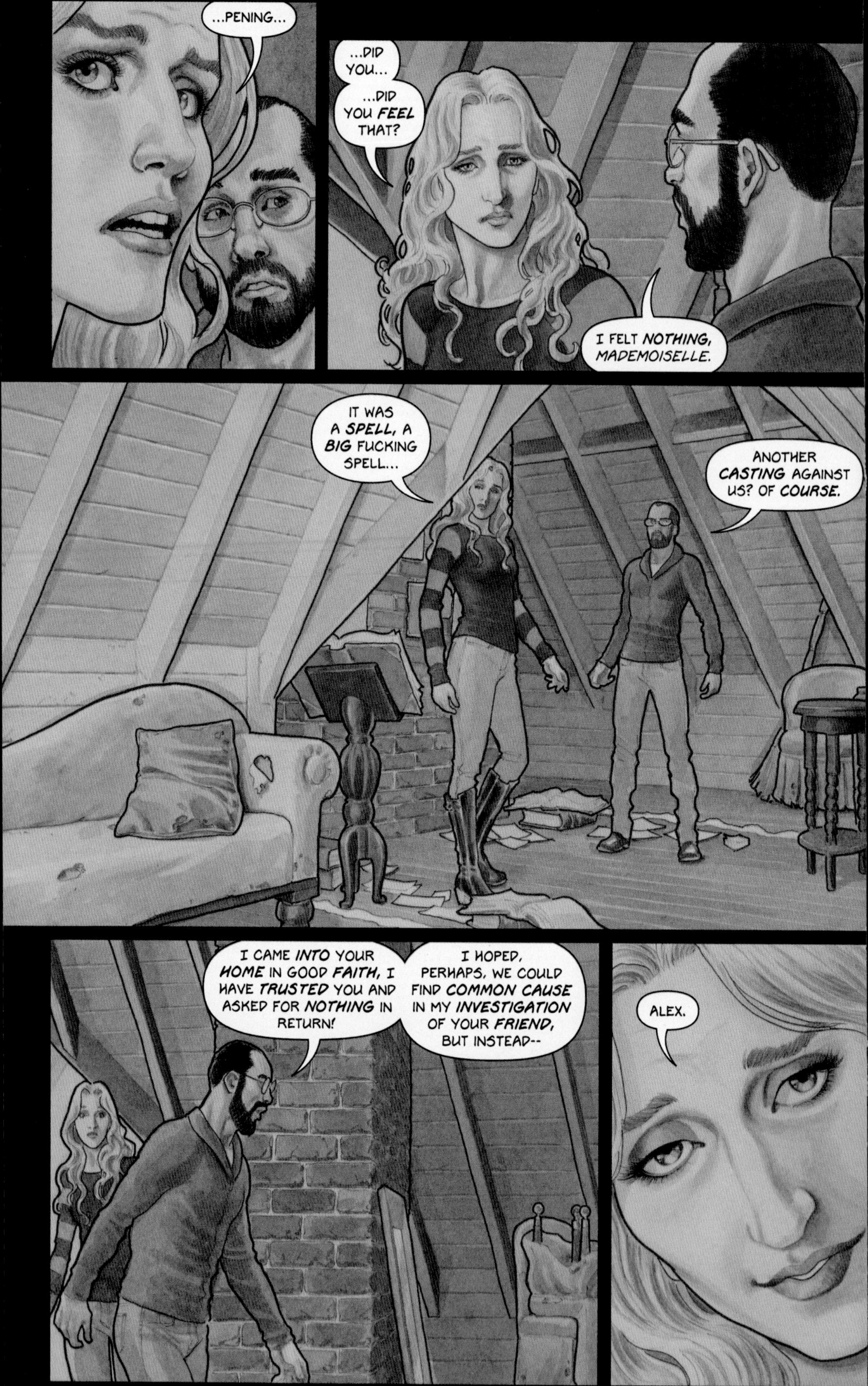
...PENING...
...DID YOU...
...DID YOU FEEL THAT?
I FELT NOTHING, MADEMOISELLE.
IT WAS A SPELL, A BIG FUCKING SPELL...
ANOTHER CASTING AGAINST US? OF COURSE.
I CAME INTO YOUR HOME IN GOOD FAITH, I HAVE TRUSTED YOU AND ASKED FOR NOTHING IN RETURN!
I HOPED, PERHAPS, WE COULD FIND COMMON CAUSE IN MY INVESTIGATION OF YOUR FRIEND, BUT INSTEAD--
ALEX.

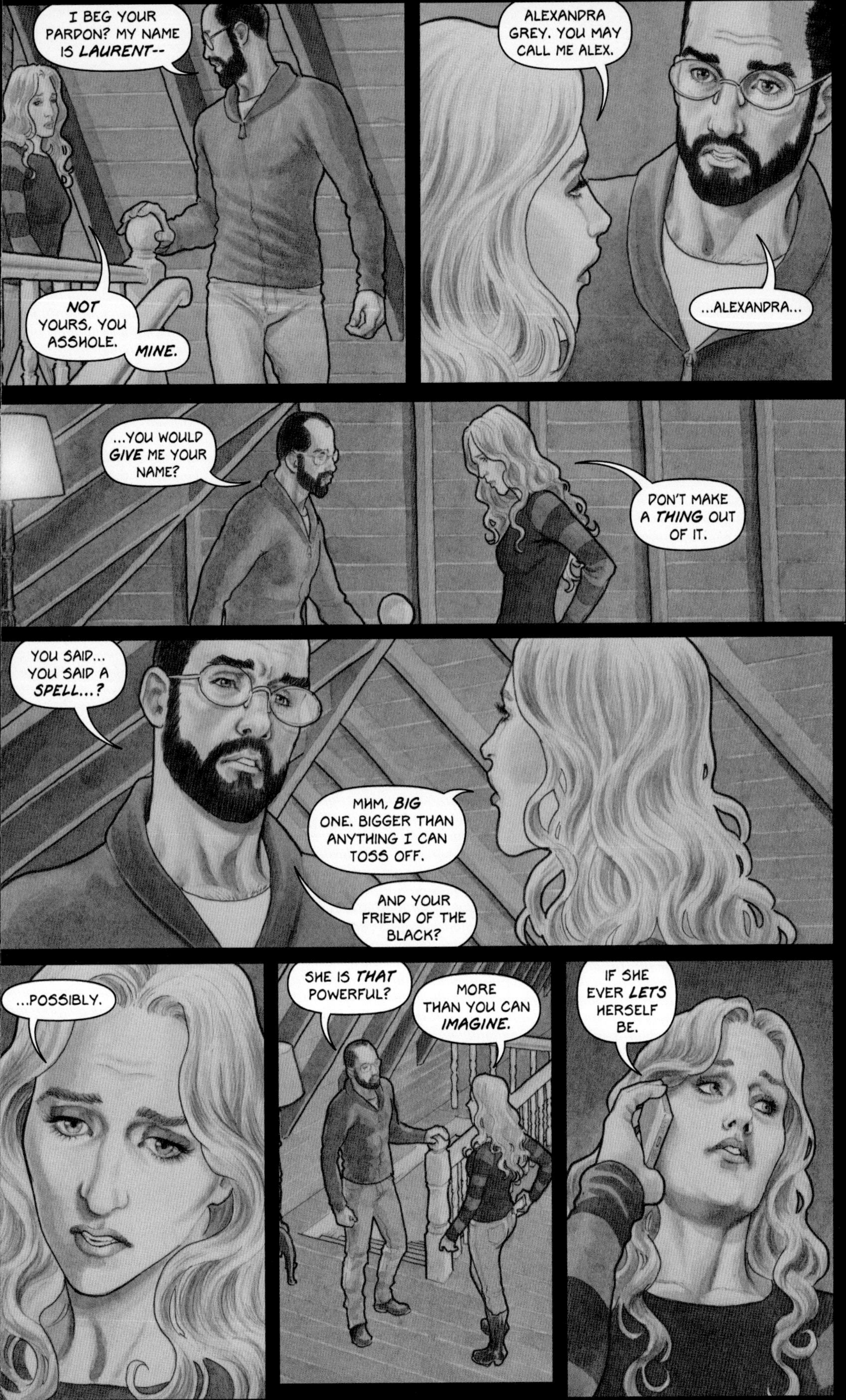
I BEG YOUR PARDON? MY NAME IS *LAURENT*--
NOT YOURS, YOU ASSHOLE. *MINE.*
ALEXANDRA GREY. YOU MAY CALL ME ALEX.
...ALEXANDRA...
...YOU WOULD *GIVE* ME YOUR NAME?
DON'T MAKE A *THING* OUT OF IT.
YOU SAID... YOU SAID A *SPELL...?*
MHM, *BIG* ONE. BIGGER THAN ANYTHING I CAN TOSS OFF.
AND YOUR FRIEND OF THE BLACK?
...POSSIBLY.
SHE IS *THAT* POWERFUL?
MORE THAN YOU CAN *IMAGINE.*
IF SHE EVER *LETS* HERSELF BE.

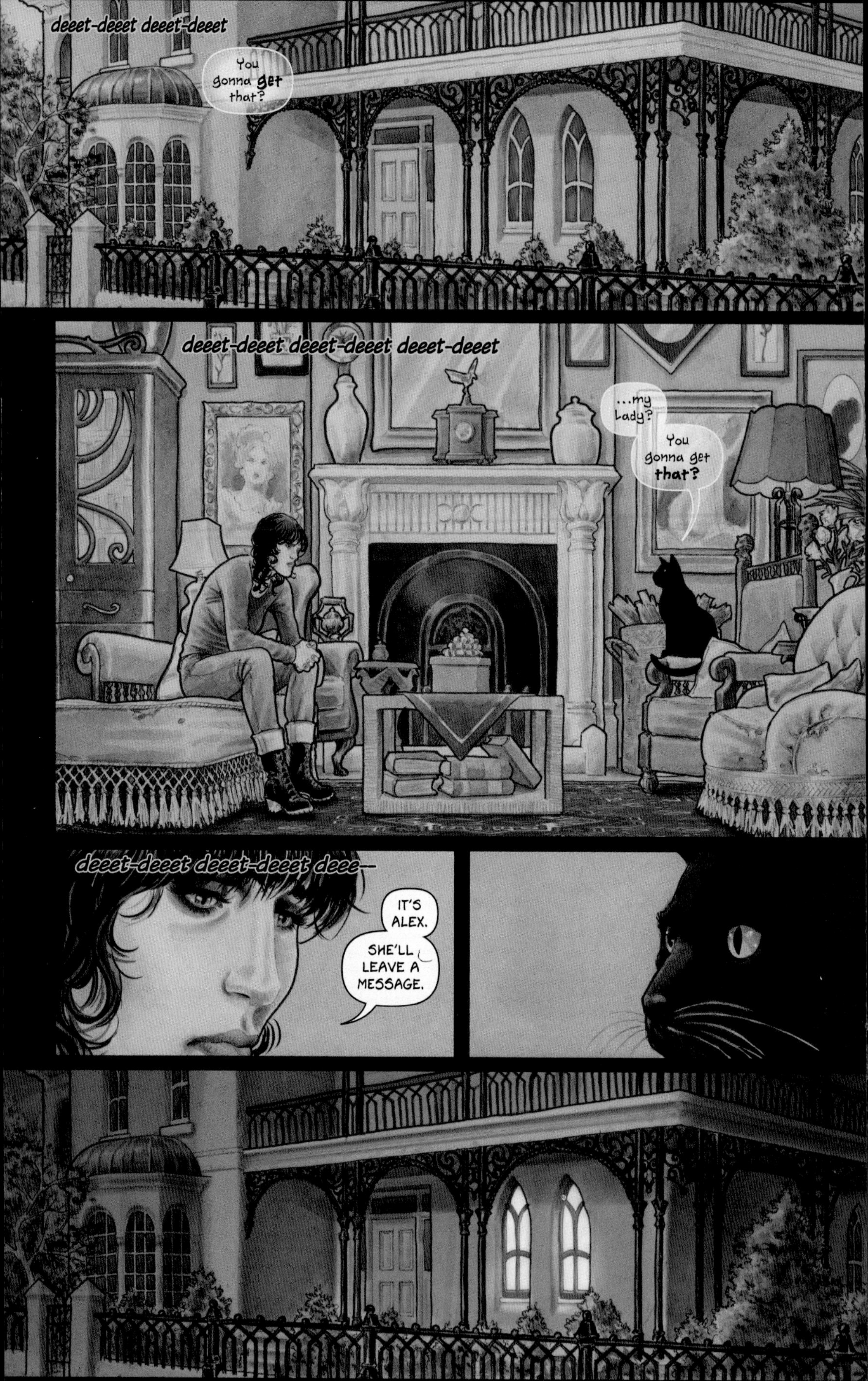
deeet-deeet deeet-deeet
You gonna get that?
deeet-deeet deeet-deeet deeet-deeet
...my Lady?
You gonna get that?
deeet-deeet deeet-deeet deee--
IT'S ALEX.
SHE'LL LEAVE A MESSAGE.

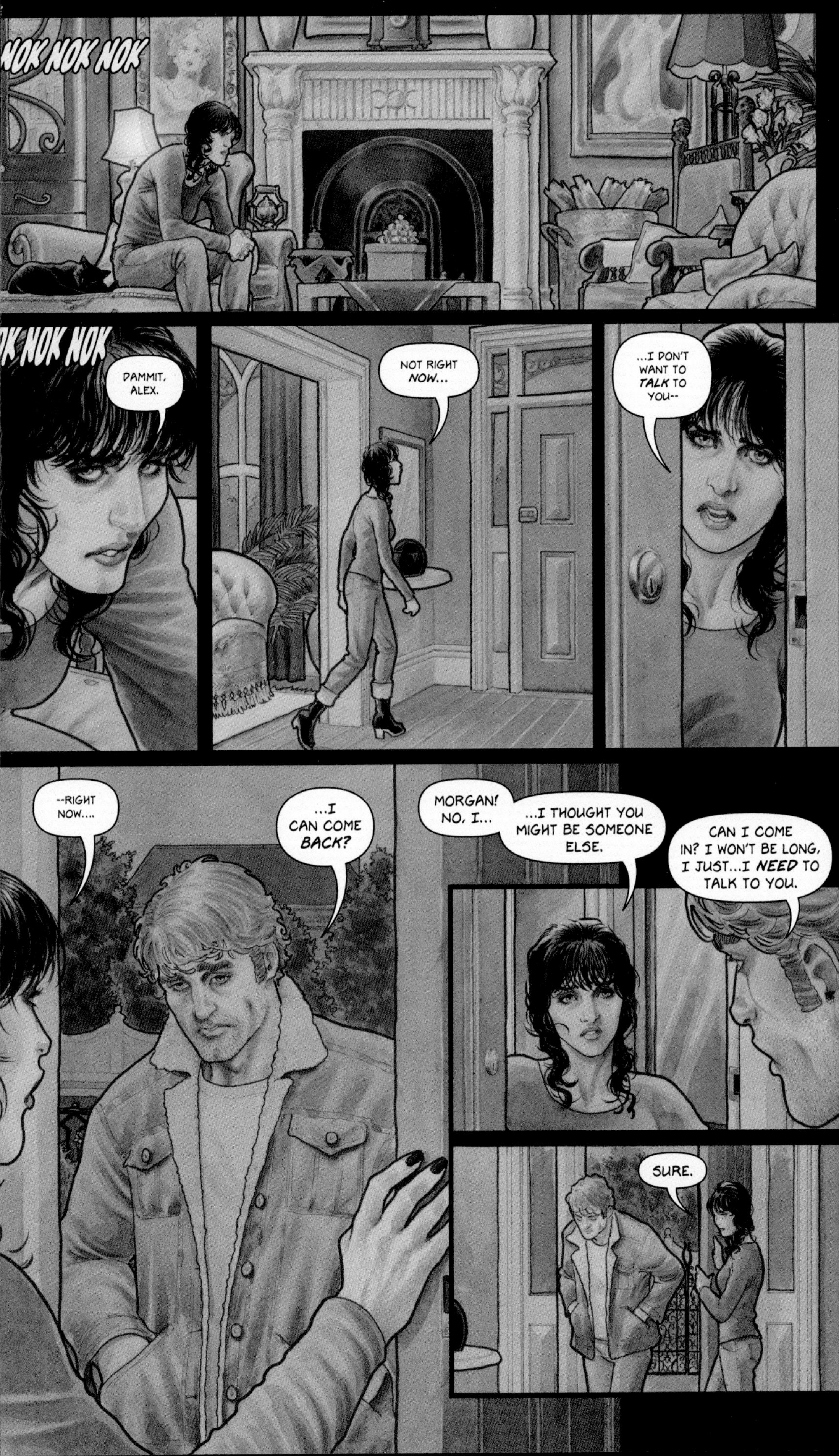
NOK NOK NOK
NOK NOK NOK
DAMMIT, ALEX.
NOT RIGHT NOW...
...I DON'T WANT TO TALK TO YOU--
--RIGHT NOW....
...I CAN COME BACK?
MORGAN! NO, I...
...I THOUGHT YOU MIGHT BE SOMEONE ELSE.
CAN I COME IN? I WON'T BE LONG, I JUST...I NEED TO TALK TO YOU.
SURE.

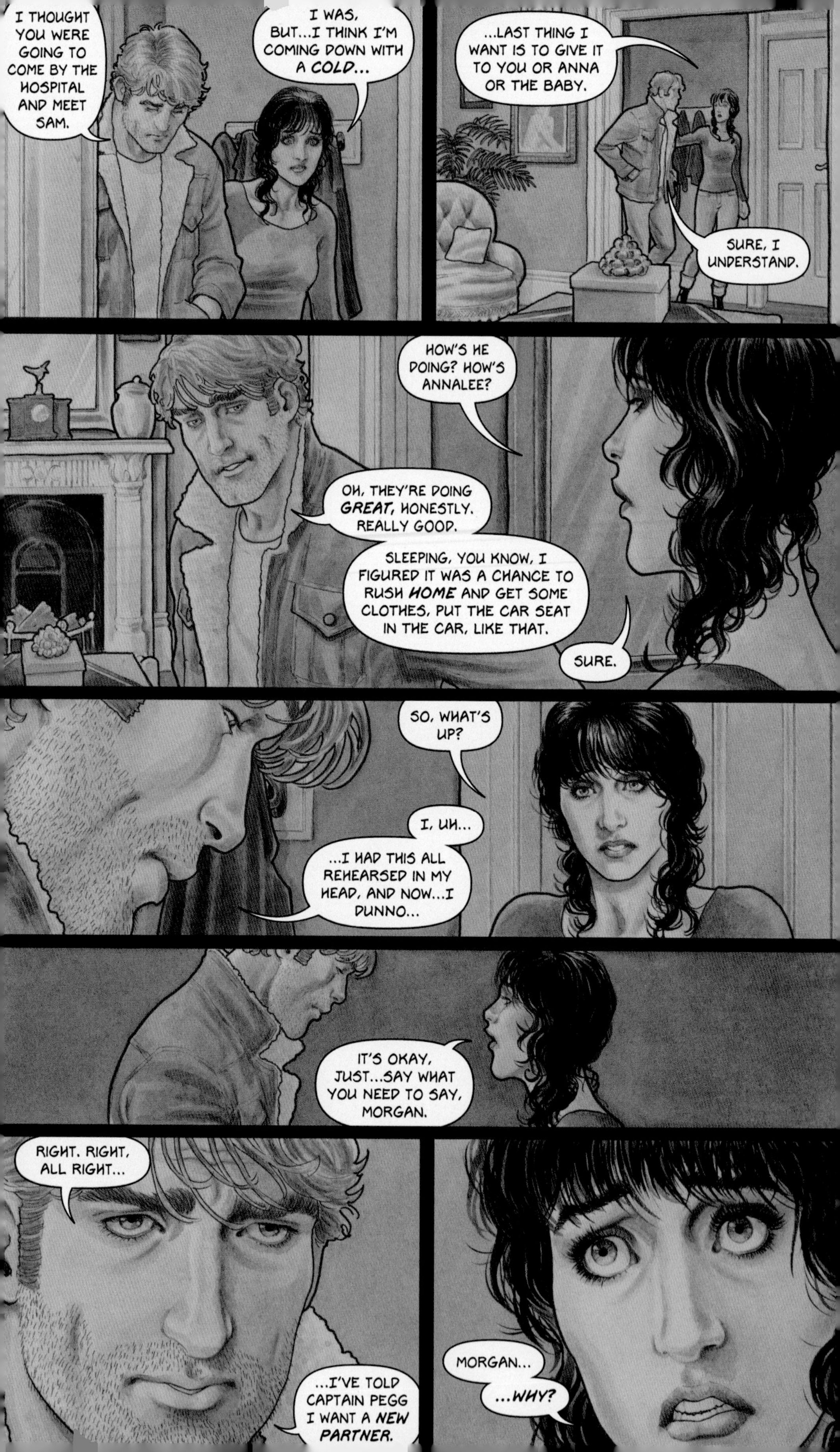
I THOUGHT YOU WERE GOING TO COME BY THE HOSPITAL AND MEET SAM.
I WAS, BUT...I THINK I'M COMING DOWN WITH A *COLD*...
...LAST THING I WANT IS TO GIVE IT TO YOU OR ANNA OR THE BABY.
SURE, I UNDERSTAND.
HOW'S HE DOING? HOW'S ANNALEE?
OH, THEY'RE DOING *GREAT,* HONESTLY. REALLY GOOD.
SLEEPING, YOU KNOW, I FIGURED IT WAS A CHANCE TO RUSH *HOME* AND GET SOME CLOTHES, PUT THE CAR SEAT IN THE CAR, LIKE THAT.
SURE.
SO, WHAT'S UP?
I, UH...
...I HAD THIS ALL REHEARSED IN MY HEAD, AND NOW...I DUNNO...
IT'S OKAY, JUST...SAY WHAT YOU NEED TO SAY, MORGAN.
RIGHT. RIGHT, ALL RIGHT...
...I'VE TOLD CAPTAIN PEGG I WANT A *NEW PARTNER.*
MORGAN...
...*WHY?*

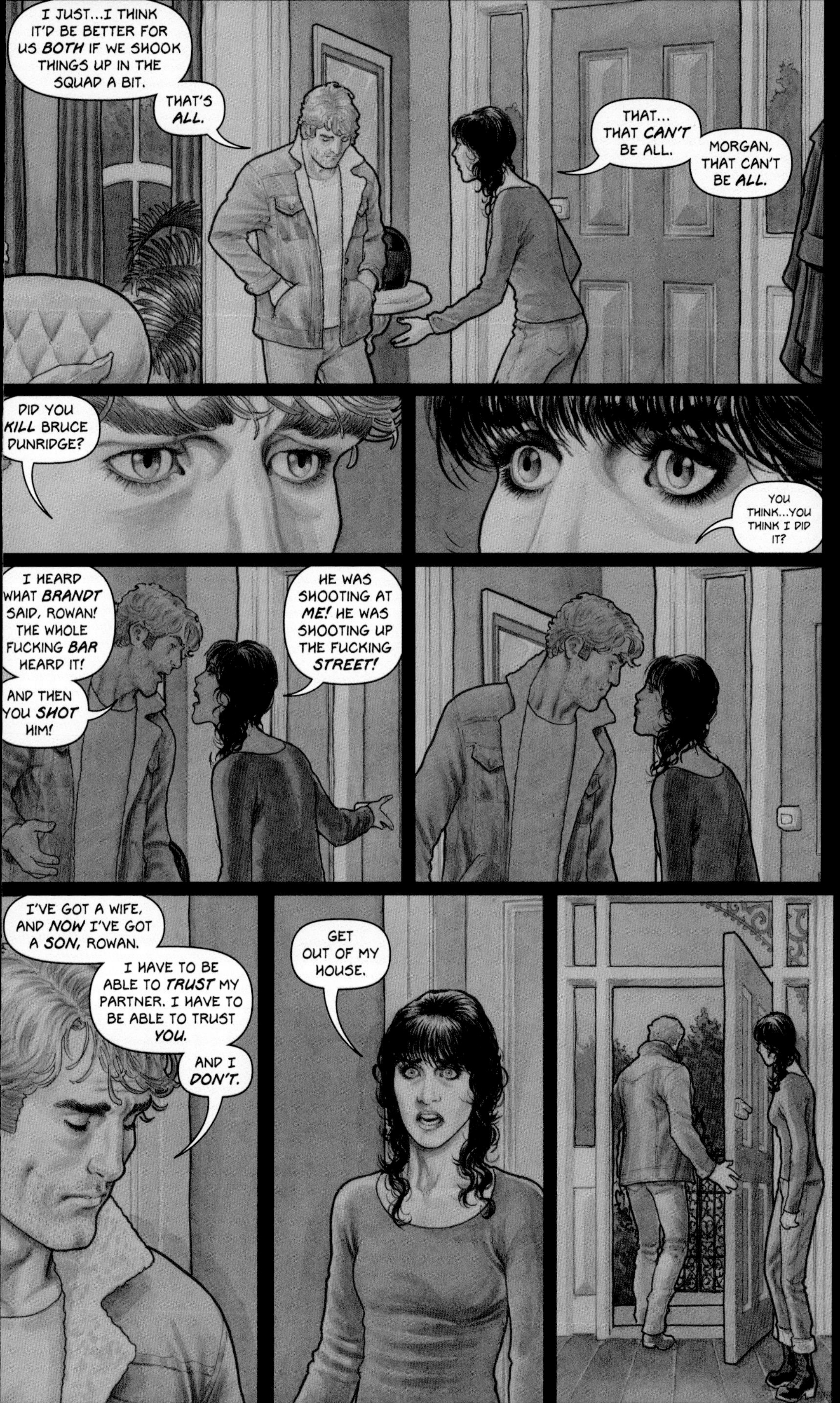
I JUST...I THINK IT'D BE BETTER FOR US BOTH IF WE SHOOK THINGS UP IN THE SQUAD A BIT.
THAT'S ALL.
THAT... THAT CAN'T BE ALL.
MORGAN, THAT CAN'T BE ALL.
DID YOU KILL BRUCE DUNRIDGE?
YOU THINK...YOU THINK I DID IT?
I HEARD WHAT BRANDT SAID, ROWAN! THE WHOLE FUCKING BAR HEARD IT!
AND THEN YOU SHOT HIM!
HE WAS SHOOTING AT ME! HE WAS SHOOTING UP THE FUCKING STREET!
I'VE GOT A WIFE, AND NOW I'VE GOT A SON, ROWAN.
I HAVE TO BE ABLE TO TRUST MY PARTNER. I HAVE TO BE ABLE TO TRUST YOU.
AND I DON'T.
GET OUT OF MY HOUSE.

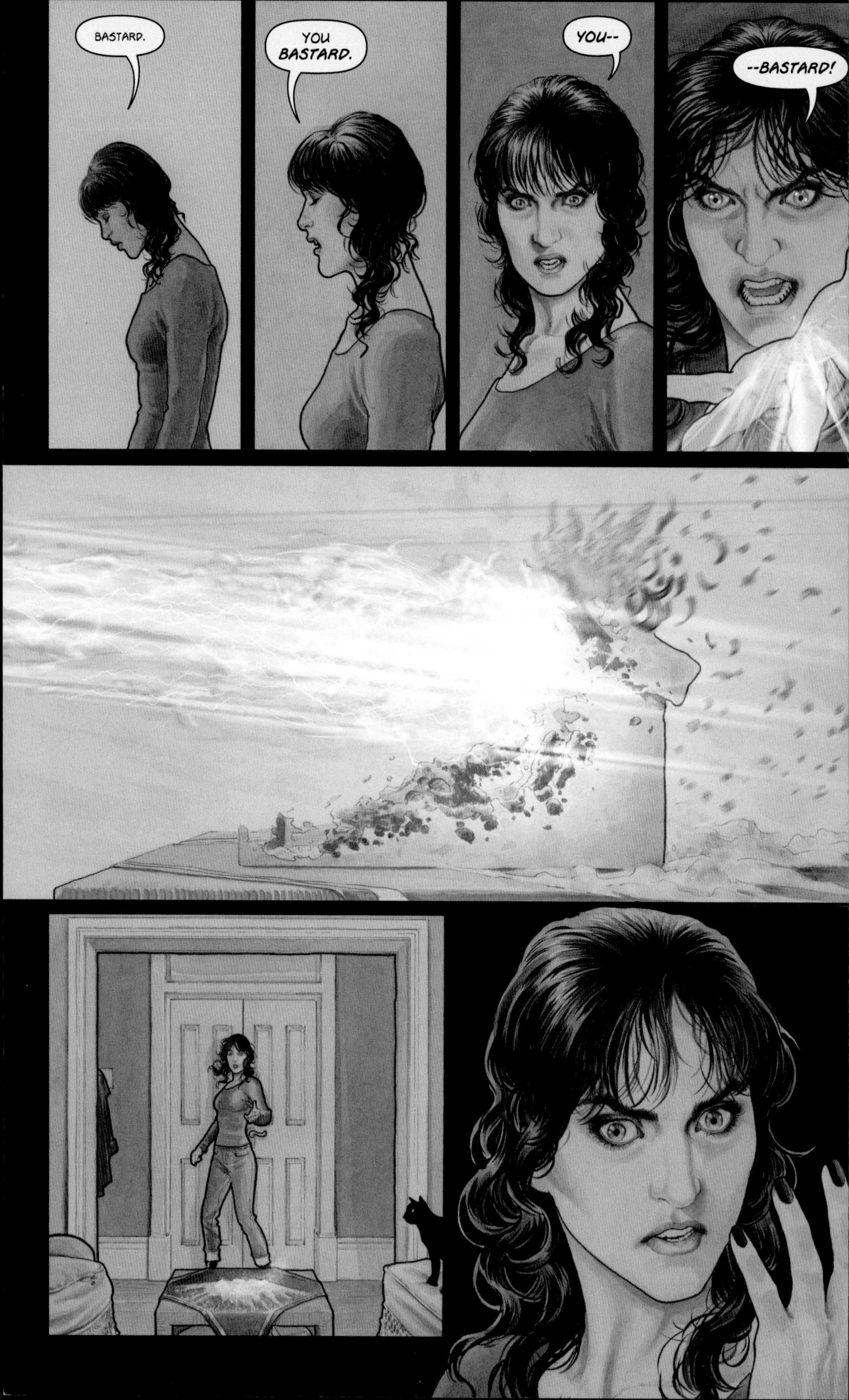
BASTARD.
YOU BASTARD.
YOU--
--BASTARD!

COVER GALLERY

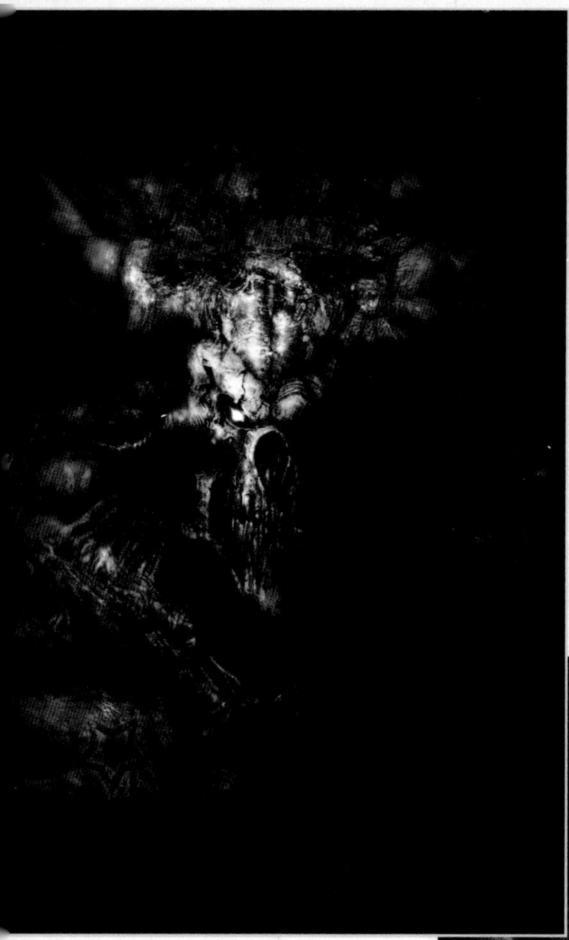

Issue 006 "B" Cover by **LIAM SHARP**

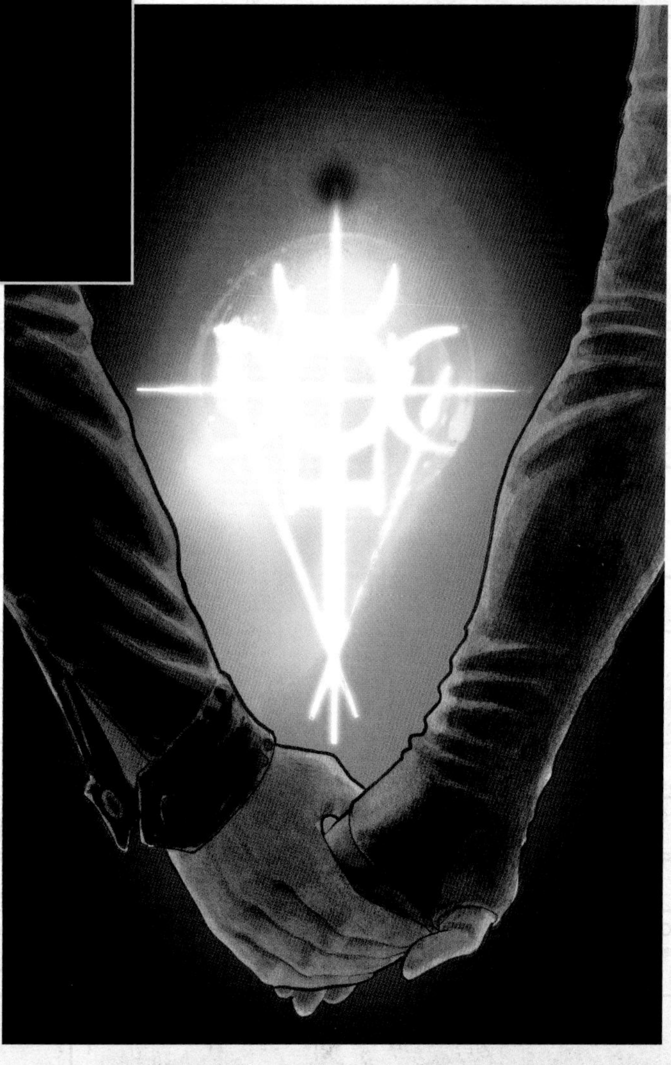

Issue 006 "Pride Month" Cover
by **NICOLA SCOTT**
(with **CHIARA ARENA**)

Issue 007 "B" Cover by **MICHAEL LARK**

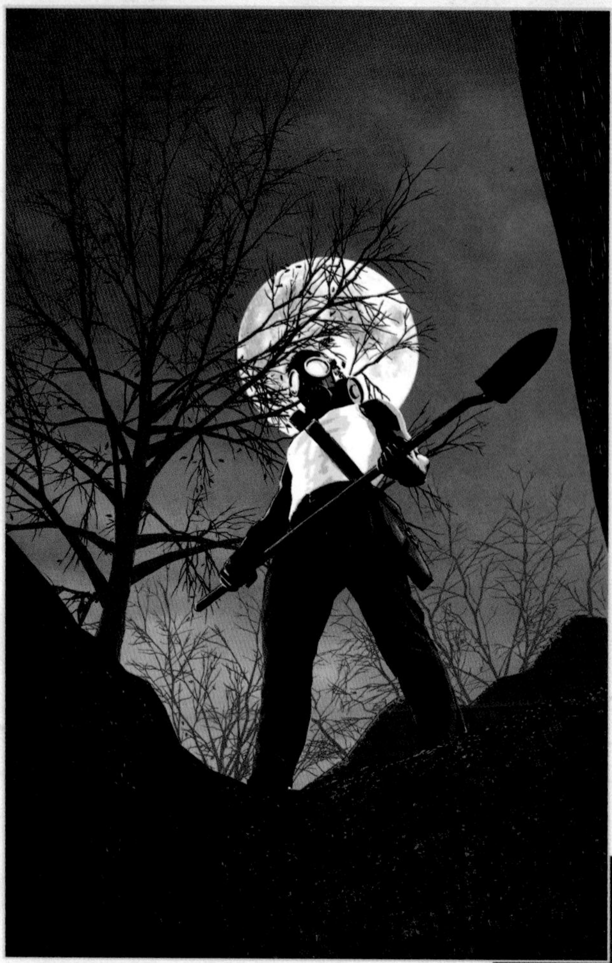

PORTSMOUTH POLICE DEPARTMENT

FORM IR RH-29181

POLICE DEP

LAST NAME OF PERSON KILLED

DOE

REPORTED BY

OFFENSE AS REPORTED (CRIME)

ASSAULT, ATTEMPTED MURDER

PLACE OF OCCURENCE — STREET AND NUM

BUDDY BURGER

2230 POTEMKIN DRIVE SE

DAY OF WEEK	DATE OF OCCURENCE	T
SUN	27 SEP 2015	2

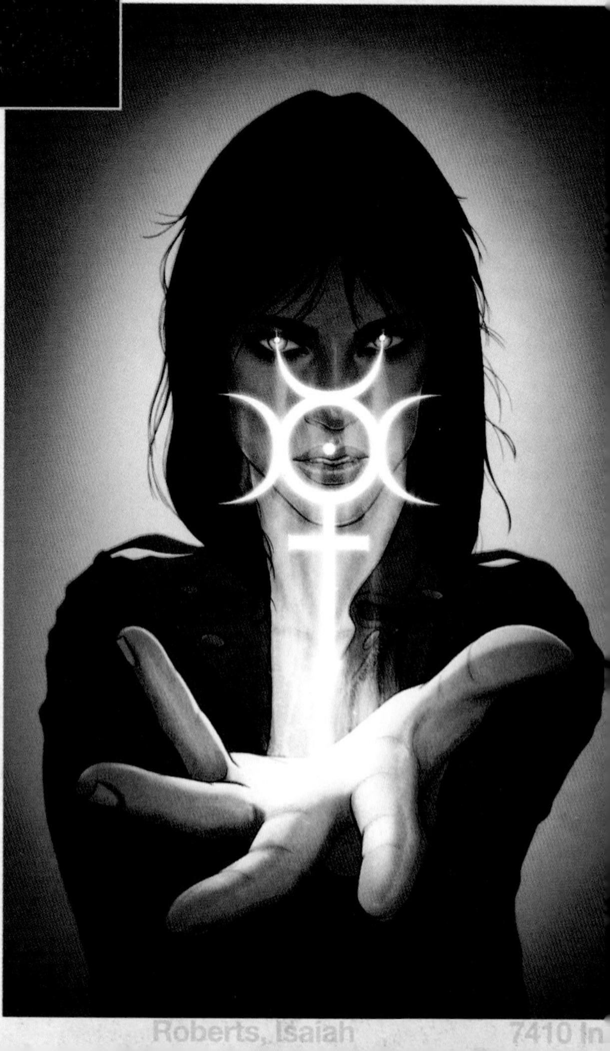

Issue 008 "B" Cover by **JENNY FRISON**

Roberts, Isaiah 7410 In

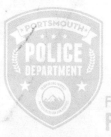

PRELIMI...
INCIDENT ...

	MIDDLE NAME	RACE	SE
		CAUC.	
TITLE OR RELATIONSHIP	RACE	SE	

TAKING

TION	DIVISION	PLATOON
	9	1

ATE REPORTED	TIME REPORTED	REPORT RE
7 SEP 2015	2230	Patrolm

NAME OF PROSECUTOR ATTENDING—TIME OF A

ADA L. CALDER

CCUSED LIVED OR ASSOCIATED

USE BOTH SIDES OF THIS SHEET.
around 2300 hours on the night of SUN
127162, recovered at scene). According
hreatened to shoot anyone attempting t

police response teams. First on scene, C
e incident area until ESU and watch co
lished contact with Subject, who demai
ed on scene at or around 1149 hours an

N INTO CUSTODY   ADDRESS

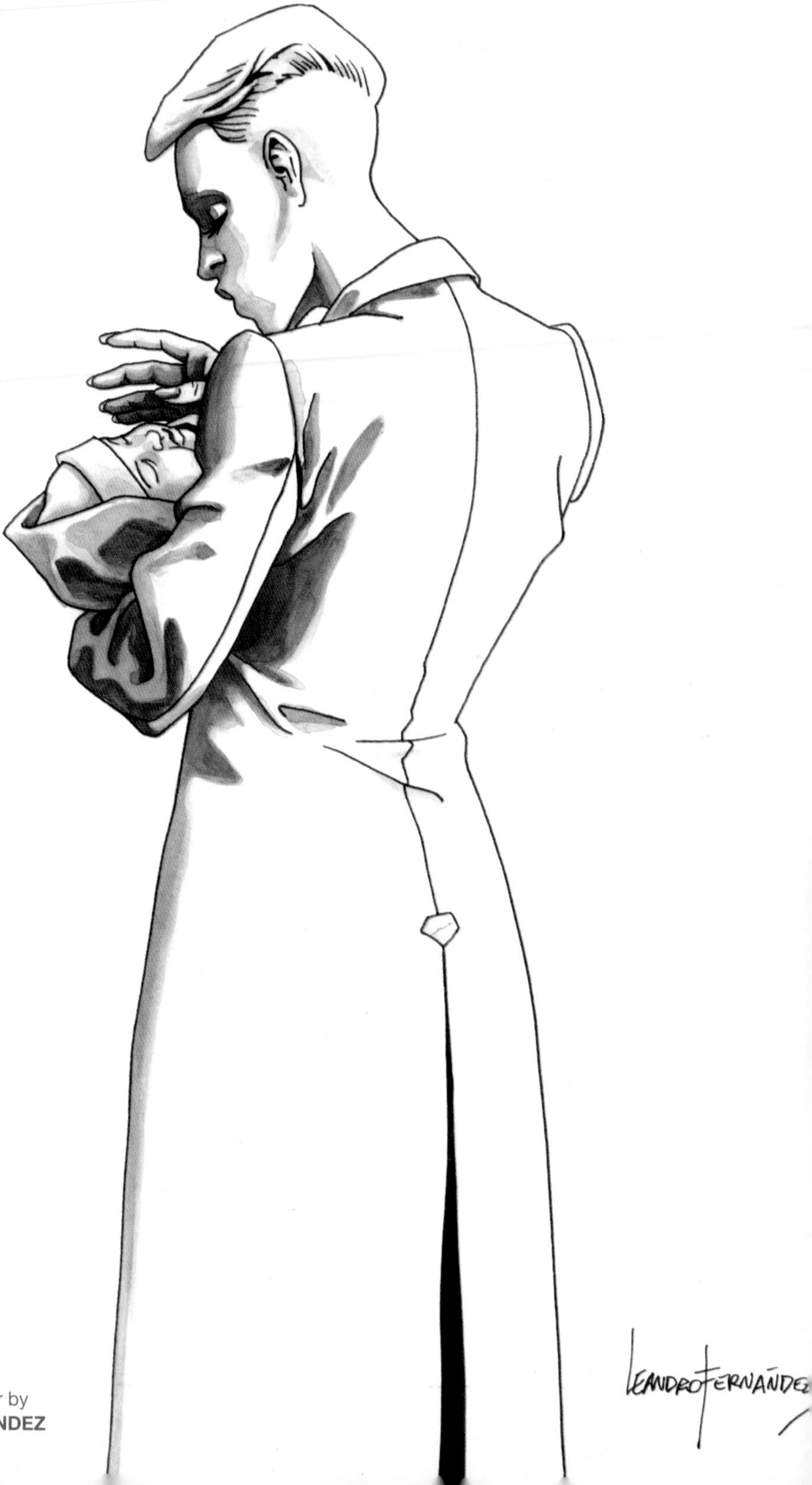
LEANDRO FERNÁNDEZ

Issue 011 “B” Cover by
LEANDRO FERNÁNDEZ